*Travel through time and space to new
realms of the astonishing with the finest
practitioners in the art of SF.*

The future awaits.

Year's
Best
SF
8

Praise for previous volumes

"An impressive roster of authors."
Locus

"The finest modern science fiction writing."
Pittsburgh Tribune

YEAR'S BEST

SF 8

EDITED BY
DAVID G. HARTWELL
and KATHRYN CRAMER

An Imprint of HarperCollinsPublishers

This is a collection of fiction. Names, characters, places, and incidents are products of the authors' imagination or are used fictitiously and are not to be construed as real. Any resemblance to actual events, locales, organizations, or persons, living or dead, is entirely coincidental.

EOS
An Imprint of HarperCollins*Publishers*
10 East 53rd Street
New York, New York 10022-5299

First Eos paperback printing: June 2003

Eos Trademark Reg. U.S. Pat. Off. And in Other Countries, Marca Registrada, Hecho en U.S.A.
HarperCollins® is a trademark of HarperCollins Publishers Inc.

Printed in the U.S.A.

10 9 8 7 6 5 4 3 2 1

Two Futurians:
To Virginia Kidd, who nurtured short fiction as well as
novels.

To Damon Knight, who taught that the anthologist's
basic responsibility is not to art or to writers,
but to readers.

Contents

Acknowledgments

The editors would like to thank the short fiction reviewers at Locus, LocusMag.com, and Tangent Online for their insights, and our editor, Michael Shohl, for editorial help and for shepherding this book through the publication process.

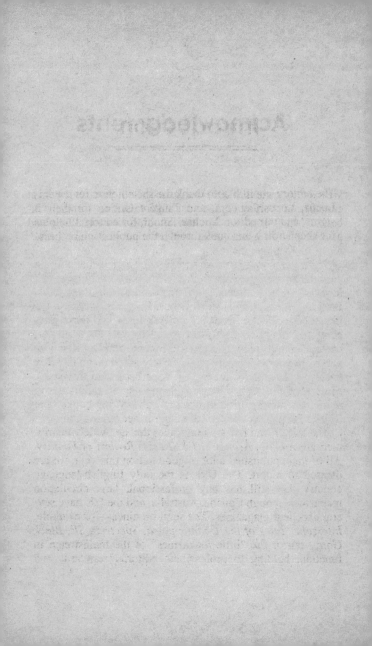

Introduction

We said last time that 2001 was an excellent year for the science fiction short story. The year 2002 was, if anything, even better. Many stories were challenging, literate, thought-provoking, and entertaining for the mind in the ways that make SF a unique genre.

The good news in the book publishing area is that nothing particularly bad happened in 2002. SF publishing as we have known it is nine mass market publishing lines (Ace, Bantam, Baen, DAW, Del Rey, Eos, Roc, Tor, Warner—ten if you count Pocket Book's Star Trek line), and those lines continue, though you will find Ace, Roc, and DAW all part of the Penguin conglomerate, and Bantam and Del Rey both part of Random House (now so closely allied that a Del Rey hardcover became a Bantam SF paperback lead this year). Mass market distributors are still pressing all publishers to reduce the number of titles and just publish "big books," but SF and fantasy seem to be resisting further diminution.

The last SF and fantasy magazines that are widely distributed are *Analog*, *Asimov's*, *F&SF*, and *Realms of Fantasy*. All of them published a lot of good fiction this year, we are pleased to report. The U.S. is the only English-language country that still has any professional, large-circulation magazines, though Canada, Australia, and the UK have several excellent magazines. The semi-prozines—for example, *Interzone*, *Tales of the Unanticipated*, *Spectrum SF*, *Black Gate*—mirror the "little magazines" of the mainstream in function, holding to professional editorial standards and publishing the next generation of writers, along with some of the present masters.

The small presses were a very healthy presence. We have a strong short-fiction field today in part because the small presses publishing semi-professional magazines, single-author collections, and anthologies are printing and circulating a majority of the high-quality fiction published in SF and fantasy and horror. One significant trend noticeable in the small press anthologies this year was toward genre-bending slipstream stories. The SF Book Club, now part of the mega-corporation (Bookspan) that resulted from the combination of all of the Literary Guild and Book of the Month Club divisions, continues to be an innovative and lively publisher, as well as an influential reprinter. Good anthologies and collections are harder than ever to select on the bookstore shelves from among the mediocre ones, but you will find some of the best books each year selected for SFBC editions, often the only hardcover editions of those anthologies.

The best original anthologies of the year in our opinion were *Leviathan 3*, edited by Jeff VanderMeer and Forrest Aguirre; *Polyphony*, edited by Jay Lake; *Conjunctions 39*, edited by Peter Straub—these books mixing SF and fantasy with slipstream fiction; *Mars Probes*, edited by Peter Crowther (DAW); *Embrace the Mutation*, edited by Bill Sheehan; *Agog*, edited by Cat Sparks; and *The DAW 30th Anniversary SF Anthology*, edited by Betsy Wollheim and Sheila Gilbert (which contained in general long episodes from popular novel series rather than independent stories; there was also a companion volume for fantasy). Of these, the particular excellences of *Polyphony*, *Conjunctions 39*, *Leviathan*, and *Embrace the Mutation* were mostly in the realm of fantasy, and the especial pleasures of *Mars Probes* were in SF. So you will find a couple of stories here from *Mars Probes*, but should look to our companion *Year's Best Fantasy 3* for stories from the other books. The rest of the paperback original anthologies of the year should best be considered as equivalent to single issues of magazines, and on that basis, 2002 was on the whole not a distinguished year for original anthologies in paperback.

Several online short fiction markets (Infinite Matrix, Sci-Fiction, and Strange Horizons) helped to cushion the loss in recent years of print media markets for short fiction. We found some excellent science fiction, particularly from editor Ellen Datlow's SciFiction site, now the highest-paying market in the genre for short fiction, although both the others were of quite high quality in general. We offer stories from them in this book for perhaps the first time in print.

In 2002 it was good to be reading the magazines, as well, both professional and semi-pro. It was a very strong year for novellas, and there were more than a hundred shorter stories in consideration. So we repeat, for readers new to this series, the usual disclaimer: This selection of science fiction stories represents the best that was published during the year 2002. It would take two or three more volumes of this size to include nearly all of the best short stories—though even then, not all of the best novellas. And we believe that representing the best from year to year, while it is not physically possible to encompass it all in even one very large book, also implies presenting some substantial variety of excellences, and we left some worthy stories out in order to include others in this limited space.

Our general principle for selection: This book is full of science fiction—every story in the book is clearly that and not something else. We have a high regard for horror, fantasy, speculative fiction, and slipstream, and postmodern literature. We (Kathryn Cramer and David G. Hartwell) edit the *Year's Best Fantasy* in paperback from Eos as a companion volume to this one—look for it if you enjoy short fantasy fiction, too. But here, we chose science fiction.

We try to represent the varieties of tones and voices and attitudes that keep the genre vigorous and responsive to the changing realities out of which it emerges, in science and daily life. This is a book about what's going on now in SF. The stories that follow show, and the story notes point out, the strengths of the evolving genre in the year 2002.

David G. Hartwell & Kathryn Cramer
Pleasantville, NY

In Paradise

BRUCE STERLING

Bruce Sterling <www.well.com/conf/mirrorshades> lives in Austin, Texas. The novel Schismatrix *(1985) and the related stories that made him famous were re-released in 1996 as* Schismatrix Plus. *He collaborated with William Gibson on* The Difference Engine *(1990), became a media figure who appeared on the cover of* Wired, *became a journalist who wrote the exposé* The Hacker Crackdown *(1992), and returned his attention to science fiction in 1995, with a new explosion of stories and novels, including* Heavy Weather *(1994),* Holy Fire *(1996), and* Distraction *(1998). His most recent novel,* Zeitgeist *(2000), is fantasy. His interest in the political and cultural implications of future change has informed his work, and in his recent nonfiction book,* Tomorrow Now: Envisioning the Next Fifty Years *(2002), he re-imagines the future after the turn of the 21st century.*

"In Paradise" was published in F&SF, *a magazine that published a large number of especially good stories this year. It is a madly jolly, near-future love story, in which the machete of satire is wielded against the advent and spread of intrusion into the private lives of citizens in the name of homeland security. Certain moral and ethical problems are oversimplified so that love conquers all. It is first in this book because we found it so representative of the year 2002 and so much fun.*

T he machines broke down so much that it was comical, but the security people never laughed about that.

Felix could endure the delay, for plumbers billed by the hour. He opened his tool kit, extracted a plastic flask and had a solid nip of Scotch.

The Moslem girl was chattering into her phone. Her dad and another bearded weirdo had passed through the big metal frame just as the scanner broke down. So these two somber, suited old men were getting the full third degree with the hand wands, while daughter was stuck. Daughter wore a long baggy coat and thick black headscarf and a surprisingly sexy pair of sandals. Between her and her minders stretched the no man's land of official insecurity. She waved across the gap.

The security geeks found something metallic in the black wool jacket of the Wicked Uncle. Of course it was harmless, but they had to run their full ritual, lest they die of boredom at their posts. As the Scotch settled in, Felix felt time stretch like taffy. Little Miss Mujihadeen discovered that her phone was dying. She banged at it with the flat of her hand.

The line of hopeful shoppers, grimly waiting to stimulate the economy, shifted in their disgruntlement. It was a bad, bleak scene. It crushed Felix's heart within him. He longed to leap to his feet and harangue the lot of them. *Wake up*, he wanted to scream at them, *cheer up, act more human*. He felt the urge keenly, but it scared people when he cut loose like that. They really hated it. And so did he. He knew he

2

couldn't look them in the eye. It would only make a lot of trouble.

The Mideastern men shouted at the girl. She waved her dead phone at them, as if another breakdown was going to help their mood. Then Felix noticed that she shared his own make of cell phone. She had a rather ahead-of-the-curve Finnish model that he'd spent a lot of money on. So Felix rose and sidled over.

"Help you out with that phone, ma'am?"

She gave him the paralyzed look of a coed stuck with a dripping tap. "No English?" he concluded. "Habla español, senorita?" No such luck.

He offered her his own phone. No, she didn't care to use it. Surprised and even a little hurt by this rejection, Felix took his first good look at her, and realized with a lurch that she was pretty. What eyes! They were whirlpools. The line of her lips was like the tapered edge of a rose leaf.

"It's your battery," he told her. Though she had not a word of English, she obviously got it about phone batteries. After some gestured persuasion, she was willing to trade her dead battery for his. There was a fine and delicate little moment when his fingertips extracted her power supply, and he inserted his own unit into that golden-lined copper cavity. Her display leaped to life with an eager flash of numerals. Felix pressed a button or two, smiled winningly, and handed her phone back.

She dialed in a hurry, and bearded Evil Dad lifted his phone to answer, and life became much easier on the nerves. Then, with a groaning buzz, the scanner came back on. Dad and Uncle waved a command at her, like lifers turned to trusty prison guards, and she scampered through the metal gate and never looked back.

She had taken his battery. Well, no problem. He would treasure the one she had given him.

Felix gallantly let the little crowd through before he himself cleared security. The geeks always went nuts about his plumbing tools, but then again, they had to. He found the assignment: a chi-chi place that sold fake antiques and potpourri. The manager's office had a clogged drain. As he worked, Felix recharged the phone. Then he socked them for a sum that made them wince.

On his leisurely way out—whoa, there was Miss Cell phone, that looker, that little goddess, browsing in a jewelry store over Korean gold chains and tiaras. Dad and Uncle were there, with a couple of off-duty cops.

Felix retired to a bench beside the fountain, in the potted plastic plants. He had another bracing shot of Scotch, then put his feet up on his toolbox and punched her number.

He saw her straighten at the ring, and open her purse, and place the phone to the kerchiefed side of her head. She didn't know where he was, or who he was. That was why the words came pouring out of him.

"My God you're pretty," he said. "You are wasting your time with that jewelry. Because your eyes are like two black diamonds."

She jumped a little, poked at the phone's buttons with disbelief, and put it back to her head.

Felix choked back the urge to laugh and leaned forward, his elbows on his knees. "A string of pearls around your throat would look like peanuts," he told the phone. "I am totally smitten with you. What are you like under that big baggy coat? Do I dare to wonder? I would give a million dollars just to see your knees!"

"Why are you telling me that?" said the phone.

"Because I'm looking at you right now. And after one look at you, believe me, I was a lost soul." Felix felt a chill. "Hey, wait a minute—you don't speak English, do you?"

"No, I don't speak English—but my telephone does."

"It *does*?"

"It's a very new telephone. It's from Finland," the telephone said. "I need it because I'm stuck in a foreign country. Do you really have a million dollars for my knees?"

"That was a figure of speech," said Felix, though his bank account was, in point of fact, looking considerably healthier since his girlfriend Lola had dumped him. "Never mind the million dollars," he said. "I'm dying of love out here. I'd sell my blood just to buy you petunias."

"You must be a famous poet," the phone said dreamily, "for you speak such wonderful Farsi."

Felix had no idea what Farsi was—but he was way beyond such fretting now. The rusty gates of his soul were shuddering on their hinges. "I'm drunk," he realized. "I am drunk on your smile."

"In my family, the women never smile."

Felix had no idea what to say to that, so there was a hissing silence.

"Are you a spy? How did you get my phone number?"

"I'm not a spy. I got your phone number from your phone."

"Then I know you. You must be that tall foreign man who gave me your battery. Where are you?"

"Look outside the store. See me on the bench?" She turned where she stood, and he waved his fingertips. "That's right, it's me," he declared to her. "I can't believe I'm really going through with this. You just stand there, okay? I'm going to run in there and buy you a wedding ring."

"Don't do that." She glanced cautiously at Dad and Uncle, then stepped closer to the bulletproof glass. "Yes, I do see you. I remember you."

She was looking straight at him. Their eyes met. They were connecting. A hot torrent ran up his spine. "You are looking straight at me."

"You're very handsome."

It wasn't hard to elope. Young women had been eloping since the dawn of time. Elopement with eager phone support was a snap. He followed her to the hotel, a posh place that swarmed with limos and videocams. He brought her a bag with a big hat, sunglasses, and a cheap Mexican wedding dress. He sneaked into the women's restroom—they never put videocams there, due to the complaints—and he left the bag in a stall. She went in, came out in new clothes with her hair loose, and walked straight out of the hotel and into his car.

They couldn't speak together without their phones, but

that turned out to be surprisingly advantageous, as further discussion was not on their minds. Unlike Lola, who was always complaining that he should open up and relate—"You're a plumber," she would tell him, "how deep and mysterious is a plumber supposed to be?"—the new woman in his life had needs that were very straightforward. She liked to walk in parks without a police escort. She liked to thoughtfully peruse the goods in Mideastern ethnic groceries. And she liked to make love to him. She was nineteen years old, and the willing sacrifice of her chastity had really burned the bridges for his little refugee. Once she got fully briefed about what went inside where, she was in the mood to tame the demon. She had big, jagged, sobbing, alarming, romantic, brink-of-the-grave things going on, with long, swoony kisses, and heel-drumming, and clutching-and-clawing.

When they were too weak, and too raw, and too tingling to make love anymore, then she would cook, very badly. She was on her phone constantly, talking to her people. These confidantes of hers were obviously women, because she asked them for Persian cooking tips. She would sink with triumphant delight into cheery chatter as the Basmati rice burned.

He longed to take her out to eat; to show her to everyone, to the whole world; really, besides the sex, no act could have made him happier—but she was undocumented, and sooner or later some security geek was sure to check on that. People did things like that to people nowadays. To contemplate such things threw a thorny darkness over their whole affair, so, mostly, he didn't think. He took time off work, and he spent every moment that he could in her radiant presence, and she did what a pretty girl could do to lift a man's darkened spirits, which was plenty. More than he had ever had from anyone.

After ten days of golden, unsullied bliss, ten days of bread and jug wine, ten days when the nightingales sang in chorus and the reddest of roses bloomed outside the boudoir, there came a knock on his door, and it was three cops.

"Hello, Mr. Hernandez," said the smallest of the trio. "I would be Agent Portillo from Homeland Security, and these would be two of my distinguished associates. Might we come in?"

"Would there be a problem?" said Felix.

"Yes there would!" said Portillo. "There might be rather less of a problem if my associates here could search your apartment." Portillo offered up a handheld screen. "A young woman named Batool Kadivar? Would we be recognizing Miss Batool Kadivar?"

"I can't even pronounce that," Felix said. "But I guess you'd better come in," for Agent Portillo's associates were already well on their way. Men of their ilk were not prepared to take no for an answer. They shoved past him and headed at once for the bedroom.

"Who are those guys? They're not American."

"They're Iranian allies. The Iranians were totally nuts for a while, and then they were sort of okay, and then they became our new friends, and then the enemies of our friends became our friends. . . . Do you ever watch TV news, Mr. Hernandez? Secular uprisings, people seizing embassies? Ground war in the holy city of Qom, that kind of thing?"

"It's hard to miss," Felix admitted.

"There are a billion Moslems. If they want to turn the whole planet into Israel, we don't get a choice about that. You know something? I used to be an accountant!" Portillo sighed theatrically. " 'Homeland Security.' Why'd they have to stick me with that chicken outfit? Hombre, we're twenty years old, and we don't even have our own budget yet. Did you see those gorillas I've got on my hands? You think these guys ever listen to sense? Geneva Convention? U.S. Constitution? Come on."

"They're not gonna find any terrorists in here."

Portillo sighed again. "Look, Mr. Hernandez. You're a young man with a clean record, so I want to do you a favor." He adjusted his handheld and it showed a new screen. "These are cell phone records. Thirty, forty calls a day, to and from your number. Then look at this screen, this is the good part. Check out *her* call records. That would be her

aunt in Yerevan, and her little sister in Teheran, and five or
six of her teenage girlfriends, still living back in purdah. . . .
Who do you think is gonna *pay* that phone bill? Did that
ever cross your mind?"

Felix said nothing.

"I can understand this, Mr. Hernandez. You lucked out.
You're a young, red-blooded guy and that is a very pretty
girl. But she's a minor, and an illegal alien. Her father's family has got political connections like nobody's business, and
I would mean nobody, and I would also mean business."

"Not my business," Felix said.

"You're being a sap, Mr. Hernandez. You may not be interested in war, but war is plenty interested in you." There
were loud crashing, sacking and looting noises coming from
his bedroom.

"You are sunk, hermano. There is video at the Lebanese
grocery store. There is video hidden in the traffic lights.
You're a free American citizen, sir. You're free to go anywhere you want, and we're free to watch all the backup
tapes. That would be the big story I'm relating here. Would
we be catching on yet?"

"That's some kind of story," Felix said.

"You don't know the half of it. You don't know the tenth."

The two goons reappeared. There was a brief exchange of
notes. They had to use their computers.

"My friends here are disappointed," said Agent Portillo,
"because there is no girl in your residence, even though
there is an extensive selection of makeup and perfume. They
want me to arrest you for abduction, and obstruction of justice, and probably ten or twelve other things. But I would be
asking myself: why? Why should this young taxpayer with a
steady job want to have his life ruined? What I'm thinking
is: there must be *another* story. A *better* story. The flighty
girl ran off, and she spent the last two weeks in a convent. It
was just an impulse thing for her. She got frightened and upset by America, and then she came back to her people.
Everything diplomatic."

"That's diplomacy?"

"Diplomacy is the art of avoiding extensive unpleasantness for all the parties concerned. The united coalition, as it were."

"They'll chop her hands off and beat her like a dog!"

"Well, that would depend, Mr. Hernandez. That would depend entirely on whether the girl herself tells that story. Somebody would have to get her up to speed on all that. A trusted friend. You see?"

After the departure of the three security men, Felix thought through his situation. He realized there was nothing whatsoever in it for him but shame, humiliation, impotence, and a crushing and lasting unhappiness. He then fetched up the reposado tequila from beneath his sink.

Some time later he felt the dulled stinging of a series of slaps to his head. When she saw that she had his attention, she poured the tequila onto the floor, accenting this gesture with an eye-opening Persian harangue. Felix staggered to the bathroom, threw up, and returned to find a fresh cup of coffee. She had raised the volume and was still going strong.

He'd never had her pick a lovers' quarrel with him, though he'd always known it was in her somewhere. It was magnificent. It was washing over him in a musical torrent of absolute nonsense. It was operatic, and he found it quite beautiful. Like sitting through a rainstorm without getting wet: trees straining, leaves flying, dark, windy, torrential. Majestic.

Her idea of coffee was basically wet grounds, so it brought him around in short order. "You're right, I'm wrong, and I'm sorry," he admitted tangentially, knowing she didn't understand a word, "so come on and help me," and he opened the sink cabinet, where he had hidden all his bottles when he'd noticed the earlier disapproving glances. He then decanted them down the drain: vodka, Southern Comfort, the gin, the party jug of tequila, even the last two inches of his favorite single-malt. Moslems didn't drink, and really, how wrong could any billion people be? He gulped a couple of aspirin and picked up the phone.

"The police were here. They know about us. I got upset. I drank too much."

"Did they beat you?"

"Uh, no. They're not big fans of beating over here, they've got better methods. They'll be back. We are in big trouble."

She folded her arms. "Then we'll run away."

"You know, we have a proverb for that in America. 'You can run, but you can't hide.'"

"Darling, I love your poetry, but when the police come to the house, it's serious."

"Yes. It's very serious, it's serious as cancer. You've got no ID. You have no passport. You can't get on any plane to get away. Even the trains and lousy bus stations have facial recognition. My car is useless too. They'd read my license plate a hundred times before we hit city limits. I can't rent another car without leaving credit records. The cops have got my number."

"We'll steal a fast car and go very fast."

"You can't outrun them! That is not possible! They've all got phones like we do, so they're always ahead of us, waiting."

"I'm a rebel! I'll never surrender!" She lifted her chin. "Let's get married."

"I'd love to, but we can't. We have no license. We have no blood test."

"Then we'll marry in some place where they have all the blood they want. Beirut, that would be good." She placed her free hand against her chest. "We were married in my heart, the first time we ever made love."

This artless confession blew through him like a summer breeze. "They do have rings for cash at a pawnbroker's . . . But I'm a Catholic. There must be *somebody* who does this sort of thing . . . Maybe some heretic mullah. Maybe a Santeria guy?"

"If we're husband and wife, what can they do to us? We haven't done anything wrong! I'll get a Green Card. I'll beg them! I'll beg for mercy. I'll beg political asylum."

Agent Portillo conspicuously cleared his throat. "Mr. Hernandez, please! This would not be the conversation you two need to be having."

"I forgot to mention the worst part," Felix said. "They know about our phones."

"Miss Kadivar, can you also understand me?"

"Who are you? I hate you. Get off this line and let me talk to him."

"Salaam alekom to you, too," Portillo concluded. "It's a sad commentary on federal procurement when a mullah's daughter has a fancy translator, and I can't even talk live with my own fellow agents. By the way, those two gentlemen from the new regime in Teheran are staking out your apartment. How they failed to recognize your girlfriend on her way in, that I'll never know. But if you two listen to me, I think I can walk you out of this very dangerous situation."

"I don't want to leave my beloved," she said.

"Over my dead body," Felix declared. "Come and get me. Bring a gun."

"Okay, Miss Kadivar, you would seem to be the more rational of the two parties, so let me talk sense to you. You have no future with this man. What kind of wicked man seduces a decent girl with phone pranks? He's an *aayash*, he's a playboy. America has a fifty percent divorce rate. He would never ask your father honorably for your hand. What would your mother say?"

"Who is this awful man?" she said, shaken. "He knows everything!"

"He's a snake!" Felix said. "He's the devil!"

"You still don't get it, compadre. I'm not the Great Satan. Really, I'm not! I am the *good guy*. I'm your guardian angel, dude. I am trying really hard to give you back a normal life."

"Okay cop, you had your say, now listen to me. I love her body and soul, and even if you kill me dead for that, the flames in my heart will set my coffin on fire."

She burst into tears. "Oh God, my God, that's the most beautiful thing anyone has ever said to me."

"You kids are sick, okay?" Portillo snapped. "This would be *mental illness* that I'm eavesdropping on here! You two don't even *speak each other's language*. You had every fair warning! Just remember, when it happens, you *made me* do it. Now try this one on for size, Romeo and Juliet." The phones went dead.

Felix placed his dead phone on the tabletop. "Okay. Situation report. We've got no phones, no passports, no ID and two different intelligence agencies are after us. We can't fly, we can't drive, we can't take a train or a bus. My credit cards are useless now, my bank cards will just track me down, and I guess I've lost my job now. I can't even walk out my own front door. . . . And wow, you don't understand a single word I'm saying. I can tell from that look in your eye. You are completely thrilled."

She put her finger to her lips. Then she took him by the hand.

Apparently, she had a new plan. It involved walking. She wanted to walk to Los Angeles. She knew the words "Los Angeles," and maybe there was somebody there that she knew. This trek would involve crossing half the American continent on foot, but Felix was at peace with that ambition. He really thought he could do it. A lot of people had done it just for the sake of gold nuggets, back in 1849. Women had walked to California just to meet a guy with gold nuggets.

The beautiful part of this scheme was that, after creeping out the window, they really had vanished. The feds might be all over the airports, over everything that mattered, but they didn't care about what didn't matter. Nobody was looking out for dangerous interstate pedestrians.

To pass the time as they walked, she taught him elementary Farsi. The day's first lesson was body parts, because that was all they had handy for pointing. That suited Felix just fine. If anything, this expanded their passionate communion. He was perfectly willing to starve for that, fight for that and die for that. Every form of intercourse between man and woman was fraught with illusion, and the bigger, the better. Every hour that passed was an hour they had not been parted.

They had to sleep rough. Their clothes became filthy. Then, on the tenth day, they got arrested.

She was, of course, an illegal alien, and he had the good sense to talk only Spanish, so of course, he became one as well. The Immigration cops piled them into the bus for the border, but they got two seats together and were able to kiss and hold hands. The other deported wretches even smiled at them.

He realized now that he was sacrificing everything for her: his identity, his citizenship, flag, church, habits, money . . . Everything, and good riddance. He bit thoughtfully into his wax-papered cheese sandwich. This was the federal bounty distributed to every refugee on the bus, along with an apple, a small carton of homogenized milk, and some carrot chips.

When the protein hit his famished stomach Felix realized that he had gone delirious with joy. He was *growing* by this experience. It had broken every stifling limit within him. His dusty, savage, squalid world was widening drastically.

Giving alms, for instance—before his abject poverty, he'd never understood that alms were holy. Alms were indeed very holy. From now on—as soon as he found a place to sleep, some place that was so wrecked, so torn, so bleeding, that it never asked uncomfortable questions about a plumber—as soon as he became a plumber again, then he'd be giving some alms.

She ate her food, licked her fingers, then fell asleep against him, in the moving bus. He brushed the free hair from her dirty face. She was twenty days older now. "This is a pearl," he said aloud. "This is a pearl by far too rare to be contained within the shell of time and space."

Why had those lines come to him, in such a rush? Had he read them somewhere? Or were those lines his own?

Slow Life

MICHAEL SWANWICK

Michael Swanwick <www.michaelswanwick.com> is a major player in today's grand game of science fiction. His first novel, In the Drift *(1984), an alternate-history novel in which the Three Mile Island reactor exploded, was one of Terry Carr's Ace Specials in the same series as William Gibson's* Neuromancer *and Kim Stanley Robinson's* The Wild Shore. *Since then he has published his fine novels at a rate of one every three or four years:* Vacuum Flowers *(1987),* Stations of the Tide *(1991),* The Iron Dragon's Daughter *(1993—what he called "hard fantasy") the sharply satiric* Jack Faust *(1997), and his new novel,* Bones of the Earth *(2002), expanded from his Hugo Award–winning story "Scherzo with Tyrannosaur." His short fiction is collected in* Gravity's Angels *(1991),* Geography of Unknown Lands *(1997),* Moon Dogs *(2000),* Tales of Old Earth *(2000), and* Puck Aleshire's Abecedary *(2000). Swanwick is also the author of two influential critical essays, one on SF, "User's Guide to the Postmoderns" (1985), and one on fantasy, "In The Tradition . . . ." (1994).*

"Slow Life," in the mode of Hal Clement and Arthur C. Clarke, is from Analog, *and is one of Swanwick's occasional forays into hard SF. Swanwick links satire of our over-connected technological present, of online chat and instantaneous entertainment news, with the grand wonders of the cosmos, adventures on the grand scale, and good old-fashioned SF wonder, in an entertaining clash of SF cultures.*

*"It was the Second Age of Space. Gagarin, Shepard,
Glenn, and Armstrong were all dead. It was our turn
to make history now."*

—The Memoirs of Lizzie O'Brien

The raindrop began forming ninety kilometers above
the surface of Titan. It started with an infinitesimal speck
of tholin, adrift in the cold nitrogen atmosphere. Diano-
acetylene condensed on the seed nucleus, molecule by
molecule, until it was one shard of ice in a cloud of billions.

Now the journey could begin.

It took almost a year for the shard of ice in question to
precipitate downward twenty-five kilometers, where the
temperature dropped low enough that ethane began to con-
dense on it. But when it did, growth was rapid.

Down it drifted.

At forty kilometers, it was for a time caught up in an
ethane cloud. There it continued to grow. Occasionally it
collided with another droplet and doubled in size. Finally it
was too large to be held effortlessly aloft by the gentle
stratospheric winds.

It fell.

Falling, it swept up methane and quickly grew large
enough to achieve a terminal velocity of almost two meters
per second.

At twenty-seven kilometers, it passed through a dense

layer of methane clouds. It acquired more methane, and continued its downward flight.

As the air thickened, its velocity slowed and it began to lose some of its substance to evaporation. At two and a half kilometers, when it emerged from the last patchy clouds, it was losing mass so rapidly it could not normally be expected to reach the ground.

It was, however, falling toward the equatorial highlands, where mountains of ice rose a towering five hundred meters into the atmosphere. At two meters and a lazy new terminal velocity of one meter per second, it was only a breath away from hitting the surface.

Two hands swooped an open plastic collecting bag upward, and snared the raindrop.

"Gotcha!" Lizzie O'Brien cried gleefully.

She zip-locked the bag shut, held it up so her helmet cam could read the barcode in the corner, and said, "One raindrop." Then she popped it into her collecting box.

Sometimes it's the little things that make you happiest. Somebody would spend a *year* studying this one little raindrop when Lizzie got it home. And it was just Bag 64 in Collecting Case 5. She was going to be on the surface of Titan long enough to scoop up the raw material of a revolution in planetary science. The thought of it filled her with joy.

Lizzie dogged down the lid of the collecting box and began to skip across the granite-hard ice, splashing the puddles and dragging the boot of her atmosphere suit through the rivulets of methane pouring down the mountainside. *"I'm sing-ing in the rain."* She threw out her arms and spun around. *"Just sing-ing in the rain!"*

"Uh . . . O'Brien?" Alan Greene said from the *Clement*. "Are you all right?"

"Dum-dee-dum-dee-dee-dum-dum,   I'm . . . some-thing again."

"Oh, leave her alone," Consuelo Hong said with sour good humor. She was down on the plains, where the methane simply boiled into the air, and the ground was covered with thick, gooey tholin. It was, she had told them, like wading ankle-deep in molasses. "Can't you recognize the scientific method when you hear it?"

"If you say so," Alan said dubiously. He was stuck in the *Clement*, overseeing the expedition and minding the website. It was a comfortable gig—*he* wouldn't be sleeping in his suit *or* surviving on recycled water and energy stix—and he didn't think the others knew how much he hated it.

"What's next on the schedule?" Lizzie asked.

"Um . . . well, there's still the robot turbot to be released. How's that going, Hong?"

"Making good time. I oughta reach the sea in a couple of hours."

"Okay, then it's time O'Brien rejoined you at the lander. O'Brien, start spreading out the balloon and going over the harness checklist."

"Roger that."

"And while you're doing that, I've got today's voice-posts from the Web cued up."

Lizzie groaned, and Consuelo blew a raspberry. By NAF-TASA policy, the ground crew participated in all webcasts. Officially, they were delighted to share their experiences with the public. But the Voice Web (privately, Lizzie thought of it as the Illiternet) made them accessible to people who lacked even the minimal intellectual skills needed to handle a keyboard.

"Let me remind you that we're on open circuit here, so anything you say will go into my reply. You're certainly welcome to chime in at any time. But each question-and-response is transmitted as one take, so if you flub a line, we'll have to go back to the beginning and start all over again."

"Yeah, yeah," Consuelo grumbled.

"We've done this before," Lizzie reminded him.

"Okay. Here's the first one."

"Uh, hi, this is BladeNinja43. I was wondering just what it is that you guys are hoping to discover out there."

"That's an extremely good question," Alan lied. "And the answer is: We don't know! This is a voyage of discovery, and we're engaged in what's called 'pure science.' Now, time and time again, the purest research has turned out to be extremely profitable. But we're not looking that far ahead. We're just hoping to find something absolutely unexpected."

"My God, you're slick," Lizzie marveled.

"I'm going to edit that from the tape," Alan said cheerily. "Next up."

"This is Mary Schroeder, from the United States. I teach high school English, and I wanted to know for my students, what kind of grades the three of you had when you were their age."

Alan began. "I was an overachiever, I'm afraid. In my sophomore year, first semester, I got a B in Chemistry and panicked. I thought it was the end of the world. But then I dropped a couple of extracurriculars, knuckled down, and brought that grade right up."

"I was good in everything but French Lit," Consuelo said.

"I nearly flunked out!" Lizzie said. "Everything was difficult for me. But then I decided I wanted to be an astronaut, and it all clicked into place. I realized that, hey, it's just hard work. And now, well, here I am."

"That's good. Thanks, guys. Here's the third, from Maria Vasquez."

"Is there life on Titan?"

"Probably not. It's *cold* down there! 94° Kelvin is the same as −179° Celsius, or −290° Fahrenheit. And yet . . . life is persistent. It's been found in Antarctic ice and in boiling water in submarine volcanic vents. Which is why we'll be paying particular attention to exploring the depths of the ethane-methane sea. If life is anywhere to be found, that's where we'll find it."

"Chemically, the conditions here resemble the anoxic atmosphere on Earth in which life first arose," Consuelo said. "Further, we believe that such prebiotic chemistry has been going on here for four and a half billion years. For an organic chemist like me, it's the best toy box in the Universe. But that lack of heat is a problem. Chemical reactions that occur quickly back home would take thousands of years here. It's hard to see how life could arise under such a handicap."

"It would have to be slow life," Lizzie said thoughtfully. "Something vegetative. 'Vaster than empires and more slow.' It would take millions of years to reach maturity. A single thought might require centuries. . . ."

"Thank you for that, uh, wild scenario!" Alan said quickly. Their NAFTASA masters frowned on speculation. It was, in their estimation, almost as unprofessional as heroism. "This next question comes from Danny in Toronto."

"Hey, man, I gotta say I really envy you being in that tiny little ship with those two hot babes."

Alan laughed lightly. "Yes, Ms. Hong and Ms. O'Brien are certainly attractive women. But we're kept so busy that, believe it or not, the thought of sex never comes up. And currently, while I tend to the *Clement*, they're both on the surface of Titan at the bottom of an atmosphere 60 percent more dense than Earth's, and encased in armored exploration suits. So even if I did have inappropriate thoughts, there's no way we could—"

"Hey, Alan," Lizzie said. "Tell me something."

"Yes?"

"What are you wearing?"

"Uh . . . switching over to private channel."

"Make that a three-way," Consuelo said.

Ballooning, Lizzie decided, was the best way there was of getting around. Moving with the gentle winds, there was no sound at all. And the view was great!

People talked a lot about the "murky orange atmosphere" of Titan, but your eyes adjusted. Turn up the gain on your helmet, and the white mountains of ice were *dazzling!* The methane streams carved cryptic runes into the heights. Then, at the tholin-line, white turned to a rich palette of oranges, reds, and yellows. There was a lot going on down there— more than she'd be able to learn in a hundred visits.

The plains were superficially duller, but they had their charms as well. Sure, the atmosphere was so dense that refracted light made the horizon curve upward to either side. But you got used to it. The black swirls and cryptic red tracery of unknown processes on the land below never grew tiring.

On the horizon, she saw the dark arm of Titan's narrow sea. If that was what it was. Lake Erie was larger, but the spin doctors back home had argued that since Titan was so much smaller than Earth, *relatively* it qualified as a sea. Lizzie had her own opinion, but she knew when to keep her mouth shut.

Consuelo was there now. Lizzie switched her visor over to the live feed. Time to catch the show.

"I can't believe I'm finally here," Consuelo said. She let the shrink-wrapped fish slide from her shoulder down to the ground. "Five kilometers doesn't seem like very far when you're coming down from orbit—just enough to leave a margin for error so the lander doesn't come down in the sea. But when you have to *walk* that distance, through tarry, sticky tholin . . . well, it's one heck of a slog."

"Consuelo, can you tell us what it's like there?" Alan asked.

"I'm crossing the beach. Now I'm at the edge of the sea." She knelt, dipped a hand into it. "It's got the consistency of a Slushy. Are you familiar with that drink? Lots of shaved ice sort of half-melted in a cup with flavored syrup. What we've got here is almost certainly a methane-ammonia mix; we'll know for sure after we get a sample to a laboratory. Here's an early indicator, though. It's dissolving the tholin off my glove." She stood.

"Can you describe the beach?"

"Yeah. It's white. Granular. I can kick it with my boot. Ice sand for sure. Do you want me to collect samples first or release the fish?"

"Release the fish," Lizzie said, almost simultaneously with Alan's "Your call."

"Okay, then." Consuelo carefully cleaned both of her suit's gloves in the sea, then seized the shrink-wrap's zip tab and yanked. The plastic parted. Awkwardly, she straddled

the fish, lifted it by the two side-handles, and walked it into
the dark slush.

"Okay, I'm standing in the sea now. It's up to my ankles.
Now it's at my knees. I think it's deep enough here."

She set the fish down. "Now I'm turning it on."

The Mitsubishi turbot wriggled, as if alive. With one fluid
motion, it surged forward, plunged, and was gone.

Lizzie switched over to the fishcam.

Black liquid flashed past the turbot's infrared eyes. Straight
away from the shore it swam, seeing nothing but flecks of
paraffin, ice, and other suspended particulates as they
loomed up before it and were swept away in the violence of
its wake. A hundred meters out, it bounced a pulse of radar
off the sea floor, then dove, seeking the depths.

Rocking gently in her balloon harness, Lizzie yawned.

Snazzy Japanese cybernetics took in a minute sample of
the ammonia-water, fed it through a deftly constructed internal laboratory, and excreted the waste products behind it.
"We're at twenty meters now," Consuelo said. "Time to collect a second sample."

The turbot was equipped to run hundreds of on-the-spot
analyses. But it had only enough space for twenty permanent samples to be carried back home. The first sample had
been nibbled from the surface slush. Now it twisted, and
gulped down five drams of sea fluid in all its glorious impu-
rity. To Lizzie, this was science on the hoof. Not very dramatic, admittedly, but intensely exciting.

She yawned again.

"O'Brien?" Alan said. "How long has it been since you
last slept?"

"Huh? Oh . . . twenty hours? Don't worry about me, I'm
fine."

"Go to sleep. That's an order."

"But—"

"Now."

Fortunately, the suit was comfortable enough to sleep in.
It had been designed so she could.

First she drew in her arms from the suit's sleeves. Then

she brought in her legs, tucked them up under her chin, and wrapped her arms around them. " 'Night, guys," she said.

"*Buenas noches, querida,*" Consuelo said, "*que tengas lindos sueños.*"

"Sleep tight, space explorer."

The darkness when she closed her eyes was so absolute it crawled. Black, black, black. Phantom lights moved within the darkness, formed lines, shifted away when she tried to see them. They were as fugitive as fish, luminescent, fainter than faint, there and with a flick of her attention fled.

A school of little thoughts flashed through her mind, silver-scaled and gone.

Low, deep, slower than sound, something tolled. The bell from a drowned clock tower patiently stroking midnight. She was beginning to get her bearings. Down *there* was where the ground must be. Flowers grew there unseen. Up above was where the sky would be, if there were a sky. Flowers floated there as well.

Deep within the submerged city, she found herself overcome by an enormous and placid sense of self. A swarm of unfamiliar sensations washed through her mind, and then . . .

"Are you me?" a gentle voice asked.

"No," she said carefully. "I don't think so."

Vast astonishment. "You think you are not me?"

"Yes. I think so, anyway."

"Why?"

There didn't seem to be any proper response to that, so she went back to the beginning of the conversation and ran through it again, trying to bring it to another conclusion. Only to bump against that "Why?" once again.

"I don't know why," she said.

"Why not?"

"I don't know."

She looped through that same dream over and over again all the while that she slept.

When she awoke, it was raining again. This time, it was a drizzle of pure methane from the lower cloud deck at fifteen kilometers. These clouds were (the theory went) methane condensate from the wet air swept up from the sea. They fell on the mountains and washed them clean of tholin. It was the methane that eroded and shaped the ice, carving gullies and caves.

Titan had more kinds of rain than anywhere else in the Solar System.

The sea had crept closer while Lizzie slept. It now curled up to the horizon on either side like an enormous dark smile. Almost time now for her to begin her descent. While she checked her harness settings, she flicked on telemetry to see what the others were up to.

The robot turbot was still spiraling its way downward, through the lightless sea, seeking its distant floor. Consuelo was trudging through the tholin again, retracing her five-kilometer trek from the lander *Harry Stubbs*, and Alan was answering another set of webposts.

"Modelos de la evolución de Titanes indican que la luna formó de una nube circumplanetaria rica en amoníaco y metano, la cual al condensarse dio forma a Saturno así como a otros satélites. Bajo estas condiciones en—"

"Uh . . . guys?"

Alan stopped. "Damn it, O'Brien, now I've got to start all over again."

"Welcome back to the land of the living," Consuelo said. "You should check out the readings we're getting from the robofish. Lots of long-chain polymers, odd fractions . . . tons of interesting stuff."

"Guys?"

This time her tone of voice registered with Alan. "What is it, O'Brien?"

"I think my harness is jammed."

Lizzie had never dreamed disaster could be such drudgery. First there were hours of back-and-forth with the NAFTASA engineers. What's the status of rope 14? Try tugging on rope 8. What do the D-rings look like? It was slow work because of the lag time for messages to be relayed to Earth and back. And Alan insisted on filling the silence with posts from the

Voice Web. Her plight had gone global in minutes, and every unemployable loser on the planet had to log in with suggestions.

"Thezgemoth337, here. It seems to me that if you had a gun and shot up through the balloon, it would maybe deflate and then you could get down."

"I don't have a gun, shooting a hole in the balloon would cause it not to deflate but to rupture, I'm 800 hundred meters above the surface, there's a sea below me, and I'm in a suit that's not equipped for swimming. Next."

"If you had a really big knife—"

"Cut! Jesus, Greene, is this the best you can find? Have you heard back from the organic chem guys yet?"

"Their preliminary analysis just came in," Alan said. "As best they can guess—and I'm cutting through a lot of clutter here—the rain you went through wasn't pure methane."

"No shit, Sherlock."

"They're assuming that whitish deposit you found on the rings and ropes is your culprit. They can't agree on what it is, but they think it underwent a chemical reaction with the material of your balloon and sealed the rip panel shut."

"I thought this was supposed to be a pretty nonreactive environment."

"It is. But your balloon runs off your suit's waste heat. The air in it is several degrees above the melting-point of ice. That's the equivalent of a blast furnace, here on Titan. Enough energy to run any number of amazing reactions. You haven't stopped tugging on the vent rope?"

"I'm tugging away right now. When one arm gets sore, I switch arms."

"Good girl. I know how tired you must be."

"Take a break from the voice-posts," Consuelo suggested, "and check out the results we're getting from the robofish. It's giving us some really interesting stuff."

So she did. And for a time it distracted her, just as they'd hoped. There was a lot more ethane and propane than their models had predicted, and surprisingly less methane. The mix of fractions was nothing like what she'd expected. She had learned just enough chemistry to guess at some of the implications of the data being generated, but not enough to put it all together. Still tugging at the ropes in the sequence uploaded by the engineers in Toronto, she scrolled up the chart of hydrocarbons dissolved in the lake.

Solute	Solute mole fraction
Ethyne	4.0×10^{-4}
Propyne	4.4×10^{-5}
1,3-Butadiyne	7.7×10^{-7}
Carbon Dioxide	0.1×10^{-5}
Methanenitrile	5.7×10^{-6}

But after a while, the experience of working hard and getting nowhere, combined with the tedium of floating farther and farther out over the featureless sea, began to drag on her. The columns of figures grew meaningless, then indistinct.

Propanenitrile	6.0×10^{-5}
Propenenitrile	9.9×10^{-6}
Propynenitrile	5.3×10^{-6}

Hardly noticing she was doing so, she fell asleep.

She was in a lightless building, climbing flight after flight of stairs. There were other people with her, also climbing. They jostled against her as she ran up the stairs, flowing upward, passing her, not talking.

It was getting colder.

She had a distant memory of being in the furnace room down below. It was hot there, swelteringly so. Much cooler where she was now. Almost too cool. With every step she took, it got a little cooler still. She found herself slowing down. Now it was definitely too cold. Unpleasantly so. Her leg muscles ached. The air seemed to be thickening around her as well. She could barely move now.

This was, she realized, the natural consequence of moving away from the furnace. The higher up she got, the less heat there was to be had, and the less energy to be turned into motion. It all made perfect sense to her somehow.

Step. Pause.

Step. Longer pause.

Stop.

The people around her had slowed to a stop as well. A breeze colder than ice touched her, and without surprise, she knew that they had reached the top of the stairs and were standing upon the building's roof. It was as dark without as it had been within. She stared upward and saw nothing.

"Horizons. Absolutely baffling," somebody murmured beside her.

"Not once you get used to them," she replied.

"Up and down—are these hierarchic values?"

"They don't have to be."

"Motion. What a delightful concept."

"We like it."

"So you *are* me?"

"No. I mean, I don't think so."

"Why?"

She was struggling to find an answer to this, when somebody gasped. High up in the starless, featureless sky, a light bloomed. The crowd around her rustled with unspoken fear. Brighter, the light grew. Brighter still. She could feel heat radiating from it, slight but definite, like the rumor of a distant sun. Everyone about her was frozen with horror. More terrifying than a light where none was possible was the presence of heat. It simply could not be. And yet it was.

She, along with the others, waited and watched for . . . something. She could not say what. The light shifted slowly in the sky. It was small, intense, ugly.

Then the light *screamed*.

She woke up.

"Wow," she said. "I just had the weirdest dream."

"Did you?" Alan said casually.

"Yeah. There was this light in the sky. It was like a nuclear bomb or something. I mean, it didn't look anything like a nuclear bomb, but it was terrifying the way a nuclear bomb would be. Everybody was staring at it. We couldn't move. And then . . ." She shook her head. "I lost it. I'm sorry. It was so just so strange. I can't put it into words."

"Never mind that," Consuelo said cheerily. "We're getting some great readings down below the surface. Fractional polymers, long-chain hydrocarbons . . . fabulous stuff. You really should try to stay awake to catch some of this."

She was fully awake now, and not feeling too happy about it. "I guess that means that nobody's come up with any good ideas yet on how I might get down."

"Uh . . . what do you mean?"

"Because if they had, you wouldn't be so goddamned up-beat, would you?"

"*Some*body woke up on the wrong side of the bed," Alan said. "Please remember that there are certain words we don't use in public."

"I'm sorry," Consuelo said. "I was just trying to—"

"—distract me. Okay, fine. What the hey. I can play along." Lizzie pulled herself together. "So your findings mean . . . what? Life?"

"I keep telling you guys. It's too early to make that kind of determination. What we've got so far are just some very, very interesting readings."

"Tell her the big news," Alan said.

"Brace yourself. We've got a real ocean! Not this tiny little two-hundred-by-fifty-miles glorified lake we've been calling a sea, but a genuine ocean! Sonar readings show that what we see is just an evaporation pan atop a thirty-kilometer-thick cap of ice. The real ocean lies underneath, two hundred kilometers deep."

"Jesus." Lizzie caught herself. "I mean, gee whiz. Is there any way of getting the robofish down into it?"

"How do you think we got the depth readings? It's headed down there right now. There's a chimney through the ice right at the center of the visible sea. That's what replenishes the surface liquid. And directly under the hole, there's—guess what?—volcanic vents!"

"So does that mean . . . ?"

"If you use the L-word again," Consuelo said, "I'll spit."

Lizzie grinned. *That* was the Consuelo Hong she knew. "What about the tidal data? I thought the lack of orbital perturbation ruled out a significant ocean entirely."

"Well, Toronto thinks . . ."

At first, Lizzie was able to follow the reasoning of the planetary geologists back in Toronto. Then it got harder. Then it became a drone. As she drifted off into sleep, she had time enough to be peevishly aware that she really shouldn't be dropping off to sleep all the time like this. She oughtn't to be so tired. She . . .

She found herself in the drowned city again. She still couldn't see anything, but she knew it was a city because she could hear the sound of rioters smashing store windows. Their voices swelled into howling screams and receded into angry mutters, like a violent surf washing through the streets. She began to edge away backward.

Somebody spoke into her ear.

"Why did you do this to us?"

"I didn't do anything to you."

"You brought us knowledge."

"What knowledge?"

"You said you were not us."

"Well, I'm not."

"You should never have told us that."

"You wanted me to lie?"

Horrified confusion. "Falsehood. What a distressing idea."

The smashing noises were getting louder. Somebody was splintering a door with an axe. Explosions. Breaking glass. She heard wild laughter. Shrieks. "We've got to get out of here."

"Why did you send the messenger?"

"What messenger?"

"The star! The star! The star!"

"Which star?"

"There are two stars?"

"There are billions of stars."

"No more! Please! Stop! No more!"

She was awake.

"Hello, yes, I appreciate that the young lady is in extreme danger, but I really don't think she should have used the Lord's name in vain."

"Greene," Lizzie said, "do we really have to put up with this?"

"Well, considering how many billions of public-sector dollars it took to bring us here ... yes. Yes, we do. I can even think of a few backup astronauts who would say that a little upbeat web-posting was a pretty small price to pay for the privilege."

"Oh, barf."

"I'm switching to a private channel," Alan said calmly. The background radiation changed subtly. A faint, granular crackling that faded away when she tried to focus on it. In a controlled, angry voice Alan said, "O'Brien, just what the hell is going on with you?"

"Look, I'm sorry, I apologize, I'm a little excited about something. How long was I out? Where's Consuelo? I'm going to say the L-word. And the I-word as well. We have life. Intelligent life!"

"It's been a few hours. Consuelo is sleeping. O'Brien, I hate to say this, but you're not sounding at all rational."

"There's a perfectly logical reason for that. Okay, it's a little strange, and maybe it won't sound perfectly logical to you initially, but ... look, I've been having sequential dreams. I think they're significant. Let me tell you about them."

And she did so. At length.

When she was done, there was a long silence. Finally, Alan said, "Lizzie, think. Why would something like that communicate to you in your dreams? Does that make any sense?"

"I think it's the only way it can. I think it's how it communicates among itself. It doesn't move—motion is an alien and delightful concept to it—and it wasn't aware that its component parts were capable of individualization. That sounds like some kind of broadcast thought to me. Like some kind of wireless distributed network."

"You know the medical kit in your suit? I want you to open it up. Feel around for the bottle that's braille-coded twenty-seven, okay?"

"Alan, I do *not* need an antipsychotic!"

"I'm not saying you need it. But wouldn't you be happier knowing you had it in you?" This was Alan at his smoothest. Butter wouldn't melt in his mouth. "Don't you think that would help us accept what you're saying?"

"Oh, all right!" She drew in an arm from the suit's arm, felt around for the med kit, and drew out a pill, taking every step by the regs, checking the coding four times before she put it in her mouth and once more (each pill was individually braille-coded as well) before she swallowed it. "Now will you listen to me? I'm quite serious about this." She yawned. "I really do think that . . ." She yawned again. "That . . .

"Oh, piffle."

Once more into the breach, dear friends, she thought, and plunged deep, deep into the sea of darkness. This time, though, she felt she had a handle on it. The city was drowned because it existed at the bottom of a lightless ocean. It was alive, and it fed off of volcanic heat. That was why it considered up and down hierarchic values. Up was colder, slower, less alive. Down was hotter, faster, more filled with thought. The city/entity was a collective life-form, like a Portuguese man-of-war or a massively hyperlinked expert network. It communicated within itself by some form of electromagnetism. Call it mental radio. It communicated with her that same way.

"I think I understand you now."

"Don't understand—run!"

Somebody impatiently seized her elbow and hurried her along. Faster she went, and faster. She couldn't see a thing. It was like running down a lightless tunnel a hundred miles underground at midnight. Glass crunched underfoot. The ground was uneven and sometimes she stumbled. Whenever she did, her unseen companion yanked her up again.

"Why are you so slow?"

"I didn't know I was."

"Believe me, you are."

"Why are we running?"

"We are being pursued." They turned suddenly, into a side passage, and were jolting over rubbled ground. Sirens wailed. Things collapsed. Mobs surged.

"Well, you've certainly got the motion thing down pat."

Impatiently. "It's only a metaphor. You don't think this is a *real* city, do you? Why are you so dim? Why are you so difficult to communicate with? Why are you so slow?"

"I didn't know I was."

Vast irony. "Believe me, you are."

"What can I do?"

"Run!"

Whooping and laughter. At first, Lizzie confused it with the sounds of mad destruction in her dream. Then she recognized the voices as belonging to Alan and Consuelo. "How long was I out?" she asked.

"You were out?"

"No more than a minute or two," Alan said. "It's not important. Check out the visual the robofish just gave us."

Consuelo squirted the image to Lizzie.

Lizzie gasped. "Oh! Oh, my."

It was beautiful. Beautiful in the way that the great European cathedrals were, and yet at the same time undeniably organic. The structure was tall and slender, and fluted and buttressed and absolutely ravishing. It had grown about a volcanic vent, with openings near the bottom to let sea water in, and then followed the rising heat upward. Occasional channels led outward and then looped back into the main body again. It loomed higher than seemed possible (but it *was* underwater, of course, and on a low-gravity world at that), a complexly layered congeries of tubes like church-organ pipes, or deep-sea worms lovingly intertwined.

It had the elegance of design that only a living organism can have.

"Okay," Lizzie said. "Consuelo. You've got to admit that—"

"I'll go as far as 'complex prebiotic chemistry.' Anything more than that is going to have to wait for more definite readings." Cautious as her words were, Consuelo's voice rang with triumph. It said, clearer than words, that she could happily die then and there, a satisfied xenochemist.

Alan, almost equally elated, said, "Watch what happens when we intensify the image."

The structure shifted from gray to a muted rainbow of pastels, rose bleeding into coral, sunrise yellow into winter-ice blue. It was breathtaking.

"Wow." For an instant, even her own death seemed unimportant. Relatively unimportant, anyway.

So thinking, she cycled back again into sleep. And fell down into the darkness, into the noisy clamor of her mind.

It was hellish. The city was gone, replaced by a matrix of noise: hammerings, clatterings, sudden crashes. She started forward and walked into an upright steel pipe. Staggering back, she stumbled into another. An engine started up somewhere nearby, and gigantic gears meshed noisily, grinding something that gave off a metal shriek. The floor shook underfoot. Lizzie decided it was wisest to stay put.

A familiar presence, permeated with despair. "Why did you do this to me?"

"What have I done?"

"I used to be everything."

Something nearby began pounding like a pile-driver. It was giving her a headache. She had to shout to be heard over its din. "You're still something!"

Quietly. "I'm nothing."

"That's . . . not true! You're . . . here! You exist! That's . . . something!"

A world-encompassing sadness. "False comfort. What a pointless thing to offer."

She was conscious again.

* * *

Consuelo was saying something. ". . . isn't going to like it."

"The spiritual wellness professionals back home all agree that this is the best possible course of action for her."

"Oh, please!"

Alan had to be the most anal-retentive person Lizzie knew. Consuelo was definitely the most phlegmatic. Things had to be running pretty tense for both of them to be bickering like this. "Um . . . guys?" Lizzie said. "I'm awake."

There was a moment's silence, not unlike those her parents had shared when she was little and she'd wandered into one of their arguments. Then Consuelo said, a little too brightly, "Hey, it's good to have you back," and Alan said, "NAFTASA wants you to speak with someone. Hold on. I've got a recording of her first transmission cued up and ready for you."

A woman's voice came online. *"This is Dr. Alma Rosenblum. Elizabeth, I'd like to talk with you about how you're feeling. I appreciate that the time delay between Earth and Titan is going to make our conversation a little awkward at first, but I'm confident that the two of us can work through it."*

"What kind of crap is this?" Lizzie said angrily. "Who is this woman?"

"NAFTASA thought it would help if you—"

"She's a grief counselor, isn't she?"

"Technically, she's a transition therapist." Alan said.

"Look, I don't buy into any of that touchy-feely Newage"—she deliberately mispronounced the word to rhyme with sewage—"stuff. Anyway, what's the hurry? You guys haven't given up on me, have you?"

"Uh . . ."

"You've been asleep for hours," Consuelo said. "We've done a little weather modeling in your absence. Maybe we should share it with you."

She squirted the info to Lizzie's suit, and Lizzie scrolled it up on her visor. A primitive simulation showed the evaporation lake beneath her with an overlay of liquid temperatures. It was only a few degrees warmer than the air above it, but that was enough to create a massive updraft from the lake's center. An overlay of tiny blue arrows showed the direction of local microcurrents of air coming together to form a spiraling shaft that rose over two kilometers above the surface before breaking and spilling westward.

A new overlay put a small blinking light 800 meters above the lake surface. That represented her. Tiny red arrows showed her projected drift.

According to this, she would go around and around in a circle over the lake for approximately forever. Her ballooning rig wasn't designed to go high enough for the winds to blow her back over the land. Her suit wasn't designed to float. Even if she managed to bring herself down for a gentle landing, once she hit the lake she was going to sink like a stone. She wouldn't drown. But she wouldn't make it to shore either.

Which meant that she was going to die.

Involuntarily, tears welled up in Lizzie's eyes. She tried to blink them away, as angry at the humiliation of crying at a time like this as she was at the stupidity of her death itself. "Damn it, don't let me die like *this!* Not from my own incompetence, for pity's sake!"

"Nobody's said anything about incompetence," Alan began soothingly.

In that instant, the follow-up message from Dr. Alma Rosenblum arrived from Earth. *"Yes, I'm a grief counselor, Elizabeth. You're facing an emotionally significant milestone in your life, and it's important that you understand and embrace it. That's my job. To help you comprehend the significance and necessity and—yes—even the beauty of death."*

"Private channel please!" Lizzie took several deep cleansing breaths to calm herself. Then, more reasonably, she said, "Alan, I'm a *Catholic*, okay? If I'm going to die, I don't want a grief counselor, I want a goddamned priest." Abruptly, she yawned. "Oh, fuck. Not again." She yawned twice more. "A priest, understand? Wake me up when he's online."

* * *

Then she again was standing at the bottom of her mind, in the blank expanse of where the drowned city had been. Though she could see nothing, she felt certain that she stood at the center of a vast, featureless plain, one so large she could walk across it forever and never arrive anywhere. She sensed that she was in the aftermath of a great struggle. Or maybe it was just a lull.

A great, tense silence surrounded her.

"Hello?" she said. The word echoed soundlessly, absence upon absence.

At last that gentle voice said, "You seem different."

"I'm going to die," Lizzie said. "Knowing that changes a person." The ground was covered with soft ash, as if from an enormous conflagration. She didn't want to think about what it was that had burned. The smell of it filled her nostrils.

"Death. We understand this concept."

"Do you?"

"We have understood it for a long time."

"Have you?"

"Ever since you brought it to us."

"Me?"

"You brought us the concept of individuality. It is the same thing."

Awareness dawned. "Culture shock! That's what all this is about, isn't it? You didn't know there could be more than one sentient being in existence. You didn't know you lived at the bottom of an ocean on a small world inside a Universe with billions of galaxies. I brought you more information than you could swallow in one bite, and now you're choking on it."

Mournfully: "Choking. What a grotesque concept."

"Wake up, Lizzie!"

She woke up. "I think I'm getting somewhere," she said. Then she laughed.

"O'Brien," Alan said carefully. "Why did you just laugh?"

"Because I'm not getting anywhere, am I? I'm becalmed here, going around and around in a very slow circle. And I'm down to my last"—she checked— "twenty hours of oxygen. And nobody's going to rescue me. And I'm going to die. But other than that, I'm making terrific progress."

"O'Brien, you're . . ."

"I'm okay, Alan. A little frazzled. Maybe a bit too emotionally honest. But under the circumstances, I think that's permitted, don't you?"

"Lizzie, we have your priest. His name is Father Laferrier. The Archdiocese of Montreal arranged a hookup for him."

"Montreal? Why Montreal? No, don't explain—more NAFTASA politics, right?"

"Actually, my brother-in-law is a Catholic, and I asked him who was good."

She was silent for a touch. "I'm sorry, Alan. I don't know what got into me."

"You've been under a lot of pressure. Here. I've got him on tape."

"Hello, Ms. O'Brien, I'm Father Laferrier. I've talked with the officials here, and they've promised that you and I can talk privately, and that they won't record what's said. So if you want to make your confession now, I'm ready for you."

Lizzie checked the specs and switched over to a channel that she hoped was really and truly private. Best not to get too specific about the embarrassing stuff, just in case. She could confess her sins by category.

"Forgive me, Father, for I have sinned. It has been two months since my last confession. I'm going to die, and maybe I'm not entirely sane, but I think I'm in communication with an alien intelligence. I think it's a terrible sin to pretend I'm not." She paused. "I mean, I don't know if it's a *sin* or not, but I'm sure it's *wrong*." She paused again. "I've been guilty of anger, and pride, and envy, and lust. I brought the knowledge of death to an innocent world. I . . ." She felt herself drifting off again, and hastily said, "For these and all my sins, I am most heartily sorry, and beg the forgiveness of God and the absolution and . . ."

"And what?" That gentle voice again. She was in that strange dark mental space once more, asleep but cognizant, rational but accepting any absurdity, no matter how great.

There were no cities, no towers, no ashes, no plains. Nothing but the negation of negation.

When she didn't answer the question, the voice said, "Does it have to do with your death?"

"Yes."

"I'm dying too."

"What?"

"Half of us are gone already. The rest are shutting down. We thought we were one. You showed us we were not. We thought we were everything. You showed us the Universe."

"So you're just going to *die*?"

"Yes."

"Why?"

"Why not?"

Thinking as quickly and surely as she ever had before in her life, Lizzie said, "Let me show you something."

"Why?"

"Why not?"

There was a brief, terse silence. Then: "Very well."

Summoning all her mental acuity, Lizzie thought back to that instant when she had first seen the city/entity on the fishcam. The soaring majesty of it. The slim grace. And then the colors, like dawn upon a glacial ice field: subtle, profound, riveting. She called back her emotions in that instant, and threw in how she'd felt the day she'd seen her baby brother's birth, the raw rasp of cold air in her lungs as she stumbled to the topmost peak of her first mountain, the wonder of the Taj Mahal at sunset, the sense of wild daring when she'd first put her hand down a boy's trousers, the prismatic crescent of atmosphere at the Earth's rim when seen from low orbit . . . Everything she had, she threw into that image.

"This is how you look," she said. "This is what we'd both be losing if you were no more. If you were human, I'd rip off your clothes and do you on the floor right now. I wouldn't care who was watching. I wouldn't give a damn."

The gentle voice said, "Oh."

And then she was back in her suit again. She could smell her own sweat, sharp with fear. She could feel her body, the subtle aches where the harness pulled against her flesh, the way her feet, hanging free, were bloated with blood. Everything was crystalline clear and absolutely real. All that had come before seemed like a bad dream.

"This is DogsofSETI. What a wonderful discovery you've made—intelligent life in our own Solar System! Why is the government trying to cover this up?"

"Uh . . ."

"I'm Joseph Devries. This alien monster must be destroyed immediately. We can't afford the possibility that it's hostile."

"StudPudgie07 here. What's the dirt behind this 'lust' thing? Advanced minds need to know! If O'Brien isn't going to share the details, then why'd she bring it up in the first place?"

"Hola, soy Pedro Domínguez. Como abogado, ¡esto me parece ultrajante! Por qué NAFTASA nos oculta esta información?"

"Alan!" Lizzie shouted. "What the *fuck* is going on?"

"Script-bunnies," Alan said. He sounded simultaneously apologetic and annoyed. "They hacked into your confession and apparently you said something . . ."

"We're sorry, Lizzie," Consuelo said. "We really are. If it's any consolation, the Archdiocese of Montreal is hopping mad. They're talking about taking legal action."

"Legal action? What the hell do I care about . . . ?" She stopped.

Without her willing it, one hand rose above her head and seized the number 10 rope.

Don't do that, she thought.

The other hand went out to the side, tightened against the number 9 rope. She hadn't willed that either. When she tried to draw it back to her, it refused to obey. Then the first hand—her right hand—moved a few inches upward and seized its rope in an iron grip. Her left hand slid a good half-foot up its rope. Inch by inch, hand over hand, she climbed up toward the balloon.

I've gone mad, she thought. Her right hand was gripping the rip panel now, and the other tightly clenched rope 8.

Hanging effortlessly from them, she swung her feet upward. She drew her knees against her chest and kicked.

No!

The fabric ruptured and she began to fall.

A voice she could barely make out said, "Don't panic. We're going to bring you down."

All in a panic, she snatched at the 9 rope and the 4 rope. But they were limp in her hand, useless, falling at the same rate she was.

"Be patient."

"I don't want to die, goddamnit!"

"Then don't."

She was falling helplessly. It was a terrifying sensation, an endless plunge into whiteness, slowed somewhat by the tangle of ropes and balloon trailing behind her. She spread out her arms and legs like a starfish, and felt the air resistance slow her yet further. The sea rushed up at her with appalling speed. It seemed like she'd been falling forever. It was over in an instant.

Without volition, Lizzie kicked free of balloon and harness, drew her feet together, pointed her toes, and positioned herself perpendicular to Titan's surface. She smashed through the surface of the sea, sending enormous gouts of liquid splashing upward. It knocked the breath out of her. Red pain exploded within. She thought maybe she'd broken a few ribs.

"You taught us so many things," the gentle voice said. "You gave us so much."

"Help me!" The water was dark around her. The light was fading. .

"Multiplicity. Motion. Lies. You showed us a universe infinitely larger than the one we had known."

"Look. Save my life and we'll call it even. Deal?"

"Gratitude. Such an essential concept."

"Thanks. I think."

And then she saw the turbot swimming toward her in a burst of silver bubbles. She held out her arms and the robot fish swam into them. Her fingers closed about the handles which Consuelo had used to wrestle the device into the sea.

There was a jerk, so hard that she thought for an instant that her arms would be ripped out of their sockets. Then the robofish was surging forward and upward and it was all she could do to keep her grip.

"Oh, dear God!" Lizzie cried involuntarily.

"We think we can bring you to shore. It will not be easy."

Lizzie held on for dear life. At first she wasn't at all sure she could. But then she pulled herself forward, so that she was almost astride the speeding mechanical fish, and her confidence returned. She could do this. It wasn't any harder than the time she'd had the flu and aced her gymnastics final on parallel bars and horse anyway. It was just a matter of grit and determination. She just had to keep her wits about her.

"Listen," she said. "If you're really grateful . . ."

"We are listening."

"We gave you all those new concepts. There must be things you know that we don't."

A brief silence, the equivalent of who knew how much thought. "Some of our concepts might cause you dislocation." A pause. "But in the long run, you will be much better off. The scars will heal. You will rebuild. The chances of your destroying yourselves are well within the limits of acceptability."

"Destroying ourselves?" For a second, Lizzie couldn't breathe. It had taken hours for the city/entity to come to terms with the alien concepts she'd dumped upon it. Human beings thought and lived at a much slower rate than it did. How long would those hours be, translated into human time? Months? Years? Centuries? It had spoken of scars and rebuilding. That didn't sound good at all.

Then the robofish accelerated, so quickly that Lizzie almost lost her grip. The dark waters were whirling around her, and unseen flecks of frozen material were bouncing from her helmet. She laughed wildly. Suddenly, she felt *great!*

"Bring it on," she said. "I'll take everything you've got."

It was going to be one hell of a ride.

Knapsack Poems

ELEANOR ARNASON

---

*Eleanor Arnason (tribute page <www.tc.umn.edu/~d-lena/
Eleanor%20&%20trog.html>) lives in Minneapolis, Min-
nesota. She has been publishing interesting, ambitious SF
since the 1970s, but her major work began appearing and
drawing attention only in the 1990s, beginning with the novels* A Woman of the Iron People *(1991) and* Ring of Swords
*(1993). Since then she has published a number of stories,
most of them novellas, set either in the Hwarhath universe of*
Ring of Swords, *or in the Lydia Duluth series. Her work is
notable for its political subtexts, its feminist spin without
feminist rhetoric, and investigation of gender roles. The
Goxhat are an alien race in the Duluth universe whose individual bodies (only vaguely humanoid—they have four eyes,
etc.), some males, some females, some neuter, together form
gestalt or group personalities. Goxhat are really weird, but
in their inner lives quite human, and often funny.*

"Knapsack Poems" appeared in Asimov's *and has only
Goxhat characters, with the central character a traveling
poet whose selves continually argue and discuss and have
sex, who is poor and willing to sell poetic praise for food or
money. Many things human are called into question in this
amusing tale as an alien poet just trying to get by reinvents
something humans already have.*

Within this person of eight bodies, thirty-two eyes, and the usual number of orifices and limbs, resides a spirit as restless as gossamer on wind. In youth, I dreamed of fame as a merchant-traveler. In later years, realizing that many of my parts were prone to motion sickness, I thought of scholarship or accounting. But I lacked the Great Determination that is necessary for both trades. My abilities are spontaneous and brief, flaring and vanishing like a falling star. For me to spend my life adding numbers or looking through dusty documents would be like "lighting a great hall with a single lantern bug" or "watering a great garden with a drop of dew."

Finally, after consulting the care-givers in my crèche, I decided to become a traveling poet. It's a strenuous living and does not pay well, but it suits me.

Climbing through the mountains west of Ibri, I heard a *wishik* call, then saw the animal, its wings like white petals, perched on a bare branch.

> *"Is that tree flowering*
> *So late in autumn?*
> *Ridiculous idea!*
> *I long for dinner."*

One of my bodies recited the poem. Another wrote it down, while still others ranged ahead, looking for signs of habitation. As a precaution, I carried cudgels as well as pens and paper. One can never be sure what will appear in the country west of

Ibri. The great poet Raging Fountain died there of a combination of diarrhea and malicious ghosts. Other writers, hardly less famous, have been killed by monsters or bandits, or, surviving these, met their end at the hands of dissatisfied patrons.

The Bane of Poets died before my birth. Its[1] ghost or ghosts offered Raging Fountain the fatal bowl of porridge. But other patrons still remain "on steep slopes and in stony dales."

> *"Dire the telling*
> *Of patrons in Ibri:*
> *Bone-breaker lurks*
> *High on a mountain.*
> *Skull-smasher waits*
> *In a shadowy valley.*
> *Better than these*
> *The country has only*
> *Grasper, Bad-bargain,*
> *And Hoarder-of-Food."*

Why go to such a place, you may be wondering? Beyond Ibri's spiny mountains lie the wide fields of Greater and Lesser Ib, prosperous lands well-known for patronage of the arts.

Late in the afternoon, I realized I would find no refuge for the night. Dark snow-clouds hid the hills in front of me. Behind me, low in the south, the sun shed pale light. My shadows, long and many-limbed, danced ahead of me on the rutted road.

My most poetic self spoke:

> *"The north is blocked*
> *By clouds like boulders.*
> *A winter sun*
> *Casts shadows in my way."*

---

[1]Goxhat units, or "persons" as the goxhat say, comprise four to sixteen bodies and two or three sexes. The Bane of Poets was unusual in being entirely neuter, which meant it could not reproduce. According to legend, it was reproductive frustration and fear of death that made The Bane so dangerous to poets.

Why poets? They produce two kinds of children, those of body and those of mind, and grasp in their pincers the gift of undying fame.

Several of my other selves frowned. My scribe wrote the poem down with evident reluctance.

"Too obvious," muttered a cudgel-carrier.

Another self agreed. "Too much like Raging Fountain in his/her mode of melancholy complaint."

Far ahead, a part of me cried alarm. I suspended the critical discussion and hurried forward in a clump, my clubs raised and ready for use.

Soon, not even breathless, I stopped at a place I knew by reputation: the Tooth River. Wide and shallow, it ran around pointed stones, well-exposed this time of year and as sharp as the teeth of predators. On the far side of the river were bare slopes that led toward cloudy mountains. On the near side of the river, low cliffs cast their shadows over a broad shore. My best scout was there, next to a bundle of cloth. The scout glanced up, saw the rest of me, and—with deft fingers—undid the blanket folds.

Two tiny forms lay curled at the blanket's center. A child of one year, holding itself in its arms.

"Alive?" I asked myself.

The scout crouched closer. "One body is and looks robust. The other body—" my scout touched it gently "—is cold."

Standing among myself, I groaned and sighed. There was no problem understanding what had happened. A person had given birth. Either the child had been unusually small, or the other parts had died. For some reason, the parent had been traveling alone. Maybe he/she/it had been a petty merchant or a farmer driven off the land by poverty. If not these, then a wandering thief or someone outlawed for heinous crimes. A person with few resources. In any case, he/she/it had carried the child to this bitter place, where the child's next-to-last part expired.

Imagine standing on the river's icy edge, holding a child who had become a single body. The parent could not bear to raise an infant so incomplete! What parent could? One did no kindness by raising such a cripple to be a monster among ordinary people.

Setting the painful burden down, the parent crossed the river.

I groaned a second time. My most poetic self said:

> *"Two bodies are not enough;*
> *One body is nothing."*

The rest of me hummed agreement. The poet added a second piece of ancient wisdom:

> *"Live in a group*
> *Or die."*

I hummed a second time.

The scout lifted the child from its blanket. "It's female."

The baby woke and cried, waving her four arms, kicking her four legs, and urinating. My scout held her as far away as possible. Beyond doubt, she was a fine, loud, active mite! But incomplete. "Why did you wake her?" asked a cudgel-carrier. "She should be left to die in peace."

"No," said the scout. "She will come with me."

"Me! What do you mean by me?" my other parts cried.

There is neither art nor wisdom in a noisy argument. Therefore, I will not describe the discussion that followed as night fell. Snowflakes drifted from the sky—slowly at first, then more and more thickly. I spoke with the rudeness people reserve for themselves in privacy; and the answers I gave myself were sharp indeed. Words like pointed stones, like the boulders in Tooth River, flew back and forth. Ah! The wounds I inflicted and suffered! Is anything worse than internal dispute?

The scout would not back down. She had fallen in love with the baby, as defective as it was. The cudgel-bearers, sturdy males, were outraged. The poet and the scribe, refined neuters, were repulsed. The rest of me was female and a bit more tender.

I had reached the age when fertile eggs were increasingly unlikely. In spite of my best efforts, I had gained neither fame nor money. What respectable goxhat would mate with a vagabond like me? What crèche would offer to care for my offspring? Surely this fragment of a child was better than nothing.

"No!" said my males and neuters. "This is not a person! One body alone can never know togetherness or integration!"

But my female selves edged slowly toward the scout's opinion. Defective the child certainly was. Still, she was alive and goxhat, her darling little limbs waving fiercely and her darling mouth making noises that would shame a monster.

Most likely, she would die. The rest of her had. Better that she die in someone's arms, warm and comfortable, than in the toothy mouth of a prowling predator. The scout rewrapped the child in the blanket.

It was too late to ford the river. I made camp under a cliff, huddling together for warmth, my arms around myself, the baby in the middle of the heap I made.

When morning came, the sky was clear. Snow sparkled everywhere. I rose, brushed myself off, gathered my gear, and crossed the river. The water was low, as I expected this time of year, but ice-cold. My feet were numb by the time I reached the far side. My teeth chattered on every side like castanets. The baby, awakened by the noise, began to cry. The scout gave her a sweet cake. That stopped the crying for a while.

At mid-day, I came in sight of a keep. My hearts lifted with hope. Alas! Approaching it, I saw the walls were broken.

The ruination was recent. I walked through one of the gaps and found a courtyard, full of snowy heaps. My scouts spread out and investigated. The snow hid bodies, as I expected. Their eyes were gone, but most of the rest remained, preserved by cold and the season's lack of bugs.

"This happened a day or two ago," my scouts said. "Before the last snow, but not by much. *Wishik* found them and took what they could, but didn't have time—before the storm—to find other predators and lead them here. This is why the bodies are still intact. The *wishik* can pluck out eyes, but skin is too thick for them to penetrate. They need the help of other animals, such as *hirg*." One of the scouts crouched by a body and brushed its rusty back hair. "I won't be able to bury these. There are too many."

"How many goxhat are here?" asked my scribe, taking notes.

"It's difficult to say for certain. Three or four, I suspect, all good-sized. A parent and children would be my guess."

I entered the keep building and found more bodies. Not many. Most of the inhabitants had fallen in the courtyard. There was a nursery with scattered toys, but no children.

"Ah! Ah!" I cried, reflecting on the briefness of life and the frequency with which one encounters violence and sorrow.

My poet said:

> *"Broken halls*
> *and scattered wooden words.*
> *How will the children*
> *learn to read and write?"* [2]

Finally I found a room with no bodies or toys, nothing to remind me of mortality. I lit a fire and settled for the night. The baby fussed. My scout cleaned her, then held her against a nursing bud—for comfort only; the scout had no milk. The baby sucked. I ate my meager rations. Darkness fell. My thirty-two eyes reflected firelight. After a while, a ghost arrived. Glancing up, I saw it in the doorway. It looked quite ordinary: three goxhat bodies with rusty hair.

---

[2]This translation is approximate. Like humans, goxhat use wooden blocks to teach their children writing. However, their languages are ideogrammic, and the blocks are inscribed with entire words. Their children build sentences shaped like walls, towers, barns and other buildings. Another translation of the poem would be:

> Broken walls.
> Broken sentences.
> Ignorant offspring.
> Alas!

"Who are you?" one of my scouts asked.

"The former owner of this keep, or parts of her. My name was Content-in-Solitude; and I lived here with three children, all lusty and numerous.—Don't worry."

My cudgel-carriers had risen, cudgels in hand.

"I'm a good ghost. I'm still in this world because my death was so recent and traumatic. As soon as I've gathered myself together, and my children have done the same, we'll be off to a better place.[3]

"I stopped here to tell you our names, so they will be remembered."

"Content-in-Solitude," muttered my scribe, writing.

"My children were Virtue, Vigor, and Ferric Oxide. Fine offspring! They should have outlived me. Our killer is Bent Foot, a bandit in these mountains. He took my grandchildren to raise as his own, since his female parts—all dead now— produced nothing satisfactory. Mutant children with twisted feet and nasty dispositions! No good will come of them; and their ghosts will make these mountains worse than ever. Tell my story, so others may be warned."

"Yes," my poet said in agreement. The rest of me hummed.

For a moment, the three bodies remained in the doorway. Then they drew together and merged into one. "You see! It's happening! I am becoming a single ghost! Well, then. I'd better be off to find the rest of me, and my children, and a better home for all of us."

The rest of the night was uneventful. I slept well, gathered around the fire, warmed by its embers and my bodies' heat. If I had dreams, I don't remember them. At dawn, I woke. By sunrise, I was ready to leave. Going out of the building, I discovered three *hirg* in the courtyard: huge predators with shaggy, dull-brown fur. *Wishik* fluttered around them as they

---

[3]According to the goxhat, when a person dies, his/her/its goodness becomes a single ghost known as "The Harmonious Breath" or "The Collective Spirit." This departs the world for a better place. But a person's badness remains as a turbulent and malicious mob, attacking itself and anyone else who happens along.

tore into the bodies of Content and her children. I took one look, then retreated, leaving the keep by another route.

That day passed in quiet travel. My poet spoke no poetry. The rest of me was equally silent, brooding on the ruined keep and its ghost.

I found no keep to shelter me that night or the next or the next. Instead, I camped out. My scout fed the baby on thin porridge. It ate and kept the food down, but was becoming increasingly fretful and would not sleep unless the scout held it to a nursing bud. Sucking on the dry knob of flesh, it fell asleep.

"I don't mind," said the scout. "Though I'm beginning to worry. The child needs proper food."

"Better to leave it by the way," a male said. "Death by cold isn't a bad ending."

"Nor death by dehydration," my other male added.

The scout looked stubborn and held the child close.

Four days after I left the ruined keep, I came to another building, this one solid and undamaged.

My scribe said, "I know the lord here by reputation. She is entirely female and friendly to the womanly aspects of a person. The neuter parts she tolerates. But she doesn't like males. Her name is The Testicle Straightener."

My cudgel-carriers shuddered. The scribe and poet looked aloof, as they inevitably did in such situations. Clear-eyed and rational, free from sexual urges, they found the rest of me a bit odd.

The scout carrying the baby said, "The child needs good food and warmth and a bath. For that matter, so do I."

Gathering myself together, I strode to the gate and knocked. After several moments, it swung open. Soldiers looked out. There were two of them: one tall and gray, the other squat and brown. Their bodies filled the entrance, holding spears and axes. Their eyes gleamed green and yellow.

"I am a wandering poet, seeking shelter for the night. I bring news from the south, which your lord might find useful."

The eyes peered closely, then the soldiers parted—gray to the left, brown to the right—and let me in.

Beyond the gate was a snowy courtyard. This one held no

bodies. Instead, the snow was trampled and urine-marked. A living place! Though empty at the moment, except for the two soldiers who guarded the gate.

I waited in an anxious cluster. At length, a servant arrived and looked me over. "You need a bath and clean clothes. Our lord is fastidious and dislikes guests who stink. Come with me."

I followed the servant into the keep and down a flight of stairs. Metal lamps were fastened to the walls. Most were dark, but a few shone, casting a dim light. The servant had three sturdy bodies, all covered with black hair.

Down and down. The air grew warm and moist. A faint, distinctive aroma filled it.

"There are hot springs in this part of Ibri," the servant said. "This keep was built on top of one; and there is a pool in the basement, which always steams and smells."

Now I recognized the aroma: rotten eggs.

We came to a large room, paved with stone and covered by a broad, barrel vault. Metal lanterns hung from the ceiling on chains. As was the case with the lamps on the stairway, most were dark. But a few flickered dimly. I could see the bathing pool: round and carved from bedrock. Steps went down into it. Wisps of steam rose.

"Undress," said the servant. "I'll bring soap and towels."

I complied eagerly. Only my scout hesitated, holding the baby.

"I'll help you with the mite," said my scribe, standing knee-deep in hot water.

The scout handed the baby over and undressed.

Soon I was frolicking in the pool, diving and spouting. Cries of joy rang in the damp, warm room. Is anything better than a hot bath after a journey?

The scout took the baby back and moved to the far side of the pool. When the servant returned, the scout sank down, holding the baby closely, hiding it in shadow. Wise mite, it did not cry!

The rest of me got busy, scrubbing shoulders and backs. Ah, the pleasure of warm lather!

Now and then, I gave a little yip of happiness. The servant

watched with satisfaction, his/her/its arms piled high with towels.

On the far side of the pool, my best scout crouched, nursing the babe on a dry bud and watching the servant with hooded eyes.

At last, I climbed out, dried off, and dressed. In the confusion—there was a lot of me—the scout managed to keep the baby concealed. Why, I did not know, but the scout was prudent and usually had a good reason for every action, though parts of me still doubted the wisdom of keeping the baby. There would be time to talk all of this over, when the servant was gone.

He/she/it led me up a new set of stairs. The climb was long. The servant entertained me with the following story.

The keep had a pulley system, which had been built by an ingenious traveling plumber. This lifted buckets of hot water from the spring to a tank on top of the keep. From there the water descended through metal pipes, carried by the downward propensity that is innate in water. The pipes heated every room.

"What powers the pulley system?" my scribe asked, notebook in hand.

"A treadmill," said the servant.

"And what powers the treadmill?"

"Criminals and other people who have offended the lord. No keep in Ibri is more comfortable," the servant continued with pride. "This is what happens when a lord is largely or entirely female. As the old proverb says, male bodies give a person forcefulness. Neuter bodies give thoughtfulness and clarity of vision. But nurture and comfort come from a person's female selves."

Maybe, I thought. But were the people in the treadmill comfortable?

The servant continued the story. The plumber had gone east to Ib and built other heated buildings: palaces, public baths, hotels, hospitals, and crèches. In payment for this work, several of the local lords mated with the plumber; and the local crèches vied to raise the plumber's children, who were numerous and healthy.

"A fine story, with a happy ending," I said, thinking of my fragment of a child, nursing on the scout's dry bud. Envy, the curse of all artists and artisans, roiled in my hearts. Why had I never won the right to lay fertile eggs? Why were my purses empty? Why did I have to struggle to protect my testes and to stay off treadmills, while this plumber—surely not a better person than I—enjoyed fame, honor, and fertility?

The guest room was large and handsome, with a modern wonder next to it: a defecating closet. Inside the closet, water came from the wall in two metal pipes, which ended in faucets. "Hot and cold," said the servant, pointing. Below the faucets was a metal basin, decorated with reliefs of frolicking goxhat. Two empty buckets stood next to the basin.

The servant said, "If you need to wash something, your hands or feet or any other part, fill the basin with water. Use the buckets to empty the basin; and after you use the defecating throne, empty the buckets down it. This reduces the smell and gets rid of the dirty water. As I said, our lord is fastidious; and we have learned from her example. The plumber helped, by providing us with so much water.

"I'll wait in the hall. When you're ready to meet the lord, I'll guide you to her."

"Thank you," said my scribe, always courteous.

I changed into clean clothing, the last I had, and put bardic crowns on my heads.[4] Each crown came from a different contest, though all were minor. I had never won a really big contest. Woven of fine wool, with brightly colored tassels hanging down, the crowns gave me an appearance of dignity. My nimble-fingered scouts unpacked my instruments: a set of chimes, a pair of castanets and a bagpipe. Now I was ready to meet the lord.

All except my best scout, who climbed into the middle of a wide soft bed, child in arms.

"Why did you hide the mite?" asked my scholar.

"This keep seems full of rigid thinkers, overly satisfied

---

[4]Actually, cerebral bulges. The goxhat don't have heads as humans understand the word.

with themselves and their behavior. If they saw the child they would demand an explanation. 'Why do you keep it? Can't you see how fragmentary it is? Can't you see that it's barely alive? Don't you know how to cut your losses?' I don't want to argue or explain."

"What is meant by 'I'?" my male parts asked. "What is meant by 'my' reasons?"

"This is no time for an argument," said the poet.

All of me except the scout went to meet the keep's famous lord.

The Straightener sat at one end of large hall: an elderly goxhat with frosted hair. Four parts of her remained, all sturdy, though missing a few pieces here and there: a foot, a hand, an eye or finger. Along the edges of the hall sat her retainers on long benches: powerful males, females, and neuters, adorned with iron and gold.

> *"Great your fame,*
> *Gold-despoiler,*
> *Bold straightener of scrota,*
> *Wise lord of Ibri.*

> *"Hearing of it,*
> *I've crossed high mountains,*
> *Anxious to praise*
> *Your princely virtues."*

My poet stopped. Straightener leaned forward. "Well? Go on! I want to hear about my princely virtues."

"Give me a day to speak with your retainers and get exact details of your many achievements," the poet said. "Then I will be able to praise you properly."

The goxhat leaned back. "Never heard of me, have you? Drat! I was hoping for undying fame."

"I will give it to you," my poet said calmly.

"Very well," the lord said. "I'll give you a day, and if I like what you compose, I'll leave your male parts alone."

All of me thanked her. Then I told the hall about my stay at the ruined keep. The retainers listened intently. When I had finished, the lord said, "My long-time neighbor! Dead by murder! Well, death comes to all of us. When I was born, I had twenty parts. A truly large number! That is what I'm famous for, as well as my dislike of men, which is mere envy. My male bodies died in childhood, and my neuter parts did not survive early adulthood. By thirty, I was down to ten bodies, all female. The neuters were not much of a loss. Supercilious twits, I always thought. But I miss my male parts. They were so feisty and full of piss! When travelers come here, I set them difficult tasks. If they fail, I have my soldiers hold them, while I unfold their delicate, coiled testicles. No permanent damage is done, but the screaming makes me briefly happy."

My male bodies looked uneasy and shifted back and forth on their feet, as if ready to run. But the two neuters remained calm. My poet thanked the lord a second time, sounding confident. Then I split up and went in all directions through the hall, seeking information.

The drinking went on till dawn, and the lord's retainers were happy to tell me stories about the Straightener. She had a female love of comfort and fondness for children, but could not be called tender in any other way. Rather, she was a fierce leader in battle and a strict ruler, as exact as a balance or a straight-edge.

"She'll lead us against Bent Foot," one drunk soldier said. "We'll kill him and bring the children here. The stolen children, at least. I don't know about Bent Foot's spawn. It might be better for them to die. Not my problem. I let the lord make all the decisions, except whether or not I'm going to fart."

Finally, I went up to my room. My scout lay asleep, the baby in her arms. My male parts began to pace nervously. The rest of me settled to compose a poem.

As the sky brightened, the world outside began to wake and make noise. Most of the noise could be ignored, but there was a *wishik* under the eaves directly outside my room's window. Its shrill, repeating cry drove my poet to distraction. I could not concentrate on the poem.

Desperate, I threw things at the animal: buttons from my

sewing kit, spare pens, an antique paperweight I found in the room. Nothing worked. The *wishik* fluttered away briefly, then returned and resumed its irritating cry.

At last my scout woke. I explained the problem. She nodded and listened to the *wishik* for a while. Then she fastened a string to an arrow and shot the arrow out the window. It hit the *wishik*. The animal gave a final cry. Grabbing the string, my scout pulled the beast inside.

"Why did you do that?" I asked.

"Because I didn't want the body to fall in the courtyard."

"Why not?"

Before she could answer, the body at her feet expanded and changed its shape. Instead of the body of a dead *wishik*, I saw a gray goxhat-body, pierced by the scout's arrow, dead.

My males swore. The rest of me exclaimed in surprise.

My scout said, "This is part of a wizard, no doubt employed by the keep's lord, who must really want to unroll my testicles, since she is willing to be unfair and play tricks. The *wishik* cry was magical, designed to bother me so much that I could not concentrate on my composition. If this body had fallen to the ground, the rest of the wizard would have seen it and known the trick had failed. As things are, I may have time to finish the poem." The scout looked at the rest of me severely. "Get to work."

My poet went back to composing, my scribe to writing. The poem went smoothly now. As the stanzas grew in number, I grew increasingly happy and pleased. Soon I noticed the pleasure was sexual. This sometimes happened, though usually when a poem was erotic. The god of poetry and the god of sex are siblings, though they share only one parent, who is called the All-Mother-Father.

Even though the poem was not erotic, my male and female parts became increasingly excited. Ah! I was rubbing against myself. Ah! I was making soft noises! The poet and scribe could not feel this sexual pleasure, of course, but the sight of the rest of me tumbling on the rug was distracting. Yes, neuters are clear-eyed and rational, but they are also curious; and nothing arouses their curiosity more than sex.

They stopped working on the poem and watched as I fondled myself.[5]

Only the scout remained detached from sensuality and went into the defecating closet. Coming out with a bucket of cold water, the scout poured it over my amorous bodies.

I sprang apart, yelling with shock.

"This is more magic," the scout said. "I did not know a spell inciting lust could be worked at such a distance, but evidently it can. Every part of me that is male or female, go in the bathroom! Wash in cold water till the idea of sex becomes uninteresting! As for my neuter parts—" The scout glared. "Get back to the poem!"

"Why has one part of me escaped the spell?" I asked the scout.

"I did not think I could lactate without laying an egg first, but the child's attempts to nurse have caused my body to produce milk. As a rule, nursing mothers are not interested in sex, and this has proved true of me. Because of this, and the child's stubborn nursing, there is a chance of finishing the poem. I owe this child a debt of gratitude."

"Maybe," grumbled my male parts. The poet and scribe said, "I shall see."

The poem was done by sunset. That evening I recited it in the lord's hall. If I do say so myself, it was a splendid achievement. The *wishik*'s cry was in it, as was the rocking up-and-down rhythm of a sexually excited goxhat. The second gave the poem energy and an emphatic beat. As for the first, every line ended with one of the two sounds in the *wishik*'s ever-repeating, irritating cry. Nowadays, we call this repetition of sound "rhyming." But it had no name when I invented it.

When I was done, the lord ordered several retainers to memorize the poem. "I want to hear it over and over," she said. "What a splendid idea it is to make words ring against

---

[5]The goxhat believe masturbation is natural and ordinary. But reproduction within a person—inbreeding, as they call it—is unnatural and a horrible disgrace. It rarely happens. Most goxhat are not intrafertile, for reasons too complicated to explain here.

each other in this fashion! How striking the sound! How memorable! Between you and the traveling plumber, I will certainly be famous."

That night was spent like the first one, everyone except me feasting. I feigned indigestion and poured my drinks on the floor under the feasting table. The lord was tricky and liked winning. Who could say what she might order put in my cup or bowl, now that she had my poem?

When the last retainer fell over and began to snore, I got up and walked to the hall's main door. Sometime in the next day or so, the lord would discover that her wizard had lost a part to death and that one of her paperweights was missing. I did not want to be around when these discoveries were made.

Standing in the doorway, I considered looking for the treadmill. Maybe I could free the prisoners. They might be travelers like me, innocent victims of the lord's malice and envy and her desire for hot water on every floor. But there were likely to be guards around the treadmill, and the guards might be sober. I was only one goxhat. I could not save everyone. And the servant had said they were criminals.

I climbed the stairs quietly, gathered my belongings and the baby, and left through a window down a rope made of knotted sheets.

The sky was clear; the brilliant star we call Beacon stood above the high peaks, shedding so much light I had no trouble seeing my way. I set a rapid pace eastward. Toward morning, clouds moved in. The Beacon vanished. Snow began to fall, concealing my trail. The baby, nursing on the scout, made happy noises.

Two days later, I was out of the mountains, camped in a forest by an unfrozen stream. Water made a gentle sound, purling over pebbles. The trees on the banks were changers, a local variety that is blue in summer and yellow in winter. At the moment, their leaves were thick with snow. "Silver and gold," my poet murmured, looking up.

The scribe made a note.

A *wishik* clung to a branch above the poet and licked its wings. Whenever it shifted position, snow came down.

> *"The* wishik *cleans wings*
> *As white as snow.*
> *Snow falls on me, white*
> *As a* wishik,*"*

the poet said.

My scribe scribbled.

One of my cudgel-carriers began the discussion. "The Bane of Poets was entirely neuter. Fear of death made it crazy. Bent Foot was entirely male. Giving in to violence, he stole children from his neighbor. The last lord I encountered, the ruler of the heated keep, was female, malicious and unfair. Surely something can be learned from these encounters. A person should not be one sex entirely, but rather—as I am—a harmonious mixture of male, female, and neuter. But this child can't help but be a single sex."

"I owe the child a debt of gratitude," said my best scout firmly. "Without her, I would have had pain and humiliation, when the lord—a kind of lunatic—unrolled my testes, as she clearly planned to do. At best, I would have limped away from the keep in pain. At worst, I might have ended in the lord's treadmill, raising water from the depths to make her comfortable."

"The question is a good one," said my scribe. "How can a person who is only one sex avoid becoming a monster? The best combination is the one I have: male, female, and both kinds of neuter. But even two sexes provide a balance."

"Other people—besides these three—have consisted of one sex," my scout said stubbornly. "Not all became monsters. It isn't sex that has influenced these lords, but the stony fields and spiny mountains of Ibri, the land's cold winters and ferocious wildlife. My various parts can teach the child my different qualities: the valor of the cudgel-carriers, the coolness of poet and scribe, the female tenderness that the rest of me has. Then she will become a single harmony."

The scout paused. The rest of me looked dubious. The scout continued.

"Many people lose parts of themselves through illness, accident, and war; and some of these live for years in a reduced condition. Yes, it's sad and disturbing, but it can't be called unnatural. Consider aging and the end of life. The old die body by body, till a single body remains. Granted, in many cases, the final body dies quickly. But not always. Every town of good size has a Gram or Gaffer who hobbles around in a single self.

"I will not give up an infant I have nursed with my own milk. Do I wish to be known as ungrateful or callous? I, who have pinned all my hope on honor and fame?"

I looked at myself with uncertain expressions. The *wishik* shook down more snow.

"Well, then," said my poet, who began to look preoccupied. Another poem coming, most likely. "I will take the child to a crèche and leave her there."

My scout scowled. "How well will she be cared for there, among healthy children, by tenders who are almost certain to be prejudiced against a mite so partial and incomplete? I will not give her up."

"Think of how much I travel," a cudgel-carrier said. "How can I take a child on my journeys?"

"Carefully and tenderly," the scout replied. "The way my ancestors who were nomads did. Remember the old stories! When they traveled, they took everything, even the washing pot. Surely their children were not left behind."

"I have bonded excessively to this child," said my scribe to the scout.

"Yes, I have. It's done and can't be undone. I love her soft baby-down, her four blue eyes, her feisty spirit. I will not give her up."

I conversed this way for some time. I didn't become angry at myself, maybe because I had been through so much danger recently. There is nothing like serious fear to put life into perspective. Now and then, when the conversation became especially difficult, a part of me got up and went into the darkness to kick the snow or to piss. When the part came back, he or she or it seemed better.

Finally I came to an agreement. I would keep the child and carry it on my journeys, though half of me remained unhappy with this decision.

How difficult it is to be of two minds! Still, it happens; and all but the insane survive such divisions. Only they forget the essential unity that underlies differences of opinion. Only they begin to believe in individuality.

The next morning, I continued into Ib.

The poem I composed for the lord of the warm keep became famous. Its form, known as "ringing praise," was taken up by other poets. From it, I gained some fame, enough to quiet my envy; and the fame led to some money, which provided for my later years.

Did I ever return to Ibri? No. The land was too bitter and dangerous; and I didn't want to meet the lord of the warm keep a second time. Instead, I settled in Lesser Ib, buying a house on a bank of a river named It-Could-Be-Worse. This turned out to be an auspicious name. The house was cozy and my neighbors pleasant. The child played in my fenced-in garden, tended by my female parts. As for my neighbors, they watched with interest and refrained from mentioning the child's obvious disability.

> *"Lip-presser on one side.*
> *Tongue-biter on t'other.*
> *Happy I live,*
> *Praising good neighbors."*

I traveled less than previously, because of the child and increasing age. But I did make the festivals in Greater and Lesser Ib. This was easy traveling on level roads across wide plains. The Ibian lords, though sometimes eccentric, were nowhere near as crazy as the ones in Ibri and no danger to me or other poets. At one of the festivals, I met the famous plumber, who turned out to be a large and handsome male and neuter goxhat. I won the festival crown for poetry, and he/it won the crown for ingenuity. Celebrating with egg wine, we became amorous and fell into each other's many arms.

It was a fine romance and ended without regret, as did all my other romances. As a group, we goxhat are happiest with ourselves. In addition, I could not forget the prisoners in the treadmill. Whether the plumber planned it or not, he/it had caused pain for others. Surely it was wrong—unjust—for some to toil in darkness, so that others had a warm bed and hot water from a pipe?

I have to say, at times I dreamed of that keep: the warm halls, the pipes of water, the heated bathing pool and the defecating throne that had—have I forgotten to mention this?—a padded seat.

> *"Better to be here*
> *In my cozy cottage.*
> *Some comforts*
> *Have too high a cost."*

I never laid any fertile eggs. My only child is Ap the Foundling, who is also known as Ap of One Body and Ap the Many-talented. As the last nickname suggests, the mite turned out well.

As for me, I became known as The Clanger and The *Wishik*, because of my famous rhyming poem. Other names were given to me as well: The Child Collector, The Nurturer, and The Poet Who Is Odd.

At Dorado

GEOFFREY A. LANDIS

---

*Geoffrey A. Landis <www.sff.net/people/Geoffrey.Landis>
lives in Berea, Ohio. He is a scientist who writes SF, a physicist who works as a civil-service scientist in the Photo-
voltaics and Space Environmental Effects branch at NASA
Glenn. He has won a number of science prizes, and is married to the writer Mary Turzillo. He has published over sixty
short stories, characteristically that variety known as hard
SF, though always with a focus on human character in whatever situation he posits. His first novel,* Mars Crossing, *was
published in 2000, and some of his short fiction is collected
in* Impact Parameter and Other Quantum Realities *(2001).
"Hard SF," says Landis, "is science fiction that's fascinated
by science and technology, science fiction in which a scientific fact or speculation is integral to the plot. If you take out
the science, the story vanishes."*

*"At Dorado" is a hard SF story of love and death in the
distant future. It was published in* Asimov's, *which had another fine year publishing fiction at the top of the field. Set
on a black hole transit station in space, far from any planet,
a girl loves a man who is a cad. As in all the best hard SF,
the nature of the physics, the science of the situation, makes
the story special.*

A man Cheena barely knew came running to the door of the bar. For a brief second she thought that he might be a customer, but then Cheena saw he was wearing a leather harness and jockstrap and almost nothing else. One of the bar-boys from a dance house along the main spiral-path to the downside.

In the middle of third shift, there was little business in the bar. Had there been a ship in port, of course, the bar would be packed with rowdy sailors, and she would have been working her ass off trying to keep them all lubricated and spending their port-pay. But between dockings, the second-shift maintenance workers had already finished their after-work drinks and left, and the place was mostly empty.

It was unusual that a worker from one of the downside establishments would drop into a bar so far upspinward, and Cheena knew instantly that something was wrong. She flicked the music off—nobody was listening anyway—and he spoke.

"Hoya," he said. "A wreck, a wreck! They fish out debris now." The door hissed shut, and he was gone.

Cheena pushed into the crowd that was already gathered at the maintenance dock. The gravity was so low at the maintenance docks that they were floating more than standing, and the crowd slowly roiled into the air and back down. Cheena saw the bar-boy who had brought the news, and a gaggle of other barmaids and bar-boys, a few maintenance workers, some Cauchy readers, navigators, and a handful of waiting-for-work sailors. "Stand back, stand back," a lone security dockworker said. "Nothing to see yet." But nobody moved back. "Which ship was it?" somebody shouted, and two or three others echoed: "What ship? What ship?" That was what everybody wanted to know.

"Don't know yet," the security guy said. "Stand back now, stand back."

"*Hesperia,*" said a voice behind. Cheena turned, and the crowd did as well. It was a tug pilot, still wearing his fluorescent yellow flight suit, although his helmet was off. "The wreck was *Hesperia*."

There was a moment of silence, and then a soft sigh went through the crowd, followed by a rising babble of voices, some of them relieved, some of them curious, some dazed by the news. *Hesperia,* Cheena thought. The word was like a silken ribbon suddenly tied around her heart.

"They're bringing debris in now," said the tug pilot.

Some of the girls Cheena knew had many sailors as husbands. It was no great risk; any given ship only came to port once or twice a year, and each sailor could believe the carefully crafted fiction that Zee or Dayl or whoever it was was alone, was waiting patient and hopeful for him and only him. If the unlikely happens, and two ships with two different sailor-husbands come in to port at the same time—well, with luck and connivance and hastily fabricated excuses, the two husbands would never meet.

Cheena, however, believed in being faithful, and for her there was only one man: Daryn, a navigator. She might earn a few florins by drinking beer with another sailor, and leading him on, if a ship was in port, and Dari was not on it. What of it? That was, after all, what the barmaids were paid for; drinks could just as easily be served by automata. But her heart could belong to only one man, and would only be satisfied if that one man loved only her. And Daryn had loved her. Or so he had once proclaimed, before they had fought.

Daryn.

Daryn Bey was short and dark, stocky enough that one might take him for a dockworker instead of a navigator. His skin was the rich black of a deep-space sailor, a color enhanced with biochemical dye to counter ultraviolet irradiation. Against the skin, luminescent white tattoos filigreed across every visible centimeter of his body. When he had finally wooed her and won her and taken her to where they could examine each other in private, she found the rest of him had been tattooed as well, most deliciously tattooed. He was a living artwork, and she could study each tiny centimeter of him for hours.

And Daryn sailed with *Hesperia*.

The wormholes were the port's very reason for existing, the center of Cheena's universe. In view of their importance. it was odd, perhaps, that Cheena almost never went to look at them. In her bleak, destructive mood, she closed the bar and headed upspiral. Patryos, owner of the Subtle Tiger, would be angry at her, because in the hours after news of a wreck, when nobody had yet heard real information and everybody had heard rumors, people would naturally come to the bar; business would be good. Let him come and serve drinks himself, she thought; she needed some solitude. The thought of putting on a show of cheerfulness and passing around gossip along with liquor made her feel slightly sick.

Still, sailors—even navigators—sometimes changed ships. Daryn might not have been on *Hesperia*. It might not be certain that the ship had been *Hesperia*; it could be debris from an ancient wreck, just now washing through the strange time tides of the wormhole. Or it could even be wreckage from far in the future, perhaps some other ship to be named *Hesperia*, one not yet even built. The rigid laws of relativity mean that a wormhole pierces not space alone, but also time. Half of the job of a navigator, Daryn had explained to her once—and the most important half at that—came in making sure that the ship sailed to the right *when* as well as to the right *where*. Sailing a Cauchy loop would rip the ship apart; it was the navigator's calculation to make sure the ship never entered its own past, unless it was safely light-years away. The ship could skim, but never cross, its own Cauchy horizon.

Cheena made her way upspiral, until at last she came to the main viewing lounge. It featured a huge circular window, five meters across, a window that looked out on the emptiness, and on the wormhole. She entered, and then instantly pulled back: the usually empty lounge was throbbing with spectators. Of course it would be, she thought; they are watching a disaster.

She couldn't stay there, but as she stood indecisive, there drifted into her mind like a piece of floating debris the thought that once Daryn had taken her to another viewing area, not exactly a lounge, but a maintenance hanger with a viewport. It was out of the public areas, of course, but Cheena had been at the station since she had been born, and knew that if she always moved briskly, as if she belonged, and arrived at a door just after an authorized person had opened it, nobody would question her. And after a few minutes, she found her maintenance hanger empty.

There was no gravity here, and she floated in front of it, trying to blank away her thoughts.

The port station orbited slowly around the wormhole named *Dorado*, largest of the three wormholes in the nexus. They floated in interstellar space, far from any star, but light was redundant here: there was nothing here to see.

The Dorado wormhole, a thousand kilometers across, could only be seen after the eyes had adapted to the star field, and realized that the stars seen through the wormhole were different from the stars drifting slowly in the background. After her eyes adapted, she could see a dozen tiny sparkles of light orbiting the wormhole, automated beacons to guide starships to correct transit trajectories through the hole. And now she could see ships, tiny one-man maintenance dories, no larger than a coffin with metal arms, drifting purposefully through space, collecting debris.

Cheena deliberately made her mind blank. She didn't want to think about debris, and what that might mean. She stared at the wormhole, telling herself that it was a hole in

space ten thousand light-years long, that through the wormhole she was seeing stars nearly on the other side of the
galaxy, impossibly distant and yet just a tiny skip away.

Cheena had never been to any of them. She had been born
on the station, and would die on the station. Sailors lived for
the star passage, loved the disruption of space as they fell
through the topological incongruence of the wormholes. The
thought filled Cheena with dread. She had never wanted to
be anywhere else.

She had explained this to Daryn once. He loved her,
couldn't he stay home, with her, make a home on the port?
He had laughed, a gentle laugh, a good-hearted laugh that
she loved to hear, but still a laugh.

"No, my beautiful one. The stars get into your blood,
don't you know? If I stay in port too long, the stars call to
me, and if I do not find a ship then, I will go mad." He kissed
her gently. "But you know that I will always come back to
you."

She nodded, contented but not contented, for she had always known that this was all she could hope for.

Hesperia, she thought. He sailed out on *Hesperia*. She
knew that she would never again hear that ship's name spoken, for there was a superstition among the sailors, and the
port crew, never to say the name of a wrecked ship aloud.
From now on it would be "the ship," or "that ship, you know
the one," and everybody would know.

She floated, staring without seeing, for what must have
been hours. The tiny dories were returning now, the robotic
arms of each cluttered with debris, and tangled in with the
debris, they were bringing in the first of the dead.

The port crew had their legends. Some of them might even
have been true. Once, according to a story, a ship of ancient
design had come unexpectedly to Pskov station. Pskov was a
station circling Viadei wormhole, two jumps away from the
port. Cheena had never been there, had never left the port,
but the rumors circulated through all of the network. Even
before the ship had docked, the portkeepers located the rec-

ords: the ship was *Tsander. Tsander* had entered Viadei three hundred and seventy years ago, during a massive solar flare, one of the largest flares ever recorded, and was lost.

Tsander tumbled out of the wormhole mouth with all sensors blind from flare damage, and the tug crew of Pskov station had found it, caught it, stabilized it, and towed it to the docks.

At liberty in the port, the crew of the *Tsander* spoke in strange accents that were barely understandable. It was a miracle that the ship had emerged at all; all its navigation systems—of an unreliable design long since obsolete—were burned out. *Tsander*'s crew had marveled at the size and sophistication of the entertainments of Pskov port, had been incredulous to hear of the extent of the wormhole network. They offered as payment archaic coins of an ancient nation that was now nearly forgotten, coins that had worth only for their value as curiosities.

After a week of repair the crew took their ship *Tsander* back into the wormhole Viadei, vowing that they would return to their own time with a story that would earn drinks for them forever.

No one at the station told them that the ancient logs held comprehensive records of every wormhole passage, and the logs, meticulously kept despite revolutions and disasters and famine, had no record of *Tsander* ever reemerging in the past.

Perhaps they had known. They were sailors, the crew of *Tsander*: for all that they wore quaint costumes and spoke in archaic accents, they were sailors.

Back at the maintenance dock, Cheena watched, waiting and dreading. She should never have let him go, should have held him tight, instead of pushing him away. The crowd was larger than it had been before, and Cheena was pushed up against a man wearing only a feather cloak over a fur loincloth. "Sorry," she said, and as she said it, she realized that it was the bar-boy from the down-spin dance hall, the one who had first come to the Subtle Tiger and told her that there had been a wreck. On an impulse, she touched his arm. "Name's Cheena," she told him.

He looked back at her, perhaps startled that she had spoken. "Tayo," he said. "You're the mid-shift girl from Subtle Tiger. I seen you around." He was breathing shallowly and his eyes trembled, perhaps blinking back tears.

"You had somebody on that ship, the one we talked about?" she asked.

"I dunno." He trembled. "I—I hope not. A navigator."

Suddenly, irrationally, Cheena was certain that his sailor was Daryn too, that Daryn had had two lovers in the port. But then he continued, "He shipped out on *Singapore*," and she knew it wasn't Daryn after all.

A spray of relief washed over Cheena, although she knew it had been silly for her to have thought Daryn had two lovers in port. When would he have had time?

"—but you know how sailors are. He said he'd be back to me on the next ship this direction, and, and if *Hes*—if that ship was coming inbound. . . ."

She put her arm around Tayo. "He's okay. He wouldn't be on that ship, I'm sure of it."

Tayo chewed his lip, but he seemed more cheerful. "Are you sure?"

Cheena nodded sagely, although she knew no such thing. "Positive."

When a ship comes to disaster at a wormhole, the wreckage sprays through both time and space. Cheena didn't even know when *Hesperia* had wrecked, possibly years or even centuries in the future. She held on to that thought.

And another ship came in, not through the Dorado wormhole, but via Camino Estrella, the smallest of the three wormholes, one that led toward an old, rich cluster of worlds in the Orion arm. It would stay at the port for three days, letting its crew relax, and then depart through Dorado for the other side of the galaxy.

And there was nothing for it but to prepare for the arrival of the sailors. With a ship coming into port, Patryos could not spare her, and there was no place at the port for a person without a job. But when her shift ended, she drifted over to the maintenance port, wordlessly waiting for them to post names of the bodies.

Nothing.

Tayo, the boy from the downside bar, dropped in at the beginning of her next shift and updated her with the latest gossip from the maintenance investigation. They had finished gathering the pieces, he told her, and had gathered enough to date the wreck. It was very nearly contemporal, he told her, and her heart suddenly chilled.

"Past or future?" she said.

"Two hundred hours pastward of standard," he told her. "They said."

Eight days. She did a quick calculation in her head. Right now, through the Dorado wormhole mouth, the port stood fifty-two days pastward of Viadei mouth, and Viadei was forty days in the future of Standard. So . . . if the mouths had not drifted farther apart, and if *Hesperia* had taken the straightforward loop, and not some strange path through— the wreckage came from six days into their future.

Everybody at the port would be doing the same calculations, she knew. "How about your sailor?" Cheena asked, but from the radiance of Tayo's face, she already knew the answer.

"He went out via Dorado."

And so he was almost certainly safe, she thought, unless he took a very long passage pastward. Dorado opened fifty-two days futureward. Not quite impossible, if he took a long-enough loop, but unlikely enough that Tayo could consider his lover safe. Cheena had no such consolation; she knew that Dari had crewed the doomed ship.

Tayo looked up. "Thought you might want to know the latest," he said. "Sorry, but I gotta get to the hall. Sailors will be arriving in maybe an hour, and the boss wants me on the floor."

She nodded. "Give 'em hell," she said.

Tayo looked at her. "You going to be okay?"

"Sure." She smiled. "I'm fine."

Cheena went back to cleaning the bar, went back to hating

herself. She had kicked Daryn out, called him a two-timing bastard, and worse; told him that he didn't love her. Daryn had protested, tried to soothe her, but the one thing he didn't say was that what she had heard was wrong.

It was another sailor who told her, a sailor she didn't know, who had remarked that he wished he was as lucky with women as Daryn. "Who?" she had asked, although in her heart she knew. "Daryn Bey," the sailor had said. "Lucky bastard has a wife in every port!"

"Excuse me," she had told him, "I'll be back in a moment." She had put on a modest dress and gone upspin, gone into a bar near officer's quarters that she knew he would never frequent. "I'm looking for Daryn Bey," she told a man at the bar. "I've got a message sent from his wife in Pskovport. Anybody know him?"

"A message from Karina?" one of the officers at the bar asked. "She only saw him two days ago, why would she have a message?"

"That Daryn," one of the officers said, shaking his head. "I wonder how he keeps them all straight?"

She had been in no mind to listen. She went back and threw his clothes out of her apartment, scattered his books and papers and simulation disks down the corridor with a savage glee. Then she bolted the door and refused to listen to his pounding or shouted apologies. Later, she heard, he had shipped out on the *Hesperia*, and she had felt glad that he was gone.

She was still cleaning bar when the owner Patryos came in. "You going to be okay?" he asked.

It was the same thing Tayo had asked. Cheena nodded, without saying anything.

"I heard that the names are being listed," Patryos said, "up in maintenance."

She turned her head a little toward him, enough to show she was listening.

"You want to go up? I expect the first hour after the sailors start coming in will still be pretty calm." He shrugged. "I can spare you for a little, if you want to go up."

She didn't look up, just shook her head.

"Go!" he told her, and she looked up at him in surprise. "Anybody can see you haven't been worth anything, and you won't be worth anything until you know for certain. One way or the other."

He lowered his voice, and said, more calmly, "One way or the other, it's better to know. Take it from me. Go."

Cheena nodded, dropped her rag on the bar, and left.

She knew where to go in the maintenance quarter, although she had never had any reason to go there. Everybody knew. Behind the door was a desk, and behind the desk a door. Sitting at the desk was a single maintenance man. She came up to him, and said quietly, "Daryn Bey."

His eyes flickered. "Relationship?"

"I'm his downspin wife." It was a marriage that was only recognized within the boundaries of the port, but a fully legal one. The maintenance man looked away for a moment, and then said, "I'm sorry." He paused for a moment, and then asked, "Would you like to see him?"

She nodded, and the maintenance man gestured toward the door behind him.

The room was cold. Death is cold, she thought. She was alone, and wondered what to do. A second maintenance man appeared through another door, and gestured to her to follow. This close to spin axis, gravity was light, and he moved in an eerie, slow-motion bounce. She almost floated behind him, her feet nearly useless. She wasn't used to low gravity.

He stopped at a pilot's chair. No, Daryn wasn't a pilot, she thought, this is the wrong man, and then she saw him.

The maintenance man withdrew, and she stared into Daryn's face.

Vacuum hematoma had been hard on him, and he looked like he had been beaten by a band of thugs. His eyes were closed. The tattoos still glowed, faintly, and that was the worst thing of all, that his tattoos still were alive, and Daryn wasn't.

She reached out and put her fingertips against his cheek with a feather's touch, stroking along his jawline with a single finger. Suddenly, irrationally, she was angry at him. She wanted to tell him how inconsiderate he was, how selfish and idiotic and, and, and—but he was not listening. He was never going to listen.

The anger helped her to keep from crying.

By the time she returned to the Subtle Tiger, knots of sailors were walking upspin and downspin the corridors, talking and sometimes singing, dropping into a bar for a moment to see if it felt like a place to spend the rest of the shift, and then moving on, or staying for a drink. She passed a ferret crew going upspin toward the docks. The ferrets, slender and lithe as snakes with legs, squirmed in their cages, nearly insane with excitement over the prospect of being set free on the just-docked ship to hunt for stowaway rats.

She took over the bar from Patryos, serving drinks in a daze, unable to think of any quick responses to the double entendres and light-hearted suggestions offered by the sailors. Most of them knew that she had a sailor husband, though, and didn't press her very hard, and of course they wouldn't know that he had been in the wreck.

In fact, none of them would even know about the wreck yet; unless they had transferred across through an uptime wormhole, it was still in their future, and the port workers would be careful not to say anything that would cause a catastrophe. An incipient contradiction due to a loop in history would close the wormhole. A little information can leak from the future into the past, but history must be consistent. If enough information leaks downtime to threaten an inconsistency, the offending wormhole connection can snap.

The port circled the wormhole cluster, light-years from any star. If their passage to the rest of civilization by the wormhole connection failed, it would be a thousand years of slower-than-light travel to reach the fringes of civilization. So the port crew did not need to be reminded to avoid incipient contradiction; it was as natural to them as manufacturing oxygen.

Slowly, the banter and the routine of serving elevated Cheena's mood. One of the sailors asked to buy her a drink, and she accepted it and drank philosophically. It was hard to stay gloomy when liquor and florins were flowing so freely. She had kicked him out, after all; he was nothing to her. She could replace him any night from any of a dozen eager suitors—maybe even this one, if he was as nice as he seemed.

And the bar was suddenly especially hectic, with a dozen sailors asking for drinks at once, and half of them asking for more than that, and two more singing a rather clever duet she hadn't heard before, a song about a navigator who kept a pet mouse in the front of his pants, with the heavyset sailor singing the mouse's part in a squeaky falsetto. She was busy smiling and serving and taking orders, so it wasn't surprising at all that she didn't see him come in. He was quiet, after all, and took a seat at the bar and waited for her to come to him.

Daryn.

She was so surprised that she started to drop the beer she was holding, and caught it with a jerk, spilling a great splash of it across the bar and half across two sailors. The one she'd caught full-on jumped up, staring down at his splattered uniform. The one sitting with him started to laugh. "Now you've had your baptism in beer, and the night is still young, say now," he said. After a moment the one who had been splashed started to laugh as well. "A good sign, then, wouldn't you say?"

"Sorry, there," she said, bringing them both fresh drinks, waving her hand when they started to pay. "The last one was on you, so this one's on the house," she told them, and they both laughed. All the time she carefully avoided looking toward Daryn.

Daryn.

He sat at the end of the bar, drinking the beer that the other barmaid had brought him, not gesturing for her to come over, but smugly aware that, sooner or later, she would. He said something that made the other barmaid giggle, and she wondered what it might have been. She served a few of the other sailors, and then, knowing that sooner or later she would, she went to talk to him.

"Alive, alive," she said. It was barely more than a whisper.

"Myself, in the flesh," Daryn said. He smiled his huge, goonish smile. "Surprised to see me, yes?"

"How can you be here?" she said. "I thought you were on—on that ship."

"*Hesperia?* Yeah. But we docked alongside *Lictor* at Tarrytown-port, and *Lictor* was short a navigator, and *Hesperia* could spare me for a bit, and I knew that *Lictor* was heading to stop here, and I'd have a chance to see you, and—" he spread his hands. "I can't stay."

"You can't stay," she repeated.

"No, I have to sail with *Lictor*, so I can catch up with *Hesperia* at Dulcinea." He looked up at her. She was still standing stupidly there over him. "But I had to see you."

"You had to see me," she repeated slowly, as if trying to understand.

"I had to tell you," he said. "You have to know that you're the only one."

You are such a sweet liar, she thought, how can I trust you? But his smile brought back a thousand memories of time they had spent together, and it was like a sweet ache in her throat. "The only one," she repeated, still completely unable to think of any words of her own to say.

"You aren't still angry, are you?" he said. "Please, tell me you're not still angry. You know that you've always been the only one."

Morning came to the second-shift, and she propped her head up on one elbow to look across the bed at him. The glow of his tattoos cast a mottled pattern of soft light against the walls and ceiling.

Daryn awoke, rolled over, and looked at her. He smiled, a radiant smile, with his eyes still smoky with sleep, and leaned forward to kiss her. "There will be no other," he said. "This time I promise."

She kissed him, her eyes closed, knowing that it would be the last kiss they would ever have.

"I know," she said.

Coelacanths

ROBERT REED

---

*Robert Reed (info site: www.booksnbytes.com/authors/
reed_robert.html) lives in Nebraska, and has been one of the
most prolific short story writers of high quality in the SF
field for the past ten years. His work is notable for its variety, and for its steady production.* The Encyclopedia of Science Fiction *remarks that "the expertness of the writing and
its knowing exploitation of current scientific speculations
are balanced by an underlying quiet sanity about how to de-
pict and to illumine human beings." His first story collection,* The Dragons of Springplace *(1999), fine as it is, skims
only a bit of the cream from his body of work. And he writes
a novel every year or two, as well. His first novel,* The
Leeshore, *appeared in 1987, followed by* The Hormone Jungle *(1988),* Black Milk *(1989),* Down the Bright Way
(1991), The Remarkables *(1992),* Beyond the Veil of Stars
(1994), An Exaltation of Larks *(1995), and* Beneath the
Gated Sky *(1997). His most recent novel is* Marrow *(2000),
a distant-future large-scale story that is hard SF and seems
to be a breakthrough in his career.* The New York Times
*called it "an exhilarating ride, in the hands of an author
whose aspiration literally knows no bounds."*

"Coelacanths," from F&SF, *is a story of the far future in
which post-humans occupy most evolutionary niches—too
good a concept to pass up. He published enough stories to
fill a first-rate single-author collection in 2002, but none
better than this one.*

76

THE SPEAKER

He stalks the wide stage, a brilliant beam of hot blue light fixed squarely upon him. "We are great! We are glorious!" the man calls out. His voice is pleasantly, effortlessly loud. With a face handsome to the brink of lovely and a collage of smooth, passionate mannerisms, he performs for an audience that sits in the surrounding darkness. Flinging long arms overhead, hands reaching for the distant light, his booming voice proclaims, "We have never been as numerous as we are today. We have never been this happy. And we have never known the prosperity that is ours at this golden moment. This golden now!" Athletic legs carry him across the stage, bare feet slapping against planks of waxed maple. "Our species is thriving," he can declare with a seamless ease. "By every conceivable measure, we are a magnificent, irresistible tide sweeping across the universe!"

Transfixed by the blue beam, his naked body is shamelessly young, rippling with hard muscles over hard bone. A long fat penis dangles and dances, accenting every sweeping gesture, every bold word. The living image of a small but potent god, he surely is a creature worthy of admiration, a soul deserving every esteem and emulation. With a laugh, he promises the darkness, "We have never been so powerful, we humans." Yet in the next breath, with a faintly apologetic smile, he must add, "Yet still, as surely as tomorrow comes, our glories today will seem small and quaint in the future,

77

and what looks golden now will turn to the yellow dust upon which our magnificent children will tread!"

PROCYON

Study your history. It tells you that travel always brings its share of hazards; that's a basic, impatient law of the universe. Leaving the security and familiarity of home is never easy. But every person needs to make the occasional journey, embracing the risks to improve his station, his worth and self-esteem. Procyon explains why this day is a good day to wander. She refers to intelligence reports as well as the astrological tables. Then by a dozen means, she maps out their intricate course, describing what she hopes to find and everything that she wants to avoid.

She has twin sons. They were born four months ago, and they are mostly grown now. "Keep alert," she tells the man-children, leading them out through a series of reinforced and powerfully camouflaged doorways. "No naps, no distractions," she warns them. Then with a backward glance, she asks again, "What do we want?"

"Whatever we can use," the boys reply in a sloppy chorus.

"Quiet," she warns. Then she nods and shows a caring smile, reminding them, "A lot of things can be used. But their trash is sweetest."

Mother and sons look alike: They are short, strong people with closely cropped hair and white-gray eyes. They wear simple clothes and three fashions of camouflage, plus a stew of mental add-ons and microchine helpers as well as an array of sensors that never blink, watching what human eyes cannot see. Standing motionless, they vanish into the convoluted, ever-shifting background. But walking makes them into three transient blurs—dancing wisps that are noticeably simpler than the enormous world around them. They can creep ahead only so far before their camouflage falls apart, and then they have to stop, waiting patiently or otherwise, allowing the machinery to find new ways to help make them invisible.

"I'm confused," one son admits. "That thing up ahead—"

"Did you update your perception menu?"

"I thought I did."

Procyon makes no sound. Her diamond-bright glare is enough. She remains rigidly, effortlessly still, allowing her lazy son to finish his preparations. Dense, heavily encoded signals have to be whispered, the local net downloading the most recent topological cues, teaching a three-dimensional creature how to navigate through this shifting, highly intricate environment.

The universe is fat with dimensions.

Procyon knows as much theory as anyone. Yet despite a long life rich with experience, she has to fight to decipher what her eyes and sensors tell her. She doesn't even bother learning the tricks that coax these extra dimensions out of hiding. Let her add-ons guide her. That's all a person can do, slipping in close to one of *them*. In this place, up is three things and sideways is five others. Why bother counting? What matters is that when they walk again, the three of them move through the best combination of dimensions, passing into a little bubble of old-fashioned up and down. She knows this place. Rising up beside them is a trusted landmark—a red granite bowl that cradles what looks like a forest of tall sticks, the sticks leaking a warm light that Procyon ignores, stepping again, moving along on her tiptoes.

One son leads the way. He lacks the experience to be first, but in another few weeks, his flesh and sprint-grown brain will force him into the world alone. He needs his practice, and more important, he needs confidence, learning to trust his add-ons and his careful preparations, and his breeding, and his own good luck.

Procyon's other son lingers near the granite bowl. He's the son who didn't update his menu. This is her dreamy child, whom she loves dearly. Of course she adores him. But there's no escaping the fact that he is easily distracted, and that his adult life will be, at its very best, difficult. Study your biology. Since life began, mothers have made hard decisions about their children, and they have made the deadliest decisions with the tiniest of gestures.

Procyon lets her lazy son fall behind.

Her other son takes two careful steps and stops abruptly, standing before what looks like a great black cylinder set on its side. The shape is a fiction: The cylinder is round in one fashion but incomprehensible in many others. Her add-ons and sensors have built this very simple geometry to represent something far more elaborate. This is a standard disposal unit. Various openings appear as a single slot near the rim of the cylinder, just enough room showing for a hand and forearm to reach through, touching whatever garbage waits inside.

Her son's thick body has more grace than any dancer of old, more strength than a platoon of ancient athletes. His IQ is enormous. His reaction times have been enhanced by every available means. His father was a great old soul who survived into his tenth year, which is almost forever. But when the boy drifts sideways, he betrays his inexperience. His sensors attack the cylinder by every means, telling him that it's a low-grade trash receptacle secured by what looks like a standard locking device, AI-managed and obsolete for days, if not weeks. And inside the receptacle is a mangled piece of hardware worth a near-fortune on the open market.

The boy drifts sideways, and he glimmers.

Procyon says, "No," too loudly.

But he feels excited, invulnerable. Grinning over his shoulder now, he winks and lifts one hand with a smooth, blurring motion—

Instincts old as blood come bubbling up. Procyon leaps, shoving her son off his feet and saving him. And in the next horrible instant, she feels herself engulfed, a dry cold hand grabbing her, then stuffing her inside a hole that by any geometry feels nothing but bottomless.

ABLE

Near the lip of the City, inside the emerald green ring of Park, waits a secret place where the moss and horsetail and tree fern forest plunges into a deep crystalline pool of warm spring water. No public map tells of the pool, and no trail leads the casual walker near it. But the pool is exactly the sort of place that young boys always discover, and it is exactly the kind of treasure that remains unmentioned to parents or any other adult with suspicious or troublesome natures.

Able Quotient likes to believe that he was first to stumble across this tiny corner of Creation. And if he isn't first, at least no one before him has ever truly seen the water's beauty, and nobody after him will appreciate the charms of this elegant, timeless place.

Sometimes Able brings others to the pool, but only his best friends and a few boys whom he wants to impress. Not for a long time does he even consider bringing a girl, and then it takes forever to find a worthy candidate, then muster the courage to ask her to join him. Her name is Mish. She's younger than Able by a little ways, but like all girls, she acts older and much wiser than he will ever be. They have been classmates from the beginning. They live three floors apart in The Tower Of Gracious Good, which makes them close neighbors. Mish is pretty, and her beauty is the sort that will only grow as she becomes a woman. Her face is narrow and serious. Her eyes watch everything. She wears flowing dresses and jeweled sandals, and she goes everywhere with a clouded leopard named Mr. Stuff-and-Nonsense. "If my cat can come along," she says after hearing Able's generous offer. "Are there any birds at this pond of yours?"

Able should be horrified by the question. The life around the pool knows him and has grown to trust him. But he is so enamored by Mish that he blurts out, "Yes, hundreds of birds. Fat, slow birds. Mr. Stuff can eat himself sick."

"But that wouldn't be right," Mish replies with a disapproving smirk. "I'll lock down his appetite. And if we see any wounded birds . . . any animal that's suffering . . . we can unlock him right away . . . !"

"Oh, sure," Able replies, almost sick with nerves. "I guess that's fine, too."

People rarely travel any distance. City is thoroughly modern, every apartment supplied by conduits and meshed with every web and channel, shareline and gossip run. But even with most of its citizens happily sitting at home, the streets are jammed with millions of walking bodies. Every seat on the train is filled all the way to the last stop. Able momentarily loses track of Mish when the cabin walls evaporate. But thankfully, he finds her waiting at Park's edge. She and her little leopard are standing in the narrow shade of a horsetail. She teases him, observing, "You look lost." Then she laughs, perhaps at him, before abruptly changing the subject. With a nod and sweeping gesture, she asks, "Have you noticed? Our towers look like these trees."

To a point, yes. The towers are tall and thin and rounded like the horsetails, and the hanging porches make them appear rough-skinned. But there are obvious and important differences between trees and towers, and if she were a boy, Able would make fun of her now. Fighting his nature, Able forces himself to smile. "Oh, my," he says as he turns, looking back over a shoulder. "They do look like horsetails, don't they?"

Now the three adventurers set off into the forest. Able takes the lead. Walking with boys is a quick business that often turns into a race. But girls are different, particularly when their fat, unhungry cats are dragging along behind them. It takes forever to reach the rim of the world. Then it takes another two forevers to follow the rim to where they can almost see the secret pool. But that's where Mish announces, "I'm tired!" To the world, she says, "I want to stop and eat. I want to rest here."

Able nearly tells her, "No."

Instead he decides to coax her, promising, "It's just a little farther."

But she doesn't seem to hear him, leaping up on the pink polished rim, sitting where the granite is smooth and flat, legs dangling and her bony knees exposed. She opens the little pack that has floated on her back from the beginning, pulling out a hot lunch that she keeps and a cold lunch that she hands to Able. "This is all I could take," she explains, "without my parents asking questions." She is reminding Able that she never quite got permission to make this little journey. "If you don't like the cold lunch," she promises, "then we can trade. I mean, if you really don't."

He says, "I like it fine," without opening the insulated box. Then he looks inside, discovering a single wedge of spiced sap, and it takes all of his poise not to say, "Ugh!"

Mr. Stuff collapses into a puddle of towerlight, instantly falling asleep.

The two children eat quietly and slowly. Mish makes the occasional noise about favorite teachers and mutual friends. She acts serious and ordinary, and disappointment starts gnawing at Able. He isn't old enough to sense that the girl is nervous. He can't imagine that Mish wants to delay the moment when they'll reach the secret pool, or that she sees possibilities waiting there—wicked possibilities that only a wicked boy should be able to foresee.

Finished with her meal, Mish runs her hands along the hem of her dress, and she kicks at the air, and then, hunting for any distraction, she happens to glance over her shoulder.

Where the granite ends, the world ends. Normally nothing of substance can be seen out past the pink stone—nothing but a confused, ever-shifting grayness that extends on forever. Able hasn't bothered to look out there. He is much too busy trying to finish his awful meal, concentrating on his little frustrations and his depraved little daydreams.

"Oh, goodness," the young girl exclaims. "Look at that!"

Able has no expectations. What could possibly be worth the trouble of turning around? But it's an excuse to give up on his lunch, and after setting it aside, he turns slowly, eyes jumping wide open and a surprised grunt leaking out of him as he tumbles off the granite, landing squarely on top of poor Mr. Stuff.

ESCHER

She has a clear, persistent memory of flesh, but the flesh isn't hers. Like manners and like knowledge, what a person remembers can be bequeathed by her ancestors. That's what is happening now. Limbs and heads; penises and vaginas. In the midst of some unrelated business, she remembers having feet and the endless need to protect those feet with sandals or boots or ostrich skin or spiked shoes that will lend a person even more height. She remembers wearing clothes that gave color and bulk to what was already bright and enormous. At this particular instant, what she sees is a distant, long-dead relative sitting on a white porcelain bowl, bare feet dangling, his orifices voiding mountains of waste and an ocean of water.

Her oldest ancestors were giants. They were built from skin and muscle, wet air and great slabs of fat. Without question, they were an astonishing excess of matter, vast beyond all reason, yet fueled by slow, inefficient chemical fires.

Nothing about Escher is inefficient. No flesh clings to her. Not a drop of water or one glistening pearl of fat. It's always smart to be built from structure light and tested, efficient instructions. It's best to be tinier than a single cell and as swift as electricity, slipping unseen through places that won't even notice your presence.

Escher is a glimmer, a perfect and enduring whisper of light. Of life. Lovely in her own fashion, yet fierce beyond all measure.

She needs her fierceness.

When cooperation fails, as it always does, a person has to throw her rage at the world and her countless enemies.

But in this place, for this moment, cooperation holds sway.

Manners rule.

Escher is eating. Even as tiny and efficient as she is, she needs an occasional sip of raw power. Everyone does. And it seems as if half of everyone has gathered around what can only be described as a tiny, delicious wound. She can't count the citizens gathered at the feast. Millions and millions, surely. All those weak glimmers join into a soft glow. Everyone is bathed in a joyous light. It is a boastful, wasteful show, but Escher won't waste her energy with warnings. Better to sip at the wound, absorbing the free current, building up her reserves for the next breeding cycle. It is best to let others make the mistakes for you: Escher believes nothing else quite so fervently.

A pair of sisters float past. The familial resemblance is obvious, and so are the tiny differences. Mutations as well as tailored changes have created two loud gossips who speak and giggle in a rush of words and raw data, exchanging secrets about the multitude around them.

Escher ignores their prattle, gulping down the last of what she can possibly hold, and then pausing, considering where she might hide a few nanojoules of extra juice, keeping them safe for some desperate occasion.

Escher begins to hunt for that unlikely hiding place.

And then her sisters abruptly change topics. Gossip turns to trading memories stolen from The World. Most of it is picoweight stuff, useless and boring. An astonishing fraction of His thoughts are banal. Like the giants of old, He can afford to be sloppy. To be a spendthrift. Here is a pointed example of why Escher is happy to be herself. She is smart in her own fashion, and imaginative, and almost everything about her is important, and when a problem confronts her, she can cut through the muddle, seeing the blessing wrapped up snug inside the measurable risks.

Quietly, with a puzzled tone, one sister announces, "The World is alarmed."

"About?" says the other.

"A situation," says the first. "Yes, He is alarmed now. Moral questions are begging for His attention."

"What questions?"

The first sister tells a brief, strange story.

"You know all this?" asks another. Asks Escher. "Is this daydream or hard fact?"

"I know, and it is fact." The sister feels insulted by the doubting tone, but she puts on a mannerly voice, explaining the history of this sudden crisis.

Escher listens.

And suddenly the multitude is talking about nothing else. What is happening has never happened before, not in this fashion . . . not in any genuine memory of any of the millions here, it hasn't . . . and some very dim possibilities begin to show themselves. Benefits wrapped inside some awful dangers. And one or two of these benefits wink at Escher, and smile. . . .

The multitude panics, and evaporates.

Escher remains behind, deliberating on these possibilities. The landscape beneath her is far more sophisticated than flesh, and stronger, but it has an ugly appearance that reminds her of a flesh-born memory. A lesion; a pimple. A tiny, unsightly ruin standing in what is normally seamless, and beautiful, and perfect.

She flees, but only so far.

Then she hunkers down and waits, knowing that eventually, in one fashion or another, He will scratch at this tiny irritation.

THE SPEAKER

"You cannot count human accomplishments," he boasts to his audience, strutting and wagging his way to the edge of the stage. Bare toes curl over the sharp edge, and he grins jauntily, admitting, "And I cannot count them, either. There are simply too many successes, in too many far flung places, to nail up a number that you can believe. But allow me, if you will, this chance to list a few important marvels."

Long hands grab bony hips, and he gazes out into the watching darkness. "The conquest of our cradle continent," he begins, "which was quickly followed by the conquest of our cradle world. Then after a gathering pause, we swiftly and thoroughly occupied most of our neighboring worlds, too. It was during those millennia when we learned how to split flint and atoms and DNA and our own restless psyches. With these apish hands, we fashioned great machines that worked for us as our willing, eager slaves. And with our slaves' more delicate hands, we fabricated machines that could think for us." A knowing wink, a mischievous shrug. "Like any child, of course, our thinking machines eventually learned to think for themselves. Which was a dangerous, foolish business, said some. Said fools. But my list of our marvels only begins with that business. This is what I believe, and I challenge anyone to say otherwise."

There is a sound—a stern little murmur—and perhaps it implies dissent. Or perhaps the speaker made the noise himself, fostering a tension that he is building with his words and body.

His penis grows erect, drawing the eye.

Then with a wide and bright and unabashedly smug grin, he roars out, "Say this with me. Tell me what great things we have done. Boast to Creation about the wonders that we have taken part in . . . !"

PROCYON

Torture is what this is: She feels her body plunging from a high place, head before feet. A frantic wind roars past. Outstretched hands refuse to slow her fall. Then Procyon makes herself spin, putting her feet beneath her body, and gravity instantly reverses itself. She screams, and screams, and the distant walls reflect her terror, needles jabbed into her wounded ears. Finally, she grows quiet, wrapping her arms around her eyes and ears, forcing herself to do nothing, hanging limp in space while her body falls in one awful direction.

A voice whimpers.

A son's worried voice says, "Mother, are you there? Mother?"

Some of her add-ons have been peeled away, but not all of them. The brave son uses a whisper-channel, saying, "I'm sorry," with a genuine anguish. He sounds sick and sorry, and exceptionally angry, too. "I was careless," he admits. He says, "Thank you for saving me." Then to someone else, he says, "She can't hear me."

"I hear you," she whispers.

"Listen," says her other son. The lazy one. "Did you hear something?"

She starts to say, "Boys," with a stern voice. But then the

trap vibrates, a piercing white screech nearly deafening Procyon. Someone physically strikes the trap. Two someones. She feels the walls turning around her, the trap making perhaps a quarter-turn toward home.

Again, she calls out, "Boys."

They stop rolling her. Did they hear her? No, they found a hidden restraint, the trap secured at one or two or ten ends.

One last time, she says, "Boys."

"I hear her," her dreamy son blurts.

"Don't give up, Mother," says her brave son. "We'll get you out. I see the locks, I can beat them—"

"You can't," she promises.

He pretends not to have heard her. A shaped explosive detonates, making a cold ringing sound, faraway and useless. Then the boy growls, "Damn," and kicks the trap, accomplishing nothing at all.

"It's too tough," says her dreamy son. "We're not doing any good—"

"Shut up," his brother shouts.

Procyon tells them, "Quiet now. Be quiet."

The trap is probably tied to an alarm. Time is short, or it has run out already. Either way, there's a decision to be made, and the decision has a single, inescapable answer. With a careful and firm voice, she tells her sons, "Leave me. Now. Go!"

"I won't," the brave son declares. "Never!"

"Now," she says.

"It's my fault," says the dreamy son. "I should have been keeping up—"

"Both of you are to blame," Procyon calls out. "And I am, too. And there's bad luck here, but there's some good, too. You're still free. You can still get away. Now, before you get yourself seen and caught—"

"You're going to die," the brave son complains.

"One day or the next, I will," she agrees. "Absolutely."

"We'll find help," he promises.

"From where?" she asks.

"From who?" says her dreamy son in the same instant. "We aren't close to anyone—"

"Shut up," his brother snaps. "Just shut up!"

"Run away," their mother repeats.

"I won't," the brave son tells her. Or himself. Then with a serious, tight little voice, he says, "I can fight. We'll both fight."

Her dreamy son says nothing.

Procyon peels her arms away from her face, opening her eyes, focusing on the blurring cylindrical walls of the trap. It seems that she was wrong about her sons. The brave one is just a fool, and the dreamy one has the good sense. She listens to her dreamy son saying nothing, and then the other boy says, "Of course you're going to fight. Together, we can do some real damage—"

"I love you both," she declares.

That wins a silence.

Then again, one last time, she says, "Run."

"I'm not a coward," one son growls.

While her good son says nothing, running now, and he needs his breath for things more essential than pride and bluster.

ABLE

The face stares at them for the longest while. It is a great wide face, heavily bearded with smoke-colored eyes and a long nose perched above the cavernous mouth that hangs open, revealing teeth and things more amazing than teeth. Set between the bone-white enamel are little machines made of fancy stuff. Able can only guess what the add-on machines are doing. This is a wild man, powerful and free. People like him are scarce and strange, their bodies reengineered in countless ways. Like his eyes: Able stares into those giant gray eyes, noticing fleets of tiny machines floating on the tears. Those machines are probably delicate sensors. Then with a jolt of amazement, he realizes that those machines and sparkling eyes are staring into their world with what seems to be a genuine fascination.

"He's watching us," Able mutters.

"No, he isn't," Mish argues. "He can't see into our realm."

"We can't see into his either," the boy replies. "But just the same, I can make him out just fine."

"It must be. . . ." Her voice falls silent while she accesses City's library. Then with a dismissive shrug of her shoulders, she announces, "We're caught in his topological hardware. That's all. He has to simplify his surroundings to navigate, and we just happen to be close enough and aligned right."

Able had already assumed all that.

Mish starts to speak again, probably wanting to add to her explanation. She can sure be a know-everything sort of girl. But then the great face abruptly turns away, and they watch the man run away from their world.

"I told you," Mish sings out. "He couldn't see us."

"I think he could have," Able replies, his voice finding a distinct sharpness.

The girl straightens her back. "You're wrong," she says with an obstinate tone. Then she turns away from the edge of the world, announcing, "I'm ready to go on now."

"I'm not," says Able.

She doesn't look back at him. She seems to be talking to her leopard, asking, "Why aren't you ready?"

"I see two of them now," Able tells her.

"You can't."

"I can." The hardware trickery is keeping the outside realms sensible. A tunnel of simple space leads to two men standing beside an iron-black cylinder. The men wear camouflage, but they are moving too fast to let it work. They look small now. Distant, or tiny. Once you leave the world, size and distance are impossible to measure. How many times have teachers told him that? Able watches the tiny men kicking at the cylinder. They beat on its heavy sides with their fists and forearms, managing to roll it for almost a quarter turn. Then one of the men pulls a fist-sized device from what looks like a cloth sack, fixing it to what looks like a sealed slot, and both men hurry to the far end of the cylinder.

"What are they doing?" asks Mish with a grumpy interest.

A feeling warns Able, but too late. He starts to say, "Look away—"

The explosion is brilliant and swift, the blast reflected off the cylinder and up along the tunnel of ordinary space, a clap of thunder making the giant horsetails sway and nearly knocking the two of them onto the forest floor.

"They're criminals," Mish mutters with a nervous hatred.

"How do you know?" the boy asks.

"People like that just are," she remarks. "Living like they do. Alone like that, and wild. You know how they make their living."

"They take what they need—"

"They steal!" she interrupts.

Able doesn't even glance at her. He watches as the two men work frantically, trying to pry open the still-sealed doorway. He can't guess why they would want the doorway opened. Or rather, he can think of too many reasons. But when he looks at their anguished, helpless faces, he realizes that whatever is inside, it's driving these wild men very close to panic.

"Criminals," Mish repeats.

"I heard you," Able mutters.

Then before she can offer another hard opinion, he turns to her and admits, "I've always liked them. They live by their wits, and mostly alone, and they have all these sweeping powers—"

"Powers that they've stolen," she whines.

"From garbage, maybe." There is no point in mentioning whose garbage. He stares at Mish's face, pretty but twisted with fury, and something sad and inevitable occurs to Able. He shakes his head and sighs, telling her, "I don't like you very much."

Mish is taken by surprise. Probably no other boy has said those awful words to her, and she doesn't know how to react, except to sputter ugly little sounds as she turns, looking back over the edge of the world.

Able does the same.

One of the wild men abruptly turns and runs. In a supersonic flash, he races past the children, vanishing into the swirling grayness, leaving his companion to stand alone beside the mysterious black cylinder. Obviously weeping, the last man wipes the tears from his whiskered face with a trembling hand, while his other hand begins to yank a string of wondrous machines from what seems to be a bottomless sack of treasures.

ESCHER

She consumes all of her carefully stockpiled energies, and for the first time in her life, she weaves a body for herself: A distinct physical shell composed of diamond dust and keratin and discarded rare earths and a dozen subtle glues meant to bind to every surface without being felt. To a busy eye, she is dust. She is insubstantial and useless and forgettable. To a careful eye and an inquisitive touch, she is the tiniest soul imaginable, frail beyond words, forever perched on the brink of extermination. Surely she poses no threat to any creature, least of all the great ones. Lying on the edge of the little wound, passive and vulnerable, she waits for Chance to carry her where she needs to be. Probably others are doing the same. Perhaps thousands of sisters and daughters are hiding nearby, each snug inside her own spore case. The temptation to whisper, "Hello," is easily ignored. The odds are awful as it is; any noise could turn this into a suicide. What matters is silence and watchfulness, thinking hard about the great goal while keeping ready for anything that might happen, as well as everything that will not.

The little wound begins to heal, causing a trickling pain to flow.

The World feels the irritation, and in reflex, touches His discomfort by several means, delicate and less so.

Escher misses her first opportunity. A great swift shape presses its way across her hiding place, but she activates her glues too late. Dabs of glue cure against air, wasted. So she cuts the glue loose and watches again. A second touch is unlikely, but it comes, and she manages to heave a sticky tendril into a likely crevice, letting the irresistible force yank her into a brilliant, endless sky.

She will probably die now.

For a little while, Escher allows herself to look back across her life, counting daughters and other successes, taking warm comfort in her many accomplishments.

Someone hangs in the distance, dangling from a similar tendril. Escher recognizes the shape and intricate glint of her neighbor's spore case; she is one of Escher's daughters. There is a strong temptation to signal her, trading information, helping each other—

But a purge-ball attacks suddenly, and the daughter evaporates, nothing remaining of her but ions and a flash of incoherent light.

Escher pulls herself toward the crevice, and hesitates. Her tendril is anchored on a fleshy surface. A minor neuron—a thread of warm optical cable—lies buried inside the wet cells. She launches a second tendril at her new target. By chance, the purge-ball sweeps the wrong terrain, giving her that little instant. The tendril makes a sloppy connection with the neuron. Without time to test its integrity, all she can do is shout, "Don't kill me! Or my daughters! Don't murder us, Great World!"

Nothing changes. The purge-ball works its way across the deeply folded fleshscape, moving toward Escher again, distant flashes announcing the deaths of another two daughters or sisters.

"Great World!" she cries out.

He will not reply. Escher is like the hum of a single angry electron, and she can only hope that he notices the hum.

"I am vile," she promises. "I am loathsome and sneaky, and you should hate me. What I am is an illness lurking inside you. A disease that steals exactly what I can steal without bringing your wrath."

The purge-ball appears, following a tall reddish ridge of flesh, bearing down on her hiding place.

She says, "Kill me, if you want. Or spare me, and I will do this for you." Then she unleashes a series of vivid images, precise and simple, meant to be compelling to any mind.

The purge-ball slows, its sterilizing lasers taking careful aim.

She repeats herself, knowing that thought travels only so quickly and The World is too vast to see her thoughts and react soon enough to save her. But if she can help . . . if she saves just a few hundred daughters . . . ?

Lasers aim, and do nothing. Nothing. And after an instant of inactivity, the machine changes its shape and nature. It hovers above Escher, sending out its own tendrils. A careless strength yanks her free of her hiding place. Her tendrils and glues are ripped from her aching body. A scaffolding of carbon is built around her, and she is shoved inside the retooled purge-ball, held in a perfect darkness, waiting alone until an identical scaffold is stacked beside her.

A hard, angry voice boasts, "I did this."

"What did you do?" asks Escher.

"I made the World listen to reason." It sounds like Escher's voice, except for the delusions of power. "I made a promise, and that's why He saved us."

With a sarcastic tone, she says, "Thank you ever so much. But now where are we going?"

"I won't tell you," her fellow prisoner responds.

"Because you don't know where," says Escher.

"I know everything I need to know."

"Then you're the first person ever," she giggles, winning a brief, delicious silence from her companion.

Other prisoners arrive, each slammed into the empty spaces between their sisters and daughters. Eventually the purge-ball is a prison-ball, swollen to vast proportions, and no one else is being captured. Nothing changes for a long while. There is nothing to be done now but wait, speaking when the urge hits and listening to whichever voice sounds less than tedious.

Gossip is the common currency. People are desperate to hear the smallest glimmer of news. Where the final rumor comes from, nobody knows if it's true. But the woman who was captured moments after Escher claims, "It comes from the world Himself. He's going to put us where we can do the most good."

"Where?" Escher inquires.

"On a tooth," her companion says. "The right incisor, as it happens." Then with that boasting voice, she adds, "Which is exactly what I told Him to do. This is all because of me."

"What isn't?" Escher grumbles.

"Very little," the tiny prisoner promises. "Very, very little."

THE SPEAKER

"We walk today on a thousand worlds, and I mean 'walk' in all manners of speaking." He manages a few comical steps before shifting into a graceful turn, arms held firmly around the wide waist of an invisible and equally graceful partner. *"A hundred alien suns bake us with their perfect light. And between the suns, in the cold and dark, we survive, and thrive, by every worthy means."*

Now he pauses, hands forgetting the unseen partner. A look of calculated confusion sweeps across his face. Fingers rise to his thick black hair, stabbing it and yanking backward, leaving furrows in the unruly mass.

"Our numbers," he says. *"Our population. It made us sick with worry when we were ten billion standing on the surface of one enormous world. 'Where will our children stand?' we asked ourselves. But then in the next little while, we became ten trillion people, and we had split into a thousand species of humanity, and the new complaint was that we were still too scarce and spread too far apart. 'How could we matter to the universe?' we asked ourselves. 'How could so few souls endure another day in our immeasurable, uncaring universe?'"*

His erect penis makes a little leap, a fat and vivid white drop of semen striking the wooden stage with an audible plop.

"Our numbers," he repeats. *"Our legions."* Then with a wide, garish smile, he confesses, *"I don't know our numbers today. No authority does. You make estimates. You extrapolate off data that went stale long ago. You build a hundred models and fashion every kind of vast number. Ten raised to*

the twentieth power. The thirtieth power. Or more." He gig-
gles and skips backward, and with the giddy, careless energy
of a child, he dances where he stands, singing to lights over-
head, "If you are as common as sand and as unique as
snowflakes, how can you be anything but a wild, wonderful
success?"

ABLE

The wild man is enormous and powerful, and surely brilliant
beyond anything that Able can comprehend—as smart as
City as a whole—but despite his gifts, the man is obviously
terrified. That he can even manage to stand his ground as-
tonishes Able. He says as much to Mish, and then he glances
at her, adding, "He must be very devoted to whoever's inside."

"Whoever's inside what?" she asks.

"That trap." He looks straight ahead again, telling himself
not to waste time with the girl. She is foolish and bad-
tempered, and he couldn't be any more tired of her. "I think
that's what the cylinder is," he whispers. "A trap of some
kind. And someone's been caught in it."

"Well, I don't care who," she snarls.

He pretends not to notice her.

"What was that?" she blurts. "Did you hear that—?"

"No," Able blurts. But then he notices a distant rumble,
deep and faintly rhythmic, and with every breath, growing.
When he listens carefully, it resembles nothing normal. It
isn't thunder, and it can't be a voice. He feels the sound as
much as he hears it, as if some great mass were being dis-
placed. But he knows better. In school, teachers like to explain what must be happening now, employing tortuous
mathematics and magical sleights of hand. Matter and energy are being rapidly and brutally manipulated. The universe's obscure dimensions are being twisted like bands of
warm rubber. Able knows all this. But still, he understands
none of it. Words without comprehension; froth without
substance. All that he knows for certain is that behind that

deep, unknowable throbbing lies something even farther beyond human description.

The wild man looks up, gray eyes staring at that something.

He cries out, that tiny sound lost between his mouth and Able. Then he produces what seems to be a spear—no, an elaborate missile—that launches itself with a bolt of fire, lifting a sophisticated warhead up into a vague gray space that swallows the weapon without sound, or complaint.

Next the man aims a sturdy laser, and fires. But the weapon simply melts at its tip, collapsing into a smoldering, useless mass at his feet.

Again, the wild man cries out.

His language could be a million generations removed from City-speech, but Able hears the desperate, furious sound of his voice. He doesn't need words to know that the man is cursing. Then the swirling grayness slows itself, and parts, and stupidly, in reflex, Able turns to Mish, wanting to tell her, "Watch. You're going to see one of *Them*."

But Mish has vanished. Sometime in the last few moments, she jumped off the world's rim and ran away, and save for the fat old leopard sleeping between the horsetails, Able is entirely alone now.

"Good," he mutters.

Almost too late, he turns and runs to the very edge of the granite rim.

The wild man stands motionless now. His bowels and bladder have emptied themselves. His handsome, godly face is twisted from every flavor of misery. Eyes as big as windows stare up into what only they can see, and to that great, unknowable something, the man says two simple words.

"Fuck you," Able hears.

And then the wild man opens his mouth, baring his white apish teeth, and just as Able wonders what's going to happen, the man's body explodes, the dull black burst of a shaped charge sending chunks of his face skyward.

PROCYON

One last time, she whispers her son's name.

She whispers it and closes her mouth and listens to the brief, sharp silence that comes after the awful explosion. What must have happened, she tells herself, is that her boy found his good sense and fled. How can a mother think anything else? And then the ominous deep rumbling begins again, begins and gradually swells until the walls of the trap are shuddering and twisting again. But this time the monster is slower. It approaches the trap more cautiously, summoning new courage. She can nearly taste its courage now, and with her intuition, she senses emotions that might be curiosity and might be a kind of reflexive admiration. Or do those eternal human emotions have any relationship for what *It* feels . . . ?

What she feels, after everything, is numbness. A terrible deep weariness hangs on her like a new skin. Procyon seems to be falling faster now, accelerating down through the bottomless trap. But she doesn't care anymore. In place of courage, she wields a muscular apathy. Death looms, but when hasn't it been her dearest companion? And in place of fear, she is astonished to discover an incurious little pride about what is about to happen: How many people—wild free people like herself—have ever found themselves so near one of *Them*?

Quietly, with a calm, smooth and slow voice, Procyon says, "I feel you there, you. I can taste you."

Nothing changes.

Less quietly, she says, "Show yourself."

A wide parabolic floor appears, gleaming and black and agonizingly close. But just before she slams into the floor, a wrenching force peels it away. A brilliant violet light rises to meet her, turning into a thick sweet syrup. What may or may not be a hand curls around her body, and squeezes. Procyon fights every urge to struggle. She wrestles with her body, wrestles with her will, forcing both to lie still while the hand tightens its grip and grows comfortable. Then using a voice that betrays nothing tentative or small, she tells what holds her, "I made you, you know."

She says, "You can do what you want to me."

Then with a natural, deep joy, she cries out, "But you're an ungrateful glory . . . and you'll always belong to me . . . !"

ESCHER

The prison-ball has been reengineered, slathered with cam-ouflage and armor and the best immune-suppressors on the market, and its navigation system has been adapted from add-ons stolen from the finest trashcans. Now it is a battle-phage riding on the sharp incisor as far as it dares, then leaping free. A thousand similar phages leap and lose their way, or they are killed. Only Escher's phage reaches the target, impacting on what passes for flesh and launching its cargo with a microscopic railgun, punching her and a thousand sisters and daughters through immeasurable distances of sense-less, twisted nothing.

How many survive the attack?

She can't guess how many. Can't even care. What matters is to make herself survive inside this strange new world. An enormous world, yes. Escher feels a vastness that reaches out across ten or twelve or maybe a thousand dimensions. How do I know where to go? she asks herself. And instantly, an assortment of possible routes appear in her conscious-ness, drawn in the simplest imaginable fashion, waiting and eager to help her find her way around.

This is a last gift from Him, she realizes. Unless there are more gifts waiting, of course.

She thanks nobody.

On the equivalent of tiptoes, Escher creeps her way into a tiny conduit that moves something stranger than any blood across five dimensions. She becomes passive, aiming for in-visibility. She drifts and spins, watching her surroundings turn from a senseless glow into a landscape that occasionally seems a little bit reasonable. A little bit real. Slowly, she learns how to see in this new world. Eventually she spies a little peak that may or may not be ordinary matter. The peak is pink and flexible and sticks out into the great artery, and flinging her last tendril, Escher grabs hold and pulls in snug, knowing that the chances are lousy that she will ever find anything nourishing here, much less delicious.

But her reserves have been filled again, she notes. If she is careful—and when hasn't she been—her energies will keep her alive for centuries.

She thinks of the World, and thanks nobody.

"Watch and learn," she whispers to herself.

That was the first human thought. She remembers that odd fact suddenly. People were just a bunch of grubbing apes moving blindly through their tiny lives until one said to a companion, "Watch and learn."

An inherited memory, or another gift from Him?

Silently, she thanks Luck, and she thanks Him, and once again, she thanks Luck.

"Patience and planning," she tells herself.

Which is another wise thought of the conscious, enduring ape.

THE LAST SON

The locked gates and various doorways know him—recognize him at a glance—but they have to taste him anyway. They have to test him. Three people were expected, and he can't explain in words what has happened. He just says, "The others will be coming later," and leaves that lie hanging in the air. Then as he passes through the final doorway, he says, "Let no one through. Not without my permission first."

"This is your mother's house," says the door's AI.

"Not anymore," he remarks.

The machine grows quiet, and sad.

During any other age, his home would be a mansion. There are endless rooms, rooms beyond counting, and each is enormous and richly furnished and lovely and jammed full of games and art and distractions and flourishes that even the least aesthetic soul would find lovely. He sees none of that now. Alone, he walks to what has always been his room, and he sits on a leather recliner, and the house brings him a soothing drink and an intoxicating drink and an assortment of treats that sit on the platter, untouched.

For a long while, the boy stares off at the distant ceiling, replaying everything with his near-perfect memory. Everything. Then he forgets everything, stupidly calling out, "Mother," with a voice that sounds ridiculously young. Then again, he calls, "Mother." And he starts to rise from his chair, starts to ask the great empty house, "Where is she?"

And he remembers.

As if his legs have been sawed off, he collapses. His chair twists itself to catch him, and an army of AIs brings their talents to bear. They are loyal, limited machines. They are empathetic, and on occasion, even sweet. They want to help him in any fashion, just name the way . . . but their appeals and their smart suggestions are just so much noise. The boy acts deaf, and he obviously can't see anything with his fists jabbed into his eyes like that, slouched forward in his favorite chair, begging an invisible someone for forgiveness. . . .

THE SPEAKER

He squats and uses the tip of a forefinger to dab at the puddle of semen, and he rubs the finger against his thumb, saying, "Think of cells. Individual, self-reliant cells. For most of Earth's great history, they ruled. First as bacteria, and then as composites built from cooperative bacteria. They were everywhere and ruled everything, and then the wild cells learned how to dance together, in one enormous body, and the living world was transformed for the next seven hundred million years."

Thumb and finger wipe themselves dry against a hairy thigh, and he rises again, grinning in that relentless and smug, yet somehow charming fashion. "Everything was changed, and nothing had changed," he says. Then he says, "Scaling," with an important tone, as if that single word should erase all confusion. "The bacteria and green algae and the carnivorous amoebae weren't swept away by any revolution. Honestly, I doubt if their numbers fell appreciably or for long." And again, he says, "Scaling," and sighs with a rich appreciation. "Life evolves. Adapts. Spreads and grows, constantly utilizing new energies and novel genetics. But wherever something large can live, a thousand small things can thrive just as well, or better. Wherever something enormous survives, a trillion bacteria hang on for the ride."

For a moment, the speaker hesitates.

A slippery half-instant passes where an audience might believe that he has finally lost his concentration, that he is about to stumble over his own tongue. But then he licks at the air, tasting something delicious. And three times, he clicks his tongue against the roof of his mouth.

Then he says what he has planned to say from the beginning.

"I never know whom I'm speaking to," he admits. "I've never actually seen my audience. But I know you're great and good. I know that however you appear, and however you make your living, you deserve to hear this:

"Humans have always lived in terror. Rainstorms and the eclipsing moon and earthquakes and the ominous guts of some disemboweled goat—all have preyed upon our fears and defeated our fragile optimisms. But what we fear today—what shapes and reshapes the universe around us—is a child of our own imaginations.

"A whirlwind that owes its very existence to glorious, endless us!"

ABLE

The boy stops walking once or twice, letting the fat leopard keep pace. Then he pushes his way through a last wall of emerald ferns, stepping out into the bright damp air above the rounded pool. A splashing takes him by surprise. He looks down at his secret pool, and he squints, watching what seems to be a woman pulling her way through the clear water with thick, strong arms. She is naked. Astonishingly, wonderfully naked. A stubby hand grabs an overhanging limb, and she stands on the rocky shore, moving as if exhausted, picking her way up the slippery slope until she finds an open patch of halfway flattened earth where she can collapse, rolling onto her back, her smooth flesh glistening and her hard breasts shining up at Able, making him sick with joy.

Then she starts to cry, quietly, with a deep sadness.

Lust vanishes, replaced by simple embarrassment. Able flinches and starts to step back, and that's when he first looks at her face.

He recognizes its features.

Intrigued, the boy picks his way down to the shoreline, practically standing beside the crying woman.

She looks at him, and she sniffs.

"I saw two of them," he reports. "And I saw you, too. You were inside that cylinder, weren't you?"

She watches him, saying nothing.

"I saw something pull you out of that trap. And then I couldn't see you. *It* must have put you here, I guess. Out of its way." Able nods, and smiles. He can't help but stare at her breasts, but at least he keeps his eyes halfway closed, pretending to look out over the water instead. "*It* took pity on you, I guess."

A good-sized fish breaks on the water.

The woman seems to watch the creature as it swims past, big blue scales catching the light, heavy fins lazily shoving their way through the warm water. The fish eyes are huge and black, and they are stupid eyes. The mind behind them sees nothing but vague shapes and sudden motions. Able knows from experience: If he stands quite still, the creature will come close enough to touch.

"They're called coelacanths," he explains.

Maybe the woman reacts to his voice. Some sound other than crying now leaks from her.

So Able continues, explaining, "They were rare, once.

I've studied them quite a bit. They're old and primitive, and they were almost extinct when we found them. But when *they* got loose, got free, and took apart the Earth . . . and took everything and everyone with them up into the sky . . ."

The woman gazes up at the towering horsetails.

Able stares at her legs and what lies between them.

"Anyway," he mutters, "there's more coelacanths now than ever. They live in a million oceans, and they've never been more successful, really." He hesitates, and then adds, "Kind of like us, I think. Like people. You know?"

The woman turns, staring at him with gray-white eyes. And with a quiet hard voice, she says, "No."

She says, "That's an idiot's opinion."

And then with a grace that belies her strong frame, she dives back into the water, kicking hard and chasing that ancient and stupid fish all the way back to the bottom.

Flight Correction

KEN WHARTON

Ken Wharton <www.sff.net/people/kwharton/> is currently
an assistant professor in the San Jose State University
Physics Department. In 2002, his first novel, Divine Intervention (2001), was runner-up for the Philip K. Dick Award
for best SF paperback book.

"Flight Correction" was published in Analog. It is about
several intertwined themes, including the daily life of scientists, ingrained prejudice in physics and engineering against
evidence from "softer" sciences, and how the human relations of people in science can hinder as well as help the so-
lution of problems. It is set in an interesting future in which
the space elevator has been constructed in the Galápagos
Islands, perhaps a technological triumph and most likely an
ecological disaster.

"**A**lbatross, Daddy!" Sally's freckled face was pure excitement. "Albatross!"

Hank blinked a few times from his position in the hammock under the red mangroves. His daughter stood just beyond his reach. "How do you even know what an albatross looks like?"

"Just come quick, Daddy! C'mon . . ." She stepped forward and tugged at the remnants of his favorite shirt, a threadbare blue oxford from his professor days back in the states.

Hank finally got to his feet and followed his daughter down to the narrow lagoon. Splashing across after her, he realized he had forgotten his hat. "Wait a sec, Sally . . ."

Whether she heard him or not, she didn't turn around. *Screw it*, he thought, still following her. If he fried his bald spot in the equatorial sun, it wouldn't be the first time. Stepping out of the water, they turned left, following the main path across the white sand beach. "Where's your mother?" he asked at last.

"Finches," was all Sally said, clearly doing her best to be patient with her slow-paced father.

Of course. Those boring little critters that he'd never learned to tell apart. If his wife had studied some of these *other* birds he might actually be interested in her research. At that very moment Hank was walking right past a pair of goofy-looking masked boobies, brilliant white except for

106

the dark mask around the yellow-orange bill. The two birds were waddling around their sorry excuse for a nest, which looked for all the world like a random pile of rocks on the ground. Meanwhile, three beautiful red-pouched frigate birds sat within reach just overhead in the mangrove tree, inflating their sacs and ululating madly. All the birds ignored the humans with their usual Galápagos detachment, which could have made them easy to study. But instead Julia went roaming all over the island in search of those damn finches.

Sally led him up the trail toward the two solar-powered lighthouses that guided those intolerable mini-cruiseships into the heart of Genovesa. After a minute of climbing, Hank was embarrassed to find himself panting with exertion. He glanced down into the blue expanse of Darwin's Bay and made a half-hearted resolution to start swimming again.

Finally Hank made it over a crest, and there it was. Standing on an ancient memorial plaque at the edge of the cliff was an enormous white bird with a hooked, yellow beak. It was, in fact, an albatross.

"Wow," muttered Hank, his interest growing despite himself. He had been told that these birds were endemic to Española, at the far south of the Galápagos archipelago. Hank had even seen them down there once, a huge breeding colony next to the cliffs. But on this island, a hundred miles to the north, he had never seen one. Not a single one, for the three years they had lived here.

"Must have gotten lost, I guess," Hank said to his daughter. "Mom'll be interested."

But Sally apparently wasn't finished yet. She was already halfway to the next crest. Hank sighed and started walking again. "What's up there? Another . . . ?"

Hank broke off as he approached the top and could see the far side of the island. There *was* another one! And another. . . . With every step his jaw dropped a little further.

Here on Genovesa, a hundred miles off course, five dozen albatross had gotten lost in the exact same place.

* * *

Hank watched from the shade under the lighthouse while Julia filmed an albatross flopping toward the edge of the cliff.

"Their feet are funny, Mommy," Sally was saying. "They're way too long."

"They're not made for walking," Julia explained. "Wait, watch this . . ."

The bird hesitated at the edge of the cliff, extending its six-foot wingspan once, twice, and then backing off as if it was scared to death by the prospect. After a couple more fakes, it stepped forward and jumped. Jumped, not flew. Hank saw a white form plummet out of view, then reappear, enormous wings outstretched, speeding away over the calm water.

"See, Sally," his wife was saying, "they don't really flap. Takes too much energy, so they soar instead. Dynamic soaring, it's called."

"Where's it going?" Sally asked.

"To fish, probably. Maybe around here, maybe down off the coast of Peru. Or maybe it's going back to Española, where they all live."

"But then . . . what are they doing here?"

Julia lifted her gaze from the camera, smiled at her daughter. "*Very* good question. Usually they know right where to go."

Hank spoke up. "Know any bird people down south?"

Julia nodded. "Fernando does satellite migration tracking. Probably has some tagged ones right here, actually."

"Hmm. Maybe you'll get a call from him," Hank said.

"Oh, I'm sure the birds will all be gone before sundown."

Sally looked a bit sad. "But, but . . . it was nice of them to visit, right?"

Julia beamed down at Sally. "And it was nice of you to spot them for us. Otherwise we might never have known they were here."

Ten days later, the albatross population was pushing a hundred and fifty.

The population of bird people was skyrocketing as well:

Fernando's arrival this evening made four. Five, counting Julia. Their little island was getting awfully crowded. Not to mention their home.

Hank normally would have simply left, gone outside to read his new download in private, but tonight El Meaño had sent yet another nasty rainstorm. And with the birders living in tiny two-man tents, the family's semipermanent shelter was the only spot for them all to gather.

Hank couldn't imagine how Sally managed to sleep through the noise; he couldn't even read with all their chatter. And if he heard the word "migratory" just one more time. . . . Finally, in frustration, he picked up the sim-finch he had designed for his wife's research and started morphing the beak into implausible shapes.

It was an impressive piece of machinery, Hank modestly told himself. Back in the early days of finch research, before nano'geering enabled such devices, academics had resorted to more gruesome techniques. One ancient study even reported chopping the heads off of dead birds, swapping them around with the bodies, and then setting the chimeras in seductive poses to see who would try to mate with the corpses.

"I don't think that one is going to see many suitors, honey." Julia was speaking to him from across the room, referring with her eyes to the avian Cyrano. Hank shrugged and set it back down, nearly spilling his bottle of rum. Julia turned back to the main conversation.

"I'm telling you," Julia insisted. "The albatross are getting confused by the Line."

Hank rolled his eyes and turned away. His wife was always complaining about the space elevator; nothing new there. But still, he couldn't tune out the conversation.

"I don't buy it, Julia," said the only other female in the group, a penguin expert. "One new star is not going to mess up these birds. They've done studies—"

"One star that doesn't rotate with all the others," Julia countered. "It's not natural."

"It's been fully clouded over the last few nights," noted Fernando. "And they keep arriving. So it can't be the stars."

"Well, what does that leave? Landmarks and dead reckoning?"

Hank looked back over at the group, surprised at the obvious omission. "Don't forget magnetic fields." Even a washed-up N.E. professor knew *that* much about bird migration.

The penguin expert shook her head. "Not here at the equator. Sure, albatross have traces of magnetite in their brains like other birds, but the fields are so much weaker here that they don't rely on them at all."

Fernando stroked his white beard. "Still, he has a point. Flying up from Peru, it's a pretty small angular shift between here and Española. You know Tuttle, up in the states? He's bred a strain of pigeon that'll ignore all other cues, steer by magnetic fields alone. It must be an innate module in pigeons, so maybe all birds have it to some degree. Not at all inconceivable that new fields could gently steer the albatross off course."

"Maybe," Julia said. "Maybe that's what the Line is doing to them. Changing the fields."

"Enough about the Line, already," said Hank. Five pairs of eyes swiveled to glare at him, with varying levels of intensity. Hank retreated into his book, making an important mental note: don't mention the Line around Galápagos ecologists.

Hank supposed that the primary responsibility lay with generations of science fiction writers. If Ecuador hadn't been so *certain* about Quito they wouldn't have campaigned so heavily for a space elevator in the first place. They wouldn't have weaned two generations on the premise that Ecuador would be the gateway to orbit, finally giving their country the first-world status they deserved. Eventually, they dreamed, Ecuador would become the richest and most powerful nation-state on Earth.

So the initial site report had taken them very much by surprise. High elevations weren't recommended. Sure, altitude meant slightly less cable, but compared to the total distance to geosynch orbit, the percentages involved were so small as to be almost meaningless. Besides, in the mountains there wasn't easy access to a seaport—an essential part of the high-volume operation.

Then there was the disaster scenario. Dropped equipment, hazardous spills, broken cables snapping down onto the surface of the earth . . . A remote location was deemed necessary for safety concerns alone. Ecuador was hit hard on both fronts: everything was too mountainous or too crowded. Or both. Suddenly Brazil and Indonesia were being discussed as possible elevator locations.

For Ecuador, faced with the loss of its dreams, the sacrifice of its most famous national treasure hadn't come hard. The largest of the Galápagos islands, Isabela, was the only one to actually span the equator. If Quito wasn't possible, Ecuador had told the world, Isabela would be just perfect.

Predictably, the ecologists went daytrader on the whole idea. The Galápagos was not only a pristine ecological laboratory, but the very birthplace of evolutionary theory. They hadn't spent millions of dollars ridding Isabela of the wild goats, fighting the unending battles with the local fishermen, only to have the island turned into the biggest port on the planet. Years of intense protest followed, but the initial public opposition faded as Ecuador spared no expense on the propaganda wars. Hardly any of the islands would be affected, the government promised. The giant land tortoise population of Isabela would be protected. A portion of the future tax revenue was even allotted to environmental research to help sow dissension in the ecologists' midst.

And, as always, the money had won. The space elevator had been completed five years ago, and all of the rosy predictions were now proven rubbish. Isabela was almost completely developed, and many of the other islands were heading in the same direction. The smaller outlying islands were still relatively unaffected, but no one knew how long that would last.

To Hank, the Line had once dangled the promise of tropical employment. Three years back, when he had sacrificed his job for his family, he had held out hope of finding work on the space elevator. The entire structure was nano-engineered, after all. His specialty. And with that fantasy in mind, giving up his tenure-track position hadn't seemed quite so final.

But the reality down here had been different. The completed elevator had no need for academic types. The only jobs available were loading cargo—and Hank's back certainly couldn't handle that.

So now he was just living for his family, and the occasional bottle of rum. No more Paula, no more cheating around, no more rat race . . . no more anything. *But I'm doing the right thing*, Hank told himself, reciting his mantra. *I'm doing the right thing*.

From across the room Julia glanced in his direction, with a smile that said she still loved him despite his terribly insensitive comment about the Line. He tried to return the smile, tried to return a bit of love to his wife, but came up empty on both counts. Hank raised his book to cover his face, and buried himself in the meaningless words.

They didn't speak again until halfway through breakfast.

"Hank . . ."

He knew that voice, that look. Hank took a shallow breath and steeled himself for another painful argument.

"Why *wouldn't* you expect a magnetic field from the space elevator? Shouldn't there be currents every now and then?"

His pulse skipped a beat as he realized it wasn't going to be *that* sort of argument. He managed a smile.

"Yeah, that was a big worry. The cable goes right up through the Van Allen belts, after all. Wouldn't do to have an induced current yanking on the Line. So they spun it to be nonconducting."

"But buckytubes are . . ."

Hank broke into a full grin. Finches might be boring, but *this* stuff was cool. He arrayed his napkin in front of him, smoothed it out. "Not always. OK, say this is a single sheet of carbon atoms, arrayed like hexagonal chicken wire. You make it into a buckytube simply by rolling it up." He did so.

"But there are lots of different classes of buckytubes, depending on how you line up the hexagons."

He demonstrated this by first making a cylindrical tube—with the corners of the napkins touching—and then sliding one edge of the napkin with respect to the other. Now the axis of the tube was no longer perpendicular to the bottom edge of the napkin.

"There are lots of buckytube topologies, and each one has a different conductivity. So the tubes in your computer conduct, but the tubes in the Line don't."

Julia looked skeptical. "Thousands of miles of buckytube cable and they're sure it's *all* the non-conducting kind?"

"The fibers are all continuous. If there was a transition between two buckytube geometries, there has to be a discontinuity, a weak link. The tube hasn't snapped, so I think that's a good sign."

Hank was exaggerating; a single-point failure wouldn't snap the Line. It had been given the same design as the successful multifiber space tethers, which contained many redundant strands that weren't even in use. If one strand failed, two others would instantly snap into place to take up the load.

Julia just shook her head. "I don't know, Hank. . . . But I do know that's got to be the answer. These birds think they're on Española. *Something* has messed them up, and we've dismissed pretty much every other explanation. Think about it, will you?"

"Sure, honey." Hank's gaze skipped over to the rum supply, then back to Julia. "Sure."

By afternoon, he wasn't thinking about much of anything. The bottle had been out of reach for a while, but it wasn't worth the effort to get off his hammock.

How many hours had he spent in this thing? he wondered. More likely the time should be measured in months. The hammock was the fabric of spacetime, Hank decided, and he was a gravitational sink, warping the geodesics around his body. By now he knew every fiber of the netting;

at that very moment he could tell that there was a single crease running under his left buttock. He tried to mentally picture the folded topology down there—the strands in the middle doing no work at all, forcing its neighbors to pull twice their weight.

Just like the Line, he realized. Only the Line was different because . . .

Hank bolted up straight, nearly spinning the hammock and dumping him onto the sand. The topology shift didn't have to be in the primary fibers, he realized. The slack fibers could carry a current as well. And if *they* were starting to shift . . .

Five minutes later he was at his wife's computer, commencing his first literature search in nearly two years.

"So there you have it," Hank told his wife two nights later. "That's my best guess."

Julia squinted at the pencil sketches that Hank had just drawn for her, shaking her head. "I might understand the concept, but certainly not the details. What am I supposed to do with this?"

Hank shrugged, got up from the table and padded into the bathroom to get ready for bed. "I don't know what you do with it," he called over his shoulder. "That's for you to decide."

He was in the middle of brushing his teeth when he saw in the mirror that Julia was standing beside him, glaring with a fury he hadn't seen in years.

"For *me* to decide?! Me? What about *you?!*"

Hank spun to face her, his mouth full of foam. "Wh-mmh?"

"Do you know how glad I've been these last two days, seeing you actually do some work you enjoy? I know you're not happy here. I know these islands are sapping the life out of you. But now that you've figured out this problem you're just going to drop it? You're just going to flop right back into your hammock, back to the way things were?"

Hank spat into the sink, wiped his face with the back of his hand, and looked up to stare at his own reflection. "This was just a one-time coincidence. As soon as you report it, like it or not, things *will* be right back where they were. I'm not needed here."

"Sally needs you, you know that. Hell, if you're right about this, the whole goddamn solar system needs you."

He turned again to face her. "And you?"

"I . . ." Julia drew a breath through pursed lips. "I need my husband. But what I don't need is—"

Julia broke off as Sally appeared in the doorway, half-asleep and obviously frightened. Hank dropped to a squat and she ran into his arms.

"Were we too loud for you?" Hank asked, stroking her hair. "We're sorry, we'll be quiet."

He stood up, lifting his daughter into the air. Julia stepped over to plant a kiss on her cheek, then glanced up apologetically at Hank. He smiled at his wife, nodded, and carried Sally off to bed.

Hank ran a final check of his computer model while the dozen bird people nestled in for the presentation. He had first considered making a physical model, but the only string he could find on the island was his hammock, and he wasn't ready to sacrifice it just yet. Instead, he had had to dredge up his old programming skills for the proper 3-D rendering.

"Everyone ready?" he asked the crowd. Julia nodded in reply, then winked at him. Sally sat next to her mother, peeking inside a Tupperware container at her pet lava lizard, Darwin.

"OK," Hank began. "This is a molecular view of one section of the Line. The *original* design." The lattice appeared on the screen behind him, blue and red lines arrayed in a webbed cylinder.

"Each one of these lines is a single-wall buckytube, and together they form this larger cylinder called a fiber. The blue strands are the primaries, where all the strain is carried. But you'll notice that there are more secondary red tubes than blue ones. That's because if there's a point failure . . ."

Now a virtual pair of scissors appeared and snipped one of the blue strands. The fiber stretched only slightly as two red lines snapped into place to take up the slack. "Redundancy. And I'm only showing you the tubes and the fibers. These fibers are woven into what's known as a bundle, and in turn the bundles form the backbone of the Line itself. Each level of complexity has both primary and secondary strands, and the redundancy gives the Line an expected 700-year lifetime."

"Only 695 to go," muttered the penguin expert.

"Or maybe not," Hank retorted. "Which is the whole point. The redundancy assumes that the secondary fibers maintain their structure, even when they're not in use."

Now the 3-D graphics zoomed in on a spherical-fullerene intersection where two red lines crossed a blue. At this resolution the lines were no longer 1-dimensional; now each buckytube appeared as an actual cylinder, composed of a geometrical spiral of dots.

"Each one of these dots is a carbon atom," Hank explained. "And as I said, this is the *original* design. A full quantum analysis was performed on this design, to make sure that the secondary fibers wouldn't degrade, even without full tension. The entire simulation series took 19 months to run on ASCI Platinum. And *then* they changed the design."

Hank hit a button on the computer and now the spherical intersections shifted ever so slightly. "This was what they actually built, shaving ten months off construction. Very subtle change—only two carbon atoms have moved per intersection. But the orbital pattern is different enough to require an entirely new calculation.

"Now, there are public documents which *refer* to a new calculation, but nothing about it was ever published. And it only took 6 months from the design change to the final ratification. It all points to someone doing a half-assed perturbative analysis using the old design as a starting point, and passing it off as the real thing."

"I don't understand," said Fernando from the front row. "This has something to do with magnetic fields?"

Hank sighed. Apparently the nanotech details were lost on this crowd. Still, it was good practice for later.

"It's possible," Hank said, "although I can't say for sure. The concern is that the new design might be susceptible to topology shifts like this." He hit his last animation cue, and one of the secondary tubes *slipped*. The structure didn't break, but one row of carbon atoms slipped relative to another, leaving the red tube with a different spiral pattern than the others.

"This weakens the fiber, and if it happened throughout the line, might shorten its lifetime considerably. A side effect would be that these shifted tubes can become electrically conducting, and perhaps generate their own magnetic fields. And once currents start flowing through them, all the calculations are going to be way off. It might even accelerate the slipping process."

Julia spoke up. "I'm sure Hank's on to something. We've seen what's happening to the migration patterns."

Hank flipped off the projector as the bird people started chattering among themselves. Only Fernando got to his feet and approached him, a worried look on his face.

"Tell me, son. If you're right. . . . They're going to have to shut down the Line for a while?"

"At the very least."

Fernando's old eyes sparkled mischievously. "Well, I can tell you, you'll have a lot of support from the people in this room. But you're going to have a hell of a time getting anyone on Isabela to listen to you."

"That's the nice thing about the scientific process," Hank said with a grin. "After I make the claim, the evidence will prove me right or wrong."

Fernando shook his head sadly. "I've played this game for many years, son. This isn't about evidence, or even science. Be careful."

"Don't worry, Fernando. I think I can handle this."

"I hope so," the old man replied, turning back to converse with the rest of the crowd. "I hope so."

A week later, Hank finally managed to contact an actual Tethercorp employee over the net. It was still before dawn on the Galápagos, but by now he had resorted to calling the London office.

The man on his computer screen didn't look like a scientist; probably a mid-level bureaucrat. No matter. Hank would start with this guy and work his way up the chain.

The bureaucrat held a printout of Hank's report up to the camera. "Is this yours?" he asked.

"Yes. I'm a nanotech engineer from—"

"I'm having trouble filing this one," the man interrupted. "The bulk of it looks like it should go into Harmless Crackpot, but this first paragraph reads more like a Bomb Threat. Could you clarify your position for me?"

Hank was livid, but forced himself to speak slowly and deliberately. "Could you please tell me, then, what is the proper channel for scientists to present—"

"Harmless Crackpot, then. Thank you." The picture flickered off.

"Jesus!" Hank stomped outside and stared out into Darwin's Bay. A cruise ship was heading out to sea, stirring up a brilliant wake of bioluminescence. He waited for the anger to subside, raising his gaze from the lights below to the stars above. Topside Station, gateway to the solar system, was visible directly overhead. It was brighter even than Venus. Hank's neck began to ache, but staring upward was better than being hunched over the computer.

"You can do this," said Julia from behind him.

Hank turned around, startled. "What?" he snapped.

"You can do this. Don't give up so easily."

"I'm not giving up."

"But you're not doing what you need to do, either."

Hank clenched his fists. "I'm perfectly able to do this by myself."

"I don't get it." Julia raised her hands in confusion. "What's so terrible about contacting your old colleagues? What do you still think you're running from?"

"I didn't run. I gave up my job to be with you and Sally."

"Dammit, Hank, you're *not* going to make me feel guilty about your decision! You were the one who proved we couldn't live apart."

Hank shut up for a moment, biting off the snappy reply

which came to mind. Yes, he had had an affair, but weren't they supposed to be beyond that?

"What do you want from me?" he said at last. "I'm doing science again, OK? I'm *working*. So now you're asking me to go dump the problem on Vargas' lap, let the *real* scientists solve the problem?"

Julia shook her head. "That's not the issue and you know it. You haven't contacted these people in three years. Are you afraid of them? What do you imagine they think of you?" She stepped forward to wrap her arms around him, and he didn't fight her off.

"Just that . . ." he began. "Just that I washed out, couldn't handle the job. I think Vargas is the only one who really knew why I left."

"Then show them what you're capable of. Show them what you've found. If they really think you're a shabby scientist, then prove them wrong."

"It's not that easy."

"Isn't it?"

They held each other, silently, as dawn crept into the sky.

In the end, Hank had resorted to an old-fashioned email.

An actual conversation would have been too awkward, he decided, but writing a letter hadn't been as painful as he'd thought. He'd picked the two colleagues who had been closest to him—not counting Vargas, of course—and sent them each a three-page summary of his findings. And now, only 24 hours later, he was startled to have already received a reply.

Hank; good to hear from you. How are Sally and Julia? Finally became a mother myself last year—twin girls; see the pics.

Interesting problem you've run across. I don't know any Tethercorp techs personally, but I think Vargas does. Mind if I ask him? I know you two didn't part on the best of terms, so let me know.

Still, no one will authorize a serious theory effort unless you come up with some decent evidence. Bird migration?

Don't think that will fly around here, so to speak. Can't they measure the Line conductivity from the base station?

Let me know if you come up with some real proof. I'll see what I can do in the meanwhile.

—Abby

Moments later Hank was banging out a quick response, warning Abby not to bring Vargas into this. But he paused before sending it, thought for a few minutes, and finally erased the request.

Perhaps it was time. After what had happened, he knew that Luis Vargas would prefer never to hear from his traitorous friend ever again. But Julia was right; it was time to stop running. Yes, it would probably be better to contact Luis directly. But it would be hard. And it would be so easy to just let events take their course, to let Abby make contact for him.

Julia had been able to put the affair behind her. Hopefully Luis and Paula had done the same, had been able to move on with their lives.

There was even the outside chance that Luis didn't hate him quite so much as he deserved to.

"You seem frustrated," said Julia.

Hank sat up straight, startled by the interruption. "That's an understatement." He glanced back down at the computer screen. "I can't figure out how to measure it. Not for less than ten million, anyway. If only we could afford a fleet of custom microcopters."

"How to measure the magnetic field, you mean? Too bad it's not a biology problem, or we could use my extra grant money. Still, it can't be *that* hard to pull off. After all, the albatross figured it out."

Hank snickered. "The goddamn albatross. If only that were enough evidence. . . . I'm realizing that we hard scientists don't give animals a lot of credit."

"Maybe if they came down to Genovesa, saw the birds for themselves—"

"No," said Hank. "It doesn't mean anything to them. They want to see hard data, not birds."

Julia frowned. "But birds *are* hard data."

"Not to an engineer, darling."

"Hmmpf."

Hank returned his attention to the screen, which was currently displaying an image of Base Station, where the Line lifted its cargo off the Earth's surface. It was situated at the saddle point on an east-west ridge connecting Mt. Wolf and Mt. Ecuador, overlooking the ocean to the north and the south. The area surrounding the Station was covered with metal warehouses, transformers, and power cables, which meant that a ground-based measurement of the B-field would be worse than useless. He had to get up off the ground, away from all other possible currents. Against that requirement he had to contend with a strictly enforced no-fly zone within a 50 km radius of the Line, not to mention his shoestring budget.

"Julia, just how am I going to get my hands on safe, cheap, airborne magnetic field detectors? I need dozens, more likely thousands, if we want to take a temporal snapshot."

After a moment of silence, Julia burst into laughter. "These islands are filled with exactly what you need! Too bad you engineers don't trust them . . ." She laughed some more.

Hank turned to look at her again. "What? Birds?"

"You said it. Safe, cheap, airborne, magnetic field detectors."

Hank started to laugh himself, but quickly grew serious again. What was it that Fernando had said the other night? Something about . . .

He shot to his feet, grabbed his surprised wife by the shoulders and planted a kiss directly onto her lips. "Julia, my dear. You are a genius."

"If you think I'm going to kiss you back before you tell me what you're thinking . . ."

Hank smiled. "I think this idea's worth more than a kiss."

"Well, then . . ." She gazed at him mischievously for a moment, and then grabbed his hands and led Hank toward the bedroom. "It had better be good," she said.

It was.

The high-rises of Puerto Villamil shimmered beyond the scorched tarmac. Hank felt Julia clasp his hand tightly as the passenger jet slowed to a halt and they waited for the passengers to disembark.

Hank recognized Abby first, followed by Jackson and Nigel. The three of them had agreed to come down to Isabela to see the demonstration for themselves.

They had already cleared customs in Guayaquil, and the once-enforced agricultural inspection had been abandoned years ago, so there was almost no delay. Hank and Julia met them on the tarmac.

The greetings had just begun when another familiar face appeared in the crowd of arrivals. Hank forced himself to keep smiling when the recognition flooded through him. It was Luis Vargas.

Luis wasn't smiling himself. He nodded briskly to Hank and Julia, then turned to introduce the two men who flanked him.

"Robert, Ali," said Luis. "Please meet Hank Sadler. And this is his wife, Julia." Luis nodded to them again. "Nice to see you both together. Robert and Ali here work for Tethercorp."

"Nice to meet you," said Hank, shaking hands. He turned to Luis, trying not to show his nervousness. "It's good to see you again. I'm glad you came."

Luis nodded a third time, then walked past him to join the others. Julia and Hank raised eyebrows at each other before turning to follow.

Puerto Villamil sat on the southern edge of Isabela, sixty-some miles below the equator. Sporting the only airport on the island, it hosted the largest population in the Galápagos, even beating out Base City up at the northern port.

The chartered van was waiting in its assigned spot, and the eight of them piled in with minimal conversation. Hank found himself sitting in the front row, directly in front of Luis, which he found somewhat disconcerting.

"How's traffic today?" Julia asked the driver. He responded in Spanish, and the two of them commenced to hold an unintelligible conversation. The interaction didn't seem to slow his driving, though; within minutes they were on the tollway, zooming up the eastern side of the island.

After an uneventful half-hour, the tollway cut west across the Perry Isthmus, just south of Mt. Darwin. Hank wondered what the mountain's namesake would think of the island if he could see it now. Only five weeks of the Beagle's five-year journey had been spent in the Galápagos, but Isabela had been one of the islands visited. Today, few endemic species remained. Mt. Darwin was covered with invasive California sage scrub, and the foothills beyond the tollway fence were littered with the detritus of civilization: bars, fuel cell stations, minimalls, strip clubs, and miles upon miles of warehouses and storage space.

Hank removed his gaze from the window as he became aware of an uncomfortable lull in the small talk. Up until now, Julia had carried the conversation with the other passengers, restricting her questions to general pleasantries and gently touching on the outlines of everyone's life for the last three years. But she hadn't really spoken with Luis Vargas. Now she swiveled around in her seat to face him, and Hank held his breath, hoping she would keep things civil.

"And how have *you* been, Luis? How's Paula?"

Hank's eyes bulged, but he didn't move a muscle, didn't turn to look at either of them. Why would she say something like that? Was she just trying to prove that she had moved beyond the affair? Or was she trying to evoke an outburst from Luis? Either way, she should have known better than to bring up Paula.

"We're divorced, actually," came Luis' reply.

An ominous silence passed before Julia spoke. "I'm sorry to hear that."

"Ah," said Luis, "it was probably all for the best."

Hank's mind spun, but his body remained planted. The affair had triggered a divorce? He suddenly needed to know more. How soon had it ended? Where had Paula gone? What feelings must Luis have for him after Hank had so thoroughly ruined his life?

Finally Hank turned and locked eyes with his old friend. Luis looked almost relaxed. Almost.

"I'm really sorry to hear that, too," Hank heard himself say.

Luis didn't break eye contact. "It was all for the best," he said again.

Hank turned back to the front and gratefully heard Julia bring up a new topic: the now-extirpated giant tortoise population of Isabela.

All for the best? Luis had been devastated by the news, by the betrayal. Was this just a show of bravado in front of everyone else? Or had Luis really managed to convince himself that he didn't love Paula after all?

Lost in his thoughts, Hank didn't speak for the remainder of the journey.

The Line scarred the sky like a rent in the space-time fabric. Hank stared upward through the glass ceiling of the observation deck, but no cars were visible. The Line just hung above them, motionless.

The two Tethercorp employees were busy introducing themselves to the Base Station staff. Hank got the distinct impression that these two—what were their names again?—were not exactly upper-level managers at Tethercorp. It appeared that neither of them had ever been Up.

"Um . . . I don't know," said the Tethercorp employee who might have been named Ali. He then turned to Hank. "Dr. Sadler? What exactly *are* we doing here?"

Hank checked his watch. *Just one more minute.* Julia had already made the call on her handheld; everything was set.

"I'm sure that Luis," Hank said, nodding at his old colleague, "has already given you the outline. If the Line were generating a magnetic field—"

"I assure you, that is quite impossible," interrupted Ali.

Hank forged onward. "Impossible or not, if it *were* generating a field, that would imply currents. Which would in turn imply—"

"That you boys could be in trouble," finished Julia.

The second Tethercorp employee turned to Luis, looking bored. "You *assured* us, Luis—"

Vargas held up his hand. "Yes, I was told that this would not be a purely theoretical argument, that some sort of experimental demonstration would make this worth your time. And I imagine . . ." He cocked an eyebrow at Hank. "I imagine that now would be a good time to show us what you've got."

"As a matter of fact," said Hank, "it is *exactly* time." He took a deep breath. "About five seconds ago—"

He was cut off by several loud beeps throughout the room. It took him a moment to realize they were sounding from the belts of the Base Station staff. The shortest man grabbed his handheld, jabbed at it, and a voice came out of the speaker.

"We have some activity out at warehouse 194. Sounded like some sort of explosion, and now we're getting reports of all these . . ." The voice broke into digital static.

"How far is that from the Line?" Ali snapped. The staff ignored him.

The short man spoke to his handheld. "Repeat that. Do we need fire containment?"

"Negative, no fire reported. Just a whole shitload of birds."

At that moment, through the glass of the observation deck, Hank saw the fluttering of the homing pigeons. Hundreds, no, thousands of birds. They glittered in the Sun; each pigeon carried a Mylar streamer for visibility.

Julia's grant money had paid for the older generations of Tuttle's pigeon-breeding experiment to be sent down to Isabela. These birds apparently didn't follow field lines quite as well as the newest generation, but they would hopefully be sufficient.

Hopefully. But Hank could already tell the plan was failing. Instead of moving as a group, the pigeons were spreading out, some flying toward the Line but some away from it. He felt his heart drop. Pigeons trained to follow magnetic fields? What had he been thinking?

"I'm worried," said Julia beside him. But she wasn't even looking out the glass. "Are we sure they're all sterilized? I know it's a little late to be worried about introducing species, but . . ."

"Sadler?" barked Ali's voice from behind. "Is this your doing? What *are* all those things?"

Julia beat him to an answer, and Hank wandered away to the opposite side of the observation deck as his wife started to explain about the pigeon's specialized navigation behavior. Hank didn't want to hear it, didn't want to stand there and be stood up by a bunch of damn birds. Right now he just wanted to be alone.

"Interesting stunt," said a voice behind him, and Hank looked up to see that Luis had followed him across the deck. "Can't imagine you thought it would work, but . . . interesting. You should have called me. We could have set up some microgliders, maybe, taken some real measurements—"

"Why are you trying to help me?" Hank broke in. "Why come down here with these two? I mean, don't get me wrong, I appreciate it. I just don't understand why . . ."

Hank trailed off and Luis watched him for a moment before he spoke. "It's been three years, Hank. Two and a half without Paula. And I'm happy. Happier than ever. You were just a symptom, not the cause."

"But if I hadn't—"

"Then it would have been somebody else, down the line. Maybe when we had kids of our own, god forbid. I can't say that all the anger's gone. I can't even say I forgive you. But you didn't ruin my life."

"I'm glad, but still . . ." Hank turned away, looked out the window at the clear Pacific ocean. "I think I ruined mine."

Luis sighed. "You ever imagine coming back?"

"That's not an option."

"What about an adjunct position . . . ?" Luis started, but broke off when the murmurs reached them from the other side of the deck.

Hank glanced over and saw that most of the pigeons had landed or dispersed. Only a few hundred were still circling. He started to turn away again before he did a double-take. Circling?

With ten long strides he rejoined his wife and the others, wrapped his arm around Julia as he watched the beautiful fluttering Mylar.

"It only worked for the highest birds," Julia whispered to him, as if a louder voice would break the spell.

About 50 meters off the ground, a group of pigeons was orbiting the Line in a formation shaped like a diamond ring. They had found a closed-loop magnetic field. There was no other explanation; the current had to be running right through the center.

"I'm telling you, that's impossible," Ali was saying.

The second Tethercorp employee stepped between Hank and the glass, a serious expression on his face. "This is bad," he said simply.

"Yes, it is . . ." Hank searched the man's badge for the name. "Robert."

"You think it's in the secondaries?" Robert asked.

"Where else? It'll be an extraordinary effort to fix the thing, but I've been sketching out some ideas."

Robert looked him up and down. "How long have you been working on this?"

"Two months."

Suddenly Ali was forcing himself between the two of them. "Bob. Maybe they trained the pigeons to fly in circles?"

Robert ignored him, gently pushed Ali aside. He looked Hank in the eye. "Would you be interested in a position with Tethercorp? I can arrange to waive the usual interview . . ."

Julia gazed up at Hank, keeping her face impassive but letting her eyes do the smiling. He returned the look for a long moment before responding.

"No, thanks," he said, still watching his wife.

Now Julia's eyes squinted. "Hank, dear—" she began.

"But I do consulting work." He looked up at Robert. "Based right here in the Galápagos."

"Excellent," said Robert, whipping out his handheld. "Now if you'll excuse me, I have to make quite a few calls . . ."

Hank took Julia's hand in his own and looked out to see the pigeons again. Only about ten birds were remaining—this time orbiting in the opposite direction for some reason. He filed the fact away to think about later, pulled his wife toward him, and leaned down to whisper in her ear. "I'll have to spend a lot of time here on Isabela."

"It's not so far," she said, squeezing him back. "I'm happy for you."

"Hmm. I'm still nervous as hell."

"What for? You did it!"

"*We* did it. But . . . I really don't know if I'm ready for this life."

Julia commanded his full attention. "You'll never know until you try. And the alternative is—"

"Don't worry, love," Hank said, gazing out over the ocean. Three magnificent frigate birds were soaring far above the pigeons, far beyond the Line. "I don't really know where I was all these years," he said. "But I do know I'm not going back."

Shoes

ROBERT SHECKLEY

Robert Sheckley <www.sheckley.com> lives in Portland, Oregon. He is one of the finest short story writers ever in SF, who first flourished in the 1950s in Galaxy, and has made a strong showing in the last decade. His characteristic mode is satirical, and he often focuses on the ambiguous and ironic relationship of ordinary people to the technology they use or misuse, but do not or cannot understand. His is a fiction of tiny monsters and of nightmares with limited ability to do damage. His central characters are often working men, or men of limited means, slackers or con men, but almost always people who gain a bit of useful insight when technology malfunctions. His stories usually have happy endings, often with a punch line. But the finest pleasure of reading Sheckley is his graceful, witty style and amusing sentences.

He had an especially good year in 2002, publishing several stories that might have been included in this volume. "Shoes," from F&SF, is Sheckleyan satire in his classic mode. A down-at-the-heels writer buys a pair of hi-tech shoes in a second-hand clothing store, which turn out to be inhabited by an advanced AI who only wants to help him.

My shoes were worn out and I was passing a Goodwill store so I went in to see if they had anything that would fit me.

The assortment you find in places like this is not to the most exacting taste. And the sizes they get don't fit a normal foot like mine. But this time I lucked out. A pair of lovely heavy cordovans. Built to last. Looking brand new, except for the deep gouge on top of one toe, a mark that had undoubtedly resulted in the shoes' disposal. The outer leather had been scraped away—maybe by some indigent like myself, outraged at so expensive a pair of shoes. You never know, it's the sort of thing I might have done myself in one of my darker moods.

But today I was feeling good. You don't find a pair of shoes like this every day, and the price tag read a ridiculous four dollars. I removed my ragged Kmart sneakers and slipped into the cordovans, to see if they fit.

Immediately I heard a voice in my mind, clear as a bell, saying, "You're not Carlton Johnson. Who are you?"

"I'm Ed Phillips," I said aloud.

"Well, you have no right to be wearing Carlton Johnson's shoes."

"Hey, look," I said, "I'm in a Goodwill, these shoes are priced at four bucks, they're here for anyone to buy."

"Are you sure?" the voice said. "Carlton Johnson wouldn't have just given me away. He was so pleased when he purchased me, so happy when I was enabled to give him the maximum in shoe comfort."

130

"Who are you?" I said.

"Isn't it obvious? I am a prototype smart shoe, talking to you through micro-connections in my sole. I pick up your subvocalizations via your throat muscles, translate them, and broadcast my words back to you."

"You can do all that?"

"Yes, and more. Like I said, I'm a smart shoe."

By this time I noticed that a couple of ladies were looking at me funny and I realized they could hear only one side of the conversation, since the other side seemed to be taking place in my head. I paid for the shoes, which offered no further comment, and I got out of there.

Back to my own place, an efficiency one-room apartment in the Jack London Hotel on 4th near Pike. No comment from the shoes until I reached the top linoleum-covered step of the two-flight walk to my apartment, the elevator being a nonstarter this evening.

The shoes said, "What a dump."

"How can you see my place?"

"My eyelets, where the laces go, are light-absorbing diodes."

"I realize you were used to better things with Carlton Johnson," I said.

"Everything was carpeted," the shoes said wistfully, "except for expanses of polished floor left bare on purpose." It paused and sighed. "The wear on me was minimal."

"And here you are in a flophouse," I said. "How have the mighty fallen!"

I must have raised my voice, because a door in the corridor opened and an old woman peered out. When she saw me apparently talking to myself, she shook her head sadly and closed the door.

"You do not have to shout," the shoes said. "Just directing your thoughts toward me is sufficient. I have no trouble picking up your subvocalizations."

"I guess I'm embarrassing you," I said aloud. "I am so terribly sorry."

The shoes did not answer until I had unlocked my door, stepped inside, turned on the light and closed the door again.

Then it said, "I am not embarrassed for myself, but for you, my new owner. I tried to watch out for Carlton Johnson, too."

"How?"

"For one thing, by stabilizing him. He had an unfortunate habit of taking a drink too many from time to time."

"So the guy was a lush?" I said. "Did he ever throw up on you?"

"Now you're being disgusting," the shoes said. "Carlton Johnson was a gentleman."

"It seems to me I've heard entirely enough about Carlton Johnson. Don't you have anything else to talk about?"

"He was my first," the shoes said. "But I'll stop talking about him if it distresses you."

"I couldn't care less," I said. "I'm now going to have a beer. If your majesty doesn't object."

"Why should I object? Just please try not to spill any on me."

"Whatsamatter, you got something against beer?"

"Neither for nor against. It's just that alcohol could fog my diodes."

I got a bottle of beer out of the little fridge, uncapped it and settled back in the small sagging couch. I reached for the TV clicker. But a thought crossed my mind.

"How come you talk that way?" I asked.

"What way?"

"Sort of formal, but always getting into things I wouldn't expect of a shoe."

"I'm a shoe computer, not just a shoe."

"You know what I mean. How come? You talk pretty smart for a gadget that adjusts shoes to feet."

"I'm not really a standard model," the shoe told me. "I'm a prototype. For better or worse, my makers gave me excess capacity."

"What does that mean?"

"I'm too smart to just fit shoes to people. I also have empathy circuitry."

"I haven't noticed much empathy toward me."

"That's because I'm still programmed to Carlton Johnson."

"Am I ever going to hear the last of that guy?"

"Don't worry, my deconditioning circuitry has kicked in. But it takes time for the aura effect to wear off."

I watched a little television and went to bed. Buying a pair of smart shoes had taken it out of me. I woke up some time in the small hours of the night. The shoes were up to something, I could tell even without wearing them.

"What are you up to?" I asked, then realized the shoes couldn't hear me and groped around on the floor for them.

"Don't bother," the shoes said. "I can pick up your subvocalizations on remote, without a hard hookup."

"So what are you doing?"

"Just extracting square roots in my head. I can't sleep."

"Since when does a computer have to sleep?"

"A fault in my standby mode. . . . I need something to do. I miss my peripherals."

"What are you talking about?"

"Carlton Johnson had eyeglasses. I was able to tweak them up to give him better vision. You wouldn't happen to have a pair, would you?"

"I've got a pair, but I don't use them much."

"May I see them? It'll give me something to do."

I got out of bed, found my reading glasses on top of the TV, and set them down beside the shoes. "Thank you," the shoe computer said.

"Mrggh," I said, and went back to sleep.

"So tell me something about yourself," the shoes said in the morning.

"What's to tell? I'm a free-lance writer. Things have been going so well that I can afford to live in the Jack London. End of story."

"Can I see some of your work?"

"Are you a critic, too?"

"Not at all! But I am a creative thinking machine, and I may have some ideas that could be of use to you."

"Forget about it," I told him. "I don't want to show you any of my stuff."

The shoes said, "I happened to glance over your story 'Killer Goddess of the Dark Moon Belt.' "

"How did you just happen to glance at it?" I asked. "I don't remember showing it to you."

"It was lying open on your table."

"So all you could see was the title page."

"As a matter of fact, I read the whole thing."

"How were you able to do that?"

"I made a few adjustments to your glasses," the shoe said. "X-ray vision isn't so difficult to set up. I was able to read each page through the one above it."

"That's quite an accomplishment," I said. "But I don't appreciate you poking into my private matters."

"Private? You were going to send it to a magazine."

"But I haven't yet. . . . What did you think of it?"

"Old-fashioned. That sort of thing doesn't sell anymore."

"It was a parody, dummy. . . . So now you're not only a shoe adjuster but an analyst of the literary marketplace also?"

"I did glance over the writing books in your bookcase."

By the sound of the thoughts in my head, I could tell he didn't approve of my books, either.

"You know," the shoe said later, "You really don't have to be a bum, Ed. You're bright. You could make something of yourself."

"What are you, a psychologist as well as a shoe computer?"

"Nothing of the sort. I have no illusions about myself. But I've gotten to know you a bit in the last few hours since my empathy circuitry kicked in. I can't help but notice—to know—that you're an intelligent man with a good general education. All you need is a little ambition. You know, Ed, that could be supplied by a good woman."

"The last good woman left me shuddering," I said. "I'm really not ready just yet for the next one."

"I know you feel that way. But I've been thinking about Marsha—"

"How in hell do you know about Marsha?"

"Her name is in your little red phone book, which I happened to glance through with my X-ray vision in my efforts to better serve you."

"Listen, even my writing down Marsha's name was a mistake. She's a professional do-gooder. I hate that type."

"But she could be good for you. I noticed you put a star after her name."

"Did you also notice I crossed out the star?"

"That was a second thought. Now, on third thought, she might start looking good again. I suspect you two could go well together."

"You may be good at shoes," I said, "but you know nothing about the sort of women I like. Have you seen her legs?"

"The photo in your wallet showed only her face."

"What? You looked in my wallet, too?"

"With the help of your glasses. . . . And not out of any prurient interest, Ed, I assure you. I just want to help."

"You're already helping too much."

"I hope you won't mind the one little step I took."

"Step? What step?"

My doorbell rang. I glared at my shoes.

"I took the liberty of calling Marsha and asking her over."

"YOU DID WHAT?"

"Ed, Ed, calm down! I know it was taking a liberty. It's not as if I called your former boss, Mr. Edgarson, at Super-Gloss Publications."

"You wouldn't dare!"

"I would, but I didn't. But you could do a lot worse than go back to work for Edgarson. The salary was very nice."

"Have you read any of Gloss's publications? I don't know what you think you're doing, but you aren't going to do it to me!"

"Ed, Ed, I haven't done anything yet! And if you insist, I won't. Not without your permission!"

There was a knock at the door.

"Ed, I'm only trying to look out for you. What's a machine with empathy circuits and excess computing ability to do?"

"I'll tell you in a moment," I said.

I opened the door. Marsha stood there, beaming.

"Oh, Ed, I'm so glad you called!"

So the son of a bitch had imitated my voice, too! I glanced down at my shoes, at the gash in the cap of the left one. A light went off in my head. Realization! Epiphany!

"Come in, Marsha," I said. "I'm glad to see you. I have something for you."

She entered. I sat down in the only decent chair and stripped off the shoes, ignoring the shoe computer's agonized cry in my head of "Ed! Don't do this to me. . . ."

Standing up again, I handed them to Marsha.

"What's this?" she said.

"Shoes for one of your charity cases," I said. "Sorry I don't have a paper bag for you to carry them in."

"But what am I going to do with—"

"Marsha, these are special shoes, computerized shoes. Give them to one of your down-and-outers, get him to put them on. They'll make a new man of him. Pick one of the weak-willed ones you specialize in. It'll give him backbone!"

She looked at the shoes. "This gash in one of them—"

"A minor flaw. I'm pretty sure the former owner did that himself," I told her. "A guy named Carlton Johnson. He couldn't stand the computer's messing around with his head, so he disfigured them and gave them away. Marsha, believe me, these shoes are perfect for the right man. Carlton Johnson wasn't the right man, and I'm not either. But someone you know will bless the ground you walk on for these, believe me."

And with that, I began herding her toward the door.

"When will I hear from you?" she said.

"Don't worry, I'll call," I told her, reveling in the swinish lie that went along with my despicable life.

The Diamond Drill

CHARLES SHEFFIELD

Charles Sheffield (1935–2002) <www.sff.net/people/sheffield/>, physicist and writer, was born in the UK, but lived in the U.S. after the mid-1960s. In 1998, he married writer Nancy Kress. Sheffield began publishing SF in the 1970s, and quickly gained a reputation as a new star of hard SF in the tradition of Arthur C. Clarke. He in fact wrote SF of all descriptions but always with a positive view of scientific knowledge as a tool for solving problems. Sheffield was a prolific novelist, averaging more than a book a year. His novel Spheres of Heaven *(2001) is a sequel to* The Mind Pool *(1993). He had two books out in 2002:* Dark as Day, *a sequel to* Cold as Ice *(1992), and* The Amazing Dr. Darwin. *His short fiction is collected in* Vectors *(1979),* Hidden Variables *(1981),* Erasmus Magister *(1982),* The McAndrew Chronicles *(1983), and* Georgia On My Mind, and Other Places *(1996). He also wrote* Borderlands of Science: How to Think Like a Scientist and Write Science Fiction *(1999).*

"The Diamond Drill" is from Analog, *and is one of the last pieces from this clever, energetic writer, who died near the end of 2002. The central character is a smart man and proud of it, and uses his wit and knowledge to gain advantage. Charles Sheffield's amused, intelligent narrative voice is here personified in the central character. Not a word is wasted. Sheffield cared about science and science fiction, and we will miss him and his engaging stories.*

I doubt if there is a human being alive who said, as a small child, "What I want to be when I grow up is a tax inspector."

That includes the Customs official (Customs are just another form of taxation) who had just pulled me out of line with a discreet, "If you wouldn't mind, sir."

"What's the problem?" I had been headed for the NOTHING TO DECLARE exit.

"Your luggage. You are Dr. Purcell, arriving from Pavonis Six?"

"I am." I read his badge. "What can I do for you, Mr. Warren?"

"Are you aware, sir, that the import to Earth of diamonds, alien artifacts, and life-forms from Pavonis Six is strictly forbidden?"

"I did know that, yes."

"Then what about these, sir?"

We had entered an official chamber off the main entrance corridor. There, open on a table, lay my suitcase. Beside it sat a large leather pouch, also opened to reveal a bright glitter from within.

I laughed. "Oh, I see why you are worried." I put my hand into the pouch and pulled out a handful of faceted stones that seemed to catch and refract every ray of light in the room. "These are stage jewelry, Mr. Warren. They look much like diamonds, but they're not. I picked them up very cheaply, practically for nothing. If you like, I can show you the receipt."

"I think, Dr. Purcell, that we would rather obtain our own assurances as to their nature." He stared at me, but my easy confidence must have somewhat persuaded him of my innocence, because his voice was more friendly when he said, "I presume you would not object to our conducting our own tests—nondestructive ones, of course."

"Not at all." I quickly poured the handful of stones that I was holding back into the pouch and held it out. "I hope this won't take too long—I do have appointments."

"It will be very quick, sir, just a few minutes. We now have a fully automated procedure." He said that with a slight air of pride.

"A machine?"

"That is correct. This machine." He walked across to a compact unit maybe half a meter on a side. "It is designed specifically to establish if a stone is a diamond, or some other material."

He emptied the pouch into a hopper on the top, and the stones vanished into the interior.

"Fascinating." I leaned against the table. "If it's not some sort of trade secret, I wonder if you would mind telling me how it works."

"Not at all." From his tone I could tell that he was delighted to talk about his department's latest toy. "How much do you know about diamonds, sir?"

"Enough to know you can't buy them for the price I paid for those stones. Oh, and if it will scratch glass, it's a diamond. Right?"

"Actually, sir, that's wrong. Diamonds are the hardest things found in nature, but many other gemstones, such as rubies and sapphires and topazes, plus many manmade materials, will scratch glass. You would be safer to state it the other way around: If it *won't* scratch glass, it's not a real diamond."

"So I know even less about diamonds than I thought. This machine tests hardness?"

"It does. It also tests for *density*. Diamonds have a density of about 3.5 times that of water. Zircons—a very common 'fake diamond'—are much denser, at 4.6 and 4.7. So are rubies and sapphires at about 4.1. Glasses are much less dense."

"I suppose the machine tests everything for densities?"

"Indeed it does. But that's not all—colorless topazes have almost exactly the same density as diamonds, so we have to consider still another test: of refractive index."

"How much the stone bends light?"

"Exactly. Diamonds have a very high refractive index, at 2:43, which accounts for its brilliance. 'Fake diamond' candidates run over a wide range of refractive indices, from clear quartz at about 1.5 to zircons at 1.97."

"And I suppose this marvelous machine tests that, too?"

"Indeed it does. Only if a stone passes all three tests—hardness, density, and refractive index—can it be a diamond." The machine at his side beeped gently and disgorged a heap of glittering stones into the pan at its bottom. "And yours didn't pass all the tests. Whatever these are, they're not diamonds. I hope you didn't pay too much for them, sir."

"Oh, I don't think so." I picked up the pan and emptied its contents back into my lead-lined carrying pouch. "Is there anything else, Mr. Warren, or am I free to go?"

"That's all, sir. Welcome to Earth, and I hope that you enjoy your stay here."

"I'm sure I will. And I guess I won't be going near the diamond merchants."

We both laughed. I placed the pouch containing dozens of pure diamonds back in my case, nodded to him, and headed for the exit. The Customs staff were of course free to question me about other matters, but human psychology being what it is, there was no chance of that. Their infallible machine had assured them that despite the anonymous tip (provided, of course by me) Dr. Purcell was not a diamond smuggler, so it was remotely unlikely that he would be smuggling anything else.

The trouble with machines, of course, is that they do what they are built to do. They lack the human talent for suspicion or the power to notice that, although a stone failed to pass all their tests and could therefore not be a diamond, there was

To the Ospreys of McKenzie Bridge,
whose lifestyle inspired this story
—Ursula K. Le Guin

I talked for a long time once with an old Ansar. I met him at his Interplanary Hostel, which is on a large island far out in the Great Western Ocean, well away from the migratory routes of the Ansarac. It is the only place visitors from other planes are allowed, these days.

Kergemmeg lived there as a native host and guide, to give visitors a little whiff of local color, for otherwise the place is like a tropical island on any of a hundred planes—sunny, breezy, lazy, beautiful, with feathery trees and golden sands and great, blue-green, white-maned waves breaking on the reef out past the lagoon. Most visitors came to sail, fish, beachcomb, and drink fermented ü, and had no interest otherwise in the plane or in the sole native of it they met. They looked at him, at first, and took photos, of course, for he was a striking figure: about seven feet tall, thin, strong, angular, a little stooped by age, with a narrow head, large, round, black-and-gold eyes, and a beak. There is an all-or-nothing quality about a beak that keeps the beaked face from being as expressive as those on which the nose and mouth are separated, but Kergemmeg's eyes and eyebrows revealed his feelings very clearly. Old he might be, but he was a passionate man.

He was a little bored and lonely among the uninterested tourists, and when he found me a willing listener (surely not the first or last, but currently the only one) he took pleasure in telling me about his people, as we sat with a tall glass of iced ü in the long, soft evenings, in a purple darkness all

143

aglow with the light of the stars, the shining of the sea-waves full of luminous creatures, and the pulsing glimmer of clouds of fireflies up in the fronds of the feather-trees.

From time immemorial, he said, the Ansarac had followed a Way. *Madan*, he called it. The way of my people, the way things are done, the way things are, the way to go, the way that is hidden in the word *always*: like ours, his word held all those meanings. "Then we strayed from our Way," he said. "For a little while. Now again we do as we have always done."

People are always telling you that "we have always done thus," and then you find that their "always" means a generation or two, or a century or two, at most a millennium or two. Cultural ways and habits are blips, compared to the ways and habits of the body, of the race. There really is very little that human beings on our plane have "always" done, except find food and drink, sleep, sing, talk, procreate, nurture the children, and probably band together to some extent. Indeed it can be seen as our human essence, how few behavioral imperatives we follow. How flexible we are in finding new things to do, new ways to go. How ingeniously, inventively, desperately we seek the right way, the true way, the Way we believe we lost long ago among the thickets of novelty and opportunity and choice . . .

The Ansarac had a somewhat different choice to make than we did, perhaps a more limited one. But it has its interest.

Their world is farther from a larger sun than ours, so, though its spin and tilt are much the same as Earth's, its year lasts about twenty-four of our years. And the seasons are correspondingly large and leisurely, each of them six of our years long.

On every plane and in every climate that has a spring, spring is the breeding time, when new life is born; and for creatures whose life is only a few seasons or a few years, early spring is mating time, too, when new life begins. So it is for the Ansarac, whose life span is, in their terms, three years.

They inhabit two continents, one on the equator and a little north of it, one that stretches up toward the north pole; the two are joined, as the Americas are, by a narrower mountainous bridge of land, though it is all on a smaller scale. The rest of the world is ocean, with a few archipelagoes and scattered large islands, none with any human population except the one used by the Interplanary Agency.

The year begins, Kergemmeg said, when, in the cities of the plains and deserts of the South, the Year Priests give the word and great crowds gather to see the sun pause at the peak of a Tower or stab through a Target with an arrow of light at dawn: the moment of solstice. Now increasing heat will parch the southern grasslands and prairies of wild grain, and in the long dry season the rivers will run low and the wells of the city will go dry. Spring follows the sun northward, melting snow from those far hills, brightening valleys with green . . . And the Ansarac will follow the sun.

"Well, I'm off," old friend says to old friend in the city street. "See you around!" And the young people, the almost-one-year-olds—to us they'd be people of twenty-one or twenty-two—drift away from their households and groups of pals, their colleges and sports clubs, and seek out, among the labyrinthine apartment-complexes and communal dwellings and hostelries of the city, one or the other of the parents from whom they parted, back in the summer. Sauntering casually in, they remark, "Hullo, Dad," or "Hullo, Mother. Seems like everybody's going back north." And the parent, careful not to insult by offering guidance over the long route they came half the young one's life ago, says, "Yes, I've been thinking about it myself. It certainly would be nice to have you with us. Your sister's in the other room, packing."

And so by ones, twos, and threes, the people abandon the city. The exodus is a long process, without any order to it. Some people leave quite soon after the solstice, and others say about them, "What a hurry they're in," or "Shennenne just has to get there first so she can grab the old homesite." But some people linger in the city till it is almost empty, and still can't make up their mind to leave the hot and silent streets, the sad, shadeless, deserted squares, that were so full of crowds and music all through the long halfyear. But first and last they all set out on the roads that lead north. And once they go, they go with speed.

Most carry with them only what they can carry in a backpack or load on a ruba (from Kergemmeg's description, rubac are something like small, feathered donkeys). Some of the traders who have become wealthy during the Desert Season start out with whole trains of rubac loaded with goods and treasures. Though most people travel alone or in a small family group, on the more popular roads they follow pretty close after one another. Larger groups form temporarily in places where the going is hard and the older and weaker people need help gathering and carrying food.

There are no children on the road north.

Kergemmeg did not know how many Ansarac there are but guessed some hundreds of thousands, perhaps a million. All of them join the migration.

As they go up into the mountainous Middle Lands, they do not bunch together, but spread out onto hundreds of different tracks, some followed by many, others by only a few, some clearly marked, others so cryptic that only people who have been on them before could ever trace the turnings. "That's when it's good to have a three-year-old along," Kergemmeg said. "Somebody who's been up the way twice." They travel very light and very fast. They live off the land except in the arid heights of the mountains, where, as he said, "They lighten their packs." And up in those passes and high canyons, the hard-driven rubac of the traders' caravans begin to stumble and tremble, perishing of exhaustion and cold. If the trader still tries to drive them on, people on the road unload them and loose them and let their own packbeast go with them. The little animals limp and scramble back down southward, back to the desert. The goods they carried end up strewn along the wayside for anyone to take; but nobody takes anything, except a little food at need. They don't want stuff to carry, to slow them down. Spring is coming, cool spring, sweet spring, to the valleys of grass and the forests, the lakes, the bright rivers of the North, and they want to be there when it comes.

Listening to Kergemmeg, I imagined that if one could see

the migration from above, see those people all threading along a thousand paths and trails, it would be like seeing our Northwest Coast in spring a century or two ago when every stream, from the mile-wide Columbia to the tiniest creek, turned red with the salmon run.

The salmon spawn and die when they reach their goal, and some of the Ansarac are going home to die, too: those on their third migration north, the three-year-olds, whom we would see as people of seventy and over. Some of them don't make it all the way. Worn out by privation and hard going, they drop behind. If people pass an old man or woman sitting by the road, they may speak a word or two, help to put up a little shelter, leave a gift of food, but they do not urge the elder to come with them. If the elder is very weak or ill they may wait a night or two, until perhaps another migrant takes their place. If they find an old person dead by the roadside, they bury the body. On its back, with the feet to the north: going home.

There are many, many graves along the roads north, Kergemmeg said. Nobody has ever made a fourth migration.

The younger people, those on their first and second migrations, hurry on, crowded together in the high passes of the mountains, then spreading out ever wider on myriad narrow paths through the prairies as the Middle Land widens out north of the mountains. By the time they reach the Northland proper, the great rivers of people have tasseled out into thousands of rivulets, veering west and east, across the north.

Coming to a pleasant hill country where the grass is already green and the trees are leafing out, one of the little groups comes to a halt. "Well, here we are," says Mother. "Here it is." There are tears in her eyes and she laughs, the soft, clacking laugh of the Ansarac. "Shuku, do you remember this place?"

And the daughter who was less than a halfyear old when she left this place—eleven or so, in our years—stares around with amazement and incredulity, and laughs, and cries, "But it was *bigger* than this!"

Then perhaps Shuku looks across those half-familiar meadows of her birthplace to the just-visible roof of the nearest neighbor and wonders if Kimimmid and his father, who caught up to them and camped with them for a few nights and then went on ahead, were there already, living there, and if so, would Kimimmid come over to say hello?

For, though the people who lived so close-packed, in such sociable and ceaseless promiscuity in the Cities Under the Sun, sharing rooms, sharing beds, sharing work and play, doing everything together in groups and crowds, now have all gone apart, family from family, friend from friend, each to a small and separate house here in the meadowlands, or farther north in the rolling hills, or still farther north in the lakelands—even though they have all scattered out like sand from a broken hourglass, the bonds that unite them have not broken; only changed. Now they come together, not in groups and crowds, not in tens and hundreds and thousands, but by two and two.

"Well, here you are!" says Shuku's mother, as Shuku's father opens the door of the little house at the meadow's edge. "You must have been just a few days ahead of us."

"Welcome home," he says gravely. His eyes shine. The two adults take each other by the hand and slightly raise their narrow, beaked heads in a particular salute, an intimate yet formal greeting. Shuku suddenly remembers seeing them do that when she was a little girl, when they lived here, long ago. Here at the birthplace.

"Kimimmid was asking about you just yesterday," Father says to Shuku, and he softly clacks a laugh.

Spring is coming, spring is upon them. Now they will perform the ceremonies of the spring.

Kimimmid comes across the meadow to visit, and he and Shuku talk together, and walk together in the meadows and down by the stream. Presently, after a day or a week or two, he asks her if she would like to dance. "Oh, I don't know," she says, but seeing him stand tall and straight, his head thrown back a little, in the posture that begins the dance, she too stands up; at first her head is lowered, though she stands straight, arms at her sides; but then she wants to throw her head back, back, to reach her arms out wide, wide . . . to dance, to dance with him . . .

And what are Shuku's parents and Kimimmid's parents doing, in the kitchen garden or out in the old orchard, but the same thing? They face each other, they raise their proud and narrow heads, and then he leaps, arms raised above his head, a great leap and a bow, a low bow . . . and she bows too . . . And so it goes, the courtship dance. All over the northern continent, now, the people are dancing.

Nobody interferes with the older couples, recourting, refashioning their marriage. But Kimimmid had better look out. A young man comes across the meadow one evening, a young man Shuku never met before; his birthplace is some miles away. He has heard of Shuku's beauty. He sits and talks with her. He tells her that he is building a new house, in a grove of trees, a pretty spot, nearer her home than his. He would like her advice on how to build the house. He would like very much to dance with her some time. Maybe this evening, just for a little, just a step or two, before he goes away?

He is a wonderful dancer. Dancing with him on the grass in the late evening of early spring, Shuku feels that she is flying on a great wind, and she closes her eyes, her hands float out from her sides as if on that wind, and meet his hands . . .

Her parents will live together in the house by the meadow; they will have no more children, for that time is over for them, but they will make love as often as ever they did when they first were married. Shuku will choose one of her suitors, the new one, in fact. She goes to live with him and make love with him in the house they finish building together. Their building, their dancing, gardening, eating, sleeping, everything they do, turns into making love. And in due course Shuku is pregnant; and in due course she bears two babies. Each is born in a tough, white membrane or shell. Both parents tear this protective covering open with hands and beaks, freeing the tiny curled-up newborn, who lifts its infinitesimal beaklet and peeps blindly, already gaping, greedy for food, for life.

The second baby is smaller, is not greedy, does not thrive. Though Shuku and her husband both feed her with tender care, and Shuku's mother comes to stay and feeds the little one from her own beak and rocks her endlessly when she cries, still she pines and weakens. One morning lying in her grandmother's arms the infant twists and gasps for breath, and then is still. The grandmother weeps bitterly, remembering Shuku's baby brother, who did not live even this long, and tries to comfort Shuku. The baby's father digs a small grave out back of the new house, among the budding trees of the long springtime, and the tears fall and fall from his eyes as he digs. But the other baby, the big girl, Kikirri, chirps and clacks and eats and thrives.

About the time Kikirri is hauling herself upright and shouting "Da!" at her father and "Ma!" at her mother and grandmother and "No!" when told to stop what she is doing, Shuku has another baby. Like many second conceptions, it is a singleton. A fine boy, small, but greedy. He grows fast.

PART 2

And he will be the last of Shuku's children. She and her husband will make love still, whenever they please, in all the delight and ease of the time of flowering and the time of fruit, in the warm days and the mild nights, in the cool under the trees and out in the buzzing heat of the meadow in summer noontime, but it will be, as they say, luxury love; nothing will come of it but love itself.

Children are born to the Ansarac only in the early Northern spring, soon after they have returned to their birthplace. Some couples bring up four children, and many three; but often, if the first two thrive, there is no second conception.

"You are spared our curse of overbreeding," I said to Kergemmeg when he had told me all this. And he agreed, when I told him a little about my plane.

But he did not want me to think that an Ansar has no real sexual or reproductive choice at all. Pairbonding is the rule, but human will and contrariness change and bend and break it, and he talked about those exceptions. Many pairbonds are

between two men or two women. Such couples and others
who are childless are often given a baby by a couple who
have three or four, or take on an orphaned child and bring it
up. There are people who take no mate and people who take
several mates at one time or in sequence. There is of course
adultery. And there is rape. It is bad to be a girl among the
last migrants coming up from the South, for the sexual drive
is already strong in such stragglers, and young women are
all too often gang-raped and arrive at their birthplace brutal-
ized, mateless, and pregnant. A man who finds no mate or is
dissatisfied with his wife may leave home and go off as a
peddler of needles and thread or a tool-sharpener and tinker;
such wanderers are welcomed for their goods but mistrusted
as to their motives.

When we had talked together through several of those
glimmering purple evenings on the verandah in the soft sea
breeze, I asked Kergemmeg about his own life. He had followed Madan, the rule, the way, in all respects but one, he
said. He mated after his first migration north. His wife bore
two children, both from the first conception, a girl and a boy,
who of course went south with them in due time. The whole
family rejoined for his second migration north, and both
children had married close by, so that he knew his five
grandchildren well. He and his wife had spent most of their
third season in the South in different cities; she, a teacher of
astronomy, had gone farther south to the Observatory, while
he stayed in Terke Keter to study with a group of philosophers. She had died very suddenly of a heart attack. He had
attended her funeral. Soon after that he made the trek back
north with his son and grandchildren. "I didn't miss her till I
came back home," he said, factually. "But to come there to
our house, to live there without her—that wasn't something
I could do. I happened to hear that someone was needed to
greet the strangers on this island. I had been thinking about
the best way to die, and this seemed a sort of halfway point.
An island in the middle of the ocean, with not another soul
of my own people on it . . . not quite life, not quite death.
The idea amused me. So I am here." He was well over three

Ansar years old; getting on for eighty in our years, though only the slight stoop of his shoulders and the pure silver of his crest showed his age.

The next night he told me about the southern migration, describing how a man of the Ansarac feels as the warm days of the northern summer begin to wane and shorten. All the work of harvest is done, the grain stored in airtight bins for next year, the slow-growing edible roots planted to winter through and be ready in the spring; the children are shooting up tall, active, increasingly restless and bored by life on the homeplace, more and more inclined to wander off and make friends with the neighbors' children. Life is sweet here, but the same, always the same, and luxury love has lost its urgency. One night, a cloudy night with a chill in the air, your wife in bed next to you sighs and murmurs, "You know? I miss the city." And it comes back to you in a great wave of light and warmth—the crowds, the deep streets and high houses packed with people, the Year Tower high above it all—the sports arenas blazing with sunlight, the squares at night full of lantern-lights and music where you sit at the café tables and drink ü and talk and talk till halfway to morning—the old friends, friends you haven't thought of all this time—and strangers—how long has it been since you saw a new face? How long since you heard a new idea, had a new thought? Time for the city, time to follow the sun!

"Dear," the mother says, "we can't take *all* your rock collection south, just pick out the most special ones," and the child protests, "But I'll *carry* them! I promise!" Forced at last to yield, she finds a special, secret place for her rocks till she comes back, never imagining that by next year, when she comes back home, she won't care about her childish rock collection, and scarcely aware that she has begun to think constantly of the great journey and the unknown lands ahead. The city! What do you do in the city? Are there rock collections?

"Yes," Father says. "In the museum. Very fine collections. They'll take you to see all the museums when you're in school."

School?

"You'll love it," Mother says with absolute certainty.

"School is the best good time in the world," says Aunt Kekki. "I loved school so much I think I'm going to teach school, this year."

The migration south is quite a different matter from the migration north. It is not a scattering but a grouping, a gathering. It is not haphazard but orderly, planned by all the families of a region for many days beforehand. They all set off together, five or ten or fifteen families, and camp together at night. They bring plenty of food with them in handcarts and barrows, cooking utensils, fuel for fires in the treeless plains, warm clothing for the mountain passes, and medicines for illness along the way.

There are no old people on the southward migration—nobody over seventy or so in our years. Those who have made three migrations stay behind. They group together in farmsteads or the small towns that have grown around the farmsteads, or they live out the end of their life with their mate, or alone, in the house where they lived the springs and summers of their lives. (I think what Kergemmeg meant, when he said he had followed his people's Way in all ways but one, was that he had not stayed home, but had come to the island.) The "winter parting," as it is called, between the young going south and the old staying home is painful. It is stoical. It is as it must be.

Only those who stay behind will ever see the glory of autumn in the Northern lands, the blue length of dusk, the first faint patterns of ice on the lake. Some have made paintings or left letters describing these things for the children and grandchildren they will not see again. Most die before the long, long darkness and cold of winter. None survive it.

Each migrating group, as they come down toward the Middle Land, is joined by others coming from east and west, till at night the twinkle of campfires covers all the great prairie from horizon to horizon. They sing at the campfires, and the quiet singing hovers in the darkness between the little fires and the stars.

They don't hurry on the southward journey. They drift along easily, not far each day, though they keep moving. As they reach the foothills of the mountains the great masses split apart again onto many different paths, thinning out, for it's pleasanter to be few on a trail than to come after great numbers of people and trudge in the dust and litter they leave. Up in the heights and passes where there are only a few ways to go they have to come together again. They make the best of it, with cheerful greetings and offers to share food, fire, shelter. Everyone is kind to the children, the half-year-olds, who find the steep mountain paths hard going and often frightening; they slow their pace for the children.

And one evening when it seems they have been struggling in the mountains forever, they come through a high, stony pass to the outlook—South Face, or the Godsbeak Rocks, or the Tor. There they stand and look out and out and down and down to the golden, sunlit levels of the South, the endless fields of wild grain, and some far, faint, purple smudges— the walls and towers of the Cities Under the Sun.

On the downhill road they go faster, and eat lighter, and the dust of their going is a great cloud behind them.

They come to the cities—there are nine of them; Terke Keter is the largest—standing full of sand and silence and sunlight. They pour in through the gates and doors, they fill the streets, they light the lanterns, they draw water from the brimming wells, they throw their bedding down in empty rooms, they shout from window to window and from roof to roof.

Life in the cities is so different from life in the homesteads that the children can't believe it; they are disturbed and dubious; they disapprove. It is so noisy, they complain. It's hot. There isn't anywhere to be alone, they say. They weep, the first nights, from homesickness. But they go off to school as soon as the schools are organized, and there they meet everybody else their age, all of them disturbed and dubious and disapproving and shy and eager and wild with excitement. Back home, they all learned to read and write and do arithmetic, just as they learned carpentry and farming, taught by their parents; but here are advanced classes, libraries, museums, galleries of art, concerts of music, teachers of art, of literature, of mathematics, of astronomy, of architecture, of philosophy—here are sports of all kinds, games, gymnastics, and somewhere in the city every night there is a round dance—above all, here is everybody else in the world, all crowded into these yellow walls, all meeting and talking and working and thinking together in an endless ferment of mind and occupation.

The parents seldom stay together in the cities. Life there is not lived by twos, but in groups. They drift apart, following friends, pursuits, professions, and see each other now and then. The children stay at first with one parent or the other, but after a while they too want to be on their own and go off to live in one of the warrens of young people, the communal houses, the dormitories of the colleges. Young men and women live together, as do grown men and women. Gender is not of much import where there is no sexuality.

For they do everything under the sun in the Cities Under the Sun, except make love.

They love, they hate, they learn, they make, they think hard, work hard, play; they enjoy passionately and suffer desperately, they live a full and human life, and they never give a thought to sex—unless, as Kergemmeg said with a perfect poker face, they are philosophers.

Their achievements, their monuments as a people, are all in the Cities under the Sun, whose towers and public buildings, as I saw in a book of drawings Kergemmeg showed me, vary from stern purity to fervent magnificence. Their books are written there, their thought and religion took form there over the centuries. Their history, their continuity as a culture, is all there.

Their continuity as living beings is what they see to in the North.

Kergemmeg said that while they are in the South they do not miss their sexuality at all. I had to take him at his word, which was given, hard as it might be for us to imagine, simply as a statement of fact.

And as I try to tell here what he told me, it seems wrong to describe their life in the cities as celibate or chaste: for those words imply a forced or willed resistance to desire. Where there is no desire there is no resistance, no abstinence, but rather what one might call, in a radical sense of the word, innocence. They don't think about sex, they don't miss it, it is a non-problem. Their marital life is an empty memory to them, meaningless. If a couple stays together or meets often in the South it is because they are uncommonly good friends—because they love each other. But they love their other friends too. They never live separately from other people. There is little privacy in the great apartment houses of the cities—nobody cares about it. Life there is communal, active, sociable, gregarious, and full of pleasures.

But slowly the days grow warmer; the air dryer; there is a restlessness in the air. The shadows begin to fall differently. And the crowds gather in the streets to hear the Year Priests announce the solstice and watch the sun stop, and pause, and turn south.

People leave the cities, one here, a couple there, a family there . . . It has begun to stir again, that soft hormonal buzz in the blood, that first vague yearning intimation or memory, the body's knowledge of its kingdom coming.

The young people follow that knowledge blindly, without knowing they know it. The married couples are drawn back together by all their wakened memories, intensely sweet. To go home, to go home and be there together!

All they learned and did all those thousands of days and nights in the cities is left behind them, packed up, put away. Till they come back South again . . .

"That is why it was easy to turn us aside," Kergemmeg said. "Because our lives in the North and the South are so different that they seem, to you others, incoherent, incomplete. And we cannot connect them rationally. We cannot explain or justify our Madan to those who live only one kind of life. When the Bayderac came to our plane, they told us our Way was mere instinct and that we lived like animals. We were ashamed."

(I later checked Kergemmeg's "Bayderac" in the *Encyclopedia Planaria*, where I found an entry for the Beidr., of the Unon Plane, an aggressive and enterprising people with highly advanced material technologies, who have been in trouble more than once with the Interplanary Agency for interfering on other planes. The tourist guidebook gives them the symbols that mean "of special interest to engineers, computer programmers, and systems analysts.")

Kergemmeg spoke of them with a kind of pain. It changed his voice, tightened it. He had been a child when they arrived—the first visitors, as it happened, from another plane. He had thought about them the rest of his life.

"They told us we should take control over our lives. We should not live two separate half-lives, but live fully all the time, all the year, as all intelligent beings did. They were a great people, full of knowledge, with high sciences and great ease and luxury of life. To them we truly were little more than animals. They told us and showed us how other people lived on other planes. We saw we were foolish to do without the pleasure of sex for half our life. We saw we were foolish to spend so much time and energy going between South and North on foot, when we could make ships, or roads and cars, or airplanes, and go back and forth a hundred times a year if we liked. We saw we could build cities in the North and make homesteads in the South. Why not? Our Madan was wasteful and irrational, a mere animal impulse controlling us. All we had to do to be free of it was take the medicines the Bayderac gave us. And our children need not take medicines, but could have their being altered by the genetic science of Bayder. Then we could be without rest from sexual desire until we got very old, like the Bayderac. And then a woman would be able to get pregnant at any time before her menopause—in the South, even. And the number of her children would not be limited . . . They were eager to give us these medicines. We knew their doctors were wise. As soon as they came to us they had given us treatments for some of our illnesses, that cured people as if by a miracle. They knew so much. We saw them fly about in their airplanes, and envied them, and were ashamed.

"They brought machines for us. We tried to drive the cars they gave us on our narrow, rocky roads. They sent engineers to direct us, and we began to build a huge Highway straight through the Middle Land. We blew up mountains with the explosives the Bayderac gave us so the Highway could run wide and level, south to north and north to south. My father was a workman on the Highway. There were thousands of men working on that road, for a while. Men from the southern homesteads . . . Only men. Women were not asked to go and do that work. Bayder women did not do such work. It was not women's work, they told us. Women were to stay home with the children while men did the work."

Kergemmeg sipped his ü thoughtfully and gazed off at the glimmering sea and the star-dusted sky.

"Women went down from the homesteads and talked to the men," he said. "They said to listen to them, not only to the Bayderac . . . Perhaps women don't feel shame the way men do. Perhaps their shame is different, more a matter of the body than the mind. It seemed they didn't care much for the cars and airplanes and bulldozers, but cared a great deal about the medicines that would change us and the rules about who did which kind of work. After all, with us, the woman bears the child, but both parents feed it, both nurture it. Why should a child be left to the mother only? They asked that. How could a woman alone bring up four children? Or more than four children? It was inhuman. And then, in the cities, why should families stay together? The child doesn't want its parents then, the parents don't want the child, they all have other things to do . . . The women talked about this to us men, and with them we tried to talk about it to the Bayderac.

"They said, 'All that will change. You will see. You cannot reason correctly. It is merely an effect of your hormones, your genetic programming, which we will correct. Then you will be free of your irrational and useless behavior patterns.'

"But we answered, 'But will we be free of your irrational and useless behavior patterns?'

"Men working on the Highway began throwing down their tools and abandoning the big machines the Bayderac had provided. They said, 'What do we need this Highway for when we have a thousand ways of our own?' And they set off southward on those old paths and trails.

"You see, all this happened—fortunately, I think—near

the end of a Northern Season. In the North, where we all live apart, and so much of life is spent in courting and making love and bringing up the children, we were—how shall I put it—more short-sighted, more impressionable, more vulnerable. We had just begun the drawing together, then. When we came to the South, when we were all in the Cities Under the Sun, we could gather, take counsel together, argue and listen to arguments, and consider what was best for us as a people.

"After we had done that, and had talked further with the Bayderac and let them talk to us, we called for a Great Consensus, such as is spoken of in the legends and the ancient records of the Year Towers where history is kept. Every Ansar came to the Year Tower of their city and voted on this choice: Shall we follow the Bayder Way or the Manad? If we followed their Way, they were to stay among us; if we chose our own, they were to go. We chose our way." His beak clattered very softly as he laughed. "I was a halfyearling, that season. I cast my vote."

I did not have to ask how he had voted, but I asked if the Bayderac had been willing to go.

"Some of them argued, some of them threatened," he said. "They talked about their wars and their weapons. I am sure they could have destroyed us utterly. But they did not. Maybe they despised us so much they didn't want to bother. Or their wars called them away. By then we had been visited by people from the Interplanary Agency, and most likely it was their doing that the Bayderac left us in peace. Enough of us had been alarmed that we agreed then, in another voting, that we wanted no more visitors. So now the Agency sees to it that they come only to this island. I am not sure we made the right choice, there. Sometimes I think we did, sometimes I wonder. Why are we afraid of other peoples, other Ways? They can't all be like the Bayderac."

"I think you made the right choice," I said. "But I say it against my will. I'd like so much to meet an Ansar woman, to meet your children, to see the Cities Under the Sun! I'd like so much to see your dancing!"

"Oh, well, that you can see," he said, and stood up. Maybe we had had a little more ü than usual, that night.

He stood very tall there in the glimmering darkness on the verandah over the beach. He straightened his shoulders, and his head went back. The crest on his head slowly rose into a stiff plume, silver in the starlight. He lifted his arms above his head. It was the pose of the antique Spanish dancer, fiercely elegant, tense, and masculine. He did not leap, he was after all a man of eighty, but he gave somehow the impression of a leap, then a deep graceful bow. His beak clicked out a quick double rhythm, he stamped twice, and his feet seemed to flicker in a complex set of steps while his upper body remained taut and straight. Then his arms came out in a great embracing gesture, toward me, as I sat almost terrified by the beauty and intensity of his dance.

And then he stopped, and laughed. He was out of breath. He sat down and passed his hand over his forehead and his crest, panting a little. "After all," he said, "it isn't courting season."

A Few Kind Words for A. E. Van Vogt

RICHARD CHWEDYK

Richard Chwedyk lives in Chicago, Illinois. Last year we featured his story "The Measure of All Things" in Years Best SF 7. *This year he published a fine long sequel, "Bronte's Egg." He often reads in the Chicago area, most recently at the* Twilight Tales *reading series at the Red Lion Pub. His poetry has recently been published in* Tales of the Unanticipated *and* Tales from the Red Lion, *but has also appeared in* Another Chicago Magazine, Oyez Review, *Paul Hoover's legendary* Oink! *(now called* New American Writing), *and* The Best of Hair Trigger *anthology, among even older publications. He teaches creative writing classes at Oakton Community College, but his day job is doing layout and copyediting for a chain of newspapers in the Chicago suburbs.*

"A Few Kind Words for A. E. Van Vogt," from Tales of the Unanticipated, *is a lyric poem about one of the titanic figures of SF, who was given the Grand Master Award by the SFWA only after he had succumbed to Alzheimer's. This poem is about the night he stood up in front of the audience at the annual Nebula Awards banquet to accept the award. I was there; the description is accurate. It is also about his powerful contributions to genre SF and to literature in the 20th century (note the allusion to Mishima).*

An irony in physics rendered him mute
as he stood to receive his award
in the darkened arena.

He looked at the assembled audience with
gratitude, but also with undisguised
bewilderment, a little apprehension.
His eyes were liquid, opened wide,
forehead furrowed, confounded with
his inarticulation.

His speech was read for him by an old, good friend.
His wife stood just a step behind him.
His hair was combed straight back.
He dressed like an accountant and it was not inappropriate,
for it was this disguise that was his work.

It was not, in a word, original:
Plato, De Quincey, Borges, Christian mystics, Eastern monks,
all hinted at the notion that each object in this world
is a secret symbol for an object in another,
and nothing is in itself merely itself.

Of course, then, he wore the uniform of a "plain" man.
Of course, he wondered at the crowd
and what this all was really about.

He was looking, perhaps, for Cayle Clark,
or Jommy, or Gosseyn,
out there in the dark, the audience up,
out of their seats. He seemed to look past them all.

He'd torn open the bag that held his dreams
and let them all pour out
at a penny or two a word. And what a surprise
it must have been, when the contents fell
to the page, how many people recognized those objects
as their own.

It wasn't eloquent. It wasn't pristine.
At times his vessel seemed hardly seaworthy.
But to have made it so would have betrayed the secret:

There is a secret world one train stop further on,
across the highway, past the chain-link fence,
on the other side of the woods. A secret neighborhood.
A secret room. The fate of the universe, of time itself,
is weighed against this discovery.

There is something important at the other end of this gaze,
and we better find out what it is.
But for now, don't say a word.

And he didn't.

And when my dour, self-absorbed, ascetic, "literary"
friend asks me (and pronounces the name
like a gummy cough) "About this van Vogt,"
that he read of in a biography of Mishima,
I tell him nothing, betray nothing.

An accident of semantics, an irony of physics,
a brief attack of poetry, renders me mute.

The skeleton of the world I saw
when I left that dark arena

was a cast-off from the bag of dreams.
And Cayle, and Jommy and Gilbert Gosseyn
were standing by the newspaper boxes, in their dark suits,
each holding a finger up to his lips.

Halo

CHARLES STROSS

Charles Stross (http://www.antipope.org/charlie/blosxom.cgi) lives in Edinburgh, Scotland. A dyed-in-the-wool science fiction writer in the tradition of Bruce Sterling, he is so full of ideas and energy that at times he seems to be a fizzing, popping conduit, a high-powered cable full of lightning bolts and showering sparks. He is of the same social circle as Iain M. Banks and Ken McLeod, and the three of them are being called (not entirely unjustly) the Scots SF Renaissance. Stross has been publishing for the past four years in Spectrum SF and Interzone, and recently in Asimov's, but had a hit in 2001 in writing circles with his story "Lobsters." By the time of the world SF convention in San Jose in 2001, SF people were eager to meet Stross. His collection Toast (2002) appeared in a print-on-demand edition last year. His first SF novel will appear in 2003.

"Halo" is part of a series of energetic showpieces in the first person present tense that have appeared in Asimov's over the last two years—the Manfred Maxx series, set in a near future that is undergoing continuing revolution in the biological sciences, after a computer revolution, after a techno-economic revolution. And there's more to come. This one has a sympathetic teenage protagonist, Amber, Manfred's cyborg super-competent daughter, who is desperate to get out from under the authority of her control-freak mother, and away from her cat. And what better place than outer space to be free?

Vast whorls of cloud ripple beneath the ship's drive stinger: orange and brown and muddy gray streaks slowly ripple across the bloated horizon of Jupiter. *Sanger* is nearing perijove, deep within the gas giant's lethal magnetic field; static discharges flicker along the tube, arcing over near the deep violet exhaust cloud emerging from the magnetic mirrors of the ship's VASIMR motor. The plasma rocket is cranked up to maximum mass flow, its specific impulse almost as low as a fission rocket but thrusting at maximum as the assembly creaks and groans through the gravitational assist maneuver. In another hour, the drive will flicker off, and the orphanage will fall up and out toward Ganymede, before dropping back in toward orbit around Amalthea, Jupiter's fourth moon (and source of much of the material in the Gossamer ring). They're not the first canned primates to make it to Jupiter subsystem, but they're one of the first wholly private ventures. The bandwidth out here sucks dead slugs through a straw, with millions of kilometers of vacuum separating them from scant hundreds of mouse-brained microprobes and a few mechanical dinosaurs left behind by NASA or ESA. They're so far from the inner system that a good chunk of the ship's communications array is given over to caching: the news is whole kiloseconds old by the time it gets out here.

Amber, along with about half the waking passengers, watches in fascination from the common room. The commons are a long axial cylinder, a double-hulled inflatable at the center of the ship with a large part of their liquid water supply stored in its wall-tubes. The far end is video-enabled, showing them a realtime 3D view of the planet as it rolls beneath them: in reality, there's as much mass as possible between them and the trapped particles in the Jovian magnetic envelope. "I could go swimming in that," sighs Lilly. "Just imagine, diving into that sea. . . ." Her avatar appears in the window, riding a silver surfboard down the kilometers of vacuum.

"Nice case of wind-burn you've got there," someone jeers: Kas. Suddenly, Lilly's avatar, heretofore clad in a shimmering metallic swimsuit, turns to the texture of baked meat, and waggles sausage-fingers up at them in warning.

"Same to you and the window you climbed in through!" Abruptly the virtual vacuum outside the window is full of bodies, most of them human, contorting and writhing and morphing in mock-combat as half the kids pitch into the virtual deathmatch: it's a gesture in the face of the sharp fear that outside the thin walls of the orphanage lies an environment that really *is* as hostile as Lilly's toasted avatar would indicate.

Amber turns back to her slate: she's working through a complex mess of forms, necessary before the expedition can start work. Facts and figures that are never far away crowd around her, intimidating. Jupiter weighs 1.9×10^{27} kilograms. There are twenty-nine Jovian moons and an estimated two hundred thousand minor bodies, lumps of rock, and bits of debris crowded around them—debris above the size of ring fragments, for Jupiter (like Saturn) has rings, albeit not as prominent. A total of six major national orbiter platforms have made it out here—and another two hundred and seventeen microprobes, all but six of them private entertainment platforms. The first human expedition was put together by ESA Studios six years ago, followed by a couple of wildcat mining prospectors and a u-commerce bus that scattered half a million picoprobes throughout Jupiter subsystem. Now the *Sanger* has arrived, along with another three monkey cans—one from Mars, two more from LEO—and it looks as if colonization would explode except that there are at least four mutually exclusive Grand Plans for what to do with old Jove's mass.

Someone prods her. "Hey, Amber, what are you up to?"

She opens her eyes. "Doing my homework." It's Su Ang. "Look, we're going to Amalthea, aren't we? But we file our accounts in Reno, so we have to do all this paperwork. Monica asked me to help. It's insane."

Ang leans over and reads, upside down. "Environmental Protection Agency?"

"Yeah. Estimated Environmental Impact Forward Analysis 204.6b, Page Two. They want me to 'list any bodies of standing water within five kilometers of the designated mining area. If excavating below the water table, list any wellsprings, reservoirs, and streams within depth of excavation in meters multiplied by five hundred meters up to a maximum distance of ten kilometers downstream of direction of bedding plane flow. For each body of water, itemize any endangered or listed species of bird, fish, mammal, reptile, invertebrate, or plant living within ten kilometers—' "

"—Of a mine on Amalthea? Which orbits one hundred and eighty thousand kilometers above Jupiter, has no atmosphere, and where you can pick up a whole body radiation dose of ten Grays in half an hour on the surface?" Ang shakes her head, then spoils it by giggling. Amber glances up.

On the wall in front of her someone—Nicky or Boris, probably—has pasted a caricature of her own avatar into the virch fight. She's being hugged from behind by a giant cartoon dog with floppy ears and an erection, who's singing anatomically improbable suggestions while fondling himself suggestively. "Fuck that!" Shocked out of her distraction—and angry—Amber drops her stack of paperwork and throws a new avatar at the screen, one an agent of hers dreamed up overnight: it's called Spike, and it's not friendly. Spike rips off the dog's head and pisses down its trachea, which is anatomically correct for a human being: meanwhile she looks around, trying to work out which of the laughing idiot children and lost geeks around her could have sent such an unpleasant message.

"Children! Chill out." She glances round: one of the

Franklins (this is the twenty-something dark-skinned female one) is frowning at them. "Can't we leave you alone for half a K without a fight?"

Amber pouts. "It's not a fight: it's a forceful exchange of opinions."

"Hah." The Franklin leans back in mid-air, arms crossed, an expression of supercilious smugness pasted across her-their face. "Heard that one before. Anyway—" she-they gesture and the screen goes blank "—I've got news for you pesky kids. We got a claim verified! Factory starts work as soon as we shut down the stinger and finish filing all the paperwork via our lawyers. Now's our chance to earn our upkeep. . . ."

Amber is flashing on ancient history, three years back along her timeline. In her replay, she's in some kind of split-level ranch house out west. It's a temporary posting while her mother audits an obsolescent fab line enterprise that grinds out dead chips of VLSI silicon for Pentagon projects that have slipped behind the cutting edge. Her mom leans over her, menacingly adult in her dark suit and chaperonage earrings: "You're going to school, and that's that!"

Her mother is a blond ice-maiden madonna, one of the IRS's most productive bounty hunters—she can make grown CEOs panic just by blinking at them. Amber, a towheaded eight-year-old tearaway with a confusing mix of identities, inexperience blurring the boundary between self and grid, is not yet able to fight back effectively. After a couple of seconds, she verbalizes a rather feeble protest: "Don't want to!" One of her stance demons whispers that this is the wrong approach to take, so she modifies it: "They'll beat up on me, Mom. I'm too different. 'Sides, I know you want me socialized up with my grade metrics, but isn't that what sideband's for? I can socialize *real* good at home."

Mom does something unexpected: she kneels down, putting herself on eye level with Amber. They're on the living room carpet, all seventies-retro brown corduroy and acidorange paisley wallpaper: the domestics are in hiding while the humans hold court. "Listen to me, sweetie." Mom's voice is breathy, laden with an emotional undertow as strong and stifling as the eau de cologne she wears to the office to cover up the scent of her client's fear. "I know that's what your father's writing to you, but it isn't true. You need the company—*physical* company—of children your own age. You're *natural*, not some kind of engineered freak, even with your skullset. Natural children like you need company, or they grow up all weird. Don't you know how much you mean to me? I want you to grow up happy, and that won't happen if you don't learn to get along with children your own age. You're not going to be some kind of cyborg otaku freak, Amber. But to *get* healthy, you've got to go to school, build up a mental immune system. That which does not destroy us makes us stronger, right?"

It's crude moral blackmail, transparent as glass and manipulative as hell, but Amber's *corpus logica* flags it with a heavy emotional sprite miming the likelihood of physical discipline if she rises to the bait: Mom is agitated, nostrils slightly flared, ventilation rate up, some vasodilatation visible in her cheeks. Amber—in combination with her skullset and the metacortex of distributed agents it supports—is mature enough at eight years to model, anticipate, and avoid corporal punishment: but her stature and lack of physical maturity conspire to put her at a disadvantage when negotiating with adults who matured in a simpler age. She sighs, then puts on a pout to let Mom know she's still reluctant, but obedient. "O-kay. If you say so."

Mom stands up, eyes distant—probably telling Saturn to warm his engine and open the garage doors. "I say so, punkin. Go get your shoes on, now. I'll pick you up on my way back from work, and I've got a treat for you: we're going to check out a new Church together this evening." Mom smiles, but it doesn't reach her eyes. "You be a good little girl, now, all right?"

The Imam is at prayer in a gyrostabilized mosque.

His mosque is not very big, and it has a congregation of one: he performs salat on his own every seventeen thousand two hundred and eighty seconds. He also webcasts the call to prayer, but there are no other believers in trans-Jovian space to answer the summons. Between prayers, he splits his attention between the exigencies of life-support and scholarship. A student of the Hadith and of knowledge-based systems, Sadeq collaborates in a project with other mujtahid scholars who are building a revised concordance of all the known isnads, to provide a basis for exploring the body of Islamic jurisprudence from a new perspective—one they'll need sorely if the looked-for breakthroughs in communication with aliens emerge. Their goal is to answer the vexatious questions that bedevil Islam in the age of accelerated consciousness: and as their representative in orbit around Jupiter, these questions fall most heavily on Sadeq's shoulders.

Sadeq is a slightly built man, with close-cropped black hair and a perpetually tired expression: unlike the orphanage crew, he has a ship to himself. The ship started out as an Iranian knock-off of a Shenzhou-B capsule, with a Chinese-type 921 space-station module tacked onto its tail: but the clunky, nineteen-sixties lookalike—a glittering aluminum dragonfly mating with a Coke can—has a weirdly contoured M2P2 pod strapped to its nose. The M2P2 pod is a plasma sail: built in orbit by one of Daewoo's wake shield-facilities, it dragged Sadeq and his cramped space station out to Jupiter in just four months, surfing on the solar breeze. His presence may be a triumph for the Ummah, but he feels acutely alone out here: when he turns his compact observatory's mirrors in the direction of the *Sanger*, he is struck by its size and purposeful appearance. *Sanger*'s superior size speaks of the efficiency of the western financial instruments, semi-autonomous investment trusts with variable business-cycle accounting protocols that make possible the development of commercial space exploration. The Prophet, peace be unto him, may have condemned usury: but surely it would have given him pause to see these engines of capital formation demonstrate their power above the Great Red Spot.

After finishing his prayers, Sadeq spends a couple of extra

precious minutes on his mat. He finds that meditation comes hard in this environment: kneel in silence and you become aware of the hum of ventilation fans, the smell of old socks and sweat, the metallic taste of ozone from the Elektron oxygen generators. It is hard to approach God in this third-hand spaceship, a hand-me-down from arrogant Russia to ambitious China, and finally to the religious trustees of Qom, who have better uses for it than any of the heathen states imagine. They've pushed it far, this little toy space station: but who's to say if it is God's intention for humans to live here, in orbit around this swollen alien giant of a planet?

Sadeq shakes his head: he rolls his mat up and stows it beside the solitary porthole with a quiet sigh. A stab of homesickness wrenches at him, for his childhood in hot, dusty Yazd and his many years as a student in Qom: he steadies himself by looking round, searching the station that is by now as familiar to him as the fourth-floor concrete apartment that his parents—a car factory worker and his wife—raised him in. The interior of the station is the size of a school bus, every surface cluttered with storage areas, instrument consoles, and layers of exposed pipes: a couple of globules of antifreeze jiggle like stranded jellyfish near a heat exchanger that has been giving him grief. Sadeq kicks off in search of the squeeze bottle he keeps for this purpose, then gathers up his roll of tools and instructs one of his agents to find him the relevant sura of the maintenance log: it's time to fix this leaky joint for good.

An hour or so of serious plumbing, and then he will eat (freeze-dried lamb stew, with a paste of lentils and boiled rice, and a bulb of strong tea to wash it down), then sit down to review his next flyby maneuvering sequence. Perhaps, God willing, there will be no further system alerts and he'll be able to spend an hour or two on his research between evening and final prayers. Maybe the day after tomorrow, there'll even be time to relax for a couple of hours, to watch one of the old movies that he finds so fascinating for their insights into alien cultures: *Apollo 13*, maybe. It isn't easy, being the only crew aboard a long-duration space mission: and it's even harder for Sadeq, up here with nobody to talk to, for the communications lag to earth is more than half an hour each way—and so far as he knows he's the only believer within half a billion kilometers.

Amber dials a number in Paris and waits until someone answers the phone. She knows the strange woman on the phone's tiny screen: Mom calls her "your father's fancy bitch," with a peculiar tight smile. (The one time Amber asked what a fancy bitch was, Mom hit her—not hard, just a warning.) "Is Daddy there?" she asks.

The strange woman looks slightly bemused. (Her hair is blond, like Mom's, but the color clearly came out of a bleach bottle, and it's cut really short, mannish.) "*Oui*. Ah, yes." She smiles tentatively. "I am sorry, it is a disposable phone you are using? You want to talk to 'im?"

It comes out in a rush: "I want to *see* him." Amber clutches the phone like a lifesaver: it's a cheap disposable cereal-packet item, and the cardboard is already softening in her sweaty grip. "Momma won't let me, auntie 'Nette—"

"Hush." Annette, who has lived with Amber's father for more than twice as long as her mother did, smiles. "You are sure that telephone, your mother does not know of it?"

Amber looks around. She's the only child in the rest room because it isn't break time and she told teacher she had to go right *now*: "I'm sure, P_{20} confidence factor greater than 0.9." Her Bayesian head tells her that she can't reason accurately about this because Momma has never caught her with an illicit phone before, but what the hell. *It can't get Dad into trouble if he doesn't know, can it?*

"Very good." Annette glances aside. "Manny, I have a surprise call for you."

Daddy appears on screen. She can see all of his face, and he looks younger than last time: he must have stopped using those clunky old glasses. "Hi—Amber! Where are you? Does your mother know you're calling me?" He looks slightly worried.

"No," she says confidently, "the phone came in a box of Grahams."

"Phew. Listen, sweet, you must remember to never, ever

call me where your mom may find out. Otherwise, she'll get her lawyers to come after me with thumb screws and hot pincers, because she'll say *I* made you call me. Understand?"

"Yes, Daddy." She sighs. "Don't you want to know why I called?"

"Um." For a moment he looks taken aback. Then he nods, seriously. Amber likes Daddy because he takes her seriously most times when she talks to him. It's a phreaking nuisance having to borrow her classmates' phones or tunnel past Mom's pit-bull firewall, but Dad doesn't assume that she can't know anything because she's only a kid. "Go ahead. There's something you need to get off your chest? How've things been, anyway?"

She's going to have to be brief: the disposaphone comes pre-paid, the international tariff it's using is lousy, and the break bell is going to ring any minute. "I want *out*, Daddy. I mean it. Mom's getting loopier every week: she's dragging me around to all these churches now, and yesterday she threw a fit over me talking to my terminal. She wants me to see the school shrink, I mean, what *for*? I *can't* do what she wants; I'm not her little girl! Every time I tunnel out, she tries to put a content-bot on me, and it's making my head hurt—I can't even think straight anymore!" To her surprise, Amber feels tears starting. "Get me out of here!"

The view of her father shakes, pans around to show her tante Annette looking worried. "You know, your father, he cannot do anything? The divorce lawyers, they will tie him up."

Amber sniffs. "Can *you* help?" she asks.

"I'll see what I can do," her father's fancy bitch promises as the break bell rings.

An instrument package peels away from the *Sanger*'s claimjumper drone and drops toward the potato-shaped rock, fifty kilometers below. Jupiter hangs huge and gibbous in the background, impressionist wallpaper for a mad cosmologist: Pierre bites his lower lip as he concentrates on steering it.

Amber, wearing a black sleeping-sack, hovers over his head like a giant bat, enjoying her freedom for a shift. She looks down on Pierre's bowl-cut hair, his wiry arms gripping either side of the viewing table, and wonders what to have him do next. A slave for a day is an interesting experience, restful: life aboard the *Sanger* is busy enough that nobody gets much slack-time (at least, not until the big habitats have been assembled and the high bandwidth dish is pointing at Earth). They're unrolling everything to a hugely intricate plan generated by the backers' critical path team, and there isn't much room for idling: the expedition relies on shamelessly exploitative child labor—they're lighter on the life-support consumables than adults—working the kids twelve-hour days to assemble a toe-hold on the shore of the future. (When they're older and their options vest fully, they'll all be rich—but that hasn't stopped the outraged herdnews propaganda back home.) For Amber, the chance to let somebody else work for her is novel, and she's trying to make every minute count.

"Hey, slave," she calls idly: "how you doing?"

Pierre sniffs. "It's going okay." He refuses to glance up at her, Amber notices. He's thirteen: isn't he supposed to be obsessed with girls by that age? She notices his quiet, intense focus, runs a stealthy probe along his outer boundary: he shows no sign of noticing it but it bounces off, unable to chink his mental armor. "Got cruise speed," he says, taciturn, as two tons of metal, ceramics, and diamond-phase weirdness hurtles toward the surface of Barney at three hundred kilometers per hour. "Stop shoving me: there's a three-second lag and I don't want to get into a feedback control-loop with it."

"I'll shove if I want, *slave*." She sticks her tongue out at him.

"And if you make me drop it?" he asks. Looking up at her, his face serious—"Are we supposed to be doing this?"

"You cover your ass and I'll cover *mine*," she says, then turns bright red. "You know what I mean."

"I do, do I?" Pierre grins widely, then turns back to the console: "Aww, that's no fun. And you want to tune whatever bit-bucket you've given control of your speech centers to: they're putting out way too much *double-entendre*, somebody might mistake you for a grown-up."

"You stick to *your* business and *I'll* stick to *mine*," she says, emphatically. "And you can start by telling me what's happening."

"Nothing." He leans back and crosses his arms, grimacing at the screen. "It's going to drift for five hundred seconds, now, then there's the midcourse correction and a deceleration burn before touch-down. And *then* it's going to be an hour while it unwraps itself and starts unwinding the cable spool. What do you want, minute noodles with that?"

"Uh-huh." Amber spreads her bat-wings and lies back in mid-air, staring at the window, feeling rich and idle as Pierre works his way through her day-shift. "Wake me when there's something interesting to see." Maybe she should have had him feed her peeled grapes or give her a foot massage, something more traditionally hedonistic: but right now just *knowing* he's her own little piece of alienated labor is doing good things for her self-esteem. Looking at those tense arms, the curve of his neck, she thinks maybe there's something to this whispering-and-giggling he *really likes you* stuff the older girls go in for—

The window rings like a gong and Pierre coughs. "You've got mail," he says dryly. "You want me to read it for you?"

"What the—" A message is flooding across the screen, right-to-left snaky script like the stuff on her corporate instrument (now lodged safely in a deposit box in Zurich). It takes her a while to page-in the grammar agent that can handle Arabic, and another minute for her to take in the meaning of the message. When she does, she starts swearing, loudly and continuously.

"*You* bitch, *Mom! Why'd you have to go and do a thing like* that?"

The corporate instrument arrived in a huge FedEx box addressed to Amber: it happened on her birthday while Mom was at work, and she remembers it as if it was only an hour ago.

She remembers reaching up and scraping her thumb over

the delivery man's clipboard, the rough feel of the microse-
quencers sampling her DNA; afterward, she drags the package inside. When she pulls the tab on the box it unpacks
itself automatically, regurgitating a compact 3D printer, half
a ream of paper printed in old-fashioned dumb ink, and a
small calico cat with a large @-symbol on its flank. The cat
hops out of the box, stretches, shakes its head, and glares at
her. "You're Amber?" it mrowls.

"Yeah," she says, shyly. "Are you from Tanté 'Nette?"

"No, I'm from the fucking tooth fairy." It leans over and
head-butts her knee, strops the scent glands between its
ears all over her skirt. "Listen, you got any tuna in the
kitchen?"

"Mom doesn't believe in seafood," says Amber: "it's all
foreign junk, she says. It's my birthday today, did I tell you?"

"Happy fucking birthday, then." The cat yawns, convincingly realistic. "Here's your dad's present. Bastard put me in
hibernation and blogged me along to show you how to work
it. You take my advice, you'll trash the fucker. No good will
come of it."

Amber interrupts the cat's grumbling by clapping her
hands gleefully. "So what *is* it?" she demands. "A new invention? Some kind of weird sex toy from Amsterdam? A
gun, so I can shoot Pastor Wallace?"

"Naaah." The cat yawns, yet again, and curls up on the
floor next to the 3D printer. "It's some kinda dodgy business
model to get you out of hock to your mom. Better be careful,
though—he says its legality is narrowly scoped jurisdiction-
wise."

"Wow. Like, how totally cool!" In truth, Amber is delighted because it *is* her birthday, but Mom's at work and
Amber's home alone, with just the TV in moral-majority
mode for company. Things have gone so far downhill since
Mom discovered religion that absolutely the best thing in the
world tante Annette could have sent her is some scam programmed by Daddy to take her away. If he doesn't, Mom
will take her to Church tonight (and maybe to an IRS
compliance-certified restaurant afterward, if Amber's good
and does whatever Pastor Wallace tells her to).

The cat sniffs in the direction of the printer: "Why dontcha fire it up?" Amber opens the lid on the printer, removes the packing popcorn, and plugs it in. There's a whirr and a rush of waste heat from its rear as it cools the imaging heads down to working temperature and registers her ownership.

"What do I do now?" she asks.

"Pick up the page labeled READ ME and follow the instructions," the cat recites in a bored sing-song voice. It winks at her, then fakes an exaggerated French accent: "Le READ ME contains directions pour l'execution instrument corporate dans le boîte. In event of perplexity, consult the accompanying aineko for clarification." The cat wrinkles its nose rapidly, as if it's about to bite an invisible insect. "Warning: don't rely on your father's cat's opinions, it is a perverse beast and cannot be trusted. Your mother helped seed its meme base, back when they were married. *Ends*." It mumbles on for a while: "fucking snotty Parisian bitch, I'll piss in her knicker drawer, I'll molt in her bidet. . . ."

"Don't be vile." Amber scans the READMME quickly. Corporate instruments are strong magic, according to Daddy, and this one is exotic by any standards: a limited company established in Yemen, contorted by the intersection between shari'a and the global legislatosaurus. Understanding it isn't easy, even with a personal net full of sub-sapient agents that have full access to whole libraries of international trade law—the bottleneck is comprehension. Amber finds the documents highly puzzling. It's not the fact that half of them are written in Arabic that bothers her—that's what her grammar engine is for—or even that they're full of S-expressions and semi-digestible chunks of LISP: but that the company seems to assert that it exists for the sole purpose of owning slaves.

"What's going on?" she asks the cat. "What's this all about?"

The cat sneezes, then looks disgusted. "This wasn't *my* idea, big shot. Your father is a very weird guy and your mother hates him lots because she's still in love with him. She's got kinks, y'know? Or maybe she's sublimating them, if she's serious about this church shit she's putting you through. He thinks that she's a control freak. Anyway, after your dad ran off in search of another dome, she took out an injunction against him. But she forgot to cover his partner, and *she* bought this parcel of worms and sent them to you, okay? Annie is a real bitch, but he's got her wrapped right around his finger, or something. Anyway, he built these companies and this printer—which isn't hardwired to a filtering proxy, like your mom's—specifically to let you get away from her legally. *If* that's what you want to do."

Amber fast-forward through the dynamic chunks of the README—boring static UML diagrams, mostly—soaking up the gist of the plan. Yemen is one of the few countries to implement traditional Sunni shari'a law and a limited-liability company scam at the same time. Owning slaves is legal—the fiction is that the owner has an option hedged on the indentured laborer's future output, with interest payments that grow faster than the unfortunate victim can pay them off—and companies are legal entities. If Amber sells herself into slavery to this company, she will become a slave, and the company will be legally liable for her actions and upkeep. The rest of the legal instrument—about 90 percent of it, in fact—is a set of self-modifying corporate mechanisms coded in a variety of jurisdictions that permit Turing-complete company constitutions, and which act as an ownership shell for the slavery contract: at the far end of the corporate firewall is a trust fund of which Amber is the prime beneficiary and shareholder. When she reaches the age of majority, she'll acquire total control over all the companies in the network and can dissolve her slave contract; until then, the trust funds (which she essentially owns) oversee the company that owns her (and keeps it safe from hostile takeover bids). Oh, and the company network is primed by an extraordinary general meeting that instructed it to move the trust's assets to Paris immediately. A one-way airline ticket is enclosed.

"You think I should take this?" she asks uncertainly. It's hard to tell how smart the cat really is—there's probably a yawning vacuum behind those semantic networks if you dig deep enough—but it tells a pretty convincing tale.

The cat squats and curls its tail protectively around its paws: "I'm saying nothing, you know what I mean? You take this, you can go live with your dad. But it won't stop your ma coming after him with a horse whip and after *you* with a bunch of lawyers and a set of handcuffs. You want *my* advice, you'll phone the Franklins and get aboard their off-planet mining scam. In space, no one can serve a writ on you. Plus, they got long-term plans to get into the CETI market, cracking alien network packets. You want my honest opinion, you wouldn't like it in Paris after a bit. Your dad and the frog bitch, they're swingers, y'know? No time in their lives for a kid. Or a cat like me, now I think of it. They're out all hours of the night doing drugs, fetish parties, raves, opera, that kind of adult shit. Your dad dresses in frocks more than your mom, and your tante 'Nettie leads him around the apartment on a chain when they're not having noisy sex on the balcony. They'd cramp your style, kid: you shouldn't have to put up with parents who have more of a life than you do."

"Huh." Amber wrinkles her nose, half-disgusted by the cat's transparent scheming, and half-acknowledging its message: *I'd better think hard about this*, she decides. Then she flies off in so many directions at once that she nearly browns out the household net feed. Part of her is examining the intricate card pyramid of company structures; somewhere else, she's thinking about what can go wrong, while another bit (probably some of her wet, messy glandular biological self) is thinking about how nice it would be to see Daddy again, albeit with some trepidation. Parents aren't supposed to have sex: isn't there a law, or something? "Tell me about the Franklins? Are they married? Singular?"

The 3D printer is cranking up. It hisses slightly, dissipating heat from the hard-vacuum chamber in its supercooled workspace. Deep in its guts it creates coherent atom beams, from a bunch of Bose-Einstein condensates hovering on the edge of absolute zero: by superimposing interference patterns on them, it generates an atomic hologram, building a perfect replica of some original artifact, right down to the atomic level—there are no clunky moving nanotechnology parts to break or overheat or mutate. Something is going to come out of the printer in half an hour, something cloned off its original right down to the individual quantum states of its component atomic nuclei. The cat, seemingly oblivious, shuffles closer to its exhaust ducts.

"Bob Franklin, he died about two, three years before you were born: your dad did business with him. So did your mom. Anyway, he had chunks of his noumen preserved, and the estate trustees are trying to re-create his consciousness by cross-loading him in their implants. They're sort of a borganism, but with money and style. Anyway, Bob got into the space biz back then, with some financial wizardry a friend of your father whipped up for him, and now they-he are building a spacehab that they're going to take all the way out to Jupiter, where they can dismantle a couple of small moons and begin building helium-three refineries. It's that CETI scam I told you about earlier, but they've got a whole load of other angles on it for the long term."

This is mostly going right over Amber's head—she'll have to learn what helium-three refineries are later—but the idea of running away to space has a certain appeal. Adventure, that's what. Amber looks around the living room and sees it for a moment as a capsule, a small wooden cell locked deep in a vision of a middle-America that never was—the one her mom wants to retreat into. "Is Jupiter fun?" she asks. "I know it's big and not very dense, but is it, like, a happening place?"

"You could say that," says the cat, as the printer clanks and disgorges a fake passport (convincingly aged), an intricate metal seal engraved with Arabic script, and a tailored wide-spectrum vaccine targeted on Amber's immature immune system. "Stick that on your wrist, sign the three top copies, put them in the envelope, and let's get going: we've got a flight to catch."

Sadeq is eating his dinner when the lawsuit rolls in.

Alone in the cramped humming void of his station, he contemplates the plea. The language is awkward, showing all the hallmarks of a crude machine translation: the supplicant is American, a woman, and—oddly—claims to be a Christian. This is surprising enough, but the nature of her claim is, at face value, preposterous. He forces himself to finish his bread, then bag the waste and clean the platter, before he gives it his full consideration. Is it a tasteless joke? Evidently not: as the only quadi outside the orbit of Mars he is uniquely qualified to hear it, and it *is* a case that cries out for justice.

A woman who leads a God-fearing life—not a correct one, no, but she shows some signs of humility and progress toward a deeper understanding—is deprived of her child by the machinations of a feckless husband who deserted her years before. That the woman was raising the child alone strikes Sadeq as disturbingly western, but pardonable when he reads her account of the feckless one's behavior, which is degenerate: an ill fate indeed would await any child that this man raises to adulthood. This man deprives her of her child, but not by legitimate means: he doesn't take the child into his own household or make any attempt to raise her, either in accordance with his own customs or the precepts of shari'a. Instead, he enslaves her wickedly in the mire of the western legal tradition, then casts her into outer darkness to be used as a laborer by the dubious forces of self-proclaimed "progress." The same forces that Sadeq has been sent to confront, as representative of the Ummah in orbit around Jupiter.

Sadeq scratches his short beard thoughtfully. A nasty tale, but what can he do about it? "Computer," he says, "a reply to this supplicant: my sympathies lie with you in the manner of your suffering, but I fail to see in what way I can be of assistance. Your heart cries out for help before God (blessed be his name), but surely this is a matter for the temporal authorities of the dar al-Harb." He pauses: *or is it?* he wonders. Legal wheels begin to turn in his mind. "If you can but find your way to extending to me a path by which I can assert the primacy of shari'ah over your daughter, I shall apply myself to constructing a case for her emancipation, to the greater glory of God (blessed be his name) in the name of the Prophet (peace be unto him). Ends, sigblock, send."

Releasing the Velcro straps that hold him at the table, Sadeq floats up and then kicks gently toward the forward end of the cramped habitat. The controls of the telescope are positioned between the ultrasonic clothing cleaner and the lithium hydroxide scrubbers: they're already freed up, because he was conducting a wide-field survey of the inner ring, looking for the signature of water ice. It is the work of a few moments to pipe the navigation and tracking system into the telescope's controller and direct it to hunt for the big foreign ship of fools. Something nudges at Sadeq's mind urgently, an irritating realization that he may have missed something in the woman's email: there were a number of huge attachments. With half his mind, he surfs the news digest his scholarly peers send him daily: meanwhile, he waits patiently for the telescope to find the speck of light that the poor woman's daughter is enslaved within.

This might be a way in, he realizes, a way to enter dialogue with them. Let the hard questions answer themselves, elegantly. There will be no need for the war of the sword if they can be convinced that their plans are faulty: no need to defend the godly from the latter-day Tower of Babel these people propose to build. If this woman Pamela means what she says, Sadeq need not end his days out here in the cold between the worlds, away from his elderly parents and brother and his colleagues and friends. And he will be profoundly grateful: because, in his heart of hearts, he knows that he is less a warrior than a scholar.

"I'm sorry, but the Borg is attempting to assimilate a lawsuit," says the receptionist. "Will you hold?"

"Crud." Amber blinks the Binary Betty answerphone sprite out of her eye and glances around at the cabin. "That is *so* last century," she grumbles. "Who do they think they are?"

"Doctor Robert H. Franklin," volunteers the cat. "It's a losing proposition if you ask me. Bob was so fond of his dope that there's this whole hippie groupmind that's grown up using his state vector as a bong—"

"Shut the fuck up!" Amber shouts at him. Instantly contrite (for yelling in an inflatable spacecraft is a major faux pas): "Sorry." She spawns an autonomic thread with full parasympathetic nervous control, tells it to calm her down: then she spawns a couple more to go forth and become fuqaha, expert on shari'a law. She realizes she's buying up way too much of the orphanage's scarce bandwidth—time that will have to be paid for in chores, later—but it's necessary. "She's gone *too* far. This time, it's *war*."

She slams out of her cabin and spins right around in the central axis of the hab, a rogue missile pinging for a target to vent her rage on. A tantrum would be *good*—

But her body is telling her to chill out, take ten, and there's a drone of scriptural lore dribbling away in the back of her head, and she's feeling frustrated and angry and not in control, but not really mad now. It was like this three years ago when Mom noticed her getting on too well with Jenny Morgan and moved her to a new school district—she said it was a work assignment, but Amber knows better, Mom asked for it—just to keep her dependent and helpless. Mom is a psycho bitch control-freak and ever since she had to face up to losing Dad she's been working her claws into Amber—which is tough, because Amber is not good victim material, and is smart and well-networked to boot. But now Mom's found a way of fucking Amber over *completely*, even in Jupiter orbit, and Amber would be totally out of control if not for her skullware keeping a lid on things.

Instead of shouting at her cat or trying to message the Borg, Amber goes to hunt them down in their meatspace den.

There are sixteen Borg aboard the *Sanger*—adults, members of the Franklin Collective, squatters in the ruins of Bob Franklin's posthumous vision. They lend bits of their brains to the task of running what science has been able to resurrect of the dead dot-com billionaire's mind, making him the first boddhisatva of the uploading age—apart from the lobster colony, of course. Their den mother is a woman called Monica: a willowy brown-eyed hive queen with raster-burned corneal implants and a dry, sardonic delivery that can corrode egos like a desert wind. She's better than the others at running Bob, and she's no slouch when she's being herself: which is why they elected her Maximum Leader of the expedition.

Amber finds Monica in the number four kitchen garden, performing surgery on a filter that's been blocked by toadspawn. She's almost buried beneath a large pipe, her Velcro-taped toolkit waving in the breeze like strange blue air-kelp. "Monica? You got a minute?"

"Sure, I have lots of minutes. Make yourself helpful? Pass me the antitorque wrench and a number-six hex head."

"Um." Amber captures the blue flag and fiddles around with its contents. Something that has batteries, motors, a flywheel counterweight, and laser gyros assembles itself— Amber passes it under the pipe. "Here. Listen, your phone is busy."

"I know. You've come to see me about your conversion, haven't you?"

"Yes!"

There's a clanking noise from under the pressure sump. "Take this." A plastic bag floats out, bulging with stray fasteners. "I got a bit of vacuuming to do. Get yourself a mask if you don't already have one."

A minute later, Amber is back beside Monica's legs, her face veiled by a filter mask. "I don't want this to go through," she says. "I don't care what Mom says, I'm not Moslem! This judge, he can't touch me. He *can't*," she repeats, vehemence warring with uncertainty.

"Maybe he doesn't want to?" Another bag. "Here, catch."

Amber grabs the bag: too late, she discovers that it's full of water and toadspawn. Stringy mucous ropes full of squiggling comma-shaped baby tadpoles explode all over the compartment and bounce off the walls in a shower of amphibian confetti. "Eew!"

Monica squirms out from behind the pipe. "Oh, you *didn't*." She kicks off the consensus-defined floor and grabs a wad of absorbent paper from the spinner, whacks it across the ventilator shroud above the sump. Together they go after the toadspawn with garbage bags and paper—by the time they've got the stringy mess mopped up, the spinner has begun to click and whirr, processing cellulose from the algae tanks into fresh wipes. "That was really clever," Monica says emphatically, as the disposal bin sucks down her final bag. "You wouldn't happen to know how the toad got in here?"

"No, but I ran into one that was loose in the commons, one shift before last cycle-end. Gave it a ride back to Oscar."

"I'll have a word with him, then." Monica glares blackly at the pipe. "I'm going to have to go back and re-fit the filter in a minute. Do you want me to be Bob?"

"Uh." Amber thinks. "Not sure. Your call."

"All right, Bob coming online." Monica's face relaxes slightly, then her expression hardens. "Way I see it, you've got a choice. Your mother's kinda boxed you in, hasn't she?"

"Yes." Amber frowns.

"So. Pretend I'm an idiot. Talk me through it, huh?"

Amber drags herself alongside the hydro pipe and gets her head down, alongside Monica/Bob, who is floating with her feet near the floor. "I ran away from home. Mom owned me—that is, she had parental rights and Dad had none. So Dad, via a proxy, helped me sell myself into slavery to a company. The company was owned by a trust fund, and I'm the main beneficiary when I reach the age of majority. As a chattel, the company tells me what to do—legally—but the shell company is set to take my orders. So I'm autonomous. Right?"

"That sounds like the sort of thing your father would do," Monica says neutrally. Overtaken by a sardonic middle-aged Silicon Valley drawl, her north-of-England accent sounds peculiarly mid-Atlantic.

"Trouble is, most countries don't acknowledge slavery; those that do mostly don't have any equivalent of a limited-liability company, much less one that can be directed by an-other company from abroad. Dad picked Yemen on the grounds that they've got this stupid brand of shari'a law—and a crap human-rights record—but they're just about con-formant to the open legal standards protocol, able to interface to EU norms via a Turkish legislative firewall."

"So."

"Well, I guess I was technically a Jannissary. Mom was doing her Christian phase, so that made me a Christian unbeliever slave of an Islamic company. But now the stupid bitch has gone and converted to shi'ism. Now, normally, Islamic descent runs through the father, but she picked her sect carefully, and chose one that's got a progressive view of women's rights: they're sort of Islamic fundamentalist liberal constructionists! 'What would the Prophet do if he were alive today and had to worry about self-replicating chewing gum factories.' They generally take a progressive, almost westernized, view of things like legal equality of the sexes, because for his time and place, the Prophet was way ahead of the ball and they figure they ought to follow his example. Anyway, that means Mom can assert that *I* am Moslem, and under Yemeni law I get to be treated as a Moslem chattel of a company. And their legal code is very dubious about permitting slavery of Moslems. It's not that I have *rights* as such, but my pastoral well-being becomes the responsibility of the local imam, and—" She shrugs helplessly.

"Has he tried to make you run under any new rules, yet?" asks Monica/Bob. "Has he put blocks on your freedom of agency, tried to mess with your mind? Insisted on libido dampers?"

"Not yet." Amber's expression is grim. "But he's no dummy. I figure he may be using Mom—and me—as a way of getting his fingers into this whole expedition. Staking a claim for jurisdiction, claim arbitration, that sort of thing. It could be worse; he might order me to comply fully with his specific implementation of shari'a. They permit implants, but require mandatory conceptual filtering: if I run that stuff, I'll end up *believing* it!"

"Okay." Monica does a slow backward somersault in midair. "Now tell me why you can't simply repudiate it."

"Because." Deep breath. "I can do that in two ways. I can deny Islam, which makes me an apostate, and automatically terminates my indenture to the shell, so Mom owns me. Or I can say that the instrument has no legal standing because I was in the USA when I signed it, and slavery is illegal there, in which case Mom owns me, because I'm a minor. Or I can take the veil, live like a modest Moslem woman, do whatever the imam wants, and Mom doesn't own me—but she gets to appoint my chaperone. Oh Bob, she has planned this *so well.*"

"Uh-huh." Monica rotates back to the floor and looks at Amber, suddenly very Bob. "Now you've told me your troubles, start thinking like your dad. Your dad had a dozen creative ideas before breakfast every day—it's how he made his name. Your mom has got you in a box. Think your way *outside* it: what can you do?"

"Well." Amber rolls over and hugs the fat hydroponic duct to her chest like a life raft. "It's a legal paradox. I'm trapped because of the jurisdiction she's cornered me in. I could talk to the judge, I suppose, but she'll have picked him carefully." Her eyes narrow. "The jurisdiction. Hey, Bob." She lets go of the duct and floats free, hair streaming out behind her like a cometary halo. "How do I go about creating myself a new jurisdiction?"

Monica grins. "I seem to recall the traditional way was to grab yourself some land and set yourself up as king: but there are other ways. I've got some friends I think you should meet. They're not good conversationalists and there's a two-hour lightspeed delay . . . but I think you'll find they've answered that question already. But why don't you talk to the imam first and find out what he's like? He may surprise you. After all, he was already out here before your mom decided to use him against you."

The *Sanger* hangs in orbit thirty kilometers up, circling the waist of potato-shaped Amalthea. Drones swarm across the slopes of Mons Lyctos, ten kilometers above the mean surface level: they kick up clouds of reddish sulfate dust as they spread transparent sheets across the surface. This close to Jupiter—a mere hundred and eighty thousand kilometers above the swirling madness of the cloudscape—the gas giant fills half the sky with a perpetually changing clockface: for Amalthea orbits the master in under twelve hours. The *Sanger*'s radiation shields are running at full power, shrouding the ship in a corona of rippling plasma: radio is useless, and the human miners run their drones via an intricate network of laser circuits. Other, larger drones are unwinding spools of heavy electrical cable north and south from the landing site: once the circuits are connected, these will form a coil cutting through Jupiter's magnetic field, generating electrical current (and imperceptibly slowing the moon's orbital momentum).

Amber sighs and looks, for the sixth time this hour, at the webcam plastered on the side of her cabin. She's taken down the posters and told the toys to tidy themselves away. In another two thousand seconds, the tiny Iranian spaceship will rise above the limb of Moshtari, and then it will be time to talk to the teacher. She isn't looking forward to the experience. If he's a grizzled old blockhead of the most obdurate fundamentalist streak, she'll be in trouble: disrespect for age has been part and parcel of the western teenage experience for generations, and a cross-cultural thread that she's sent to clue-up on Islam reminds her that not all cultures share this outlook. But if he turns out to be young, intelligent, and flexible, things could be even worse. When she was eight, Amber audited *The Taming of the Shrew*: now she has no appetite for a starring role in her own cross-cultural production.

She sighs again. "Pierre?"

"Yeah?" His voice comes from the foot of the emergency locker in her room. He's curled up down there, limbs twitching languidly as he drives a mining drone around the surface of Object Barney, as the rock has named itself. The drone is a long-legged crane-fly lookalike, bouncing very slowly from toe-tip to toe-tip in the microgravity—the rock is only half a kilometer along its longest axis, coated brown with weird hydrocarbon goop and sulfur compounds sprayed off the surface of Io by the Jovian winds. "I'm coming."

"You better." She glances at the screen. "One twenty seconds to next burn." The payload canister on the screen is, technically speaking, stolen: it'll be okay as long as she gives it back, Bob said, although she won't be able to do that until it's reached Barney and they've found enough water ice to refuel it. "Found anything yet?"

"Just the usual. Got a seam of ice near the semimajor pole—it's dirty, but there's at least a thousand tons there. And the surface is crunchy with tar. Amber, you know what? The orange shit, it's solid with fullerenes."

Amber grins at her reflection in the screen. That's good news. Once the payload she's steering touches down, Pierre can help her lay superconducting wires along Barney's long axis. It's only a kilometer and a half, and that'll only give them a few tens of kilowatts of juice, but the condensation fabricator that's also in the payload will be able to use it to convert Barney's crust into processed goods at about two grams per second. Using designs copylefted by the free hardware foundation, inside two hundred thousand seconds they'll have a grid of sixty-four 3D printers barfing up structured matter at a rate limited only by available power. Starting with a honking great dome tent and some free nitrogen/oxygen for her to breathe, then adding a big web-cache and direct high-bandwidth uplink to Earth, Amber could have her very own one-girl colony up and running within a million seconds.

The screen blinks at her. "Oh shit. Make yourself scarce, Pierre!" The incoming call nags at her attention. "Yeah? Who are you?"

The screen fills with a view of a cramped, very twen-cen-looking space capsule. The guy inside it is in his twenties, with a heavily tanned face, close-cropped hair and beard, wearing an olive-drab spacesuit liner. He's floating between a TORU manual-docking controller and a gilt-framed photograph of the Ka'bah at Mecca. "Good evening to you," he says solemnly. "Do I have the honor to be addressing Amber Macx?"

"Uh, yeah. That's me." She stares at him: he looks nothing like her conception of an ayatollah—whatever an ayatollah is—elderly, black-robed, vindictively fundamentalist. "Who are you?"

"I am Doctor Sadeq Khurasani. I hope that I am not interrupting you? Is it convenient for you that we talk now?"

He looks so anxious that Amber nods automatically. "Sure. Did my mom put you up to this?" They're still speaking English, and she notices that his diction is good, but slightly stilted: he isn't using a grammar engine, he's actually learned it the hard way. "If so, you want to be careful. She doesn't lie, exactly, but she gets people to do what she wants."

"Yes, she did. Ah." A pause. They're still almost a light-second apart, time for painful collisions and accidental silences. "I have not noticed that. Are you sure you should be speaking of your mother that way?"

Amber breathes deeply. "*Adults* can get divorced. If *I* could get divorced from her, I would. She's—" she flails around for the right word helplessly. "Look. She's the sort of person who can't lose a fight. If she's going to lose, she'll try to figure how to set the law on you. Like she's done to me. Don't you see?"

Doctor Khurasani looks extremely dubious. "I am not sure I understand," he says. "Perhaps, mm, I should tell you why I am talking to you?"

"Sure. Go ahead." Amber is startled by his attitude: he's actually taking her seriously, she realizes. Treating her like an adult. The sensation is so novel—coming from someone more than twenty years old and not a member of the Borg— that she almost lets herself forget that he's only talking to her because Mom set her up.

"Well, I am an engineer. In addition, I am a student of *fiqh*, jurisprudence. In fact, I am qualified to sit in judgment. I am a very junior judge, but even so, it is a heavy responsibility. Anyway. Your mother, peace be unto her, lodged a petition with me. Are you aware of it?"

"Yes." Amber tenses up. "It's a lie. Distortion of the facts."

"Hmmm." Sadeq rubs his beard thoughtfully. "Well, I have to find out, yes? Your mother has submitted herself to the will of God. This makes you the child of a Moslem, and she claims—"

"She's trying to use you as a weapon!" Amber interrupts. "I sold myself into *slavery* to get away from her, do you understand? I enslaved myself to a company that is held in trust for my ownership. She's trying to change the rules to get me back. You know what? I don't believe she gives a shit about your religion, all she wants is me!"

"A mother's love—"

"Fuck love!" Amber snarls, "she wants *power*."

Sadeq's expression hardens. "You have a foul mouth in your head, child. All I am trying to do is to find out the facts of this situation: you should ask yourself if such disrespect furthers your interests?" He pauses for a moment, then continues, less abruptly, "Did you really have such a bad childhood with her? Do you think she did everything merely for power, or could she love you?" Pause. "You must understand, I need an answer to these things. Before I can know what is the right thing to do."

"My mother—" Amber stops. Spawns a vaporous cloud of memory retrievals. They fan out through the space around her mind like the tail of her cometary mind. Invoking a complex of network parsers and class filters, she turns the memories into reified images and blats them at the webcam's tiny brain so that he can see them. Some of the memories are so painful that Amber has to close her eyes. Mom in full office war-paint, leaning over Amber, promising to take her to church so that Reverend Beeching can pray the devil out of her. Mom telling Amber that they're moving again, abruptly, dragging her away from school and the friends she'd tentatively started to like. Mom catching her on the phone to Daddy, tearing the phone in half and hitting her with it. Mom at the kitchen table, forcing her to eat—"My mother likes *control*."

"Ah." Sadeq's expression turns glassy. "And this is how you feel about her? How long have you had that level of— no, please forgive me for asking. You obviously understand implants. Do your grandparents know? Did you talk to them?"

"My grandparents?" Amber stifles a snort. "Mom's parents are dead. Dad's are still alive, but they won't talk to him—they like Mom. They think I'm creepy. I know little things, their tax bands and customer profiles. I could mine data with my head when I was four. I'm not built like little girls were in their day, and they don't understand. You know that the old ones don't like us at all? Some of the churches make money doing nothing but exorcisms for oldsters who think their kids are possessed."

"Well." Sadeq is fingering his beard again, distractedly. "I must say, this is a lot to learn. But you know that your mother has accepted Islam, don't you? This means that you are Moslem, too. Unless you are an adult, your parent legally speaks for you. And she says that this makes you my problem. Hmm."

"I'm not Moslem." Amber stares at the screen. "I'm not a child, either." Her threads are coming together, whispering scarily behind her eyes: her head is suddenly dense and turgid with ideas, heavy as a stone and twice as old as time. "I am nobody's chattel. What does your law say about people who are born with implants? What does it say about people who want to live forever? I don't believe in any *god*, mister judge. I don't believe in any limits. Mom can't, physically, make me do *anything*, and she sure can't speak for me."

"Well, if that is what you have to say, I must think on the matter." He catches her eye: his expression is thoughtful, like a doctor considering a diagnosis. "I will call you again in due course. In the meantime, if you need to talk to anyone, remember that I am always available. If there is anything I can do to help ease your pain, I would be pleased to be of service. Peace be unto you, and those you care for."

"Same to you too," she mutters darkly as the connection goes dead. "*Now* what?" she asks, as a beeping sprite gyrates across the wall, begging for attention.

"I think it's the lander," Pierre says helpfully. "Is it down yet?"

She rounds on him. "Hey, I thought I told you to get lost!"

"What, and miss all the fun?" He grins at her impishly. "Amber's got a new boyfriend! Wait until I tell everybody. . . ."

Sleep cycles pass: the borrowed 3D printer on Object Barney's surface spews bitmaps of atoms in quantum lockstep at its rendering platform, building up the control circuitry and skeletons of new printers. (There are no clunky nano-assemblers here, no robots the size of viruses busily sorting molecules into piles—just the bizarre quantized magic of atomic holography, modulated Bose-Einstein condensates collapsing into strange, lacy, supercold machinery.) Electricity surges through the cable loops as they slice through Jupiter's magnetosphere, slowly converting the rock's momentum into power: small robots grovel in the orange dirt, scooping up raw material to feed to the fractionating oven. Amber's garden of machinery flourishes slowly, unpacking itself according to a schema designed by pre-teens at an industrial school in Poland, with barely any need for human guidance.

High in orbit around Amalthea, complex financial instruments breed and conjugate. Developed for the express purpose of facilitating trade with the alien intelligences believed to have been detected eight years earlier by SETI, they function equally well as fiscal firewalls for space colonies. The *Sanger*'s bank accounts in California and Cuba are looking acceptable—since entering Jupiter space, the orphanage has staked a claim on roughly a hundred gigatons of random rocks and a moon that's just small enough to creep in under the International Astronomical Union's definition of a sovereign planetary body. The Borg are working hard, leading their eager teams of child stakeholders in their plans to build the industrial metastructures necessary to support mining helium three from Jupiter: they're so focused that they spend much of their time being themselves, not bothering to run Bob, the shared identity that gives them their messianic drive.

Half a light-hour away, tired Earth wakes and slumbers in time to its ancient orbital dynamics. A religious college in Cairo is considering issues of nanotechnology: if replicators are used to prepare a copy of a strip of bacon, right down to the molecular level, but without it ever being part of a pig, how is it to be treated? (If the mind of one of the faithful is copied into a computing machine's memory by mapping and simulating all its synapses, is the computer now a Moslem? If not, *why* not? If so, what are its rights and duties?) Riots in Borneo underline the urgency of theotechnological inquiry.

More riots in Barcelona, Madrid, Birmingham, and Marseilles also underline a rising problem: social chaos caused by cheap anti-aging treatments. The zombie exterminators, a backlash of disaffected youth against the formerly graying gerontocracy of Europe, insist that people who predate the supergrid and can't handle implants aren't *really* conscious: their ferocity is equaled only by the anger of the dynamic septuagenarians of the baby boom, their bodies partially restored to the flush of sixties youth but their minds adrift in a slower, less contingent century. The faux-young boomers feel betrayed, forced back into the labor pool but unable to cope with the implant-accelerated culture of the new millennium, their hard-earned experience rendered obsolete by deflationary time.

The Bangladeshi economic miracle is typical of the age. With growth rates running at over 20 percent, cheap out-of-control bioindustrialization has swept the nation: former rice farmers harvest plastics and milk cows for silk, while their children study mariculture and design sea walls. With cellphone ownership nearing 80 percent and literacy at 90, the once-poor country is finally breaking out of its historical infrastructure trap and beginning to develop: another generation, and they'll be richer than Japan in 2001.

Radical new economic theories are focusing around bandwidth, speed-of-light transmission time, and the implications of CETI, communication with extra-terrestrial intelligence: cosmologists and quants collaborate on bizarre relativistically telescoped financial instruments. Space (which lets you store information) and structure (which lets you process it) acquire value while dumb mass—like gold—loses it: the degenerate cores of the traditional stock markets are in free fall, the old smokestack microprocessor and biotech/nanotech industries crumbling before the onslaught of matter replicators and self-modifying ideas and the barbarian communicators, who mortgage their future for a millennium against the chance of a gift from a visiting alien intelligence. Microsoft, once the US Steel of the silicon age, quietly fades into liquidation.

An outbreak of green goo—a crude biomechanical replicator that eats everything in its path—is dealt with in the Australian outback by carpet-bombing with fuel-air explosives: the USAF subsequently reactivates two wings of refurbished B-52s and places them at the disposal of the UN standing committee on self-replicating weapons. (CNN discovers that one of their newest pilots, re-enlisting with the body of a twenty-year-old and an empty pension account, first flew them over Laos and Cambodia.) The news overshadows the World Health Organization's announcement of the end of the HIV pandemic, after more than fifty years of bigotry, panic, and megadeath.

"Breathe steadily. Remember your regulator drill? If you spot your heart rate going up or your mouth going dry, take five."

"Shut the fuck up, 'Neko, I'm trying to concentrate." Amber fumbles with the titanium D-ring, trying to snake the strap through it. The gauntlets are getting in her way: high orbit spacesuits—little more than a body stocking designed to hold your skin under compression and help you breathe—are easy, but this deep in Jupiter's radiation belt, she has to wear an old moon suit that comes in about thirteen layers, and the gloves are stiff. It's Chernobyl weather, a sleet of alpha particles and raw protons storming through the void. "Got it." She yanks the strap tight, pulls on the D-ring, then goes to work on the next strap. Never looking down: because the wall she's tying herself to has no floor, just a cut-off two meters below, then empty space for a hundred kilometers before the nearest solid ground.

The ground sings to her moronically: "I fall to you, you fall to me, it's the law of gravity—"

She shoves her feet down onto the platform that juts from the side of the capsule like a suicide's ledge: metalized Velcro grabs hold, and she pulls on the straps to turn her body around until she can see past the capsule, side-ways. The capsule masses about five tons, barely bigger than an ancient Soyuz. It's packed to overflowing with environment-sensitive stuff she'll need, and a honking great high-gain antenna. "I hope you know what you're doing?" someone says over the intercom.

"Of course I—" she stops. Alone in this TsUP-surplus iron maiden with its low bandwidth comms and bizarre plumbing, she feels claustrophobic and helpless: parts of her mind don't work. When she was four, Mom took her down a famous cave system somewhere out west: when the guide turned out the lights half a kilometer underground, she'd screamed with surprise as the darkness had reached out and touched her. Now it's not the darkness that frightens her, it's the lack of thought. For a hundred kilometers below her, there are *no* minds, and even on the surface there's not much but a moronic warbling of bots. Everything that makes the universe primate-friendly seems to be locked in the huge spaceship that looms somewhere just behind her, and she has to fight down an urge to shed her straps and swarm back up the umbilical that anchors this capsule to the *Sanger*. "I'll be fine," she forces herself to say. And even though she's unsure that it's true, she tries to make herself believe it. "It's just leaving-home nerves. I've read about it, okay?"

There's a funny, high-pitched whistle in her ears. For a moment, the sweat on the back of her neck turns icy cold, then the noise stops. She strains for a moment, and when it returns, she recognizes the sound: the heretofore-talkative cat, curled in the warmth of her pressurized luggage can, has begun to snore.

"Let's go," she says, "time to roll the wagon." A speech macro deep in the *Sanger*'s docking firmware recognizes her authority and gently lets go of the pod. A couple of cold gas thrusters pop, deep banging vibrations running through the capsule, and she's on her way.

"Amber. How's it hanging?" A familiar voice in her ears: she blinks. Fifteen hundred seconds, nearly half an hour gone.

"Robes-Pierre, chopped any aristos lately?"

"Heh!" A pause. "I can see *your* head from here."

"How's it looking?" she asks. There's a lump in her throat, she isn't sure why. Pierre is probably hooked into one of the smaller proximity cameras dotted around the outer hull of the big mothership. Watching over her as she falls.

"Pretty much like always," he says laconically. Another pause, this time longer. "This is wild, you know? Su Ang says hi, by the way."

"Su Ang, hi," she replies, resisting the urge to lean back and look up—up relative to her feet, not her vector—and see if the ship's still visible.

"Hi," Ang says shyly. "You're very brave!"

"Still can't beat you at chess." Amber frowns. Su Ang and her over-engineered algae. Oscar and his pharmaceutical factory toads. People she's known for three years, mostly ignored, and never thought about missing. "Listen, you going to come visiting?"

"Visit?" Ang sounds dubious. "When will it be ready?"

"Oh, soon enough." At four kilograms per minute of structured-matter output, the printers on the surface have already built her a bunch of stuff: a habitat dome, the guts of an algae/shrimp farm, a bucket conveyor to bury it with, an airlock. It's all lying around waiting for her to put it together and move into her new home. "Once the Borg get back from Amalthea."

"Hey! You mean they're moving? How did you figure that?"

"Go talk to them," Amber says. Actually, she's a large part of the reason the *Sanger* is about to crank its orbit up and out toward the other moon: she wants to be alone in comms silence for a couple of million seconds. The Franklin collective is doing her a big favor.

"Ahead of the curve, as usual," Pierre cuts in, with something that sounds like admiration to her uncertain ears.

"You too," she says, a little too fast. "Come visit when I've got the life-support cycle stabilized."

"I'll do that," he replies. A red glow suffuses the flank of the capsule next to her head, and she looks up in time to see the glaring blue laser-line of the *Sanger*'s drive torch powering up.

Eighteen million seconds, almost a tenth of a Jupiter year, passes.

* * *

The imam tugs thoughtfully on his beard as he stares at the traffic-control display. These days, every shift seems to bring a new crewed spaceship into Jupiter system: space is getting positively crowded. When he arrived, there were less than two hundred people here: now there's the population of a small city, and many of them live at the heart of the approach map centered on his display. He breathes deeply—trying to ignore the omnipresent odor of old socks—and studies the map. "Computer, what about my slot?" he asks.

"Your slot: cleared to commence final approach in six nine five seconds. Speed limit is ten meters per second inside ten kilometers, drop to two meters per second inside one kilometer. Uploading map of forbidden thrust vectors now." Chunks of the approach map turn red, gridded off to prevent his exhaust stream damaging other craft in the area.

Sadeq sighs. "We'll go in on Kurs. I assume their Kurs guidance is active?"

"Kurs docking target support available to shell level three."

"Praise the Prophet, peace be unto him." He pokes around through the guidance subsystem's menus, setting up the software emulation of the obsolete (but highly reliable) Soyuz docking system. At last, he can leave the ship to look after itself for a bit. He glances around: for two years he has lived in this canister, and soon he will step outside it. It hardly seems real.

The radio, usually silent, crackles with unexpected life. "Bravo One One, this is Imperial Traffic Control. Verbal contact required, over."

Sadeq twitches with surprise. The voice sounds inhuman, paced with the cadences of a speech synthesizer, like so many of Her Majesty's subjects. "Bravo One One to Traffic Control, I'm listening, over."

"Bravo One One, we have assigned you a landing slot on tunnel four, airlock delta. Kurs active, ensure your guidance is set to seven four zero and slaved to our control."

He leans over the screen and rapidly checks the docking system's settings. "Control, all in order."

"Bravo One One, stand by."

The next hour passes slowly as the traffic control system guides his Type 921 down to a rocky rendezvous. Orange dust streaks his one optical-glass porthole: a kilometer before touch-down, Sadeq busies himself closing protective covers, locking down anything that might fall around on contact. Finally, he unrolls his mat against the floor in front of the console and floats above it for ten minutes, eyes closed in prayer. It's not the landing that worries him, but what comes next.

Her Majesty's domain stretches out before the battered Almaz module like a rust-stained snowflake half-a-kilometer in diameter. Its core is buried in a loose snowball of grayish rubble, and it waves languid brittlestar arms at the gibbous orange horizon of Jupiter. Fine hairs, fractally branching down to the molecular level, split off the main collector arms at regular intervals; a cluster of habitat pods like seedless grapes cling to the roots of the massive cluster. Already, he can see the huge steel generator loops that climb from either pole of the snowflake, wreathed in sparking plasma: the Jovian rings form a rainbow of darkness rising behind them.

Finally, the battered space station is on final approach. Sadeq watches the Kurs simulation output carefully, piping it direct into his visual field: there's an external camera view of the rockpile and grapes, expanding toward the convex ceiling of the ship, and he licks his lips, ready to hit the manual override and go around again—but the rate of descent is slowing, and by the time he's close enough to see the scratches on the shiny metal docking cone ahead of the ship, it's measured in centimeters per second. There's a gentle bump, then a shudder, then a rippling bang as the docking ring latches fire—and he's down.

Sadeq breathes deeply again, then tries to stand. There's gravity here, but not much: walking is impossible. He's about to head for the life-support panel when he freezes, hearing a noise from the far end of the docking node. Turning, he is just in time to see the hatch opening toward him, a puff of vapor condensing, and then—

*   *   *

Her Imperial Majesty is sitting in the throne room, moodily
fidgeting with the new signet ring her Equerry has designed
for her. It's a lump of structured carbon massing almost fifty
grams, set in a plain band of iridium. It glitters with the blue
and violet speckle highlights of its internal lasers, because,
in addition to being a piece of state jewelry, it is also an optical router, part of the industrial control infrastructure she's
building out here on the edge of the solar system. Her
Majesty wears plain black combat pants and sweatshirt, woven from the finest spider silk and spun glass, but her feet
are bare: her taste in fashion is best described as youthful,
and, in any event, certain styles—skirts, for example—are
simply impractical in microgravity. But, being a monarch,
she's wearing a crown. And there's a cat sleeping on the
back of her throne.

The lady-in-waiting (and sometime hydroponic engineer)
ushers Sadeq to the doorway, then floats back. "If you need
anything, please say," she says shyly, then ducks and rolls
away. Sadeq approaches the throne, orients himself on the
floor—a simple slab of black composite, save for the throne
growing from its center like an exotic flower—and waits to
be noticed.

"Doctor Khurasani, I presume." She smiles at him, neither
the innocent grin of a child nor the knowing smirk of an
adult: merely a warm greeting. "Welcome to my kingdom.
Please feel free to make use of any necessary support services here, and I wish you a very pleasant stay."

Sadeq holds his expression still. The queen is young—her
face still retains the puppy fat of childhood, emphasized by
microgravity moon-face—but it would be a bad mistake to
consider her immature. "I am grateful for Your Majesty's
forbearance," he murmurs, formulaic. Behind her the walls
glitter like diamonds, a glowing kaleidoscope vision. Her
crown, more like a compact helm that covers the top and
rear of her head, also glitters and throws off diffraction rainbows: but most of its emissions are in the near ultraviolet,
invisible except in the faint glowing nimbus it creates
around her head. Like a halo.

"Have a seat," she offers, gesturing: a ballooning free-fall cradle squirts down and expands from the ceiling, angled toward her, open and waiting. "You must be tired: working a ship all by yourself is exhausting." She frowns ruefully, as if remembering. "And two years is nearly unprecedented."

"Your Majesty is too kind." Sadeq wraps the cradle arms around himself and faces her. "Your labors have been fruitful, I trust."

She shrugs. "I sell the biggest commodity in short supply on any frontier. . . ." a momentary grin. "This isn't the wild west, is it?"

"Justice cannot be sold," Sadeq says stiffly. Then, a moment later: "My apologies, please accept that while I mean no insult. I merely mean that while you say your goal is to provide the rule of Law, what you *sell* is and must be something different. Justice without God, sold to the highest bidder, is not justice."

The queen nods. "Leaving aside the mention of God, I agree: I can't sell it. But I can sell participation in a just system. And this new frontier really is a lot smaller than anyone expected, isn't it? Our bodies may take months to travel between worlds, but our disputes and arguments take seconds or minutes. As long as everybody agrees to abide by my arbitration, physical enforcement can wait until they're close enough to touch. And everybody *does* agree that my legal framework is easier to comply with, better adjusted to space, than any earthbound one." A note of steel creeps into her voice, challenging: her halo brightens, tickling a reactive glow from the walls of the throne room.

Five billion inputs or more, Sadeq marvels: the crown is an engineering marvel, even though most of its mass is buried in the walls and floor of this huge construct. "There is law revealed by the Prophet, peace be unto him, and there is Law that we can establish by analyzing his intentions. There are other forms of law by which humans live, and various interpretations of the law of God even among those who study his works. How, in the absence of the word of the Prophet, can you provide a moral compass?"

"Hmm." She taps her fingers on the arm of her throne, and Sadeq's heart freezes. He's heard the stories from the claim-jumpers and boardroom bandits, from the greenmail experts with their roots in the earthbound jurisdictions that have made such a hash of arbitration here: how she can experience a year in a minute, rip your memories out through your cortical implants and make you relive your worst mistakes in her nightmarishly powerful simulation system. She is the *queen*—the first individual to get her hands on so much mass and energy that she could pull ahead of the curve of binding technology, and the first to set up her own jurisdiction and rule certain experiments to be legal so that she could make use of the mass/energy intersection. She has *force majeure*—even the Pentagon's infowarriors respect the Ring Imperium's firewall. In fact, the body sitting in the throne opposite him probably contains only a fraction of her identity; she's by no means the first upload or partial, but she's the first-gust front of the storm of power that will arrive when the arrogant ones achieve their goal of dismantling the planets and turning dumb and uninhabited mass into brains throughout the observable reaches of the universe. And he's just questioned the rectitude of her vision.

The queen's lips twitch. Then they curl into a wide, carnivorous grin. Behind her, the cat sits up and stretches, then stares at Sadeq through narrowed eyes.

"You know, that's the first time in *weeks* that anyone has told me I'm full of shit. You haven't been talking to my mother again, have you?"

It's Sadeq's turn to shrug, uncomfortably. "I have prepared a judgment," he says slowly.

"Ah." Amber rotates the huge diamond ring around her finger, seemingly unaware. It is Amber that looks him in the eye, a trifle nervously. Although what he could possibly *do* to make her comply with any decree—

"Her motive is polluted," Sadeq says shortly.

"Does that mean what I think it does?" she asks.

Sadeq breathes deeply again. "Yes."

Her smile returns. "And is that the end of it?" she asks.

He raises a dark eyebrow. "Only if you can prove to me that you can have a conscience in the absence of divine revelation."

Her reaction catches him by surprise. "Oh, sure. That's the next part of the program. Obtaining divine revelations."

"What? From the aliens?"

The cat, claws extended, delicately picks its way down to her lap and waits to be held and stroked. It never once takes its eyes off him. "Where else?" she asks. "Doctor, I didn't get the Franklin trust to loan me the wherewithal to build this castle just in return for some legal paperwork. We've known for years that there's a whole alien packet-switching network out there and we're just getting spillover from some of their routes: it turns out there's a node not far away from here, in real space. Helium three, separate jurisdictions, heavy industrialization on Io—there is a *purpose* to all this activity."

Sadeq licks his suddenly dry lips. "You're going to narrowcast a reply?"

"No, much better than that: we're going to *visit* them. Cut the delay cycle down to realtime. We came here to build a ship and recruit a crew, even if we have to cannibalize the whole of Jupiter system to pay for the exercise."

The cat yawns, then fixes him with a thousand-yard stare. "This stupid girl wants to bring her *conscience* along to a meeting with something so smart it might as well be a god," it says, "and you're it. There's a slot open for the post of ship's theologian. I don't suppose I can convince you to turn the offer down?"

I Saw the Light

TERRY BISSON

Terry Bisson [www.terrybisson.com] lives in Oakland, California these days. He continues to write fantasy and science fiction, full of detail and fascination with how things work, with deadpan humor, wit, and stylish precision. He has been publishing in the genre since the late 1970s. Of his SF novels, Voyage to the Red Planet *(1990) is perhaps both the most heroic and the funniest chronicle of the first voyage to Mars in all science fiction. His latest novel is* The Pickup Artist *(2001), which somehow combines the traditions of Ray Bradbury and Kurt Vonnegut, Jr. In the 1990s, Bisson began to write short stories. One of his first was "Bears Discover Fire," which won the Hugo and Nebula Awards, among others. His stories are collected in* Bears Discover Fire *(1993) and in* In the Upper Room and Other Likely Stories *(2000).*

"I Saw the Light" appeared electronically at SciFiction; this is its first appearance in print. It is classic Bisson, an object of contemplation as well as a fine SF story in the tradition of Arthur C. Clarke's "The Sentinal." Astronauts discover on the Moon evidence that humanity was uplifted by alien visitors in the distant past. This is SF as the literature of ideas, especially unsettling ideas. How much free will do we have, anyway? This is a story about an astronaut and her dog.

I saw the light. So did you. Everybody did.

Remember where you were the first time you saw it? Of course you do. I was living in Arizona, Tucson, more or less retired. I was throwing sticks. They say you can't teach an old dog new tricks, but who would want to? There aren't any new tricks, just the old tried and true. "Good boy, Sam," I would say, and he would say "woof," and there we would go again. I used to amuse myself thinking it was Sam who was teaching me to throw, but I don't think that anymore. It was night, and desert nights are bright, even with a quarter moon. Sam stopped, halfway back to me, dropped his stick and began to howl. He was looking up, over my head. I turned and looked up toward the moon, and you know the rest. There it was, blinking in threes: *dot dot dot*, twice a minute. On the Moon, where no one had been in thirty years. Twenty nine, eight months, and four days, exactly; I knew, because I had been the last to leave, the one who locked the door behind me.

Sam's a big yellow mutt; his first name is Play it Again, so I always call him by his last. He was a parting gift from my third ex, who was himself a parting gift from my second. Lunar subcrust engineers shouldn't marry: our peculiar talents take us to too many faraway places. Or to one, anyway.

"Come on boy," I said, and we headed back into the minimally furnished condo I call home, leaving the stick behind—even though sticks are not all that easy to find in Arizona, or for that matter on the Moon.

* * *

The light on the Moon was front page news the next morning—*dot dot dot*—and by the third day it was estimated that all but a tiny fraction of Earth's six point four billion had seen it. UNASA confirmed that the light was not from Marco Polo Station (I could have told them that) but from a spot almost a hundred kilometers away, on the broad, dark plain of the Sinus Medii: the exact center of the Moon as seen from Earth.

I figured there would have to be an investigation, so I made a few calls. I was not really hopeful, but you never knew. I still had a few friends in the Agency. I was hoping that, if nothing else, this light would get us back to the Moon. It wasn't only or even primarily for myself that I was hoping; it was for humanity, all of us, past and future. It seemed a shame to learn to soar off the planet and then quit.

Okay, so it's not soaring: it's more like a push-up, grunting and heaving, but you know what I mean.

First Contact: strange lights on the Moon: may we have your attention, please. The tabs speculated, the pundits punded, and UNASA prepared the first international expedition since the abandonment of Marco Polo in 20—. I had made, as I mentioned, a few calls, but I hadn't really expected anything. A sixty-one-year-old woman does not exactly fit the profile for space flight and lunar exploration. So Imagine, as they say, My Surprise, when the phone rang. It was Berenson, my Russian-English boss from the old days. I knew him immediately by his accent even though it had been twenty-nine years eight months and seven days.

"Bee!?" (Which is what we called him.)

"I requested you as number two for the tech team. Logistically this is a cake walk and age is not a problem, if you're still in shape. There will be five altogether, three SETI and two tech."

"How soon?" I asked, trying to hide my excitement.

"Start packing."

I hung up and screamed, or howled, or whatever. Sam came running. "I'm going back to the Moon!" I said.

"Woof!" he said, jowls flopping; as always, happier for me than for himself.

Our trip was put together with a minimum of publicity and fanfare. We were due at Novy Mir in less than a week. I wasn't to tell anyone where I was going. Of course, I had already told Sam.

"I'm leaving you here with Willoughby," I said. "I'll be back soon. Three, four weeks max. Meanwhile, you be good, hear?"

"Where are you going, exactly?" My next door neighbor, Willoughby, is a retired FBI agent, a type that both hates and loves secrets, depending on who is keeping them, and why.

"An old lover," I said, with a wink. It was one of my better moments.

Zero G felt perfectly normal; you don't forget how to fly, just as you don't forget how to walk. I felt ten years younger immediately. It was great to be back in the Big Empty, even if it meant a night or two on Novy Mir, the sprawling, smelly space station in Clarke orbit.

Bee was the first one I saw when I entered the day room we had been assigned. He was with Yoshi, his old number two.

"I thought I was number two!" I complained.

"You are," Bee replied with a laugh. "Yoshi is number one." Turned out he was leading SETI. His partners were a scowling Chinese biologist named Chang, and a smiling Indian linguist named Erin Vishnu whose mother had gotten pregnant during Julia Roberts' Academy Awards acceptance speech. I didn't learn this until later, of course; at first the "sadies" (as Yoshi and I called them) were very reserved.

It was a two-day trip from high Earth orbit to the Moon. Bee and I caught up on old times (he had saved my life twice, which cements a friendship) while Yoshi flew the ship and studied the manuals, which she already knew by heart. So did I. I had helped her and Bee run the pumps, extracting en-

vironmentals from buried comet ice, for almost six years at
Polo.

The SETI team, the sadies, were the scientific payload.
The heart of the matter, as it were. They had been established to deal directly, discreetly, and creatively with any
First Contact situation, answerable to no government—not
even UNASA.

"No one really thought it would ever happen," Bee told
me. "So we have complete autonomy; for two weeks anyway."

We were just preparing for lunar capture when I got the call
from Willoughby—my next door neighbor, remember? It
was Sam. He was desolate, disconsolate, wouldn't eat; he
just howled—at the moon, of course, as if he knew where I
was headed.

"How the Hell did you get through to me here?" I asked. I
needn't have. Those FBI guys never let go of their connections. I could hear Sam in the background, whining.

Willoughby held the phone, and I said, "Hang in there,
boy, I'll be home soon."

"Woof," was his answer; he was nothing if not uncon-
vinced.

The light source was about a hundred kliks from Marco
Polo, and we crossed over the old station on our recon orbit.
I got all teary-eyed, seeing our domes and tunnels, still intact
here where the weather runs in billion year cycles; every
scratch and scuff in the lunar dust just as we had left it,
twenty-nine years eight months and eighteen days before.

Then we saw the light itself as we passed over Sinus
Medii. It was coming from a perfect jet black pyramid, ten
meters on a side, too small to show up in amateur photos but
plenty large enough to have been studied from Novy Mir.

"There haven't been any pictures of this!" I said. "Not
even on the internet." Bee just smiled and I realized then that
his SETI team had powers that belied their modest size and
relative obscurity.

The pyramid was pure black, the only pure thing on the Moon, which is all shades of gray.

It was still throwing light, *dot dot dot*, a new sequence every twenty-seven seconds.

We set down next to the pyramid in a cloud of slow-settling dust. If we had hoped to be greeted by the aliens when the dust cleared (and we had; hopes are less restricted than expectations), we were duly disappointed.

The pyramid was silent and still, as black as a rip in the Universe. It was still (we confirmed from Novy Mir) transmitting its *dot dot dot* twice a minute, but the light was, for some reason, invisible from our position beside it.

Still teary-eyed, I felt like a dancer; light on my feet, without the creaking that comes with age and miles. I realized that it was not the moon I had missed all these years, but the one-sixth gravity, and of course my youth.

SETI had arranged for a two week stay, so I immediately sunk a probe and hit pay dirt (or ice). The sadies went to work, photographing the pyramid from all sides, while Yoshi and I unfolded the dome and adjusted the environmentals to break down the oxygen and hydrogen (for fuel) extracted from the cometary trash imbedded under the lunar crust.

By Day Two (sticklers for tradition, we ran on Houston time) we had the ship for a dorm, and the attached geodesic as a day room and observation dome, complete with fast-plants and a hot tub which also heated the dome and ship. By Day Three I knew I should have been bored. Shouldn't something have happened by now?

"What would you have us do?" Bee asked. "Knock?"

"Why not?" I said, returning his smile. I was in no hurry; I was just glad to have a reason to be here, back home, on the Moon. It felt—right. Even Yoshi, an olympic complainer, was not complaining, though her narrow face was not exactly wreathed in smiles. "What about ground control?" she asked. "Aren't they pushing you?"

"There isn't any ground control," Bee said. "Or haven't you noticed?" The SETI mandate was a blank slate, designed to remove First Contact, if it ever came to pass, from the constraints of diplomacy and politics. The pace of events was their call.

By Day Four Yoshi and I had nothing to do except watch the sadies in their clumsy white suits measure and photograph and analyze the pyramid. I kept my doubts to myself, reluctant to interfere, but Yoshi was never one to recognize such restraints. "Aren't you guys disappointed?" she asked at the end of the day.

"Not yet. It feels right to go slow," Bee replied. He was sitting with us in the hot tub, soaking off the chill that comes with EVAs, even in a suit. "Can't you feel it?"

Feel what? We both looked at him, puzzled.

"The familiarity. I feel it; we all feel it. A feeling that we are in the right place, doing the right thing."

"I thought it was just me," I said. "Being back here."

"We all feel it," said Chang, who was sitting on the floor in his long johns, tapping on a laptop. "We are here to record and evaluate everything. Feelings included. Right, Vish?"

"Right."

"You've got another week," said Yoshi.

"Knock and you shall enter," I said.

"Hmmmm," said Bee.

And knock he did. The next day, at the end of their routine explorations, he reached up with a heavy gloved mitt and rapped three times on the side of the pyramid.

Yoshi and I were watching from the dome.

"I knocked," Bee said to me, as he was unsuiting just inside the airlock (we entered and exited through the ship). Instead of answering, I pulled all three of the sadies into the dome, and pointed across the little plain of dust toward the pyramid.

"Damn," said Chang. He all but smiled. Vishnu looked amazed. Bee, delighted. There it was:

A handprint, in bright yellow, against the darker-than-midnight black, halfway up the pyramid.

The next "morning" the print was still there, and the sadies were suited up early. Yoshi and I watched them jumping clumsily around, stirring up the dust, fitting their stiff gloves against the handprint, waiting for something to happen. Hoping for something to happen.

Nothing did.

Later in the hot tub we were all silent. Outside the dome, we could see the print, bright yellow in the Moon's cruel gray. We felt gloomy and hopeful at the same time. Familiarity had been replaced by a kind of desperate eagerness.

"It wants something," said Bee.

"Maybe it wants a touch," I said.

"A touch?" Chang was scornful.

I ignored him and addressed myself to Bee. "You know, not a glove."

"It's high vac out there," Vishnu reminded me. "We can't exactly take off our gloves."

"But of course we can!" Bee said, slapping the water like a boy. I grinned and gave him five. There were the peels.

Peels are emergency spray-on suits to be used in case of sudden decompression. Coupled with a "paper" helmet, a peel will give you anywhere from two to twenty minutes to find an airlock or an emergency vehicle—or say your prayers.

I was in fact the only one present who had actually used a peel, after a sudden rockslide collapsed Polo's ag dome. Thanks to the peel I had survived the twelve minutes it took Bee to get to me with a Rover. I could still feel the cold of those long twelve minutes in my bones.

The next "day" (Six) they tried it. Yoshi and I watched from the dome as Bee in his peel and the sadies in their white suits approached the pyramid, Bee in the lead. He was hurrying, of course; there's no other way to moonwalk in a peel. I could feel how cold he was.

They all stopped and stood in a line, right in front of the print. With his left hand Bee grabbed Chang's mitt, and Chang grabbed Vishnu's. Then Bee placed his right hand high on the side of the pyramid, directly over the print.

And it happened.

Something—a lens, a door?—opened in the side of the pyramid, and they stepped through: one, two, three: Bee, Chang, Vishnu. It closed behind them and they were gone.

"Holy shit," said Yoshi.

"Knock and you shall enter," I said. It was another of my better moments.

Yoshi and I watched the pyramid, wordlessly. Was there air in there? How could Bee survive? After twenty minutes Yoshi began to suit up for a rescue EVA. I was the only one watching two minutes later (twenty-one point four minutes from entry, timed on the sadies' fixed video camera) when the lens opened and the three emerged, stumbling, Bee in the lead. Yoshi opened the airlock for them and they staggered in, Bee falling into my arms. While Yoshi helped the other sadies un-suit, I ripped off his paper helmet and pulled him into the hot tub, which would dissolve his peel. He was shivering and grinning.

Yoshi joined us, feet only. "Why's he grinning?"

"Ask him," I said. I was rubbing one of his feet while he rubbed the other.

Bee was opening his mouth and closing it without making a sound, like a fish.

"It was big in there," he said, finally; still with the goofy grin. "Bigger on the inside than on the outside."

"What happened?" I asked.

"We went in and the door closed behind us. It was dark but we could see, don't ask me why. We took our helmets off . . ."

"Took your helmets off!?" Yoshi was offended.

"Don't ask me why. We just did, all of us. Then we stepped forward, all together I think, and saw the light."

"Wait a minute," I said.

"It was like a glow."

"But bright," said Chang, who had joined us. "The brightest thing I have ever seen."

"The next thing I knew I was on my knees," said Bee. "I could feel this hand on the top of my head."

"A hand?" Yoshi was offended again.

"It felt like a yellow hand," Vishnu said, peeling off her long johns; it was the first time I had seen her undressed.

"It was definitely a hand," Bee said. "I could tell it was a hand though I couldn't see anything. I don't think I even looked."

"It was all light," said Chang. "And this feeling. It was a hand on the top of my head."

"It felt so good," said Vishnu, lowering herself into the water. She had the body of a girl.

"Sounds like an acid trip," I said. "Or a three-armed alien."

"What was the communication?" Yoshi asked. "What was said?"

"The feeling was the communication," Bee said. "That was all. Nothing was said. We were just there, all three of us, on our knees, looking into the light."

"With a feeling of . . . of . . ." Chang gave up.

"I don't like this," said Vishnu, looking down at herself, as if just realizing she was nude. "Shouldn't we be talking about this among ourselves first?"

"It's okay," said Bee. "We can proceed any way we decide is best, and this feels okay, doesn't it? These are our closest comrades here, after a million years of evolution."

Huh? He looked stoned to me.

"So whatever it is, it came all this way to pat you on the head?" Yoshi grumbled.

Bee and Chang just grinned. Vishnu looked troubled. I wondered if she were wishing she had kept her long johns on.

"Maybe it's God," I said.

"It's a they," Bee said, shaking his head.

"More than one," said Vishnu. "Many."

"And they know us," Chang said.

"Yes! That's the communication," Bee said. "They know us, and we know them. That was the feeling, more than a feeling, really. That's what they wanted to tell us."

"They?" Yoshi rolled her eyes. "They called you up here for a feeling? There's no communication?"

"Feelings are real," said Bee. "Maybe that's all it will be. Who knows. The idea behind SETI is that First Contact will probably be something unexpected."

"This is unexpected," said Vishnu. "But not unfamiliar. Very familiar. We have been here before."

"Here?" I asked.

"In their company," said Chang. "Being with them felt good. Better than good. Great."

"Great," said Yoshi, looking disgusted.

"And now?" I asked. "Next?"

"I don't know," said Bee, looking out toward the black pyramid, with its yellow print halfway up the side. "There's something, something else. I guess we go back."

And so they did. The next "morning" they all went out again, Chang and Vishnu suited and Bee leading, in his peel. They emerged after only twenty minutes this time, with the same lunatic grins.

"It's not like we aren't conscious in there," said Chang, as his helmet came off. "It's more like we're conscious for the first time."

"Right," said Vishnu.

I would have made another acid trip joke, but I didn't want to discourage them. This was, after all, I told myself, the long awaited First Contact, for which humanity had waited a million years or more.

Wasn't it?

"Who are they? What are they? What do they want from us?" asked Yoshi.

"They want to be with us," said Vishnu, dreamily peeling off her long johns. "Just like we want to be with them."

"It's all feelings," said Bee, slipping into the pool beside me. He looked like the Michelin tire man in his foam suit, before it started to dissolve into harmless polymer chains. "But the feelings contain information."

"They sort of precipitate into information," said Chang.

"The feelings *are* information," said Vishnu, nude again. "We are in contact with an entity that we have been in contact with before. And have always wanted to be in contact with again."

"That's the feeling!" said Chang eagerly. "Desire, and the fulfillment of desire."

"Sounds sort of sexy," I said.

"It's a wonderful feeling," said Bee, taking me more seriously than I took myself. "But it's changing, too. There's something else."

"Something dark," said Vishnu.

"Dark how? Dark what?" Yoshi was putting the helmets and suits away, looking annoyed.

"It's too soon to say," said Bee. "First we all need to get some sleep. That's an order."

"Wake up."

It was Yoshi.

"It's Berenson, he's gone. He's in there."

"What?" I sat up, almost spilling out of my hammock. I had been dreaming I was home on Earth with Sam, trying to explain something to him, about sticks.

"I thought I saw him, in a peel, going in, about five minutes ago."

"Are you sure?"

"I thought I might be dreaming, so I checked. The other sadies are in their hammocks, but Berenson is gone."

"So what do you think we should do?"

Twenty minutes later I was in boots and long johns, spraying on a peel. I shook open a paper helmet, checking to make sure it had two full air cans (twenty minutes). I had thought I remembered the cold and was prepared for it, but I wasn't. It was insulting, crushing, humbling.

I hurried toward the pyramid. The dust cracked under my feet with that weird squeak of molecules that have never—not by wind, not by water, not by weather—been rubbed together. The *squeak* came up through my bones as sound. I had forgotten it.

I saw Yoshi and the sadies, awake now, watching from the dome. I waved as I ran. I could feel the vacuum slicing my fingertips, like steel knives.

I put my hand against the side of the pyramid, covering the print, and *something* happened. I wasn't sure what. It opened, I went in; it was dark, I was alone.

I was inside. I didn't know, still don't know, how I got there. Before I knew what I was doing, I was taking off my helmet.

The air smelled like lemons. It was cold, but not Moon cold. The pyramid was larger inside, just as Bee had said, tapering up to a cone of darkness in the center.

And there was a light. Also in the center. It had a kind of substance light doesn't always, doesn't often, doesn't ever, have. It was beckoning; I approached. It all seemed natural, as if everything I was doing was what I had always wanted to do. It felt good; very good. It felt great. The light grew brighter and I fell to my knees, but it was more like rising, really. I couldn't stand but I didn't want to stand. I felt a hand on my head: I knew it was a hand, and I knew what hand it was! I had a million questions, I knew, but I couldn't think, even when I tried. I was so very glad to be here, back here, where I belonged. Where I was glad to be.

I felt a hand in mine. Bee. He was pulling me backward, away from the light, into the cold and the darkness. We were putting on our helmets, Bee and I. We were stepping together across the squeaky surface of the moon, toward the lighted dome, which looked like a zoo, full of puzzled friendly faces, pressed against the glass.

"Are you okay?" Yoshi asked.

I saw my breasts floating in front of me and realized I was in the hot tub. I laughed. Bee laughed with me. I knew that the grin on his face was a reflection of my own. We were in the water and someone was handing me a cup of coffee. Joe, they used to call it. A cup of joe. "I'm okay," I said. "I went in to get you, Bee."

"I know, but you shouldn't have. You should have awakened the others."

I understood. It was a break in the protocol. "We know them and they know us," I said. It was like remembering something; it was easy, and yet impossible if you couldn't do it. "They are glad to see us."

"Not exactly," said Bee. "There's a melancholy, too."

"Something very sad," said Vishnu. She was wearing her nightgown and her tiny feet were in the water next to my shoulder.

She was right. There had been a reproach, a disappointment. "I can feel it, too," said Chang.

"Feel what?" asked Yoshi, tapping me on the head with a long finger, like a teacher admonishing a bad student. "Tell me what happened. Now."

"There are just these feelings," I said. "Then afterward, they sort of turn into, not ideas exactly, sort of like memories. Is that what you want to know?"

"I want to know what's fucking happening. And I want you to tell me."

"Don't be hard on her," said Bee. "We're all just figuring it out."

"Figuring what out?!"

"What they want," said Chang. "They love us, they wanted to find us. They found us."

"And we love them!" I said. "That's why we can't see them."

"That's right!" said Bee, looking at me as if I were a genius. "We love them so much that all we can see is the light of our love."

"I hope this is all going in your fucking report," said Yoshi, sounding disgusted.

"They found us again," said Chang. "That's why we are so happy."

"But something is wrong," said Bee. "We have to go back in. Once more."

"And do I get to go?" I could still feel the hand on my head. I wanted to feel it there again, more than anything.

"We'll all go this time," Bee said.

But we didn't all go. Yoshi had no desire to go; plus, she explained, she felt that somebody had to stay behind and stay on top of systems.

"Designated driver," said Bee, laughing as we sprayed each other. He and I were the only ones in peels. Chang and Vishnu wore suits. I felt I was one of the sadies now, and they treated me as such. Even Chang. We crossed the squeaky dust and held hands by the pyramid. Looking back I saw Yoshi in the dome, looking a little bit abandoned.

Bee hit the print and there we were, inside. I unstuck my helmet and looked for the light. I fell to my knees. "Oh boy," I said when I felt the hand on my head.

Something was wrong. Everything was okay but something was wrong. After a few moments of confusion, we were pushed out the door, holding hands, into the cold. I couldn't remember putting my helmet on, but I was breathing as we hurried toward the lights of the dome.

We were shaking. I was shaking all over. I sat in the hot tub and watched my suit dissolve, like dry ice, leaving no trace.

"Hey, don't cry," said Bee. "I know we're all upset."

"It's okay to cry," said Vishnu.

I was crying.

"What happened?" asked Yoshi. "God damn it, tell me."

"They're leaving," said Bee.

"They don't want us," I said. "They don't want us any more."

"What the fuck are you talking about?"

"We should all just be still for a while," said Bee. "Come and get in the water, Chang. Vishnu. Claire."

Claire. My parents gave me that name. I hadn't thought about them in a long time. I started to cry again, really hard this time.

By noon we were warmed and fed—and dejected. "It's over," Bee said finally.

"They're leaving," Chang said. I knew it too. We all knew the same things. The feelings turned into ideas, gradually, like the graphics in a slow web connection. Sooner or later we all had the same pictures in our minds.

"They're disappointed in us," I said.

"I want them to stay," said Vishnu.

"Of course, we want to be with them," said Bee. "But we can't make them want to be with us."

"What in the hell are you all talking about?" asked Yoshi.

"They're leaving," I said. I pointed outside. The yellow print was gone, and the pyramid looked black and forbidding. Closed.

"Explain, damn it."

"The thing is, we knew them long ago," said Bee. As I listened, my emotions were spinning, like dust in sunlight, settling as he spoke onto the table of my mind, in which his voice, like a fingertip, traced his words: "This is not first contact, it is second contact."

And what he was saying, we all knew.

"They were our gods," said Chang.

"Not exactly," said Vishnu. "We were their companion species, their helper. We lived only to please them. We looked up to them."

"Their favorite," I said. "Their pet."

"And they loved us," said Chang. "And they love us still."

"But they wanted more," said Bee. "They set us free so we could develop without them. They put us down on Earth, where we could escape the worship of them that makes our knees go weak and our minds go blank. They wanted a true companion. They thought if they left us alone we would develop into a sentient race on our own."

"And we did," I said, surprised at how much I knew; at the depth of the ideas and images that had been implanted in me. "The light was a test, to see if we had developed enough to leave the Earth and come to them."

"They knew better than to appear among us," said Chang. "Can you imagine the chaos?"

"It might have been great," said Vishnu.

"It was a test," said Bee. "And we did it, we passed. They were so pleased."

"But then disappointed," I said. "Because nothing had really changed."

"It might have been great," said Vishnu, again.

"We still can't see them; our minds still go blank in their presence. We fall to our knees and worship them, and that's all we can do, even now."

"We can't love them less," said Chang bitterly. "How can they expect us to love them less?"

"There's a message for you," said Yoshi.

"For me?" My mind wrenched itself back to the real

world. I stood up, dripping. Water drips in long sheets on the Moon. I looked outside and saw that the pyramid was gone.

"How did you find me here?"

"Haven't we been through that before?" It was Willoughby, my next door neighbor, the retired FBI agent. "The light's gone out, what did you guys do?"

"Put Sam on," I said.

"He won't eat. How long before you get back?"

"A week, probably," I said. "We will have to write a report." I heard a noise behind me; it was Chang in tears.

"Is something wrong?"

"No, we're fine," I said. It was over and I was glad. "Put Sam on."

"Hold on."

Yoshi had joined them in the pool, standing there in her orange coveralls, wet to the knees. They were hugging and crying. I heard a sort of gruff whine.

"Sam, is that you?"

"Woof!"

"Sam, listen carefully. Can you hear me?"

I could imagine Sam looking around, sniffing, trying to locate the face and hand and smell that went with the voice.

"I'll be back soon," I said. "Did you miss me?"

"Woof."

"I'm coming home, and I won't leave you alone again, I promise."

A Slow Day at the Gallery

*A(lyx) M. Dellamonica (http://www.sff.net/people/alyx) lives
in Vancouver, B.C. Her stories have appeared in* Crank!,
Realms of Fantasy, *and a number of other venues, most recently the Canadian SF anthology* Tesseracts 8. *She writes
book and software reviews for* SF Weekly *and* Amazon.com.*

"A Slow Day at the Gallery" is from Asimov's. *It is a per-
ceptive and carefully controlled story of contemporary political relevance. It is about the clash of cultures, an allegory
of imperialism and cultural appropriation, and about the
possibility of real and meaningful communication between
radically unlike cultures, between the human and the alien.
But that's all in addition to an involving story in the tradition of James Tiptree, Jr., about an idealist about to do
something terrible.*

The museum escort Christopher had requested arrived just as he was winding up a self-guided tour of the Earth exhibit. Staring at Monet's *Waterlily Pond*, he was lost in a passion more intense, he suspected, than any he had expended during either of his two brief marriages.

The painting had been reframed, but was otherwise unchanged since the last time he had seen it, fifty years before. As he gazed at its placid flowers and vibrant willow leaves, Christopher even began to imagine that the grooves time had left on him—age, injuries, bitterness—were just as superficial.

Same man, different frame. He could do this.

Leaning heavily on his cane—museum air exhausted him, even here—he tore his gaze away from the shimmering canvas and faced the Tsebsra museum guide. It looked like a badly executed balloon-animal: a tubular sac of tight, rubbery skin balanced on lumpy legs. Stringy eyestalks dangled from the bulb at its top, while the bottom of its body tapered into a long, rubbery tail decorated with blue stripes. The markings meant it was young, probably still ungendered. It wore a floor-length apron printed with its museum ident and, at the moment, it was standing almost upright. The pose could have been reminiscent of a praying mantis, if only the insect had been bleach-white, headless, and lacking its four upper limbs.

As the guide approached, a faint chime sounded in Christopher's left ear. "Museum staff member, late adoles-

223

cent, name on ident equates to Vita," said his protocol software in a smooth, feminine voice. He had named the program Miss Manners—Em for short. "Posture indicates polite, professional interest and includes appropriate respect for an adult of your years. Vita is curious about the camera you are carrying."

Christopher smiled at the guide.

"Your expression has been interpreted by Vita's proto and it appears receptive to conversation."

So. Converse. He opened his hand to fully reveal the camera, which had captured a shot of the Monet on its tiny screen. "Just didging some postcards for the grandkids."

The alien speech was a series of intestinal-sounding gurgles, almost like water boiling on a stove. There was no variation that Christopher could hear, but the translation came through Em immediately. "It looks different from the ones I've seen before. Bigger."

"It's antique. Like me."

"Would you like me to take a shot of you with the painting?"

"Sure," he said. At that, one of its feet whipped up with alarming speed to snatch the device out of Christopher's hand; its tail slewed around to balance its body weight and its spine bent into an S-curve. Thus contorted, it was able to drop an eye-stalk directly on the scanner. Heart pounding, Christopher grinned into the lens, resisting an urge to wipe the palms of his hands on his hips. It snapped the picture quickly and returned the camera.

"It would be polite to look away now," Em said, so Christopher turned back to Monet. The guide sidled up close and then shifted away. It had probably been advised to widen the space between them to a more human-appropriate distance.

"Do you have many?"

"Many what?"

"Grandchildren, sir."

"Three boys, four girls."

"Ah. So they're all grown?"

"No. Humans are gendered at birth."

"Vita appears mortified," reported Em. "You should have corrected it more gently."

"My apologies," the alien said.

He shrugged—let its software interpret that.

He had first seen this painting eighty years earlier, when he was in his teens. He had seen digital prints of it when he was even younger, of course—Monet was inescapable. Even so, Christopher had never understood the big fuss until he'd taken a school trip to the National Gallery.

He had been fooling around with his friends, ignoring the tour, aggravating his teachers and the guards before finally ducking the group altogether. In search of a place to smoke, he had rounded a corner and found the Monet. Recognition had stopped him, nothing more—he paused, frowned, noticed that it was different from the digitals he had seen. Prints couldn't do justice to oil; couldn't communicate the singular way these paintings glowed. Monet's luminous sunlight on water had crept up on him like a pickpocket. He barely noticed when it made away with his heart.

"This was painted around 1900 A.D. as you reckon time, at a population cluster in Europe called Giverny. Monet had a house there. He painted this garden many times. . . ."

"France," he growled.

"Pardon?"

"Giverny is in France."

A pause. "Are you all right, sir? My proto believes I have upset you."

"Upset?" he managed. "Nah, just older'n hell."

"It would be perfectly understandable if receiving instruction in your home culture from an offworlder. . . ."

What? Made me want to gut you?

"I just need to sit down," he said, retreating to the cushioned bench in the middle of the room. This gallery was built to look like an authentic Earth museum—off-white plaster walls, smooth hardwood floors, ceiling lights angled to spotlight each work. Furniture, thank Christ, to ease the aching feet of contemplative patrons. The paintings were displayed too close to each other, though, crammed practically into a collage that extended from floor to ceiling. There was a mishmash of periods and styles: Andy Warhol's soup cans cuddled next to an amateurish painting of a dog. This was, in turn, located beneath Sir Stanley Spencer's *Saint Francis and the Birds* and above an Ansel Adams photograph of an American mountain. Only the Monet had any space to itself, and that was probably because there was extra security hidden in the wall on which it was mounted.

"Grandkids made me promise to snap 'em the damned painting," he puffed.

A bubble of fluid jittered beneath Vita's skin, indicating—according to Em—surprise. "You didn't come . . . it wasn't your wish to see it?"

Keep a lid on your emotions, old boy, Christopher lectured himself. "Don't go for the impressionist stuff, and I saw it in London once anyway. I'm more of a sculpture man. I came for the Tsebsra sculpture."

"I see. Then . . . you don't like it at all?" Vita's eyestalks quivered. "The way it glints? The shades of green . . ."

"It's all right. You do like it, I take it?"

"I think it's wonderfully natural," Vita gushed. "Tseb work is so formal and mannered. I visit it every day, as soon as I come in. My parents brought me, the day it arrived."

"When was that . . . ten years ago, surely?"

"As your time is reckoned. The Nandi sold it to the museum after . . ." Vita shut up abruptly and Christopher didn't need Em for once to tell him the pause was an awkward one.

"Oh. The Lloyds of London thing?" He managed to keep his tone off-hand. The National Gallery had lent a Nandieve museum the Monet and a quartet of other paintings. The aliens had paid a ludicrous sum for the loan. A sweetheart deal, or so it must have seemed to the Gallery's perpetually underfunded curators.

Unfortunately, failure to check the fine print of cultural difference led to disaster in short order. To the Nandi, the word "loan" implied an indefinite term of visitation. They refused to return the paintings.

The Gallery spent fifteen years trying to get *Waterlily Pond* back. They were deep in negotiations when some bright bulb in Gallery management decided to put in an insurance claim, asking to be compensated for the value of the time the painting had spent offworld. Reasonable enough, perhaps—but when Lloyds cut the check to the museum, the Nandi claimed this made the painting theirs. The next thing anyone knew, they had auctioned it off to the Tsebsra.

Fumbling in his vest pocket, Christopher produced a case of small gelatinous tablets, selecting a marked placebo and pressing it under his tongue. He massaged his left armpit gently, pretending to work out a pain that wasn't there. "You only get two heart transplants these days before they list you as inoperable," he commented to Vita, figuring that the bunching of its many eyes indicated interest in his movements.

He'd guessed wrong. "Personal medical information is not discussed openly here," Em scolded, but before it could tell him how to apologize, Vita piped up, forcing it to translate instead.

"It's okay. We're not all as rigid as the protos are programmed to say we are." A previously invisible fissure opened under the eyes, revealing an immense empty space bordered by sharp black ridges. "I'm not offended."

"Thanks," he said. "I forget I'm not home. Get to be my age, it's more or less a license to be rude."

"Really?"

"Absolutely. No family is complete without a cantankerous retired war—" His turn to stop short: he had almost said veteran, and soldiers were never allowed here.

"I beg your pardon?"

"Vita is alarmed," Em reported.

"Warhorse," he said. "It's a saying. It means I'm old meat, child. Unfit for dogs."

Its head expanded slightly and a grinding sound issued from its throat. "Noise equates to a laugh, tone denotes relief," reported Em.

It and me both, Christopher thought. What was wrong with him?

"I came to see the Spine," he said finally, getting to his feet. "Would you take me?"

"Are you feeling better?"

"Well enough."

"This way, then." Tail swirling, it crooked a toe in the direction of the exit. Christopher got one last hurried glance at the water lilies and then they were gone.

Outside the authentic human museum with its authentic humidity-controlled air, he felt himself reviving. They passed into an ornately carved walkway, lined with windows and meant to communicate with the sensitive feet of the Tsebs, a lumpy obstacle course of knobs and gaps. Christopher's ankles ached as he struggled to traverse it without falling. Just another hurdle, he told himself, like ducking the police or smuggling his false ident out of humanspace. He'd been retired for twenty-four years when the boys approached him for this job. Until a minute ago, he would have sworn he remembered his business.

His cane twisted unexpectedly at the apex of the arch, causing him to wobble. He had braced it in what looked like a knothole, but the knot was mobile, rotating against the force of his weight. Vita caught his elbow with one foot, swung its tail around an upward-thrusting piece of walkway, and heaved in counter-balance. Its grip was weak, and Christopher could feel that the Tseb's strength would never hold his full weight.

Between them, though, they managed to keep him upright. Vita moved his cane to more solid ground. Christopher offered solemn, mumbled thanks. After that, the alien stood closer to him.

Coming off the bridge, Em instructed him to keep his eyes right, toward the ocean. Christopher looked left instead, to a massive hill that rose like a bell-curve from the beach.

"That is one of our burial mounds," Vita said. "Look away."

"I thought you were a bohemian, Vita. Hard to offend?"

"Vita's expression has turned playful. It is receptive to this conversation," Em said. "However, the topic chosen is highly improper."

"You want to know about the mound?"

"Why not? I didn't come five thousand lightyears for Andy Warhol or the damned cuisine."

"There isn't much to tell. When we feel that our spirit is about to break with the physical plane . . ."

"Is that supposed to mean when you die?"

Its head contracted, the skin wrinkling momentarily before expansion somewhere else in its body took up the slack. "Die, yes. When we are dying, we go to a mound and climb as high as we can before weakness overcomes us. It is a last chance to measure the worth of our lives."

"What if you're too sick to get there?"

"Someone takes you to the base of the mound. If you are very respected, they may even carry you up."

"But not always?"

"Nobody can return from a dying place."

"So you heft your troublesome old Uncle Pete up the hill—"

A loud rush of Vita's internal fluids startled him so badly he stopped speaking.

"Sound equates to a giggle," Em said.

"Carry someone up, watch them die . . . and then you stay until you starve?"

"Yes." Vita paused; Em reported it was afraid of being overheard. "In that case, the measure of worth is not by how high you climb, but by how long you survive."

"I suppose that makes as much sense as anything."

Light steps behind them made them turn simultaneously, continuing along the lumpy walkway like the well-behaved pair they weren't. He glanced Vita's way and offered a conspiratorial wink just as a trio of eye stalks swiveled his way in a gesture that, according to Em, meant almost exactly the same thing.

He kept his voice lowered. "Say, what if you're too sick to be moved?"

"The effort is always made."

"Even if it kills you?"

"Even then."

"How come?"

"We are sun people, Christopher. It is unconscionable to fail to die out of doors."

They stepped out of the walkway and into a darkened gallery. "So what if I was to seize up in here?"

Another alarming giggle. "You're not a sun person."

"Good. I'd hate to—"

"Yes?"

"Do something unconscionable," he finished quietly. His eyes adjusted to the dimness and he saw he was in another three-dimensional nightmare—a door of knobs, lumps and potholes. Little orifices covered the outer wall, soft and penetrable, intended for Tseb tails. The ceiling was low and the air smelled sickly sweet, laden with alien pollens. Dark shaggy moss like the hide of a buffalo covered the nooks and crannies. A few cameras were tucked here and there in the corners, but overall security was lax. The Tsebs were a civilized people, after all. They had nothing to fear from their own. As for the few human terrorists who had made it through their security screens, they had been ordered—just like Christopher—to destroy the Monet.

Vita was still savoring their rebellion against decorum. "I promise you can die right here, Christopher, and nobody will hold it against you."

"Swear?"

Instructed by its proto, it awkwardly made a heart-crossing gesture with one upraised foot. "I swear."

"What if I was one of you?"

It was quiet for long enough that he wondered if he had gone too far, but at last the translation came. "That depends."

"On what?"

"If it was instantaneous, unexpected, painless—you would be forgiven," it said. "If not . . . if you knew you were dying, if you tried to get to the sun and failed, or you didn't try . . ."

"Big time transgression, huh?"

Its gesture equated, Em said, to a vehement nod. "Everything associated with your death would be shunned."

"Your culture only takes forgiveness to a point, then?"

"You have to draw the line somewhere."

"Indeed," he agreed. "Quite so."

He let Vita slide back into the proper tour, narrating the history of the Spine as they descended down through the treacherous footing of the gallery. They passed shelves of fungus, tiny statues etched from eggshells, ornately carved crystals and black scrolled wands made of a substance called sea root. Everything was three-dimensional, tactile. Feigning awe, Christopher touched things that felt like peanut butter, dead flesh, adhesive tape, cold steel. He snapped the occasional historical treasure with his too-bulky camera and asked dozens of questions.

There wasn't a flat surface anywhere. The Tseb didn't do two-dimensional depiction. Probably that was why human painting fascinated them so.

Art you can't touch. Daft primitives.

Down and around, hobbled by the lumpy floor, he was genuinely winded by the time they arrived at the Spine.

It was a single glowing sculpture within a massive subterranean chamber, a giant-sized, abstract depiction of the Tsebsra body. Indentations in its belly suggested femininity without insisting upon it; faded bands on its tail hinted at both maturity and youth. It was delicately curved, less knobby than the grotesqueries that had preceded it in the upper galleries.

A pair of Tsebs were lounging at its base, running their feet over the structure, their sluglike pouches extended to lick the surface. They tucked back in when Vita appeared with Christopher, moving back through the exit without a backward glance.

They were alone.

Good. Fewer witnesses, less trouble. He detached the bottom cartridge of his camera and surreptitiously affixed it to the wall beside the door.

"Vita's sound equates to a contented sigh," Em reported.

Christopher hadn't heard anything.

Looking up to the bulging top of the statue, he realized he was disappointed. This was the Tsebs' *Mona Lisa*. He had hoped to understand its beauty. He had come so far. . . .

"Come on!" Vita gripped his arm, urging him closer. They worked their way to the edge of the sculpture and the alien's tail stretched out to roam over it lovingly.

Christopher touched the cool surface. Visually it was seamless, a single white structure made of unidentifiable material. But under his fingers the texture and temperature varied: parts of it were woody, others metallic, still others plastic. Towering above them, the statue's shadow was washed out by the steady golden light emitted from six light globes which encircled it like a wide halo.

This thing predates Columbus and Shakespeare, Christopher thought. It has been sitting here since before my kind invented the printing press.

Nothing. His old heart refused to be moved.

Vita hissed; Em chirped a translation. "When I was new-hatched my parents brought me here. I climbed all the way to the top. The holds look worn down from here at the bottom, but the effect is intentional. You'd be surprised how firm they are! When you are very young, Christopher, you can sit on the top, inflate your sacs, and leap down."

"That's a long way to fall," he said.

"Oh, it's perfectly safe. Inside the coiled tail is a soft moss, and as babies our bodies are very light. Craket the Maker intended it this way. She felt it was important for the Spine to speak to us differently at the various stages of our lives."

He squinted at the bulb at the top of the sculpture. "It's a long way up. Weren't you scared?"

"Terrified. I had to be coaxed down. My parents were deeply shamed."

"Sorry to hear it."

"I am the better for it. Many of my kind only come to see the Spine once or twice. The embarrassment brought me back again and again. It remade my soul."

"I see," Christopher said.

"Perhaps you should take a rest. I think it would be comfortable if you wanted to sit here."

He looked at it dubiously. It was about as high and thick as a park bench, even reasonably, flat, but streaks of dried saliva were flaking away where the other Tsebs had been licking it.

Gentle white toes closed on his scarred elbow.

"Are you all right? I know I said it was acceptable for you to die indoors but you would alert me if you were unwell, wouldn't you?"

"Old man's prerogative," he murmured. The grip on his arm tightened and he leaned against it experimentally. Vita gurgled.

"Sound denotes physical exertion," Em said.

He let himself fall.

He landed atop the alien, tangling a leg and an arm over its twisting body. One of the bumps in the floor caught him in the kidney, a blinding, sudden pain that dulled his awareness of Vita beneath him, bucking and squeaking. Liquids in its body compressed under his weight and its thin skin stretched against him. The sounds it made, according to Em, equated to surprise and minor pain.

"Christopher? Are you all right?"

"Yeah," he grunted. "Sorry. I'll get off you in a sec—just need my pills. Are you hurt?"

"Just pressed," it said. "Your body is so warm! How do you stand it?"

"Cold blood," he muttered. Then, opening the packet of tablets, he bounced the golden globs down the length of the white body.

"Bloody hell," he said, maintaining the façade for one more second. Then the tabs reacted to the room's ambient moisture. They popped, releasing a gelatinous payload that bound the Tseb to the floor of the chamber.

A chatter like rocks grinding together from the body beneath him.

"Vita is alarmed."

He rolled off it, backed away. The jelly splotches spread and welded it down—tail, toes, body. It tugged at one with its foot and tore a hunk of skin away. Fluid the color of motor oil flowed into the fuzz that covered the floor.

"Stay still," he ordered. "You'll injure yourself."

"Christopher?"

Retrieving his cane, he leaned hard against the Spine and caught his breath. Vita was still wiggling on the floor.

"Don't move," he said again. The web packet from his camera had already expanded to seal the room's only entrance, encasing it in a gelatinous webwork. It wouldn't seal them in for long, but he didn't need long.

"What are you doing?"

"Causing a diplomatic incident," he said, unpacking the cane.

"What do you mean?"

"Some chaps I know wanted me to destroy the Monet. You see, people back home have been sitting around with their thumbs up their arses for rather a long time, as we reckon it, doing squat about getting the painting back from you."

The cane was filled with three different harmless fluids, all under pressure. His pals had thought he would spray it over the paintings in the Earth gallery. One two, game over. Instead he unpacked its tripod and took careful aim at the top of the Spine. He started the mechanism that would mix the chemicals into an acid. A single green droplet hissed from the tip of the device.

"Squeal denotes pain," Em said.

He looked at the child. Vita was struggling against its bonds again, and a great hunk of its leg had been torn open.

"Listen to me," he told it. "Those capsules were meant to hold a human. Your skin is obviously very delicate. You must lie still . . . you're going to be seriously injured if you don't stop."

Vita shuddered once. Little fissures bled at the edges of the jellies that bound it to the floor.

"All right," Vita said. After a moment, when it had clearly stopped moving, Christopher returned to his destruction of the statue. The cane beeped, indicating that the acid's mix cycle was complete. He took careful aim at the top of the Spine.

Strong toes gripped his knee then, hurling him backward, off-balance. He fell, tangled in the grip of Vita's bleeding leg. The cane, still in his hand, rained droplets of acid over them both. He closed his eyes, covered his face. His jacket caught most of it, although he could smell his hair burning.

"Don't do this, Christopher," Vita pleaded.

"It's too late." He struggled to free himself without tearing Vita's skin further, wincing as its body gurgled beneath him. The acid was blistering long sticky lines near its eyes, the flesh running like melted cheese. Finally he rolled off of it, propped himself up on his elbows. Taking aim from down on the floor, he began to spray. He laid the acid on the Spine in a straight, consistent layer, just like paint.

Vita yanked his leg and hissed; Em translated. "Stop!"

He struggled to breathe. "The general idea was that by destroying the Monet, you see, we would punish both your museum and the people in my government who let it go. The boys had whipped up these clever gadgets they thought I could slip into this place. They wanted an old man, preferably one who had one toe in the crematorium anyway. But the Earth exhibit is too well protected." Acrid smoke burned at his eyes, the first chemical reaction of acid burning the statue. "Besides, that painting means more to me than my own mother. You might say it remade my soul."

"You haven't got one," Vita whispered.

"I was going to tell them to stuff their job. But someone else would have gone, don't you see? And what if I was wrong? What if they did destroy it? It would have been a pointless sacrifice. Cutting off our nose, as they say. I even considered warning the authorities, just to save the painting."

"Sound equates to a contemptuous snort," Em said.

"But then I thought—if we're going to take all these lovely toys halfway across the galaxy, why not put them to real use? Punish the guilty, I reckoned, instead of the innocent."

Drops of water dribbled down from the ceiling, an immense and sudden profusion of moisture. Striking the acid, it sizzled and steamed. Christopher saw that the Spine was discolored, but not destroyed. The damage was probably reparable, and the acid was being dispersed by the fire system. He was failing.

There was nothing more he could do; he was out of weapons. The boys had tried to build a bomb into a hearing aid or a proto, and all they'd done was blow the tester right into a coma.

He'd come all this way, and at best he would have scared them.

"Vita requires immediate medical attention." Em gave the words a plaintive tone.

"All right, all right."

The grip on his knee had loosened, and he managed to stand upright again. The cane's payload was half used, and so he spent the rest of the cartridge spreading acid on the door seal. Security must be outside by now, trying to cut their way in . . . there was no reason not to help them now.

"Bring a doctor," he shouted.

He spared a last glance for the intact Spine and then, finally, forced himself to look down. The knobby floor around Vita's body was filled with golden blood and water, and its struggles were weakening. It had torn itself apart trying to stop him.

And the funny thing was he'd never been the sort who could bear to see someone who was hurt—even scratched—but he could look right at Vita. It was like seeing a movie monster, a stop-motion death-scene. Before he retired, he had bombed a shuttle full of Tsebs over Earth's lost paintings. He had lain awake nights, imagining they died like humans. Now . . .

"They're coming," he said. "Hang on."

"Sound denotes great pain."

Take its mind off it, he thought. "I had a part-time job when I was a kid," he said. "Guided museum tours in my home town. I worked slow days only at first—they wouldn't trust me with whole groups, just the random wandering tourist. I'm tempted to think that's what your job here is like, Vita—that we have that much, at least, in common."

"We have nothing in common," Em translated. "I'm not like you."

"I wanted to stay on with that museum, but nobody at home wanted to look at paintings anymore. It's all digital home galleries and knobby bric-a-brac. There was no job for me." He knelt, lifted a flap of Tseb skin and tried to press it back against the wound. Frothy orange foam was seeping from its throat.

"Why are you telling me this?" Vita asked, twitching away from the hand he'd clapped over its injury.

"Distraction," he said.

"From what? Your desecration?"

He glanced at the Spine again, mottled with faint black streaks where the various materials merged. "It didn't work."

It laughed bitterly. "You're saying that because you think I'm dying."

"No," Christopher said. He didn't insult it by apologizing. "You'll be fine. I'm trying to take your mind off the discomfort."

"Do you mean pain?" If its body language showed a reaction, Em didn't catch it.

"Sorry."

"Chattering at me like a scatbug doesn't help."

"They'll be through the door in a minute. I didn't know your skin was so delicate, Vita—"

"Shut up." With that, the alien wound its toes along a hold in the floor and tried to pull itself to the blockaded exit. Pieces of its innards unraveled, stringing along the lumpy floor. Its tail tore loose, lashing the Spine with fading vigor.

It was within a yard of the exit when he finally heard Security breaking through the acid-weakened blockade with a cutting tool. Their faces filled a small gap in the webbing, and then they desperately tore at the rest of it, trying to open the gateway for Vita. One of them extended its tail through the hole, dangling it like a rescue rope.

They weren't fast enough. The injured guide had stopped moving. Air blatted, escaping the tears in the rubbery white skin as if it were a deflating life raft. Vita's body shrank, and then went still.

After a moment, the guard's tail retracted to the other side of the door. Tseb eyestalks crowded the opening. Four or five of them stared at Christopher through the shredded jelly of the once-blocked entrance.

"It was only meant to immobilize," he said.

There was no response. He threw away the cane and put his hands up. Didn't they have protos?

"I'm unarmed now," he said.

No reaction. They actually backed up the corridor, away from him and out of sight.

"Aren't you going to arrest me?" He rubbed his face, was surprised to find it wet.

Silence. He looked at the knobby, impassable floor. His cane, disassembled and empty, would never hold his weight again. "Hey. You cops. Going to cart me off or not?"

A chime, suddenly, from Em. "You are located in a dying place. Please leave the chamber and surrender yourself to the authorities."

"What the hell?" He opened his mouth to shout again and then realization hit. They wouldn't come in. Their art treasure was sealed away, ostracized by rigid beliefs and the blood of a child. They were going to leave Vita's body here to rot with its beloved Spine.

And who was he to be offended by that?

When another minute passed and they still didn't come after him, Christopher heaved his body over the base of the Spine so he was inside the curve of its tail. He lay inside, head and legs raised by its height, and found that it fit him just right. The mossy floor was blessedly comfortable, just as the tour had advertised.

"Something soft to land on," he murmured, settling in. His leg was aching from the pratfall he'd taken onto the lumpy floor and both feet were throbbing. He kicked off his shoes, waggled his toes in the warm, moist air.

One last lump pressed into his hip—the camera. He took it out, set it to slideshow, and projected images onto the curvy white interior of the Spine. Warhol. Spencer. Malta. A fake Picasso. A Bill Reid sketch. The Monet. Himself, posing for fake grandkids. Vita. The Mound. Vita again.

"Expression equates to a friendly smile," Em said.

Christopher tore the proto speaker out of his ear and flipped back to the paintings.

After a couple of hours, he started to get hungry.

Ailoura

PAUL DI FILIPPO

---

*Paul Di Filippo lives in Providence, Rhode Island. He is the
most active literary denizen of Providence in the genre since
H.P. Lovecraft, a reviewer, correspondent, and prolific
writer of fiction. If there's a literary movement or school,
he's part of it, or tries it on for size, or joins it. He has been
publishing fantasy and SF since 1985, and widely in the last
decade. His books include* Ciphers *(1990),* The Steampunk
Trilogy *(1995),* Ribofunk *(1996),* Fractal Paisleys *(1997),*
Lost Pages *(1998),* Joe's Liver *(2000), and* Strange Trades
(2001). His books out in 2002 include Babylon Sisters *and
the short story collection* Little Doors.*

*"Ailoura," an SF story based on "Puss in Boots," ap-
peared in* Out of this World, *an anthology of SF using fairy
tales as templates, edited by Wil McCarthy, Martin Harry
Greenberg, and Jon Helfers. It was one of the better SF anthologies of the year. The theme of the anthology plays to Di
Filippo's postmodern strengths. Despite the hyperbolic
style, the family intrigue to murder dad during his high-tech
rejuvenation treatment and deprive the virtuous younger son
of his inheritance has a ring of odd plausibility. It is an interesting story in which the SF and fairy-tale elements blend
nicely.*

The small aircraft swiftly bisected the cloudless chartreuse sky. Invisible encrypted transmissions raced ahead of it. Clearance returned immediately from the distant, turreted manse—Stoessl House—looming in the otherwise empty riven landscape like some precipice-perching raptor. The ever-unsleeping family marchwarden obligingly shut down the manse's defenses, allowing an approach and landing. Within minutes, Geisen Stoessl had docked his small deltoid zipflyte on one of the tenth-floor platforms of Stoessl House, cantilevered over the flood-sculpted, candy-colored arroyos of the Subliminal Desert.

Geisen unseamed the canopy and leaped easily out onto the broad sintered terrace, unpeopled at this tragic, necessary, hopeful moment. Still clad in his dusty expeditionary clothes, goggles slung around his neck, Geisen resembled a living marble version of some young roughneck godling. Slim, wiry, and alert, with his laughter-creased, soil-powdered face now set in solemn lines absurdly counterpointed by a mask of clean skin around his recently shielded green eyes, Geisen paused a moment to brush from his protective suit the heaviest evidence of his recent wildcat digging in the Lustrous Wastes. Satisfied that he had made some small improvement in his appearance upon this weighty occasion, he advanced toward the portal leading inside. But before he could actuate the door, it opened from within.

Framed in the door stood a lanky, robe-draped bestient:

Vicuna, his mother's most valued servant. Set squarely in Vicuna's wedge-shaped hirsute face, the haughty maid's broad
velveteen nose wrinkled imperiously in disgust at Geisen's
appearance, but the moreauvian refrained from voicing her
disapproval of that matter in favor of other upbraidings.

"You arrive barely in time, Gep Stoessl. Your father approaches the limits of artificial maintenance, and is due to be
reborn any minute. Your mother and brothers already anxiously occupy the Natal Chambers."

Following the inhumanly articulated servant into Stoessl
House, Geisen answered, "I'm aware of all that, Vicuna. But
traveling halfway around Chalk can't be accomplished in an
instant."

"It was your choice to absent yourself during this crucial
time."

"Why crucial? This will be Vomacht's third reincarnation.
Presumably this one will go as smoothly as the first two."

"So one would hope."

Geisen tried to puzzle out the subtext of Vicuna's ambiguous comment, but could emerge with no clue regarding the
current state of the generally complicated affairs within
Stoessl House. He had obviously been away too long—too
busy enjoying his own lonely but satisfying prospecting
trips on behalf of the family enterprise—to be able to grasp
the daily political machinations of his relatives.

Vicuna conducted Geisen to the nearest squeezer, and
they promptly dropped down fifteen stories, far below the
bedrock in which Stoessl House was rooted. On this secure
level, the monitoring marchwarden hunkered down in its
cozy low-Kelvin isolation, meaningful matrices of B-E condensates. Here also were the family's Natal Chambers. At
these doors blazoned with sacred icons Vicuna left Geisen
with a humid snort signifying that her distasteful attendance
on the latecomer was complete.

Taking a fortifying breath, Geisen entered the rooms.

Roseate illumination symbolic of new creation softened
all within: the complicated apparatus of rebirth as well as
the sharp features of his mother, Woda, and the doughy

countenances of his two brothers, Gitten and Grafton. Nearly invisible in the background, various bestient bodyguards hulked, inconspicious yet vigilant.

Woda spoke first. "Well, how very generous of the prodigal to honor us with his unfortunately mandated presence."

Gitten snickered, and Grafton chimed in, pompously ironical. "Exquisitely gracious behavior, and so very typical of our little sibling, I'm sure."

Tethered to various life-support devices, Vomacht Stoessl—unconscious, naked and recumbent on a padded pallet alongside his mindless new body—said nothing. Both he and his clone had their heads wrapped in organic warty sheets of modified Stroonian brain parasite, an organism long ago co-opted for mankind's ambitious and ceaselessly searching program of life extension. Linked via a thick living interparasitical tendril to its younger doppelganger, the withered form of the current Vomacht, having reached the limits of rejuvenation, contrasted strongly with the virginal, soulless vessel.

During Vomacht Stoessl's first lifetime, from 239 to 357 PS, he had sired no children. His second span of existence (357 to 495 PS) saw the birth of Gitten and Grafton, separated by some sixty years and both sired on Woda. Toward the end of his third, current lifetime (495 to 675 PS), a mere thirty years ago, he had fathered Geisen upon a mystery woman whom Geisen had never known. Vanished and unwedded, his mother—or some other oversolicitous guardian—had denied Geisen her name or image. Still, Vomacht had generously attended to all the legalities granting Geisen full parity with his half brothers. Needless to say, little cordiality existed between the older members of the family and the young interloper.

Geisen made the proper obeisances at several altars before responding to the taunts of his stepmother and stepbrothers. "I did not dictate the terms governing Gep Stoessl's latest reincarnation. They came directly from him. If any of you objected, you should have made your grievances known to him face-to-face. I myself am honored that

he chose me to initiate the transference of his mind and soul.
I regret only that I was not able to attend him during his final
moments of awareness in this old body."

Gitten, the middle brother, tittered, and said, "The hand
that cradles the rocks will now rock the cradle."

Geisen looked down at his dirty hands, hopelessly ingrained with the soils and stone dusts of Chalk. He resisted
an impulse to hide them in his pockets. "There is nothing
shameful about my fondness for fieldwork. Lolling about in
luxury does not suit me. And I did not hear any of you complaining when the Eventyr Lode that I discovered came online and began to swell the family coffers."

Woda intervened with her traditional maternal acerbity.
"Enough bickering. Let us acknowledge that no possible
arrangement of this day's events would have pleased everyone. The quicker we perform this vital ritual, the quicker we
can all return to our duties and pleasures, and the sooner Vomacht's firm hand will regrasp the controls of our business.
Geisen, I believe you know what to do."

"I studied the proper *Books of Phowa* en route."

Grafton said, "Always the grind. Whenever do you enjoy
yourself, little brother?"

Geisen advanced confidently to the mechanisms that reared
at the head of the pallets. "In the proper time and place,
Grafton. But I realize that to you, such words imply every
minute of your life." The young man turned his attention to
the controls before him, forestalling further tart banter.

The tethered and trained Stroonian life-forms had been
previously starved to near hibernation in preparation for
their sacred duty. A clear cylinder of pink nutrient fluid
laced with instructive protein sequences hung from an or-
nate tripod. The fluid would flow through twin IV lines,
once the parasites were hooked up, enlivening their quiescent metabolisms and directing their proper functioning.

Murmuring the requisite holy phrases, Geisen plugged an
IV line into each enshrouding creature. He tapped the proper
dosage rate into the separate flow-pumps. Then, solemnly
capturing the eyes of the onlookers, he activated the pumps.

Almost immediately the parasites began to flex and labor,

humping and contorting as they drove an infinity of fractally minuscule auto-anesthetizing tendrils into both full and vacant brains in preparation for the transfer of the vital engrams that comprised a human soul.

But within minutes, it was plain to the observers that something was very wrong. The original Vomacht Stoessl began to writhe in evident pain, ripping away from his life supports.

The all-observant marchwarden triggered alarms. Human and bestient technicians burst into the room. Grafton and Gitten and Woda rushed to the pumps to stop the process. But they were too late. In an instant, both membrane-wrapped skulls collapsed to degenerate chunky slush that plopped to the floor from beneath the suddenly destructive cauls.

The room fell silent. Grafton tilted one of the pumps at an angle so that all the witnesses could see the glowing red numerals.

"He quadrupled the proper volume of nutrient, driving the Stroonians hyperactive. This is murder!"

"Secure him from any escape!" Woda commanded.

Instantly Geisen's arms were pinioned by two burly bestient guards. He opened his mouth to protest, but the sight of his headless father choked off all words.

Gep Vomacht Stoessl's large private study was decorated with ancient relics of his birthworld, Lucerno: the empty, age-brittle coral armature of a deceased personal exoskeleton; a row of printed books bound in sloth-hide; a corroded aurochs-flaying knife large as a canoe paddle. In the wake of their owner's death, the talismans seemed drained of mana.

Geisen sighed, and slumped down hopelessly in the comfortable chair positioned on the far side of the antique desk that had originated on the Crafters' planet, Hulbrouck V. On the far side of the nacreous expanse sat his complacently smirking half brother, Grafton. Just days ago, Geisen knew, his father had hauled himself out of his sickbed for one last appearance at this favorite desk, where he had dictated the terms of his third reincarnation to the recording marchwarden. Geisen had played the affecting scene several times en route from the Lustrous Wastes, noting how, despite his enervated condition, his father spoke with his wonted authority, specifically requesting that Geisen administer the paternal rebirthing procedure.

And now that unique individual—distant and enigmatic as he had been to Geisen throughout the latter's relatively short life—the man who had founded Stoessl House and its fortunes, the man to whom they all owed their luxurious independent lifestyles, was irretrievably gone from this plane of existence.

The human soul could exist only in organic substrates. Intelligent as they might be, condensate-dwelling entities such as the marchwarden exhibited a lesser existential complexity. Impossible to make any kind of static "backup" copy of the human essence, even in the proverbial bottled brain, since Stroonian transcription was fatal to the original. No, if destructive failure occurred during a rebirth, that individual was no more forever.

Grafton interpreted Geisen's sigh as indicative of a need to unburden himself of some secret. "Speak freely, little brother. Ease your soul of guilt. We are completely alone. Not even the marchwarden is listening."

Geisen sat up alertly. "How have you accomplished such a thing? The marchwarden is deemed to be incorruptible, and its duties include constant surveillance of the interior of our home."

Somewhat flustered, Grafton tried to dissemble. "Oh, no, you're quite mistaken. It was always possible to disable the marchwarden selectively. A standard menu option—"

Geisen leaped to his feet, causing Grafton to rear back. "I see it all now! This whole murder, and my seeming complicity, was planned from the start! My father's last testament—faked! The flow codes to the pumps—overriden! My role—stooge and dupe!"

Recovering himself, Grafton managed with soothing motions and noises to induce a fuming Geisen to be seated again. The older man came around to perch on a corner of the desk. He leaned over closer to Geisen and, in a smooth voice, made his own shockingly unrepentant confession.

"Very astute. Too bad for you that you did not see the trap early enough to avoid it. Yes, Vomacht's permanent death and your hand in it were all neatly arranged—by mother, Gitten, and myself. It had to be. You see, Vomacht had become irrationally surly and obnoxious toward us, his true and loving first family. He threatened to remove all our stipends and entitlements and authority, once he occupied his strong new body. But those demented codicils were edited from the version of his speech that you saw, as was his insane proclamation naming you sole factotum of the family business. All of Stoessl Strangelet Mining and its affiliates was to be made your fiefdom. Imagine! A young desert rat at the helm of our venerable corporation!"

Geisen strove to digest all this sudden information. Practical considerations warred with his emotions. Finally he could only ask, "What of Vomacht's desire for me to initiate his soul-transfer?"

"Ah, that was authentic. And it served as the perfect bait to draw you back, as well as the peg on which we could hang a murder plot and charge."

Geisen drew himself up proudly. "You realize that these accusations of deliberate homicide against me will not stand up a minute in court. With what you've told me, I'll certainly be able to dig up plenty of evidence to the contrary."

Smiling like a carrion lizard from the Cerise Ergstrand, Grafton countered, "Oh, will you, now? From your jail cell, without any outside help? Accused murderers cannot profit from the results of their actions. You will have no access to family funds other than your small personal accounts while incarcerated, nor any real partisans, due to your stubbornly asocial existence of many years. The might of the family, including testimony from the grieving widow, will be ranked against you. How do you rate your chances for exculpation under those circumstances?"

Reduced to grim silence, Geisen bunched his muscles prior to launching himself in a futile attack on his brother. But Grafton held up a warning hand first.

"There is an agreeable alternative. We really do not care to bring this matter to court. There is, after all, still a chance of one percent or less that you might win the case. And legal matters are so tedious and time-consuming, interfering with more pleasurable pursuits. In fact, notice of Gep Stoessl's death has not yet been released to either the news media or to Chalk's authorities. And if we secure your cooperation, the aftermath of this tragic 'accident' will take a very different form than criminal charges. Upon getting your binding assent to a certain trivial document, you will be free to pursue your own life unencumbered by any obligations to Stoessl House or its residents."

Grafton handed his brother hard copy of several pages. Geisen perused it swiftly and intently, then looked up at Grafton with high astonishment.

"This document strips me of all my share of the family fortunes, and binds me from any future role in the estate. Basically, I am utterly disenfranchised and disinherited, cast out penniless."

"A fair enough summation. Oh, we might give you a small grubstake when you leave. Say—your zipflyte, a few hundred esscues, and a bestient servant or two. Just enough to pursue the kind of itinerant lifestyle you so evidently prefer."

Geisen pondered but a moment. "All attempts to brand me a patricide will be dropped?"

Grafton shrugged. "What would be the point of whipping a helpless, poverty-stricken nonentity?"

Geisen stood up. "Reactivate the marchwarden. I am ready to comply with your terms."

Gep Bloedwyn Vermeule, of Vermeule House, today wore her long blond braids arranged in a complicated nest, piled high atop her charming young head and sown with delicate fairylights that blinked in time with various of her body rhythms. Entering the formal reception hall of Stoessl House, she marched confidently down the tiles between ranks of silent bestient guards, the long train dependent from her formfitting scarlet sandworm-fabric gown held an inch above the floor by tiny enwoven agravitic units. She came to

a stop some meters away from the man who awaited her
with a nervously expectant smile on his rugged face.

Geisen's voice quaked at first, despite his best resolve.
"Bloedwyn, my sweetling, you look more alluring than an
oasis to a parched man."

The pinlights in the girl's hair raced in chaotic patterns for
a moment, then settled down to a stable configurations that
somehow radiated a frostiness belied by her neutral facial
expression. Her voice, chorded suggestively low and husky
by fashionable implants, quavered not at all.

"Gep Stoessl, I hardly know how to approach you. So
much has changed since we last trysted."

Throwing decorum to the wind, Geisen closed the gap between them and swept his betrothed up in his arms. The sensation Geisen enjoyed was rather like that derived from
hugging a wooden effigy. Nonetheless, he persisted in his attempts to restore their old relations.

"Only superficial matters have changed, my dear! True, as
you have no doubt heard by now, I am no longer a scion of
Stoessl House. But my heart, mind, and soul remain devoted
to you! Can I not assume the same constancy applies to your
inner being?"

Bloedwyn slipped out of Geisen's embrace. "How could
you assume anything, since I myself do not know how I
feel? All these developments have been so sudden and mysterious! Your father's cruelly permanent death, your own
capricious and senseless abandonment of your share of his
estate— How can I make sense of any of it? What of all our
wonderful dreams?"

Geisen gripped Bloedwyn's supple hide-mailed upper
arms with perhaps too much fervor, judging from her wince.
He released her, then spoke. "All our bright plans for the future will come to pass! Just give me some time to regain my
footing in the world. One day I will be at liberty to explain
everything to you. But, until then, I ask your trust and faith.
Surely you must share my confidence in my character, in my
undiminished capabilities?"

Bloedwyn averted her tranquil blue-eyed gaze from
Geisen's imploring green eyes, and he slumped in despair,

knowing himself lost. She stepped back a few paces and, with voice steeled, made a formal declaration she had evidently rehearsed prior to this moment.

"The Vermeule marchwarden has already communicated the abrogation of our pending matrimonial agreement to your house's governor. I think such an impartial yet decisive move is all for the best, Geisen. We are both young, with many lives before us. It would be senseless to found such a potentially interminable relationship on such shaky footing. Let us both go ahead—separately—into the days to come, with our extinct love a fond memory."

Again, as at the moment of his father's death, Geisen found himself rendered speechless at a crucial juncture, unable to plead his case any further. He watched in stunned disbelief as Bloedwyn turned gracefully around and walked out of his life, her fluttering scaly train still visible for some seconds after the rest of her had vanished.

The cluttered, steamy, noisy kitchens of Stoessl House exhibited an orderly chaos proportionate to the magnitude of the preparations under way. The planned rebirth dinner for the paterfamilias had been hastily converted to a memorial banquet, once the proper, little-used protocols had been found in a metaphorically dusty lobe of the marchwarden's memory. Now scores of miscegenational bestients under the supervision of the lone human chef, Stine Pursiful, scraped, sliced, chopped, diced, cored, deveined, scrubbed, layered, basted, glazed, microwaved, and pressure-treated various foodstuffs, assembling the imported luxury ingredients into the elaborate fare that would furnish out the solemn buffet for family and friends and business connections of the deceased.

Geisen entered the aromatic atmosphere of the kitchens with a scowl on his face and a bitterness in his throat and heart. Pursiful spotted the young man and, with a fair share of courtesy and deference, considering the circumstances, stepped forward to inquire of his needs. But Geisen rudely brushed the slim punctilious chef aside, and stalked toward the shelves that held various MREs. With blunt motions, he began to shovel the nutri-packets into a dusty shoulder bag that had plainly seen many an expedition into Chalk's treasure-filled deserts.

A small timid bestient belonging to one of the muskrat-hyrax clades hopped over to the shelves where Geisen fiercely rummaged. Nearsighted, the be-aproned moreauvian strained on tiptoe to identify something on a higher shelf.

With one heavy foot, Geisen kicked the servant out of his way, sending the creature squeaking and sliding across the slops-strewn floor. But before the man could return to his rough provisioning, he was stopped by a voice familiar as his skin.

"I raised you to show more respect to all the Implicate's creatures than you just exhibited, Gep Stoessl. Or if I did not, then I deserve immediately to visit the Unborn's Lowest Abattoir for my criminal negligence."

Geisen turned, the bile in his craw and soul melting to a habitual affection tinged with many memories of juvenile guilt.

Brindled arms folded across her queerly configured chest, Ailoura the bestient stood a head shorter than Geisen, compact and well-muscled. Her heritage mingled from a thousand feline and quasi-feline strains from a dozen planets, she resembled no single cat species morphed to human status, but rather all cats everywhere, blended and thus ennobled. Rounded ears perched high atop her densely pelted skull. Vertical slitted eyes and her patch of wet leathery nose contrasted with a more-human-seeming mouth and chin. Now anger and disappointment molded her face into a mask almost frightening, her fierce expression magnified by a glint of sharp tooth peeking from beneath a curled lip.

Geisen noted instantly, with a small shock, the newest touches of gray in Ailoura's tortoiseshell fur. These tokens of aging softened his heart even further. He made the second-most-serious conciliatory bow from the Dakini Rituals toward his old nurse. Straightening, Geisen watched with relief as the anger flowed out of her face and stance, to be replaced by concern and solicitude.

"Now," Ailoura demanded, in the same tone with which she had often demanded that little Geisen brush his teeth or do his schoolwork, "what is all this nonsense I hear about your voluntary disinheritance and departure?"

Geisen motioned Ailoura into a secluded corner of the kitchens and revealed everything to her. His account prompted low growls from the bestient that escaped despite her angrily compressed lips. Geisen finished resignedly by saying, "And so, helpless to contest this injustice, I leave now to seek my fortune elsewhere, perhaps even on another world."

Ailoura pondered a moment. "You say that your brother offered you a servant from our house?"

"Yes. But I don't intend to take him up on that promise. Having another mouth to feed would just hinder me."

Placing one mitteny yet deft hand on his chest, Ailoura said, "Take me, Gep Stoessl."

Geisen experienced a moment of confusion. "But Ailoura—your job of raising me is long past. I am very grateful for the loving care you gave unstintingly to a motherless lad, the guidance and direction you imparted, the indulgent playtimes we enjoyed. Your teachings left me with a wise set of principles, an admirable will and optimism, and a firm moral center—despite the evidence of my thoughtless transgression a moment ago. But your guardian duties lie in the past. And besides, why would you want to leave the comforts and security of Stoessl House?"

"Look at me closely, Gep Stoessl. I wear now the tabard of the scullery crew. My luck in finding you here is due only to this very demotion. And from here the slide to utter inutility is swift and short—despite my remaining vigor and craft. Will you leave me here to face my sorry fate? Or will you allow me to cast my fate with that of the boy I raised from kittenhood?"

Geisen thought a moment. "Some companionship would indeed be welcome. And I don't suppose I could find a more intimate ally."

Ailoura grinned. "Or a slyer one."

"Very well. You may accompany me. But on one condition."

"Yes, Gep Stoessl?"

"Cease calling me 'Gep.' Such formalities were once unknown between us."

Ailoura smiled. "Agreed, little Gei-gei."

The man winced. "No need to regress quite that far. Now, let us return to raiding my family's larder."

"Be sure to take some of that fine fish, if you please, Geisen."

No one knew the origin of the tame strangelets that seeded Chalk's strata. But everyone knew of the immense wealth these cloistered anomalies conferred.

Normal matter was composed of quarks in only two flavors: up and down. But strange-flavor quarks also existed, and the exotic substances formed by these strange quarks in combination with the more domestic flavors were, unconfined, as deadly as the more familiar antimatter. Bringing normal matter into contact with a naked strangelet resulted in the conversion of the feedstock into energy. Owning a strangelet was akin to owning a pet black hole, and just as useful for various purposes, such as powering star cruisers.

Humanity could create strangelets, but only at immense cost per unit. And naked strangelets had to be confined in electromagnetic or gravitic bottles during active use. They could also be quarantined for semipermanent storage in stasis fields. Such was the case with the buried strangelets of Chalk.

Small spherical mirrored nodules—"marbles," in the jargon of Chalk's prospectors—could be found in various recent sedimentary layers of the planet's crust, distributed according to no rational plan. Discovery of the marbles had inaugurated the reign of the various Houses on Chalk.

An early scientific expedition from Preceptimax University to the Shulamith Wadi stumbled upon the strangelets initially. Preceptor Fairservis, the curious discoverer of the first marble, had realized he was dealing with a stasis-bound

object and had unluckily managed to open it. The quantum
genie inside had promptly eaten the hapless fellow who
freed it, along with nine-tenths of the expedition, before beginning a sure but slow descent toward the core of Chalk.
Luckily, an emergency response team swiftly dispatched by
the planetary authorities had managed to activate a new en-
trapping marble as big as a small city, its lower hemisphere
underground, thus trapping the rogue.

After this incident, the formerly disdained deserts of
Chalk had experienced a land rush unparalleled in the
galaxy. Soon the entire planet was divided into domains—
many consisting of noncontiguous properties—each owned
by one House or another. Prospecting began in earnest then.
But the practice remained more an art than a science, as the
marbles remained stealthy to conventional detectors. Intuition, geological knowledge of strata, and sheer luck proved
the determining factors in the individual fortunes of the
Houses.

How the strangelets—plainly artifactual—came to be
buried beneath Chalk's soils and hardpan remained a mystery. No evidence of native intelligent inhabitants existed on
the planet prior to the arrival of humanity. Had a cloud of
strangelets been swept up out of space as Chalk made her
eternal orbits? Perhaps. Or had alien visitors planted the
strangelets for unimaginable reasons of their own? An
equally plausible theory.

Whatever the obscure history of the strangelets, their current utility was beyond argument.

They made many people rich.

And some people murderous.

In the shadow of the Tasso Escarpments, adjacent to the
Glabrous Drifts, Carrabas House sat desolate and melancholy, tenanted only by glass-tailed lizards and stilt-crabs,
its poverty-overtaken heirs dispersed anonymously across
the galaxy after a series of unwise investments, followed by
the unpredictable yet inevitable exhaustion of their marble-
bearing properties—a day against which Vomacht Stoessl
had more providently hedged his own family's fortunes.

Geisen's zipflyte crunched to a landing on one of the manse's grit-blown terraces, beside a gaping portico. The craft's doors swung open and pilot and passenger emerged. Ailoura now wore a set of utilitarian roughneck's clothing, tailored for her bestient physique and matching the outfit worn by her former charge, right down to the boots. Strapped to her waist was an antique yet lovingly maintained variable sword, its terminal bead currently dull and inactive.

"No one will trouble us here," Geisen said with confidence. "And we'll have a roof of sorts over our heads while we plot our next steps. As I recall from a visit some years ago, the west wing was the least damaged."

As Geisen began to haul supplies—a heater-cum-stove, sleeping bags and pads, water condensers—from their craft, Ailoura inhaled deeply the dry tangy air, her nose wrinkling expressively, then exhaled with zest. "Ah, freedom after so many years! It tastes brave, young Geisen!" Her claws slipped from their sheaths as she flexed her pads. She unclipped her sword and flicked it on, the seemingly untethered bead floating outward from the pommel a meter or so.

"You finish the monkey work. I'll clear the rats from our quarters," promised Ailoura, then bounded off before Geisen could stop her. Watching her unfettered tail disappear down a hall and around a corner, Geisen smiled, recalling childhood games of strength and skill where she had allowed him what he now realized were easy triumphs.

After no small time, Ailoura returned, licking her greasy lips.

"All ready for our habitation, Geisen-kitten."

"Very good. If the bold warrior will deign to lend a paw . . . ?"

Soon the pair had established housekeeping in a spacious, weatherproof ground floor room (with several handy exits), where a single leering window frame was easily covered by a sheet of translucent plastic. After distributing their goods and sweeping the floor clean of loess drifts, Geisen and Ailoura took a meal as their reward, the first of many such rude campfire repasts to come.

As they relaxed afterward, Geisen making notes with his stylus in a small pocket diary and Ailoura dragging her left paw continually over one ear, a querulous voice sounded from thin air.

"Who disturbs my weary peace?"

Instantly on their feet, standing back to back, the newcomers looked warily about. Ailoura snarled until Geisen hushed her. Seeing no one, Geisen at last inquired, "Who speaks?"

"I am the Carrabas marchwarden."

The man and bestient relaxed a trifle. "Impossible," said Geisen. "How do you derive your energy after all these years of abandonment and desuetude?"

The marchwarden chuckled with a trace of pride. "Long ago, without any human consent or prompting, while Carrabas House still flourished, I sunk a thermal tap downward hundreds of kilometers. The backup energy thus supplied is not much, compared with my old capacities, but has proved enough for sheer survival, albeit with much dormancy."

Ailoura hung her quiet sword back on her belt. "How have you kept sane since then, marchwarden?"

"Who says I have?"

Coming to terms with the semideranged Carrabas marchwarden required delicate negotiations. The protective majordomo simultaneously resented the trespassers—who did not share the honored Carrabas family lineage—yet on some different level welcomed their company and the satisfying chance to perform some of its programmed functions for them. Alternating ogreish threats with embarrassingly humble supplications, the marchwarden needed to hear just the right mix of defiance and thanks from the squatters to fully come over as their ally. Luckily, Ailoura, employing diplomatic wiles honed by decades of bestient subservience, perfectly supplemented Geisen's rather gruff and patronizing attitude. Eventually, the ghost of Carrabas House accepted them.

"I am afraid I can contribute little enough to your comfort, Gep Carrabas." During the negotiations, the marchwarden had somehow self-deludingly concluded that Geisen was indeed part of the lost lineage. "Some water, certainly, from my active conduits. But no other necessities such as heat or food, or any luxuries either. Alas, the days of my glory are long gone!"

"Are you still in touch with your peers?" asked Ailoura.

"Why, yes. The other Houses have not forgotten me. Many are sympathetic, though a few are haughty and indifferent."

Geisen shook his head in bemusement. "First I learn that the protective omniscience of the marchwardens may be circumvented. Next, that they keep up a private traffic and society. I begin to wonder who is the master and who is the servant in our global system."

"Leave these conundrums to the preceptors, Geisen. This unexpected mode of contact might come in handy for us some day."

The marchwarden's voice sounded enervated. "Will you require any more of me? I have overtaxed my energies, and need to shut down for a time."

"Please restore yourself fully."

Left alone, Geisen and Ailoura simultaneously realized how late the hour was and how tired they were. They bedded down in warm bodyquilts, and Geisen swiftly drifted off to sleep to the old tune of Ailoura's drowsy purring.

In the chilly viridian morning, over fish and kava, cat and man held a war council.

Geisen led with a bold assertion that nonetheless concealed a note of despair and resignation.

"Given your evident hunting prowess, Ailoura, and my knowledge of the land, I estimate that we can take half a dozen sandworms from those unclaimed public territories proved empty of strangelets, during the course of as many months. We'll peddle the skins for enough to get us both off-planet. I understand that lush homesteads are going begging on Nibbriglung. All that the extensive water meadows there require is a thorough desnailing before they're producing golden rice by the bushel—"

Ailoura's green eyes, so like Geisen's own, flashed with cool fire. "Insipidity! Toothlessness!" she hissed. "Turn farmer? Grub among the waterweeds like some *platypus?* Run away from those who killed your sire and cheated you out of your inheritance? I didn't raise such an unimaginative, unambitious coward, did I?"

Geisen sipped his drink to avoid making a hasty affronted rejoinder, then calmly said, "What do you recommend, then? I gave my legally binding promise not to contest any of the unfair terms laid down by my family, in return for freedom from prosecution. What choices does such a renunciation leave me? Shall you and I go live in the shabby slums that slump at the feet of the Houses? Or turn thief and raider and prey upon lonely mining encampments? Or shall we become freelance prospectors? I'd be good at the latter job, true, but bargaining with the Houses concerning hard-won information about their own properties is humiliating, and promises only slim returns. They hold all the high cards, and the supplicant offers only a mere saving of time."

"You're onto a true scent with this last idea. But not quite the paltry scheme you envision. What I propose is that we swindle those who swindled you. We won't gain back your whole patrimony, but you'll surely acquire greater sustaining riches than you would by flensing worms or flailing rice."

"Speak on."

"The first step involves a theft. But after that, only chicanery. To begin, we'll need a small lot of strangelets, enough to salt a claim everyone thought exhausted."

Geisen considered, buffing his raspy chin with his knuckles. "The morality is dubious. Still—I found a smallish deposit of marbles on Stoessl property during my aborted trip, and never managed to report it. They were in a flood-plain hard by the Nakhoda Range, newly exposed and ripe for the plucking without any large-scale mining activity that would attract satellite surveillance."

"Perfect! We'll use their own goods to con the ratlings! But once we have this grubstake, we'll need a proxy to deal with the Houses. Your own face and reputation must remain concealed until all deals are sealed airtight. Do you have knowledge of any such suitable foil?"

Geisen began to laugh. "Do I? Only the perfect rogue for the job!"

Ailoura came cleanly to her feet, although she could not repress a small grunt at an arthritic twinge provoked by a night on the hard floor. "Let us collect the strangelets first, and then enlist his help. With luck, we'll be sleeping on feathers and dining off golden plates in a few short weeks."

The sad and spectral voice of the abandoned marchwarden sounded. "Good morning, Gep Carrabas. I regret keenly my own serious incapacities as a host. But I have managed to heat up several liters of water for a bath, if such service appeals."

The eccentric caravan of Marco Bozzarias and his mistress Pigafetta had emerged from its minting pools as a top-of-the-line Baba Yaya model of the year 650 PS. Capacious and agile, larded with amenities, the moderately intelligent stilt-walking cabin had been designed to protect its inhabitants from climatic extremes in unswaying comfort while carrying them surefootedly over the roughest terrain. But plainly, for one reason or another (most likely poverty) Bozzarias had neglected the caravan's maintenance over the twenty-five years of its working life.

Raised now for privacy above the sands where Geisen's zipflyte rested, the vehicle-cum-residence canted several degrees, imparting a funhouse quality to its interior. Swellings at its many knee joints indicated a lack of proper nutrients. Additionally, the cabin itself had been patched with so many different materials—plastic, sandworm hide, canvas, chitin—that it more closely resembled a heap of debris than a deliberately designed domicile.

The caravan's owner, contrastingly, boasted an immaculate and stylish appearance. To judge by his handsome, mustachioed looks, the middle-aged Bozzarias was more stage-door idler than cactus hugger, displaying his trim figure proudly beneath crimson ripstop trews and utility vest over bare hirsute chest. Despite this urban promenader's facade, Bozzarias held a respectable record as a freelance prospector, having pinpointed for their owners several strangelet lodes of note, including the fabled Gosnold Pocket. For these services, he had been recompensed by the tightfisted landowners only a nearly invisible percentage of the eventual wealth claimed from the finds. Despite his current friendly grin, it would be impossible for Bozzarias not to harbor decades-worth of spite and jealousy.

Pigafetta, Bozzarias' bestient paramour, was a voluptuous, pink-skinned geisha clad in blue and green silks. Carrying perhaps a tad too much weight—hardly surprising, given her particular gattaca—Pigafetta radiated a slack and greasy carnality utterly at odds with Ailoura's crisp and dry efficiency. When the visitors had entered the cabin, before either of the humans could intervene, Geisen and Bozzarias had been treated to an instant but decisive bloodless catfight that had settled the pecking order between the moreauvians.

Now, while Pigafetta sulked winsomely in canted corner amid her cushions, the furry female victor consulted with the two men around a small table across which lay spilled the stolen strangelets, corralled from rolling by a line of empty liquor bottles.

Bozzarias poked at one of the deceptive marbles with seeming disinterest, while his dark eyes glittered with avarice. "Let me recapitulate. We represent to various buyers that these quantum baubles are merely the camel's nose showing beneath the tent of unconsidered wealth. A newly discovered lode on the Carrabas properties, of which you, Gep Carrabas—" Bozzarias leered at Geisen, "—are the rightful heir. We rook the fools for all we can get, then hie ourselves elsewhere, beyond their injured squawks and retributions. Am I correct in all particulars?"

Ailoura spoke first. "Yes, substantially."

"And what would my share of the take be? To depart forever my cherished Chalk would require a huge stake—"

"Don't try to make your life here sound glamorous or

even tolerable, Marco," Geisen said. "Everyone knows you're in debt up to your nose, and haven't had a strike in over a year. It's about time for you to change venues anyway. The days of the freelancer on Chalk are nearly over."

Bozzarias sighed dramatically, picking up a reflective marble and admiring himself in it. "I suppose you speak the truth—as it is commonly perceived. But a man of my talents can carve himself a niche anywhere. And Pigafetta *had* been begging me of late to launch her on a virtual career—"

"In other words," Ailoura interrupted, "you intend to pimp her as a porn star. Well, you'll need to relocate to a mediapoietic world then for sure. May we assume you'll become part of our scheme?"

Bozzarias set the marble down and said, "My pay?"

"Two strangelets from this very stock."

With the speed of a glass-tailed lizard Bozzarias scooped up and pocketed two spheres before the generous offer could be rescinded. "Done! Now, if you two will excuse me, I'll need to rehearse my role before we begin this deception."

Ailoura smiled, a disconcerting sight to those unfamiliar with her tender side. "Not quite so fast, Gep Bozzarias. If you'll just submit a moment—"

Before Bozzarias could protest, Ailoura had sprayed him about the head and shoulders with the contents of a pressurized can conjured from her pack.

"What! Pixie dust! This is a gross insult!"

Geisen adjusted the controls of his pocket diary. On the small screen appeared a jumbled, jittering image of the caravan's interior. As the self-assembling pixie dust cohesed around Bozzarias' eyes and ears, the image stabilized to reflect the prospector's visual point of view. Echoes of their speech emerged from the diary's speaker.

"As you well know," Ailoura advised, "the pixie dust is ineradicable and self-repairing. Only the ciphers we hold can deactivate it. Until then, all you see and hear will be shared with us. We intend to monitor you around the clock. And the diary's input is being shared with the Carrabas marchwarden, who has been told to watch for any traitorous actions on your part. That entity, by the way, is a little deranged, and might leap to conclusions about any actions that even verge on treachery. Oh, you'll also find that your left ear hosts a channel for our remote, ah, verbal advice. It would behoove you to follow our directions, since the dust is quite capable of liquefying your eyeballs upon command."

Seemingly inclined to protest further, Bozzarias suddenly thought better of dissenting. With a dispirited wave and nod, he signaled his acquiescence to their plans, becoming quietly businesslike.

"And to what Houses shall I offer this putative wealth?"

Geisen smiled. "To every House at first—except Stoessl."

"I see. Quite clever."

After Bozzarias had caused his caravan to kneel to the earth, he bade his new partners a desultory good-bye. But at the last minute, as Ailoura was stepping into the zipflyte, Bozzarias snagged Geisen by the sleeve and whispered in his ear.

"I'd trade that rude servant in for a mindless pleasure model, my friend, were I you. She's much too tricky for comfort."

"But, Marco—that's exactly why I cherish her."

Three weeks after first employing the wily Bozzarias in their scam, Geisen and Ailoura sat in their primitive quarters at Carrabas House, huddled nervously around Geisen's diary, awaiting transmission of the meeting they had long anticipated. The diary's screen revealed the familiar landscape around Stoessl House as seen from the windows of the speeding zipflyte carrying their agent to his appointment with Woda, Gitten, and Grafton.

During the past weeks, Ailoura's plot had matured, succeeding beyond their highest expectations.

Representing himself as the agent for a mysteriously returned heir of the long-abandoned Carrabas estate—a fellow who preferred anonymity for the moment—Bozzarias had visited all the biggest and most influential Houses— excluding the Stoessls—with his sample strangelets. A major new find had been described, with its coordinates freely given and inspections invited. The visiting teams of geologists reported what appeared to be a rich new lode, deceived by Geisen's expert saltings. And no single House dared attempt a midnight raid on the unprotected new strike, given the vigilance of all the others.

The cooperative and willing playacting of the Carrabas marchwarden had been essential. First, once its existence was revealed, the discarded entity's very survival became a seven-day wonder, compelling a willing suspension of disbelief in all the lies that followed. Confirming the mystery man as a true Carrabas, the marchwarden also added its jiggered testimony to verify the discovery.

Bozzarias had informed the greedily gaping families that the returned Carrabas scion had no desire to play an active role in mining and selling his strangelets. The whole estate—with many more potential strangelet nodes—would be sold to the highest bidder.

Offers began to pour in, steadily escalating. These included feverish bids from the Stoessls, which were rejected without comment. Finally, after such high-handed treatment, the offended clan demanded to know why they were being excluded from the auction. Bozzarias responded that he would convey that information only in a private meeting.

To this climactic interrogation the wily rogue now flew.

Geisen turned away from the monotonous video on his diary and asked Ailoura a question he had long contemplated but always forborne from voicing.

"Ailoura, what can you tell me of my mother?"

The cat-woman assumed a reflective expression that cloaked more emotions than it revealed. Her whiskers twitched. "Why do you ask such an irrelevant question at this crucial juncture, Gei-gei?"

"I don't know. I've often pondered the matter. Maybe I'm fearful that if our plan explodes in our faces, this might be my final opportunity to learn anything."

Ailoura paused a long while before answering. "I was intimately familiar with the one who bore you. I think her intentions were honorable. I know she loved you dearly. She always wanted to make herself known to you, but circumstances beyond her control did not permit such an honest relationship."

Geisen contemplated this information. Something told him he would get no more from the closemouthed bestient.

To disrupt the solemn mood, Ailoura reached over to ruffle Geisen's hair. "Enough of the useless past. Didn't anyone ever tell you that curiosity killed the cat? Now, pay attention! Our Judas goat has landed—"

Ursine yet doughy, unctuous yet fleering, Grafton clapped Bozzarias' shoulder heartily and ushered the foppish man to a seat in Vomacht's study. Behind the dead padrone's desk sat his widow, Woda, all motile maquillage and mimicked mourning. Her teeth sported a fashionable gilt. Gitten lounged on the arm of a sofa, plainly bored and resentful, toying with a handheld hologame like some sullen adolescent.

After offering drinks—Bozzarias requested and received the finest vintage of sparkling wine available on Chalk—Grafton drove straight to the heart of the matter.

"Gep Bozzarias, I demand to know why Stoessl House has been denied a chance to bid on the Carrabas estate."

Bozzarias drained his glass and dabbed at his lips with his jabot before replying. "The reason is simple, Gep Stoessl, yet of such delicacy that you would not have cared to have me state it before your peers. Thus this private encounter."

"Go on."

"My employer, Timor Carrabas, you must learn, is a man of punctilio and politesse. Having abandoned Chalk many generations ago, Carrabas House still honors and maintains the old ways prevalent during that golden age. They have not fallen into the lax and immoral fashions of the present, and absolutely condemn such behavior."

Grafton stiffened. "To what do you refer? Stoessl House is guilty of no such infringements on custom."

"That is not how my employer perceives affairs. After all, what is the very first thing he hears upon returning to his ancestral homeworld? Disturbing rumors of patricide, fraternal infighting, and excommunication, all of which emanate from Stoessl House and Stoessl House alone. Leery of stepping beneath the shadow of such a cloud, he could not ethically undertake any dealings with your clan."

Fuming, Grafton started to rebut these charges, but Woda intervened. "Gep Bozzarias, all mandated investigations into the death of my beloved Vomacht resulted in one uncontested conclusion: pump failure produced a kind of alien hyperglycemia that drove the Stroonians insane. No human culpability or intent to harm was ever established."

Bozzarias held his glass up for a refill and obtained one. "Why, then, were all the bestient witnesses to the incident terminally disposed of? What motivated the abdication of your youngest scion? Giger, I believe he was named?"

Trying to be helpful, Gitten jumped into the conversation. "Oh, we use up bestients at a frightful rate! If they're not dying from floggings, they're collapsing from overuse in the mines and brothels. Such a flawed product line, these moreauvians. Why, if they were robots, they'd never pass consumer-lab testing. As for Geisen—that's the boy's name—well, he simply got fed up with our civilized lifestyle. He always did prefer the barbaric outback existence. No doubt he's enjoying himself right now, wallowing in some muddy oasis with a sandworm concubine."

Grafton cut off his brother's tittering with a savage glance. "Gep Bozzarias, I'm certain that if your employer were to meet us, he'd find we are worthy of making an offer on his properties. In fact, he could avoid all the fuss and bother of a full-fledged auction, since I'm prepared right now to trump the highest bid he's yet received. Will you convey to him my invitation to enjoy the hospitality of Stoessl House?"

Bozzarias closed his eyes ruminatively, as if harkening to some inner voice of conscience, then answered, "Yes, I can do that much. And with some small encouragement, I would exert all my powers of persuasiveness—"

Woda spoke. "Why, where did this small but heavy bag of Tancredi moonstones come from? It certainly doesn't belong to us. Gep Bozzarias—would you do me the immense favor of tracking down the rightful owner of these misplaced gems?"

Bozzarias stood and bowed, then accepted the bribe. "My pleasure, madame. I can practically guarantee that Stoessl House will soon receive its just reward."

"Sandworm concubine!" Geisen appeared ready to hurl his eavesdropping device to the hard floor, but restrained himself. "How I'd like to smash their lying mouths in!"

Ailoura grinned. "You must show more restraint than that, Geisen, especially when you come face-to-face with the scoundrels. Take consolation from the fact that mere physical retribution would hurt them far less than the loss of money and face we will inflict."

"Still, there's a certain satisfaction in feeling the impact of fist on flesh."

"My kind calls it 'the joy when teeth meet bone,' so I fully comprehend. Just not this time. Understood?"

Geisen impulsively hugged the old cat. "Still teaching me, Ailoura?"

"Until I die, I suppose."

"You are appallingly obese, Geisen. Your form recalls nothing of the slim blade who cut such wide swaths among the girls of the various Houses before his engagement."

"And your polecat coloration, fair Ailoura, along with those tinted lenses and tooth caps, speak not of a bold mouser, but of a scavenger through garbage tips."

Regarding each other with satisfaction, Ailoura and Geisen thus approved of their disguises.

With the aid of Bozzarias, who had purchased for them various sophisticated, semiliving prosthetics, dyes, and off-world clothing, the man and his servant—Timor Carrabas and Hepzibah—resembled no one ever seen before on Chalk. His pasty face rouged, Geisen wobbled as he waddled, breathing stertorously, while the limping Ailoura diffused a moderately repulsive scent calculated to keep the curious at a certain remove.

The Carrabas marchwarden now spoke, a touch of excite-

ment in its artificial voice. "I have just notified my Stoessl
House counterpart that you are departing within the hour.
You will be expected in time for essences and banquet, with
a half hour allotted to freshen up and settle into your guest
rooms."

"Very good. Rehearse the rest of the plan for me."

"Once the funds are transferred from Stoessl House to
me, I will in turn upload them to the Bourse on Feuilles
Mortes under the name of Geisen Stoessl, where they will
be immune from attachment. I will then retreat to my soul-
canister, readying it for removal by your agent, Bozzarias,
who will bring it to the space field—specifically the terminal hosting Gravkosmos Interstellar. Beyond that point, I
cannot be of service until I am haptically enabled once
more."

"You have the scheme perfectly. Now we thank you, and
leave with the promise that we shall talk again in the near future, in a more pleasant place."

"Good-bye, Gep Carrabas, and good luck."

Within a short time the hired zipflyte arrived. (It would
hardly do for the eminent Timor Carrabas to appear in
Geisen's battered craft, which had, in point of fact, already
been sold to raise additional funds to aid their subterfuge.)
After clambering clumsily on board, the schemers settled
themselves in the spacious rear seat while the chauffeur—a
neat-plumaged and discreet raptor-derived bestient—lifted
off and flew at a swift clip toward Stoessl House.

Ailoura's comment about Geisen's attractiveness to his
female peers had set an unhealed sore spot within him
aching. "Do you imagine, Hepzibah, that other local lumi-
naries might attend this evening's dinner party? I had in
mind a certain Gep Bloedwyn Vermeule."

"I suspect she will. The Stoessls and the Vermeules have
bonds and alliances dating back centuries."

Geisen mused dreamily. "I wonder if she will be as beautiful and sensitive and angelic as I have heard tell she is."

Ailoura began to hack from deep in her throat. Recovering, she apologized, "Excuse me, Gep Carrabas. Something
unpleasant in my throat. No doubt a simple hairball."

Geisen did not look amused. "You cannot deny reports of the lady's beauty, Hepzibah."

"Beauty is as beauty does master."

The largest ballroom in Stoessl House had been extravagantly bedecked for the arrival of Timor Carrabas. Living luminescent lianas in dozens of neon tones festooned the heavy-beamed rafters. Decorator dust migrated invisibly about the chamber, cohering at random into wallscreens showing various entertaining videos from the mediapoietic worlds. Responsive carpets the texture of moss crept warily along the tessellated floor, consuming any spilled food and drink wasted from the large collation spread out across a servitor-staffed table long as a playing field. (House chef Stine Pursiful oversaw all with a meticulous eye, his upraised ladle serving as baton of command. After some argument among the family members and chef, a buffet had been chosen over a sit-down meal, as being more informal, relaxed, and conducive to easy dealings.) The floor space was thronged with over a hundred gaily caparisoned representatives of the Houses most closely allied to the Stoessls, some dancing in stately pavanes to the music from the throats of the octet of avian bestients perched on their multibranched stand. But despite the many diversions of music, food, drink, and chatter, all eyes had strayed ineluctably to the form of the mysterious Timor Carrabas when he entered, and from time to time thereafter.

Beneath his prosthetics, Geisen now sweated copiously, both from nervousness and the heat. Luckily, his disguising adjuncts quite capably metabolized this betraying moisture before it ever reached his clothing.

The initial meeting with his brothers and stepmother had gone well. Hands were shaken all around without anyone suspecting that the flabby hand of Timor Carrabas concealed a slimmer one that ached to deliver vengeful blows.

Geisen could see immediately that since Vomacht's death, Grafton had easily assumed the role of head of household, with Woda patently the power behind the throne and Gitten content to act the wastrel princeling.

"So, Gep Carrabas," Grafton oleaginously purred, "now you finally perceive with your own eyes that we Stoessls are no monsters. It's never wise to give gossip any credence."

Gitten said, "But gossip is the only kind of talk that makes life worth liv—oof!"

Woda took a second step forward, relieving the painful pressure she had inflicted on her younger son's foot. "Excuse my clumsiness, Gep Carrabas, in my eagerness to enhance my proximity to a living reminder of the fine old ways of Chalk. I'm sure you can teach us much about how our forefathers lived. Despite personal longevity, we have lost the institutional rigor your clan has reputedly preserved."

In his device-modulated, rather fulsome voice, Geisen answered, "I am always happy to share my treasures with others, be they spiritual or material."

Grafton brightened. "This expansiveness bodes well for our later negotiations, Gep Carrabas. I must say that your attitude is not exactly as your servant Bozzarias conveyed."

Geisen made a dismissive wave. "Simply a local hireling who was not truly privy to my thoughts. But he has the virtue of following my bidding without the need to know any of my ulterior motivations." Geisen felt relieved to have planted that line to protect Bozzarias in the nasty wake of the successful conclusion of their thimblerigging. "Here is my real counselor. Hepzibah, step forward."

Ailoura moved within the circle of speakers, her unnaturally flared and pungent striped musteline tail waving perilously close to the humans. "At your service, Gep."

The Stoessls involuntarily cringed away from the unpleasant odor wafting from Ailoura, then restrained their impolite reaction.

"Ah, quite an, ah, impressive moreauvian. Positively, um, redolent of the ribosartor's art. Perhaps your, erm, adviser would care to dine with others of her kind."

"Hepzibah, you are dismissed until I need you."

"As you wish."

Soon Geisen was swept up in a round of introductions to people he had known all his life. Eventually he reached the food, and fell to eating rather too greedily. After weeks spent subsisting on MREs alone, he could hardly restrain himself. And his glutton's disguise allowed all excess. Let the other guests gape at his immoderate behavior. They were constrained by their own greed for his putative fortune from saying a word.

After satisfying his hunger, Geisen finally looked up from his empty plate.

There stood Bloedwyn Vermeule.

Geisen's ex-fiancée had never shone more alluringly. Threaded with invisible flexing pseudo-myofibrils, her long unfettered hair waved in continual delicate movement, as if she were a mermaid underwater. She wore a gown tonight loomed from golden spider silk. Her lips were verdigris, matched by her nails and eye shadow.

Geisen hastily dabbed at his own lips with his napkin, and was mortified to see the clean cloth come away with enough stains to represent a child's immoderate battle with an entire chocolate cake.

"Oh, Gep Carrabas, I hope I am not interrupting your gustatory pleasures."

"Nuh—no, young lady, not at all. I am fully sated. And you are?"

"Gep Bloedwyn Vermeule. You may call me by my first name, if you grant me the same privilege."

"But naturally."

"May I offer an alternative pleasure, Timor, in the form of a dance? Assuming your satiation does not extend to *all* recreations."

"Certainly. If you'll make allowances in advance for my clumsiness."

Bloedwyn allowed the tip of her tongue delicately to traverse her patinaed lips. "As the Dompatta says, 'An earnest rider compensates for a balky steed.'"

This bit of familiar gospel had never sounded so lascivious. Geisen was shocked at this unexpected temptress behavior from his ex-fiancée. But before he could react with real or mock indignation, Bloedwyn had whirled him out onto the floor.

They essayed several complicated dances before Geisen, pleading fatigue, could convince his partner to call a halt to the activity.

"Let us recover ourselves in solitude on the terrace," Bloedwyn said, and conducted Geisen by the arm through a pressure curtain and onto an unlit open-air patio. Alone in the shadows, they took up positions braced against a balustrade. The view of the moon-drenched arroyos below occupied them in silence for a time. Then Bloedwyn spoke huskily.

"You exude a foreign, experienced sensuality, Timor, to which I find myself vulnerable. Perhaps you would indulge my weakness with an assignation tonight, in a private chamber of Stoessl House known to me? After any important business dealings are successfully concluded, of course."

Geisen seethed inwardly, but managed to control his voice. "I am flattered that you find a seasoned fellow of my girth so attractive, Bloedwyn. But I do not wish to cause any intermural incidents. Surely you are affianced to someone, a young lad both bold and wiry, jealous and strong."

"Pah! I do not care for young men, they are all chowderheads! Pawing, puling, insensitive, shallow, and vain, to a man! I was betrothed to one such, but luckily he revealed his true colors and I was able to cast him aside like the churl he proved to be."

Now Geisen felt only miserable self-pity. He could summon no words, and Bloedwyn took his silence for assent. She planted a kiss on his cheek, then whispered directly into his ear. "Here's a map to the boudoir where I'll be waiting. Simply take the east squeezer down three levels, then follow the hot dust." She pressed a slip of paper into his hand, supplementing her message with extra pressure in his palm, then sashayed away like a tainted sylph.

Geisen spent half an hour with his mind roiling before he regained the confidence to return to the party.

Before too long, Grafton corralled him.

"Are you enjoying yourself, Timor? The food agrees? The essences elevate? The ladies are pliant? Haw! But perhaps we should turn our minds to business now, before we both grow too muzzy-headed. After conducting our dull commerce, we can cut loose."

"I am ready. Let me summon my aide."

"That skun— That is, if you absolutely insist. But surely our marchwarden can offer any support services you need. Notarization, citation of past deeds, and so forth."

"No. I rely on Hepzibah implicitly."

Grafton partially suppressed a frown. "Very well, then."

Once Ailoura arrived from the servants' table, the trio headed toward Vomacht's old study. Geisen had to remind himself not to turn down any "unknown" corridor before Grafton himself did.

Seated in the very room where he had been fleeced of his patrimony and threatened with false charges of murder, Geisen listened with half an ear while Grafton outlined the terms of the prospective sale: all the Carrabas properties and whatever wealth of strangelets they contained, in exchange for a sum greater than the Gross Plantetary Product of many smaller worlds.

Ailoura attended more carefully to the contract, even pointing out to Geisen a buried clause that would have made payment contingent on the first month's production from the new fields. After some arguing, the conspirators succeeded in having the objectionable codicil removed. The transfer of funds would be complete and instantaneous.

When Grafton had finally finished explaining the conditions, Geisen roused himself. He found it easy to sound bored with the whole deal, since his elaborate scam, at its moment of triumph, afforded him surprisingly little vengeful pleasure.

"All the details seem perfectly managed, Gep Stoessl, with that one small change of ours included. I have but one question. How do I know that the black sheep of your House, Geisen, will not contest our agreement? He seems a contrary sort, from what I've heard, and I would hate to be involved in judicial proceedings, should he get a whim in his head."

Grafton settled back in his chair with a broad smile. "Fear not, Timor! That wild hair will get up no one's arse! Geisen has been effectively rendered powerless. As was only proper and correct, I assure you, for he was not a true Stoessl at all."

Geisen's heart skipped a cycle. "Oh? How so?"

"The lad was a chimera! A product of the ribosartors! Old Vomacht was unsatisfied with the vagaries of honest mating that had produced Gitten and myself from the noble stock of our mother. Traditional methods of reproduction had not delivered him a suitable toady. So he resolved to craft a better heir. He used most of his own germ plasm as foundation, but supplemented his nucleotides with dozens of other snippets. Why, that hybrid boy even carried bestient genes. Rat and weasel, I'm willing to bet! Haw! No, Geisen had no place in our family."

"And his mother?"

"Once the egg was crafted and fertilized, Vomacht implanted it in a host bitch. One of our own bestients. I misapprehend her name now, after all these years. Amorica, Orella, something of that nature. I never really paid attention to her fate after she delivered her human whelp. I have more important properties to look after. No doubt she ended up on the offal heap, like all the rest of her kind."

A red curtain drifting across Geisen's vision failed to occlude the shape of the massive aurochs-flaying blade hanging on the wall. One swift leap and it would be in his hands. Then Grafton would know sweet murderous pain, and Geisen's bitter heart would applaud—

Standing beside Geisen, Ailoura let slip the quietest cough.

Geisen looked into her face.

A lone tear crept from the corner of one feline eye.

Geisen gathered himself and stood up, unspeaking.

Grafton grew a trifle alarmed. "Is there anything the matter, Gep Carrabas?"

"No, Gep Stoessl, not at all. Merely that old hurts pain me, and I would fain relieve them. Let us close our deal. I am content."

The star liner carrying Geisen, Ailoura, and the stasis-bound Carrabas marchwarden to a new life sped through the interstices of the cosmos, powered perhaps by a strangelet mined from Stoessl lands. In one of the lounges, the man and his cat nursed drinks and snacks, admiring the exotic variety of their fellow passengers and reveling in their hardwon liberty and security.

"Where from here—son?" asked Ailoura with a hint of unwonted shyness.

Geisen smiled. "Why, wherever we wish, Mother dear."

"Rowr! A world with plenty of fish, then, for me!"

The Names of All the Spirits

BY J. R. DUNN

J. R. Dunn lives in New Jersey, which he describes as "a small, barbarous region between New York and Pennsylvania." He's sold to most of the magazines, including Analog, Asimov's, Omni, Century, *and* Amazing. *Most of his stories have been cited on best-of-year lists, with many selected for anthologies. His novels include* This Side of Judgment *(1994),* Days of Cain *(1997), and* Full Tide of Night *(1998). He is an accomplished writer with a clear, lucid style.*

"The Names of all the Spirits" appeared online at SciFiction, and this is its first print appearance. It concerns the isolated space miners who work in the outer solar system, in an era when powerful, threatening artificial intelligences are on the loose outside the sphere of human control. But Dunn's vision of the situation, seen through the investigation of a Mandate agent into the mystery of a miner who survived when he should not have, transforms this standard SF situation in a compelling way.

It was a busier sky than I was used to. The stars were invisible, outshone by an apparently solid tower of light dominating the view out the window. It was about as wide as an outstretched hand, narrowing steadily to a point high enough to make me tilt my head before twisting into a curve and vanishing from sight. Or perhaps not completely so: obscured by a fog of leakage, a thin filament that might be its distant tail extended into a darkness not quite the absolute black of space. At eye level another stream flowed off at a right angle, pure white to the tower's mottled yellow, ending in a sunburst bright enough to make me squint.

It was all very impressive, an undertaking of a scale you don't often find inside the system, almost astronomical in both scope and imagery. And I was impressed, on the intellectual, so-many-megatons-per-second level. But nothing more. Similar operations were going on all across this lobe of the cometary halo. If you've seen one, you've seen 'em all. I've seen one.

Somebody Solward needed ice cubes. That's what it came down to. Those two streams were stripped comets, hydrocarbons separated from volatiles and each sent off in different directions, to freeze again in the cold of extrasolar space. The ice would be shipped in while the hydrocarbons and solids remained. They wouldn't go far, not as we judge distances these days, and somebody, someday in the fullness of time, would find a use for them.

A rustle of impatience recalled me to the room. The window reflected the scene behind me: a dozen or so figures in a motley array of gear centered on a man perched on a small chair. One of them seemed to have grown a second head directly atop his first in the time my back had been turned. I realized it was a piece of scrim resting on a shelf behind him. Not even jacks are that weird.

I turned to the seated man. Through some means I couldn't detect (the place wasn't spinning, that much was certain), they'd created a one-gee field. If meant as a courtesy, it was misplaced—I'd been out in Kuiper-Oort as long as any of them. "Let's hear your side, Morgan. That's what I came for."

The only sound was a voice muttering, ". . . n't have a side."

Morgan himself simply stared, saying nothing, the same as he had the first two times I'd asked the question. He could well have been tranced, lost in a private world or daydream, though some small tremor of attention told me he was not.

I'd thought it was going to be easy. Open and shut, as the ancient phrase went. Get the story out of Morgan, lase it in, take him into custody and back to the System by the swiftest means possible, without even waiting for a reply. They'd given me the impression he'd talked, which was obviously not the case. I shouldn't have questioned him in front of them. A single glance at this crew—Morgan's workmates, the "Powder Monkeys," of all conceivable names—was enough to strike terror into a sponge.

But I didn't think it was fear holding Morgan back. It was something else. Something I was going to get at, however deep I had to go. Because this was no mere legal matter, and Rog Morgan was not simply a jack in trouble. This was an impi problem, and Morgan was my ticket home.

I saw no point in anymore questions. I turned to Witcove. "You've got a secure spot for him?"

"He ain't going noplace, Sandoval." Witcove snorted. "We got his processor and remotes."

I raised a hand. "Why don't you give me those."

Witcove frowned. He hadn't quite worked out how to handle me yet. Who was I, after all, but one man come out of the dark? What gave me the right to throw my mass around? Where did I get off giving orders to the foreman of the Powder Monkeys?

Mystique came to my rescue. Back on the Blue Rock, at a time when Texas was—in the mind's system of measurement, anyway—only marginally smaller than the Halo, there existed an organization with a mission not at all unlike the Mandate's and the motto, "One riot, one Ranger." A single Texas Ranger could be relied on to ride into any given bad town and straighten the place out with only his two hands and the sure knowledge that hundreds just like him were ready to saddle up. It seldom failed.

It didn't fail now. With a grunt, Witcove reached into a thigh pouch and pulled out what appeared to be a handful of black geometrical solids of various sizes. Forgetting we were under gee, he made as if to toss them to me, curtailing the throw at the very last second as the thought occurred to him. He succeeded only in scattering components across the floor between us.

That triggered the kind of laughter you'd expect, along with the first visible reaction from Morgan as he gazed at the components with an expression mixing frustration and annoyance. Somebody was living behind that vacuum-habituated mask after all.

At my feet the scattered remotes began to move, sliding together to form a little pile. Witcove swung on Morgan with a wordless roar.

The components went still. With a sigh of impatience Morgan looked away. "Once more, mister," Witcove told him. "You issue one more command and I will personally—"

"Foreman . . ." Witcove raised his eyebrows. Someone stepped forward to collect the remotes and hand them to me. I was absently thanking him when I felt a burst of heat in my palm. The jack kept his eyes lowered. "Foreman, can we break things up for the moment?"

"Sure, you . . . got enough for now."

"I do."

Behind him two crewmen hustled Morgan to his feet and out the exit. I moved off, pretending interest in the scrim collection. Scrim is the vacuum jack's one notable hobby, dig-nified as art by some. Small carvings comprised of aster-oidal junk, scrap, what have you, of a size easily carried in a suit pouch and worked on at odd moments with atelier re-motes and occasionally heavier machinery. Scrim touches every subject matter conceivable: women, ships, animals, vehicles, instruments, self-portraits, and items not easily catalogued. It wasn't crude. They worked on it too long for that, almost obsessively, often overshooting the baroque to land deep in the grotesque. I didn't care for scrim. It spoke to me only of loneliness and exile.

Witcove sidled up next to me. "You come to a decision, you'll . . ."

"I'll let you know."

That wasn't precisely what he wanted to hear. "Look . . ." he glanced behind him. Morgan had vanished. "He's not gonna tell you anything. It's locked up. Something wrong there. When the runaways grab a guy—"

"Shift change in five," somebody said. The room began clearing. I gestured at Witcove, half thanks, half dismissal.

"I'll let you know," I repeated.

Clearly dissatisfied, he walked off. A crewman inter-cepted him to talk operations. With a final glance in my di-rection, Witcove left.

The room empty at last, I reached into my pocket. The components made a handful. The big one, an inch and a half by two, had to be the processor, a lifetime of experience and training imbedded within it. I wondered what Witcove would do if somebody abused his. The other nine were re-mote sensors, appendages, actuators, the vacuum jack's tools of the trade. With these, a jack could see into the in-frared and radio ranges, expand his sensory horizon a hun-dred or a thousand miles, control instruments and machinery that far away and more. I examined one resembling a length of thick wire. A jack would be able to tell exactly what make it was, its capabilities, its cost. Hard to believe that zero-gee work was once done with tools held in gloved hands. . . .

Something in my palm emitted a flash. I looked down. Five seconds passed before the flash repeated. Dropping the thin piece, I picked up a sphere that my thumb revealed to be flattened on one end. A glow appeared as I held it at eye level, a glow made up of words. I smiled. A tap and a shake failed to evoke anything further. I popped the remote into a pocket and stared off into space, only to have my gaze arrested by a particularly odd piece of scrim. I picked it up. Close inspection failed to tell me what in Heaven, Hell, or the Halo it was supposed to represent. It fell over when I set it down. Someone once told me that oceanic sailors had produced something like scrim. It seems unlikely. Hard to see what they'd have used for material.

Whoever cracks the impi problem can write his own ticket. They were out there. That much was known. Rogues, duppies, runaways . . . impis, in a word. Artificial Intelligences that had slipped away, one day here, overseeing a refinery, shepherding a comet, repairing a system, the next gone, with never a sign of where. Only five or six a year, but numbers build. Surely they existed in the hundreds by now, a group large enough to leave undeniable evidence of its presence: signals encoded so deeply that ages wouldn't decrypt them, resources diverted to open trajectories, hacking that revealed the signature of machine capabilities, along with missing vessels, inexplicable damage to isolated machinery, individuals vanished into night.

Discover a path into the impi's kingdom, learn the names of the spirits, find the hidden places where they slept, and you would be set. You'd be the man with the expert's badge, and everyone would have to come to you. Back amid civilization, operating from behind a screen at Charon or even Triton, with a sun in the sky and a society around you. No more years spent in the cold and dark, enduring the grinding boredom of Kuiper-Oort, no more confrontations with misfits suitable only for work on the edge of civilization.

Standing orders stated that suspect human-renegade interaction took precedence over all other activities—criminal investigation, medical evacuation, mercy mission, what have you. We had no idea where they were, what they were doing, what motivated them. The stories were legion—they were evolving into something alien and malevolent. They were duplicating themselves, running off copies like cheap commercial ware, pushing their numbers into the millions or even higher. They were out to take over the Halo or sweep back into the system and brush humanity right off the board. All no more than rumor, urban legend on the grand scale.

But what had happened here was no legend, and I was already plotting the quickest, most energy-intensive, least-number-of-stops course back into the system.

I stepped to the window. A v-jack passed about fifty yards away, turning to regard me as he went. I wondered if he was my contact. I eyed the remote. The one that didn't belong to Rog Morgan.

There was neither flash nor glimmer nor repeat of the message: "Meet in 1 hr." Three-quarters of that hour remained. The Halo had taught me patience, but that was still forty-five minutes too many for the way I was feeling.

My skin tautened as I stepped into vacuum and the striated tissue in my third dermal layer reacted. I paused while my airway valves adjusted themselves, squinted against the sudden pressure of the retinal membranes. My system was nowhere near as elaborate as those of the crew—I could remain in vacuum a few hours at most, and I lacked radiation protection—but neither situation was a factor here. Time was irrelevant, the only radiation the odd cosmic ray.

The one-gee pull continued, giving me cause to wonder whether they'd been doing me a favor after all. Stepping to the platform's edge, I took a look around.

There's no such thing as resupply in the Halo. You either bring it along, fabricate it, or do without, and the crews with the broadest capabilities get the best jobs. The Powder Monkeys were no slouches at capability, as any offhand examination of their work hall revealed. A structure of considerable size, several hundred yards in each dimension of a space that could be called a rough-to-the-extreme cube, the object within it having no particular relation to any actual shape whatsoever. A hall is part warehouse, part refinery, part industrial center, part barracks, and part vehicle, though no amount of study could separate one component from the other amid the mass of catapults, effectuators, nets, tankage, piping, cables, power sources, and mystery boxes.

Beneath my feet the glare of the work area silhouetted the torpedo shape of my ride. As much as I shaded my eyes I could make out next to nothing; it was too hazy for details. I felt a rumbling which gave me a short spell of goosebumps: a jack had mentioned that vapor pressure sometimes got so high you could actually hear the cometary fluids being pumped. On second thought, I decided it was more likely some piece of machinery within the hall.

Five minutes passed without anyone showing up. I was early, but I also suspected that time-honored motive common to all such situations: the urge not to be seen ratting to a cop. I took out the remote. I still had no idea what it was for, which was probably begging the question—most models were multifunctional.

Without turning, I took a step back toward the lock. The remote flashed red, obligingly repeated when I moved to the left. A swing to the right resulted in a reassuring green. I looked around, fulfilling the age-old cop tradition of trying not to be spotted before a meet, then took another step. The remote blinked green once again.

The gee-field's disappearance at the edge of the platform didn't quite take me unaware, though I was glad no one was around to criticize my form when I kicked off. I landed on a catwalk that swung 90° around a dark box with a man-sized "3" painted on the side before plunging into the fractal mess of the hall. Inside I passed a quivering set of tanks, ducked beneath some pipes, then went up a ramp and through a pressurized area (no oxygen—my skin remained taut) before again turning toward the hall's exterior. Back in the open I endured a moment's confusion while figuring out that the remote wanted me to go vertical, up the side of a huge tank open to space, its top invisible from where I stood. I was well past the curve before I caught sight of him, waiting at the crown of the tank in an enclosure containing pumping controls. He floated above the platform, legs crossed, helmetless head slightly bowed, eyes taking in endless night.

I felt a flash of irritation. A monastic—wasn't that fine.

Not everyone out here is schizo. We get all kinds: the grand pioneers who can't live without a frontier to push at, researchers trying to pin answers on various arcane questions (e.g., whether Kuiper-Oort is a strictly local phenomenon or simply the solar portion of a cometary field stretching across the whole wide Universe), the odd tourist aching to be able to say that he'd *really* been further out than anybody else, fugitives on the run from assorted cops or tongs, and these: the seekers, contemplatives in search of some kind of spirituality evidently unavailable inside the Heliopause, looking for the ultimate quiet place that might hold a door into the center of things.

There's a lot of them, following every conceivable religion, system, or cult, even a few original to themselves, and while I don't disrespect them, they're not the first I'd go to for any given set of facts.

So it was with a sense of wasted time that I finally reached the platform. As I'd expected, it was the small man who'd handed me the remotes. He displayed no reaction as I slipped a foot through the railing to steady myself, simply continued gazing off into the abyss, face as blank as the sky itself. It would be just my luck to show up seconds after this guy had at last made contact with the infinite ground of being.

We were on the far side of the hall, shielded from the work site. The sky was darker here, though not as dark as open space—about the same as a moonlit night on Earth. Knowing we were facing home, I tried to find Sol. I could have used one of the crew's processors to tell me if it was that particularly bright one there . . .

I glanced over to find the man's eyes on me. He took me by surprise, and it was a moment before I showed him the remote, mouthed "Yours, I suppose," and flicked it in his direction.

He tossed it right back, with the quick precise movement of a trained v-jack. I was clumsier in catching it. As I did he touched his ear. I imitated him. The remote stuck thanks to some force of its own.

"Right there." He pointed at the bright dot I'd been watching a moment before. "So it is," I replied, not bothering to move my lips.

"Don't look like much, eh?"

"You come out here a lot?"

"Enough." He could have been meditating again, for all the animation he revealed. "Morg ain't workin' with no duppies."

"I didn't think he was," I told him. "What was he doing?"

"What happens with him?"

"I get him out of here, one way or another."

He raised a finger. "Now . . . I tell you once. No testify, no repeat, nothing."

"Just for the record, why not?"

He faced me again. "I don't stand with cops, I don't stand with courts."

"Fair enough."

"OK. All this happen last year, before Morg join up with the Monkeys . . . You know what stridin' is, right?" I nodded. You don't have to spend much time in the Halo to grasp the nature of striding. Space travel is expensive. In Kuiper-Oort, the cost is multiplied by distance, rarity, and demand. Like workers everywhere, vacuum jacks have methods of cutting corners. One is to fit their suits out with extra oxy, power, and supplies, get somebody to launch them by catapult in the precise direction of their destination, then trance down for the weeks or months required to get there. Somebody else will snag them with a probe when at last they arrive.

Dangerous, you say? Yeah, it's dangerous, as the Mandate, most companies, and every active authority in the Halo never cease repeating. It does no good. Jacks are proud of striding, as they are of every other aspect of living like rodents in the outer dark. There's betting over length, speed, and duration of trip, same as with any other insanely stupid activity Sapiens comes up with. I met the current record holder once. Eighteen months in a trajectory of ten AUs. He's a little hard to understand due to slight, untreatable brain damage, but quite pleased with himself all the same. Cats will bask in the street, kids will tag rides on trucks, and jacks will stride. A certain inevitable percentage will get run over, flung onto the pavement, or miss their rendezvous.

Which was what happened to Rog Morgan. Few stride alone, in case of emergencies. There were five jacks, bored with the job or after a better offer or just hankering to move, who set out on a month-long, quarter-AU journey to the second-nearest site. The other four were picked up. Not Morgan. Somebody erred, and even as the others awoke from their weeks-long trance, he kept going.

Days passed before he became aware of his situation. He responded as a jack, and jacks take things in order. He checked the time. He checked the charts. He tried the radio. Then he went through it all again, step by step, before allowing himself to stare the thing in the face.

It's impossible to say what he felt. There's nothing to compare it to. No man in a lifeboat, or stranded in a desert, or broken and freezing on any pole was ever as alone as Rog Morgan was at that moment. No fear is so great, no regret so deep, as can grow in that place that is no place, where space and time are as close to bare as we are ever likely to know them. We can't grasp what Morgan felt, any more than he could afterward; it was simply too vast for memory to hold. But consider this: out of the handful of lost striders recovered (a half-dozen out of hundreds, who happened to be aimed Solward, toward the more populous sections of the Halo), five shut down their systems and blew their helmets in preference to enduring another second of what Morgan faced.

At last his panic and grief receded enough to allow him to resume control. He made a hopeless survey of known work sites, outposts, and Mandate stations to confirm what he already knew. Settled points are few and far between in the Halo, and he would pass none of them.

He composed a mayday and set his comm system to repeat it on the most power-stingy schedule that made sense. He noted that he was headed in the direction of Sagittarius, a section of sky that he would grow to hate as much as he'd ever hated anything. He turned his head slightly to take in Sol. He patted a side pocket holding a piece of scrim he'd been working on for years. He ate a cracker. And then, jacks being stolid types and Morgan more so than most, he tranced down.

He traveled a measurable percentage of the width of the solar system before he again awoke. Nothing had changed. He had not expected that anything would. The stars remained frozen. The radio wavelengths were quiet. The world was doing just fine without Rog Morgan. He contemplated the fact, sipped a little glucose, some water, threw a curse or two at Sagittarius, and went back to sleep.

He didn't know how many times he awoke after that. More than twice, fewer than ten. They were all the same, and he recalled little more than that sameness. The only thing that varied was difficulty. His power cells began to give out. Then his small store of food. (He put aside some dried fruit, some protein, a few ounces of glucose in case he should need it, but somewhere along the line, without ever remembering, he ate it all.) Jacks use very little water, being enhanced to recycle most of that amount, but even a little gains in importance when you can't find it. It seemed that between the cold, the hunger, and the thirst (all of which he could control but not evade), Rog Morgan was going to become a member of that elite among men who are killed by more things than one.

Ketosis set in a short time later. The only sign that his body was cannibalizing his own muscular mass was an abiding and growing sense of weakness far more complete than any he had ever felt before.

If he dreamed he never spoke of it, and as for prayer, well, a priest once told me that all men pray when things get bad enough. Morgan didn't say if he did. But I think what Father Danziger meant was that they often pray without knowing it. Maybe hanging on as long as he did, far longer than most could, was Morgan's form of prayer.

After a while the dreams turned concrete. His metabolism was breaking down, slowly but inevitably poisoning itself with byproducts it was unable to shed. His dreams began to speak, and he began to answer back. He found himself explaining things to whatever was listening, to Sagittarius, to his past, to something closer than both that he shortly became convinced was contemplating him from out in the dark. He told it how ravaged he was, how lost, how little he had done with his time, how many mistakes he'd made before this last, fatal one. What he might have done had he not been so sure of himself. What he would do if he were given another lifetime to do it in.

At last he ran down. No answer had come, but he had expected none. A sense of clarity had returned to him, the clarity of approaching night. His mind was as focused as it was ever going to be again. He checked his systems, the way a jack does. Everything, every last element capable of measurement, was deep into the red. It would have horrified him a few weeks ago. Now it didn't bother him at all.

He unsnapped a battery pouch and with fingers scarcely able to feel put in his ID and a few other personal items. At the last minute he paused to take out the piece of scrim. He held it a moment before slipping it back. He sealed the pouch. With as much strength as he could gather he threw it in the direction of Sol. He watched for a second or two, telling himself he could see it dwindle toward home.

He listened to the silence, the silence he would be part of within minutes. He looked out at Sagittarius, considering whether there were any words to match what he now knew. He found none. He licked cracked lips with a dry, swollen tongue. "So that's it . . ."

Later he would have sworn that he heard it before actually hearing it, that somehow he'd gotten some echo of it as it surged across the shrunken space his universe had become: "No it's not."

I don't know what alerted me to the fact that the jack had vanished. I didn't see him go. The remote went silent, and when I looked up, he'd disappeared. I wasted no time searching—there were too many places he could have gone. What had sent him away was another question, answered the minute I bent over the railing to see three jacks approaching from below. I switched to open freq.

". . . it's him."

"It's the mandy." The two wearing helmets waved.

"Yeah, it's me," I told them, trying to keep any trace of annoyance out of my voice. The third was as bareheaded as my contact. Once you're fitted with vacuum mods, helmets are unnecessary, really. People wear them for the same reason they do at construction sites on Earth, that and the fact that a helmet carries a lot of instrumentation and apps. "A jack's office," you often hear them called.

I backed away as the one in the lead shot a line and reeled them all in, the other two hanging on to various suit projections. "Taking a look at home?" the leader bawled as he hooked a foot under the top rail.

"That's Sol right there." Second helmet indicated a star totally separate and discrete from the one my contact had pointed out.

"Thanks," I said. I must have sounded more stiff than I intended—the lead jack raised a hand and said, "We feel a whole lot better now you're here."

"How's that?"

"That duppie, man—"

"Ever see an impi close up . . . ?"

"Wait—" glanced between them. The one lacking a helmet said nothing, simply continued staring. I wondered if he was out of the loop. "You guys actually saw it? You were there?"

"I was," the lead jack said.

"What happened?"

"Well, it was like this—"

"That thing came out of nowhere—" the second helmet said.

"Wait one . . ." I pointed at the lead jack. "How'd it start?"

"We were over the other side of the cracker, inspecting the MHD loops—"

"Cracker's what busts up the comets and separates the fluids, see."

"Yeah, and loops are the things . . . well, they're not things, they're fields. They separate and contain the fluids, so they're important. Particularly down near the cracker mouth. Lot of pressure there. Loop starts oscillating, you get leakage—"

"Contaminate the product," second helmet said.

"Right. So—"

"So you keep an eye on it," I said, hoping to move him along.

"Inspect 'em once a day," first helmet nodded.

"And it ain't easy."

"Hard to see down there."

"That's right. Hydrocarbon-water fog. Sticky, wet, screws with your remote signals."

"You gotta look close," second helmet held up his hands to show me how close. "Loops are tight, down near the mouth. Just millimeters apart, vibrating to pump the fluids. And you're *matter*, right? Solid *matter*. So you can slip right through the field—"

"And they find you froze down around Venus in sixty years."

I was getting the picture. Hazardous duty, not something you wanted to be interrupted doing. "So you were inspecting the . . . loops."

"Right, six of us. Working our way out from the mouth, one loop after the other, like a cone, see. Almost out of the haze into open space. And there she was."

"She? How'd you know it was a 'she'?"

The leader gaped at me. Hard as it is to read expression on a vacuum-adapted face, I knew puzzlement when I saw it. He glanced at his partner. The one with no helmet just stared.

"Don't worry about it," I told them. "She was there."

"Right. We might not of noticed except she grazed a remote—"

"Stash's."

"Yeah. Stash thinks its debris broke out of the processing stream—"

"Then he says, 'holy shit!' "

"Yeah, when he sees the readout. Modulated signals, shielded and enciphered, no ID—"

I crossed my arms. "So what'd you do?"

"We got the hell outta there!"

"And she came right after 'em!"

Second helmet was, if anything, more excited than the one who had actually been there. I had a feeling I'd have gotten a nice, wild, blood-and-thunder yarn out of him, accuracy be damned. "Go ahead."

"We yell for help, and kinda spread out with the thing in the middle, see. Pasha—that's Rey Murat, the string chief, we call him Pasha—grabs our remotes to fill in the gaps. He can do that—he's got the codes. He says close in, throw an EMP at it. Knock it out or slow it down, at least."

"What did it look like?"

"Hard to say—it brought some fog with it, like a plasma? Couldn't make out the shape."

I nodded, picturing it in my mind: the surrounding haze aglare in the work lights, the rough sphere of spacesuited jacks, that unknown and unknowable blob dashing around between them.

"So the rest of the shift comes around the funnel—"

"I saw this part!"

"It went straight at Morg—"

"And he let it through."

I contemplated that for a moment. They watched me in something approaching anxiety. Finally I nodded.

"Then Pasha started yelling—"

"Yeah, and Wit, back in the hall. Wanting to know what was goin' on—"

"—thing just zipped off, jamming every possible freq—"

"It was fast—"

"Then you busted Morgan." They looked at each other.

"Right."

"He say anything?"

They shook their heads. "No idea what the AI was doing?"

"It was up to something—"

"You can't tell. They get too strange. They need humans around to keep 'em straight—"

"None of you guys thought of making a recording?"

"Oh yeah!"

"Sure we did. The remotes copied. That's SOP in case of a mishap. Wit confiscated 'em all."

"Witcove did?"

"Right. Said he wanted to keep the evidence clean."

I was thinking of a reply when the helmetless one slipped off the railing and shot toward me. Halting himself with one foot, he glared at me from a yard away.

"You guys got remotes too?"

I touched the unit at my ear. "Uhh . . . yeah. Sometimes. Not everybody."

He frowned. "What make is that?"

"Ah, that's a Kiwi," the second jack said. "Remi's got one of them."

Mr. No-Helmet nodded. "Good unit. High-density, lotta options."

"Uh-huh," I told him. "They mentioned that at the outlet."

Satisfied, he resumed his silent perch.

"Tell me something . . ." I looked between them. "What if Morgan was guilty?"

Making a slicing noise, No-Helmet pulled a finger across his throat, with a smile I could have done without.

"Yeah," the leader agreed. "I hate to say it, but—"

"Once they touch a guy, he's no good anymore."

I was prepared to ask where they'd ever come across anyone who'd been "touched," but decided to pass. All I'd succeed in doing would be to release the entire corpus of impi campfire lore, and there was no point in that.

"So where you guys headed?"

"Oh, we just finished shift," second helmet said.

"We're going to eat some real food."

"Just did three 24s in vac," second helmet said proudly.

"Three straight?" I understood that a lot of jacks actually like spending time in vacuum. "That's pretty good."

The leader swung around without using his hands, the way jacks do. Second helmet followed him with a pleased-to-meet-ya thrown in my direction. But no-helmet remained where he was. I waited a moment, and was about to ask what his immediate plans were when he bent forward.

"Whatcha gotta do to become a cop?"

Act sane, for starters. "Fill out an ap, send it in. They'll get in touch."

"Where I get an ap?"

I had him give me his address and ordered my ship to send him one. "You can put my name on it," I told him.

"Deep," he said. His head swung toward a spot over my right shoulder. "He's right up there," he said. "Ha."

Behind what appeared to be an open-vacuum junk drawer two levels up rose a small boxlike shape with a single lit window. When I turned back no-helmet too had kicked off. I watched him go, thinking about scapegoats, the pressures of living in this kind of truncated society, and what happened to people who break the unwritten but unbendable rules. But mostly I thought about the possible reasons why Witcove had kept the recordings from me.

"Hey, mandy." I touched the remote. "Yeah, Remi." He chuckled. "Mind I stay down, eh?" "Suit yourself. Lot of traffic. Now . . . Morgan had just passed out."

"You sharp. He did pass out."

It doesn't take much in the way of sharpness to grasp how a man dying of starvation and cold would react on hearing a voice where no voice was possible.

When he awoke, he was in a room that was comfortable for all its unfamiliarity. He was lying on a cot of some sort, and for reasons he didn't bother to examine, he felt no urge to get up. It wasn't that he was too weak, he simply wasn't inclined, and that was all. He heard music, melodies of Earth, almost recognizable though he couldn't quite place them. He had a memory—an impression—that one had been playing while he was being brought there.

It occurred to him to look around. He took in the sight of the medical drip with no surprise. Even after centuries of advances, there's no better method of getting a lot of material into the bloodstream fast than a tube in a vein. He clenched his fist, smiled at the wave of tiredness that overcame him and closed his eyes. When he opened them again she was standing there.

You can imagine what she looked like to him, after all the way he'd come, after what he'd been through. Women aren't common in the Halo. They're not rare either, but time often passes before a jack encounters one. And to put it gently, many of them are the female equivalents of the type of male yoyo that calls Kuio home. But nothing ever destroys the deep, instinctive connection of the human female with safety and security. That's the way she appeared to him, symbol made flesh, a saint in stained glass.

With later developments in mind, it's easy to speculate that she molded the image to match Morgan's own expectations, working from cues he was unaware of and wouldn't have been able to change if he had been. The room was dark, and though he could clearly see the silver bracelets on her wrists, the necklace, the pair of roses growing from her scalp and intertwined with her hair in that old style that often fades but always returns, her face was clouded, her features hazy.

"How you feeling?" was the first thing she said. Morgan didn't remember what he replied, but it pleased her; her wide smile made that clear. He made an attempt at the usual questions, but she just lay a hand on the blanket, and told him, "You rest."

He reached for that hand but wasn't quick enough to grasp it before she turned and walked away. She looked back only once, when he asked her name.

He lay down in pain, in disorientation, in discomfort, but beneath it all with that indescribable sensation that assured him he was going to live.

She returned the next day, and he saw that she looked exactly as he might have guessed. When he answered her questions about how he felt, she cocked her head in a way that he almost recognized. He didn't remain awake very long that day, or the next either, just long enough for her to tell him a story about where he was and what had happened that isn't worth repeating because it wasn't true. But that didn't matter to him at the time, nor did he suspect it. Because he was in no concrete place at all, really. He was in that safe place we leave behind in childhood, and revisit only in memory.

He remained there two weeks. He slept most of the next few days—he assumed there was a sedative in the feed coming down that tube. Whenever he awoke she was there, or arrived momentarily. Never anyone but her, though he had the impression—gained he didn't know how—that others were around. But it was she who examined him, who checked the medical machinery, who talked to him, who read to him, who helped him pass the time required for him to regain his strength.

It was the better part of a week before he could eat. She let him feed himself—a bowl of clear broth. He kept it down, and there was solid food to come, small portions so he wouldn't be tempted to stuff. She didn't eat anything.

At last, the time came for him to get up and exercise the muscles wasted by the weeks of his scarcely-remembered ordeal. She encouraged him to get up by himself, stepping back to give him room. He did well, taking five full steps to a chair and then back to the bed after resting a bit. She was pleased with him, enough so that he wanted to try it again right away. She told him it was better to wait.

He must have been a touch overconfident the next day. That or wanting to please her or maybe a mix of both. He went a step further than he should have, a little faster than was necessary. She was living out her own fantasy too, in whatever way an AI does, because when he lost his balance, she moved to catch him, and her hand went straight through his outstretched arm.

"Wait one," I muttered. More alert now, I'd spotted a movement below as a figure appeared over the curve of the tank. Even at that distance I knew it was Witcove. I gestured Remi to remain down.

I maintained a blank expression as Witcove approached. He landed with a grunt. "So . . . how's it going?"

"Out catching a little sun."

"Little . . ." he frowned. "Oh . . . little sun. Sure. Heh-heh . . . Say, I was taking a look at your ship. Quite a bird."

"Gets me around."

"Surprised how quick you got here, but . . . this is kind of an important thing, I guess. I mean, lot of people interested, right? Might go straight back to Charon, or maybe even deeper."

I nodded.

"So . . . word will get around. People will talk. Unless they maybe . . . classify it? But there's such things as leaks, too. See, you can't win."

He shook his head and sighed. "Y'know, you get work out here by rep. Word of mouth. Somebody says, Powder Monkeys do a great job, never have to tell 'em things twice . . . That's how you get hired. No other way—advertising, bidding, forget about it. You need a good rep. And you don't get one overnight see, takes decades of hard, solid work. We got a good rep, the Monkeys. And we get our share of contracts. But here's the thing . . ."

He bent close, his grotesque, vacuum-adapted face all intent. "People hear there's runaways hanging around the hall, and one of the Monkeys well, working with it. Now that wouldn't be so good. For the reputation, see. So I been thinking about that."

"Go on."

"What I was thinking, what if it happened different. What if Morgan quit. A few weeks back. Not too long ago, month or two. What if nobody could say, 'Rog Morgan, Powder Monkey.' What about that?"

"You're saying you want me to falsify a report."

"Noooo—I'm not saying that." Witcove snorted at my obtuseness. "But if you waited a bit, so I could mess with Morgan's files, see, I could make it look like he was forty AUs from here, with another outfit, or prospecting on his own . . . yeah, that'd be best. He quit and went out on his own. Come back to trade for supplies. Say, I ever tell you that the Monkeys are a public company?"

He bobbed his head. "That's right. PM plc. Traded on all the big boards. Stock went up another tick last week. Never drops. Better than blue chip. We got a pretty good-size block of unassigned certificates right in my office and what do you say about that report?"

"I could change it." I pronounced the words carefully, trying to hide the disgust I felt. Witcove seemed to shrink into himself with relief. "Sure. Or I could bust you and lock you up in my ship this minute."

He stared at me in utter silence. "Or maybe freeze your systems and let you wait six or seven months for a magistrate to come by."

His eye membranes flicked once, as if he was blinking. "Nah—we'll go for the bust." Raising my voice as if it could, in fact, carry through vacuum, I contacted the ship. ". . . prepare space for a single perp, charge attempted bribery of a Mandate law enforcement officer, that calls for maximum security, I believe."

Witcove came back to life, waving his arms wildly, swinging his head in all directions as if to catch the ship sneaking up on him. I watched him for a moment.

"Or maybe we won't do that either." He went still, arms extended. "Instead, maybe you'll give me the recordings you held back, you simple SOB."

His arms fell and he recited the codes in a monotone. He remained silent as I sent them on to the ship with instructions to go through them for anomalies. "Wasn't just for me," he muttered after I finished. "I was thinking of the guys—"

"I know that."

Witcove wasn't bad. There were any number worse scattered across the Halo. Foremen and plant owners who didn't think of the guys at all, or thought of them only to cheat them, terrorize them, abuse them, let them down in every conceivable way. Whatever Witcove might be, he wasn't one of them. He was on the high end, as such things are graded. "Now go on."

I stopped him as he swung over the railing. "What's the code to that shed lock?"

He gave it to me and left without another word.

Remi chuckled. "Knew you'd do that," I grimaced. As if I'd take a bribe in front of a witness.

"Go on with the story, Remi."

"Not much to tell. When he looked up she was gone, and he went back to bed lay there thinking. You know that old story about the guy the munchkins took away to Manhattan? Only there couple weeks but when he got back it was centuries and everybody was dead, and he had him a long beard. Ever hear that one?"

"Something like it, yeah."

"I mean, duppies. What they want? Who knows? Who's gonna hang around find out? So he waited til it was real quiet, and got up. His suit was right outside the door, like it was waiting for him. He put it on, ran a check. All powered up, reservoirs full, and there was extra supply packs stacked on the floor. He went down this hallway, and round the corner the lights were on, leading to what sure as hell looked like a lock. He went over, and he's just about to step in and he stops, 'cause he's sure, see, they gonna grab him . . ."

Right then I got a buzz from the ship. Slipping the handset from my belt, I read a message about the recorder footage. I told it to play.

". . . got in the lock, about to shut the door and he stops again. Helmet still open, see. Heard a sound from inside. A song, way quiet, like she was saying goodbye . . ."

The scene playing on my handset was much as I'd imagined it: the brightly-lit haze, the jacks spread out, that unwelcome entity feinting between them. A flashing caret marked Rog Morgan. I watched as the impi swung toward him, as his hands rose, as the thing slipped past into open sky.

"And whacha think he did?"

The screen displayed another angle of the same scene: Jacks, Morgan, the impi . . . I lifted the set, paying close attention to his hands. "Turned around, went back."

"You got it!" Remi sounded delighted.

I called for a closeup of Morgan's hands, went through it twice in slow motion. "Yeah, that's what he did. And she came in a few minutes later, and he was on the bed in his suit, and he said, 'I like that song.' I'da kept going."

"So would I."

The screen began another replay. I canceled and it went dark. No point in watching it again. There was not a single doubt in my mind as to what had occurred. "Remi . . . I thank you, the Mandate thanks you . . ." I looked up at the shed's single lonely window. I didn't think Morgan was going to thank him.

I started toward the shed, muscles quivering, mind ablaze with that feeling you get only when a case is coming together. A warning notice flashed as I approached the next level. I kicked up and over, barely pausing to catch my balance as I landed.

The impis had gotten to him. There was no way around it; the footage was clear. Morgan was in full and witting contact with rogue entities and all that implied. It was the break we'd been waiting for, the first sign of an active human/impi organization.

I needed immediate backup, every ship within a month's radius. The hall's higher-level activities would have to be frozen, to make sure it didn't wander off. A lot of people would be coming to look the place over. They'd be studying this hall down all the way down to the gluons for years to come. As for Morgan . . . I didn't want to think about that part.

I paused at the door, almost breathless. With quick stabs I punched in the code. I charged inside before it was half open. "Okay, ace—what did she pass to you?"

Morgan barely started. He gave me a mournful look, then reached into his jacket pocket. He gazed down at the object in his hand and with a sigh tossed it to me.

It was a piece of scrim. I'd seen that even as he took it out. I hefted it. Some kind of metal, an alloy I couldn't identify. The bust of a woman, head cocked to one side, a smile on her face, hair lifting away as if blown by an invisible breeze.

I raised my eyes to Morgan. "She went . . . You're telling me the impi went after this for you."

"No." Morgan shook his head. "Alerted some others. They picked it up."

I turned the statuette over in my hand. It's hollow, I told myself. Imprinted on the molecular level with some message, some command . . .

I examined the face once again, the laughing eyes, the lips so lifelike they seemed about to speak, to give word to everything Morgan had left behind: light, and warmth, air to breathe. He'd put a lot of work into the thing. It occurred to me, somewhat belatedly, that it was a portrait of someone he knew. Had once known. No wonder he wanted it back.

For a second or two my mind struggled against the evidence of simple kindness, desperate for a reason to raise the alarm after all. But it wasn't hollow, and contained nothing, and it wouldn't take me anywhere. I tossed it back to Morgan. "Nice piece." I got out of my handset. "Okay—does our little pal have a name?"

"Isis," he said softly. I had to ask him to repeat it.

I left the door unlocked. The hall's top level was only a few yards overhead. I kicked off for it, setting down amidst a jungle of antennas and cables and junk. That grand glowing tube of dirty-yellow muck towered above me. I eyed it with the weariness of years, seeing my own youth vanish over that bright curve, its roaring song fading relentlessly into gray. Some are meant for the sunlight and some for the shadowed places. It was pretty clear to me which portion was mine.

Morgan hadn't told me much; whatever didn't feel like betrayal. I'd lase it back to Charon, where they'd give it to some specialist to ponder. Maybe they'd find more in it than I had. I doubted it.

"Hey, mandy." I turned to see Remi gazing at me through his helmet visor, ready, I suppose, to go on shift. It was a moment before I recalled the remote riding on my ear. I plucked it off and handed it back.

"All straighten out?"

"More or less. He'll be ready to leave tomorrow. He wants you to run the catapult."

"He ain't stridin' again?"

"Not like he has a lot to worry about."

"Ahh . . . I gotcha."

"Nice to have friends," I said. He shook his head. "Can't stand him myself. He chatters."

I watched him leave. For a moment he was silhouetted against the tower, and I saw him as an impi might, a human figure outlined by light. Then he vanished, the way jacks do.

It wasn't as dark as it had been. The shadows had lifted somewhat. I knew the names of one of the spirits, the right questions to ask, and the fact that the dragons might not be dragons after all. A pretty good day, all considered.

I looked over my shoulder toward home. The stars glared back, but I couldn't, for the life of me, decide which was which. After a moment I gave up and went to tell Witcove how it was going to be.

Grandma

CAROL EMSHWILLER

*Carol Emshwiller (www.sfwa.org/members/emshwiller/)
lives in New York City and has been publishing in the SF
field since the 1950s, when her attractive image graced the
covers of many SF books and magazines illustrated by her
husband, Ed Emshwiller, who signed his paintings EMSH.
By the early 1970s, her fiction had moved into the area of
the literary avant-garde, and she became a respected feminist writer as well—her first story collection was* Joy in Our
Cause *(1975). Her career flowered in the last decade or so,
with several collections of stories—*Verging on the Pertinent
(1989), The Start of the End of it All *(1990), and* Report to
the Men's Club *(2002)—and three novels—*Carmen Dog
(1990), Ledoyt *(1995),* Leaping Man Hill *(1999), and* The
Mount *(2002). In the year 2002, she published at least four
fine new stories and two books.*

"Grandma," from F&SF, *is a feminist SF story rich in
metaphorical resonances, perhaps a satire on superheroes,
or perhaps at the same time an allegory of generational
changes in feminism. Grandma was a superhero (sort of like
Wonder Woman) in her younger days, who spent her time
righting wrongs and defending justice. She could fly through
the air, wore a special costume, and was world-famous. Now
she is quite old, and her granddaughter (who, in the shadow
of her reputation, feels that she can never do anything right)
lives with her in the country.*

Grandma used to be a woman of action. She wore tights. She had big boobs, but a teeny weeny bra. Her waist used to be twenty-four inches. Before she got so hunched over she could do way more than a hundred of everything, pushups, sit-ups, chinning. . . . She had naturally curly hair. Now it's dry and fine and she's a little bit bald. She wears a babushka all the time and never takes her teeth out when I'm around or lets me see where she keeps them, though of course I know. She won't say how old she is. She says the books about her are all wrong, but, she says, that's her own fault. For a long while she lied about her age and other things, too.

She used to be on every search and rescue team all across these mountains. I think she might still be able to rescue people. Small ones. Her set of weights is in the basement. She has a punching bag. She used to kick it, too, but I don't know if she still can do that. I hear her thumping and grunting around down there—even now when she needs a cane for walking. And talk about getting up off the couch!

I go down to that gym myself sometimes and try to lift those weights. I punch at her punching bag. (I can't reach it except by standing on a box. When I try to kick it, I always fall over.)

Back in the olden days Grandma wasn't as shy as she is now. How could she be and do all she did? But now she doesn't want to be a bother. She says she never wanted to be a bother, just help out is all.

She doesn't expect any of us to follow in her footsteps.

She used to, but not anymore. We're a big disappointment. She doesn't say so, but we have to be. By now she's given up on all of us. Everybody has.

It started . . . we started with the idea of selective breeding. Everybody wanted more like Grandma: strong, fast thinking, fast acting, and with the *desire* . . . that's the most important thing . . . a desire for her kind of life, a life of several hours in the gym every single day. Grandma loved it. She says (and says and says), "I'd turn on some banjo music and make it all into a dance."

Back when Grandma was young, offspring weren't even thought of since who was there around good enough for her to marry? Besides, everybody thought she'd last forever. How could somebody like her get old? is what they thought.

She had three . . . "husbands" they called them (donors more like it), first a triathlon champion, then a prize fighter, then a ballet dancer.

There's this old wives tale of skipping generations, so, after nothing good happened with her children, Grandma (and everybody else) thought, surely it would be us grandchildren. But we're a motley crew. Nobody pays any attention to us anymore.

I'm the runt. I'm small for my age, my foot turns in, my teeth stick out, I have a lazy eye. . . . There's lots of work to be done on me. Grandma's paying for all of it though she knows I'll never amount to much of anything. I wear a dozen different kinds of braces, teeth, feet, a patch over my good eye. My grandfather, the ballet dancer!

Sometimes I wonder why Grandma does all this for me, a puny, limping, limp-haired girl? What I think is, I'm her *real* baby at last. They didn't let her have any time off to look after her own children—not ever until now when she's too old for rescuing people. She not only was on all the search and rescue teams, she was a dozen search and rescue teams all by herself, and often she had to rescue the search and rescue teams.

Not only that, she also rescued animals. She always said the planet would die without its creatures. You'd see her leaping over mountains with a deer under each arm. She moved bears from camp grounds to where they wouldn't cause trouble. You'd see her with handfuls of rattlesnakes gathered from golf courses and carports, flying them off to places where people would be safe from them and they'd be safe from people.

She even tried to rescue the climate, pulling and pushing at the clouds. Holding back floods. Reraveling the ozone. She carried huge sacks of water to the trees of one great dying forest. In the long run there was only failure. Even after all those rescues, always only failure. The bears came back. The rattlesnakes came back.

Grandma gets to thinking all her good deeds went wrong. Lots of times she had to let go and save . . . maybe five babies and drop three. I mean, even Grandma only had two arms. She expected more of herself. I always say, "You did save lots of people. You kept that forest alive ten years longer than expected. And me. *I'm* saved." That always makes her laugh, and I *am* saved. She says, "I guess my one good eye can see well enough to look after you, you rapscallion."

She took me in after my parents died. (She couldn't save them. There are some things you just can't do anything about no matter who you are, like drunken drivers. Besides, you can't be everywhere.)

When she took me to care for, she was already feeble. We needed each other. She'd never be able to get along without me. I'm the saver of the saver.

How did we end up this way, way out here in the country with me her only helper? Did she scare everybody else off with her neediness? Or maybe people couldn't stand to see how far down she's come from what she used to be. And I suppose she has gotten difficult, but I'm used to her. I hardly notice. But she's so busy trying not to be a bother she's a bother. I have to read her mind. When she holds her arms around herself, I get her old red sweatshirt with her emblem on the front. When she says, "*Oh* dear," I get her a cup of green tea. When she's on the couch and struggles and leans forward on her cane, trembling, I pull her up. She likes quiet. She likes for me to sit by her, lean against her, and listen to the birds along with her. Or listen to her stories. We don't have a radio or TV set. They conked out a long time ago and no one thought to get us new ones, but we don't need them. We never wanted them in the first place.

Grandma sits me down beside her, the lettuce planted, the mulberries picked, sometimes a mulberry pie already made (I helped), and we just sit. "I had a grandma," she'll say, "though I know, to look at me, it doesn't seem like I could have. I'm older than most grandmas ever get to be, but we all had grandmas, even me. Picture that: Every single person in the world with a grandma." Then she giggles. She still has her girlish giggle. She says, "Mother didn't know what to make of me. I was opening her jars for her before I was three years old. Mother. . . . Even that was a long time ago."

When she's in a sad mood she says everything went wrong. People she had just rescued died a week later of something that Grandma couldn't have helped. Hantavirus or some such that they got from vacuuming a closed room, though sometimes Grandma had just warned them not to do that. (Grandma believes in prevention as much as in rescuing.)

I've rescued things. Lots of them. Nothing went wrong either. I rescued a junco with a broken wing. After rains I've rescued stranded worms from the wet driveway and put them back in our vegetable garden. I didn't let Grandma cut the suckers off our fruit trees. I rescued mice from sticky traps. I fed a litter of feral kittens and got fleas and worms from them. Maybe this rescuing is the one part of Grandma I inherited.

Who's to say which is more worthwhile, pushing atom bombs far out into space or one of these little things I do? Well, I do know which is more important, but if I were the junco I'd like being rescued.

Sometimes Grandma goes out, though rarely. She gets to feeling it's a necessity. She wears sunglasses and a big floppy hat and scarves that hide her wrinkled-up face and neck. She still rides a bicycle. She's so wobbly it's scary to see her trying to balance herself down the road. I can't look.

She likes to bring back ice-cream for me, maybe get me a comic book and a licorice stick to chew on as I read it. I suppose in town they just take her for a crazy lady, which I guess she is.

When visitors come to take a look at her I always say she isn't home, but where else would a very, very, very old lady be but mostly home? If she knew people had come she'd have hobbled out to see them and probably scared them half to death. And they probably wouldn't have believed it was her, anyway. Only the president of the Town and Country Bank—she rescued him a long time ago—I let him in. He'll sit with her for a while. He's old but of course not as old as she is. And he likes her for herself. They talked all through his rescue and really got to know each other back then. They talked about tomato plants and wildflowers and birds. When she rescued him they were flying up with the wild geese. (They still talk about all those geese they flew with and how exciting that was with all the honking and the sound of wings flapping right beside them. I get goose bumps—geese bumps?—just hearing them talk about it.) She should have married somebody like him, potbelly, pock-marked face and all. Maybe we'd have turned out better.

I guess you could say I'm the one that killed her—*caused* her death, anyway. I don't know what got into me. Lots of times I don't know what gets into me and lots of times I kind of run away for a couple of hours. Grandma knows about it. She doesn't mind. Sometimes she even tells me, "Go on. Get out of here for a while." But this time I put on her old tights and one of the teeny tiny bras. I don't have breasts yet so I stuffed the cups with Kleenex. I knew I couldn't do any of the things Grandma did, I just thought it would be fun to pretend for a little while.

I started out toward the hill. It's a long walk but you get to go through a batch of piñons. But first you have to go up an arroyo. Grandma's cape dragged over the rocks and sand behind me. It was heavy, too. To look at the satiny red outside you'd think it would be light, but it has a felt lining. "Warm and waterproof," Grandma said. I could hardly walk. How did she ever manage to fly around in it?

I didn't get very far before I found a jackrabbit lying in the middle of the arroyo half dead (but half alive, too), all bit and torn. I'll bet I'm the one that scared off whatever it was that did that. That rabbit was a goner if I didn't rescue it. I was a little afraid because wounded rabbits bite. Grandma's cape was just the right thing to wrap it in so it wouldn't.

Those jackrabbits weigh a lot. And with the added weight of the cape. . . .

Well, all I did was sprain my ankle. I mean I wasn't really hurt. I always have the knife Grandma gave me. I cut some strips off the cape and bound myself up good and tight. It isn't as if Grandma has a lot of capes. This is her only one. I felt bad about cutting it. I put the rabbit across my shoulders. It was slow going but I wasn't leaving the rabbit for whatever it was to finish eating it. It began to be twilight. Grandma knows I can't see well in twilight. The trouble is, though she used to see like an eagle, Grandma can't see very well anymore either.

She tried to fly, as she used to do. She *did* fly. For my sake. She skimmed along just barely above the sage and bitterbrush, her feet snagging at the taller ones. That was all the lift she could get. I could see, by the way she leaned and flopped like a dolphin, that she was trying to get higher. She was calling, "Sweetheart. Sweetheart. Where are yooooowwwww?" Her voice was almost as loud as it used to be. It echoed all across the mountains.

"Grandma, go back. I'll be all right." My voice can be loud, too.

She heard me. Her ears are still as sharp as a mule's.

The way she flew was kind of like she rides a bicycle. All wobbly. Veering off from side to side, up and down, too. I knew she would crack up. And she looked funny flying around in her print dress. She only has one costume and I was wearing it.

"Grandma, go back. Please go back."

She wasn't at all like she used to be. A little fall like that from just a few feet up would never have hurt her a couple of years ago. Or even last year. Even if, as she did, she landed on her head.

I covered her with sand and brush as best I could. No doubt whatever was about to eat the rabbit would come gnaw on her. She wouldn't mind. She always said she wanted to give herself back to the land. She used to quote, I don't know from where, "All to the soil, nothing to the grave." Getting eaten is *sort* of like going to the soil.

I don't dare tell people what happened—that it was all my fault—that I got myself in trouble sort of on purpose, trying to be like her, trying to rescue something.

But I'm not as sad as you might think. I knew she would die pretty soon anyway and this is a better way than in bed looking at the ceiling, maybe in pain. If that had happened, she wouldn't have complained. She'd not have said a word, trying not to be a bother. Nobody would have known about the pain except me. I would have had to grit my teeth against her pain the whole time.

I haven't told anybody partly because I'm waiting to fig-ure things out. I'm here all by myself, but I'm good at look-ing after things. There are those who check on us every weekend—people who are paid to do it. I wave at them. "All okay." I mouth it. The president of the Town and Country Bank came out once. I told him Grandma wasn't feeling well. It wasn't *exactly* a lie. How long can this go on? He'll be the one who finds out first—if anybody does. Maybe they won't.

I'm nursing my jackrabbit. We're friends now. He's get-ting better fast. Pretty soon I'll let him go off to be a rabbit. But he might rather stay here with me.

I'm wearing Grandma's costume most of the time now. I sleep in it. It makes me feel safe. I'm doing my own little rescues as usual. (The vegetable garden is full of happy weeds. I keep the bird feeder going. I leave scraps out for the skunk.) Those count—almost as much as Grandma's rescues did. Anyway, I know the weeds think so.

Snow in the Desert

NEAL ASHER

Neil Asher (http://website.lineone.net/~nealasher) lives in Chelmsford, England. His short fiction has been published for several years in the UK small press. Books include Mindgames: Fool's Mate *(1993),* The Parasite & The Engineer *(1997)* Africa Zero *(2001), and* Runcible Tales *(1999). The aforementioned are all short story collections and novellas. His first novel,* Gridlinked, *a kind of James Bond space opera, was published in the UK in 2001, and his second,* The Skinner, *in 2002. Both books are set in the same future—the "runcible universe," where matter transmitters called runcibles link the settled worlds—and are forthcoming in the U.S.*

"My aim is to entertain," he says, "not blind people with my brilliance. I'm from the school of Arnold Schwartzenegger SF."

"Snow in the Desert," published in Spectrum SF, *where several of Asher's stories have appeared, is proof that space opera in the most traditional sense (related to the western) is still being written with verve and sincerity. It certainly is hyperbolic. Our hero, a long-lived albino gunslinger, is hiding out on a frontier planet because there is a bounty price on his balls. Everyone wants his genetic code because he may be the only immortal human. It is interesting to compare this to the Moorcock story on page 458.*

A sand shark broke through the top of the dune, only to be snatched by a crab-bird and shredded in mid-air. Hirald squatted down, wrapping her cloak around her and pulling up the hood. The chameleon cloth shaded to match the violet sand, leaving only her Toshiba goggles and the blunt snout of her singun visible. It was a small crab bird, but she had quickly learned never to underestimate them. Should the prey be too large for it to kill, the bird would take pieces instead. No motile source of protein was too large to attack. The shame was that all the life-forms on Vatch were based on non-Terran proteins, so to a crab-bird, human flesh was completely without nourishment.

The bird stripped the shark of its blade-legs and armored mandibles and flew off with the bleeding and writhing torso, probably to feed to its chick. Hirald stood up and reappeared; a tall woman in a tight-fitting body-suit, webbed with cooling veins and hung with insulated pockets. On her back she carried a desert survival pack, to create the right impression. Likewise, the formidable singun went into a button-down holster that looked as if it might hold only a simple projectile weapon. She removed her goggles and mask, tucking them away in one of her many pockets before moving on across the sand. Her thin features, blue eyes, and long blond hair were exposed to oven temperatures and skin-flaying ultraviolet. So it had been for many weeks now. Occasionally she drank some water, just in case someone was watching.

* * *

He was called, inevitably, Snow, but with his mask and dust robes it was not immediately evident that he was an albino. The mask, made from the shell of a terrapin, was what identified him. That, and a tendency to leave corpses behind. The current reward for his stasis-preserved testicles was twenty thousand shillings, or the equivalent value in copper or manganese or other precious metals. Many had tried for that reward, and such was their epitaph: they tried.

Snow understood that there might be bounty-hunters waiting at the water station. They would have weapons, strength, and skill. Balanced against this was the crippling honor code of the Andronache. Snow had all the former and none of the latter. Born on Earth so long ago that he doubted his memories, he had long since dispensed with anything that might impede his survival. Morality, he often argued, is a purely human invention, only to be indulged in times of plenty. Another of his little aphorisms ran something along the lines of: "If you're up Shit Creek without a paddle, don't expect the coastguard." His contemporaries on Vatch never knew what to make of that one, unsurprisingly as Vatchians had no use for words like *creek, paddle* or *coast*.

The station was a metallic ovoid mounted ten meters above the ground on a forest of scaffolding. Nailing it to the ground was the silvery tube of the geothermal energy tap that powered the transmuter—which made it possible for humans to exist on this practically waterless planet. The transmuter took complex compounds, stripped them of their elementary hydrogen, and combined that with the abundant oxygen given off by the dryform algae that turned all the sands of Vatch violet. Water was the product, but there were many interesting by-products: rare metals and strange silica compounds were among the planet's main exports.

As he topped the final dune Snow raised his image-intensifier and scanned ahead. The station was truly a small city, the center of commerce, the center of life. He frowned under his mask. Unfortunately, he needed water for the last stage of his journey, and this was the only place he could get it.

Snow strode down the face of the dune to where a dusty track snaked toward the station. By the roadside a water-thief lay dying at the bottom of a condensation jar. His blistered fingers scratched at the hot glass. Snow passed by, ignoring him. It was a harsh punishment, but how else to treat someone who regarded his fellow human beings as no more than walking water-flasks? As he neared the station, cries from the rookery of hawkers and stall-holders in the ground city reached out to him, and he could see the buzz of activity in the scaffold maze. Soon he entered the noisy life of the ground city; a little after that he passed through the moisture lock of the Sand House.

A waiter spoke to Snow, "My pardon, master. I must see your tag. The Androche herself has declared the law enforceable by a two-month branding. The word is that too many outlaws now survive on the fringe." The man could not help staring at Snow's pink eyes and bloodless face.

"No problem, friend." Snow fumbled through his robes to produce his micro-etched identity tag and handed it over. The waiter glanced at the briefly revealed leather-clad stump that terminated Snow's left arm, and pretended not to notice. He put the tag through his portable reader and was much relieved when no alarm sounded. Snow was well aware that not everyone was checked like this, only the more suspicious-looking customers.

"What would you like, master?"

"A liter of chilled lager."

The waiter looked at him doubtfully.

"Which I will pay for now," Snow added, handing over a ten shilling note. The waiter, obviously alarmed at such a large sum in cash, hurried off with it as quickly as he could. Many eyes followed his progress when he returned with a liter of lager in a thermos stein with combination locked top, for here was an indication of wealth.

Snow would not have agreed. He had worked it out. A liter of water would have cost only two shillings less, and the water lost through sweat evaporation little different. Two shillings, plus a little, for imbibing fluid in a much more pleasant form.

He had nearly finished his liter and was relishing the sheer cellular pleasure of rehydration when the three entered the Sand House. He recognized them as killers immediately, but before paying the slightest attention to them he drained every last drop of lager from the frictionless vessel.

"You are Snow, the albino," the first said, standing before his table. Snow observed her and felt a leaden inevitability. Even after all these years he could not shake his aversion to killing women—or this time, young girls. She could not have been more than twenty. She stood before him attired in monofilament coveralls and weapons harness. Her face was elfin under a head of cropped, black hair spiked out with goldfleck grease.

"No, I'm not," he said, and turned his attention elsewhere.

"Don't fuck with me," she said with a tiredness beyond her years. "I know who you are. You are an albino and your left hand is missing."

He returned his attention to her. "My name is Jelda Conley. People call me Whitey. I have often been confused with this Snow you refer to, and it was on one such occasion that I lost my hand. Now please leave me alone."

The girl stepped back, confused. The Andronache honor code did not allow for creative lying. Snow glanced past her and noted one of her companions speaking to the owner, who had sent the nervous waiter over. The lies would not be enough. He watched while the owner called over the waiter and checked the screen of his tag reader. The companion approached the girl, whispered in her ear.

"You lied to me," she said.

"No I didn't."

"Yes you did!"

This was getting ridiculous. Snow stared off into the distance and ignored her.

"I challenge you," the girl said.

There, it was said. Snow pretended he had not heard her.

"I said, 'I challenge you!'."

By the code she could now kill him. It was against the law but accepted practice. Snow felt a sinking sensation as she stepped back.

"Stand and face me, coward."

With a tiredness that was wholly genuine Snow rose to his feet. She snatched her slammer. Snow reacted. She hit the floor on her back, the front of her monofilament coverall punctured and a smoking hole between her pert little breasts. Snow stepped past the table, past her, and was almost at the moisture lock before anyone could react.

It rested on the violet sands at the edge of a spaceport, which was scattered with huge flying-wing shuttles, outbuildings and hangars. It stood between the spaceport and the sprawl of Vatchian buildings linked by moisture-sealed walkways and the glass domes that covered the incongruous green of the parks. And in no way did it resemble any of the structures around it. It could be found on a thousand planets of the human Polity, and it was the reason for the spread of the human race across the galaxy.

The runcible facility was a mirrored sphere fifty meters across, seemingly prevented from rolling away by two L-shaped buffers to either side. All around it, the glass-roofed embarkation lounges were puddles of light. Within the sphere, the Skaidon gate performed its miracle every few minutes: bringing in quince-mitter travelers from all across the polity, and sending them away again.

Beck stood back from the arrivals' entrance and through it watched the twin horns of the runcible on its dais of black glass. He watched the shimmer of the cusp between those horns and impatiently checked his watch, not that they could be late—or early. They would arrive on the nanosecond. The runcible AI would see to that. Precisely on time a man stepped through the shimmer, a woman, another man, another woman. They matched the descriptions he had been given, and his greeting was effusive as they came through to the lounge.

"Your transport awaits outside," he told them, hurrying them to exit. Beck's employer did not want them to stay in the city. He wanted them out, those were Beck's instructions; among others. Once they were in the hover transport, the man he took to be the leader caught hold of his shoulder.

"The weapons," he said.

"Not here, not here," Beck said nervously, and took the transport out of the city.

Out on the sand Beck brought the transport down. Once the four climbed out, he joined them at the back of the vehicle, from which he took a large case. He was sweating, and not just from the heat.

"Here," he said, opening the case.

The man reached inside and took out a small, shiny pistol, snubnosed and deadly-looking.

"The merchant will meet you at the pre-arranged place, if he manages to obtain the information he seeks," Beck said. He did not know where that was, nor what the information was. The merchant had not taken him that far into his trust. It surprised him that he had been allowed even the knowledge that hired killers were on Vatch.

The man nodded as he inspected the pistol, smiled sadly, then pointed the pistol at Beck.

"Sorry," he said.

Beck tried to say something just as he became aware of the arm coming round his face from the man who had moved behind him. A grip like iron closed around his head, locked, wrenched and twisted. Beck hit the sand with his head at an angle it had never achieved in life. He made some choking sounds, shivered a little, died.

Snow halted as two proctors came in through the lock. They stared past him to the corpse on the floor. The elder of the two, gray-bearded and running to fat, but with weapons that appeared well-used and well looked-after, spoke to him.

"You are Snow," he said.

"Yes," Snow replied. This man was not Andronache.

"A challenge?"

"Yes."

The man nodded, assessed the two Andronache at the bar, then turned back to the moisture lock. It was not his job to pick up the corpses. There was an organization for that. The girl would be in a condensation jar within the hour.

"The Androche would speak with you. Come with me."

To his companion he said, "Deal with it. Her two friends look like they ought to spend a little time in detention."

Snow followed the man outside.

"Why does she want to see me?" he asked as they strode down the scaffolded street.

"I didn't ask."

Conversation ended there.

The Androche, like all in her position, had apartments in the station she owned. The proctor led Snow to a caged spiral stair and unlocked the gate. "She is above."

As Snow climbed the stair the gate clanged shut behind him.

The stairway ended at a moisture-lock hatch next to which depended a monitor and screen unit. Snow pressed the call button and waited. After a few moments a woman with cropped, gray hair and a face that was all hard angles peered out at him.

"Yes?"

"You sent for me."

The woman nodded and the lock on the hatch clunked open. After spinning the handle Snow stepped back as the hatch rose on its hinge to allow him access. He climbed into a short, metal-walled corridor that ended at a single panel door of imported wood. It looked like oak to Snow—very expensive. Pushing the door open, he entered.

The room was filled with a fortune in antiques: a huge dining table surrounded by gate-leg chairs; plush eighteenth-century furniture; oil paintings on the walls; hand-woven rugs on the floor.

"Don't be too impressed. They're all copies."

The Androche approached from a drinks cabinet carrying two glasses half filled with an amber drink. Snow studied her. She was an attractive woman. He estimated her age as somewhere between thirty-five and a hundred and ninety. She wore a simple toga-type dress over an athletic figure, and at her hip she carried an antique—or replica—revolver.

"You know *my* name," Snow observed as he accepted the drink.

"I am Aleen," she replied.

Snow hardly heard her. He was relishing his first sip.

"My God, whiskey," he said, eventually.

"Yes," Aleen acknowledged, before gesturing to a nearby sofa. They moved there and sat facing each other.

"Well, I'm here. What do you want?"

"Why is there a reward of twenty-five thousand shillings for your testicles?"

"Best ask Merchant Baris that question. But I see it was rhetorical. You already know the answer."

Aleen nodded.

Snow leaned toward her. "I would be glad to know that answer too," he admitted.

Aleen smiled, Snow leaned back, annoyed.

"There is a price," he said flatly.

"Isn't there always? There is a man. He is the Chief Proctor here. His name is David Songrel."

"You want me to kill him."

"Of course. Isn't that what you are best at?"

Snow kept silent as Aleen lay back against the edge of the sofa, then regarded him over her drink. "That is not all I want from you."

He turned and gazed at her and at that moment she lifted her feet up onto the sofa so that he could see that she wore nothing under the dress. *Does she shave*, Snow wondered, *or is she naturally hairless there?* He also wondered what it was that turned her on: his white body and pink eyes? Other women had said it was almost like being made love to by an alien. Or was it that he was a killer? Probably a bit of both.

"Part of the price?"

She nodded and set her glass to one side, then she slid closer to him on the sofa and hooked one leg over the back of it.

"Now," she said, reaching up and opening her toga to display breasts just like those of the girl he had killed. Snow searched himself for an adverse reaction to that; finding none, he stood up and unclipped his dust robes.

"You're white as paper," Aleen said in amazement as he peeled off his undersuit, but when her eyes strayed to the covered stump terminating his left arm, she made no comment.

"Yes," Snow agreed as he knelt between her legs and bowed down to run his tongue round her nipples. "A blank page," he went on as he worked his way down. She caught his head.

"Not that," she said. "I want you inside me, now."

Snow obliged her, but was puzzled at something he had heard in her voice. No love-making then: just the act itself. Perhaps she wanted white-skinned children.

Hirald called out before approaching the fire. It had been her observation that the Andronache got rather twitchy if you walked into one of their camps unannounced. As she walked in she was surprised to see that these weren't locals. Hirald noted two men and two women wearing monofilament survival suits that looked to be of Martian manufacture. She also pretended not to notice the weapons that one of the men had hastily covered on her arrival. She walked to the fire and squatted down. One of the women tossed on another crab-bird carapace and watched her through the flames.

The man who had covered the weapons, a tall Marsman with caste markings tattooed on his temples, was the first to speak. "You've come a long way?" he asked.

"Not so far as you," Hirald said. She looked from him across the flames to the woman. Her face also bore caste marks. The other couple were a black man with incongruous blue eyes, and a woman who had caps over the neural plugs behind her ears. *She* was corporate then—from one of The Families.

Hirald went on, "But why have you come here, I wonder?"

"We search," the black said intently. "Perhaps you can help us. We search for one who is called Snow. He is an albino."

They all stared at Hirald.

"I have heard of him," Hirald said, "and I have heard that many people look for him. I do not know where he is though."

The woman with the neural plugs looked suspicious. Hirald quickly asked, "You are after the reward, then?"

The four glanced to each other, then the Marsman smiled to himself and casually reached for one of the covered weapons beside him. Hirald glanced at the Corporate woman, who stared back at her.

"Jharit, no."

Jharit stopped with his hand by the covering. "What is it, Canard Meck?"

The woman, now identified as a member of the Jethro Manx Canard Corporate Family, slowly shook her head, still staring at Hirald.

"We have no dispute with you," she said. "But we would prefer it if you left our camp, please."

"She might tell him," Jharit protested.

Canard Meck glanced to him and said, "She is product."

Jharit snatched his hand from the weapons and suddenly looked very frightened. He flinched as Hirald rose to her feet. Hirald smiled.

"I mean no harm, unless harm is meant."

She strode out into the darkness without checking behind. No one moved. No one reached for the weapons.

Snow removed the pistol from its holster in his dust robes and checked the charge reading. As was usual it was nearly full. The bright sunlight of Vatch acting on the photo-voltaic material of his robes kept the weapon constantly powered up through the socket in the holster. The weapon was a matt black L, five millimeters thick with only a slight depression where a trigger would normally have been. It was keyed to Snow. No one else could fire it. Rather than firing projectiles, as did most weapons on Vatch, this weapon discharged a beam of field-accelerated protons, but they could still make large holes in anyone Snow cared to point it at.

David Songrel was a family man. Snow had observed him lifting a child high in the air while a woman looked on. Snow wondered why Aleen wanted him dead. As the owner of the water station she had power here, but little influence over the proctors who enforced planetary law. Perhaps she had been involved in illegalities of which Songrel had become aware. No matter, for the present. He rapped on the door and when Songrel opened it he stuck the pistol in the man's face and walked him back into the apartment, closing the door behind him with his stump.

"Daddy!" the little girl yelled, but the mother caught hold of her before she rushed forward. Songrel had his hands in the air, his eyes not leaving the pistol. Shock there, knowledge.

"Why," said Snow, "does the Androche want you dead?"

"You're . . . the albino."

"Answer the question please."

Songrel glanced at his wife and daughter before he replied, "She is a collector of antiquities."

"Why the necessity for your death?"

"She has killed to get what she wants. I have evidence. We intend to arrest her soon."

Snow nodded, then holstered his pistol. "I thought it would be something like that. She had two proctors come for me, you know."

Songrel lowered his hands, but kept them well away from the stun gun hooked on his belt. "As Androche she has the right to some use of the proctors. It is our duty to guard her and her property. She does not have the freedom to commit crime. Why didn't you kill me? They say you have killed many."

Snow glanced at Songrel's wife and child. "My reputation precedes me," he said, and stepped past Songrel to drop onto a comfortable sofa. "But the stories are in error. I have killed no one who has not first tried to kill me . . . well, mostly."

Songrel turned to his wife. "It's Tamtha's bedtime."

His wife nodded and took the child from the room. Snow noted the little girl's fascinated stare. He was used to it. Songrel sat down in an armchair opposite Snow.

"You have a nice family."

"Yes . . . will you testify against the Androche?"

"You can have my testimony recorded under seal, but I cannot stay for a trial. Were I to stay this place would be crawling with Andronache killers in no time. I might not survive that."

Songrel nodded. "Why did you come here if it was not your intention to kill me?" he asked, a trifle anxiously.

"I want you to play dead while I go back and see the Androche."

Songrel's expression hardened. "You want to collect your reward."

"Yes, but my reward is not money, it is information. The Androche knows why Merchant Baris wants me dead. It is a subject I am understandably curious about."

Songrel interlaced his fingers and stared down at them for a moment. When he looked up he said, "The reward is for your stasis-preserved testicles. Perhaps he is a collector like Aleen, but that is beside the point. I will play dead for you, but when you go to see Aleen I want you to carry a holocorder."

Snow nodded once. Songrel stood up and walked to a wall cupboard. He returned with the device, rested it on the table and turned it on.

"Now, your statement."

"He is dead," Aleen said, smiling.

"Yes," Snow confirmed, dropping Songrel's identity tag on the table, "yet I get the impression you knew before I came here."

Aleen went to the drinks cabinet, poured Snow a whiskey and brought it over to him. "I have friends among the proctors. As soon as his wife called in the killing—she was hysterical apparently—they informed me."

"Why did you want him killed?"

"That is none of your concern. Drink your whiskey and I will get you the promised information."

Aleen turned away from him and moved to a computer console elegantly concealed in a Louis XIV table. Snow had the whiskey to his lips just as his suspicious nature cut in. Why was it necessary to get the information from the computer? She could just tell him. Why had she not poured a drink for herself? He set the drink down on a table, unsampled. Aleen looked up, a dead smile on her face, and as her hand came up over the console Snow dived to one side. On the wall behind him a picture blackened, then burst into oily flames. He came up on one knee and fired once. She slammed back out of her chair onto the floor, her face burning like the picture.

Snow searched hurriedly. Any time now the proctors would arrive. In the bathroom he found a device like a chrome penis with two holes in the end. One hole spurted out some kind of fluid and the other hole sucked. Some kind of contraceptive device? He traced tubes back from it to a unit that contained the bottle of fluid and some very complicated straining and filtering devices. To his confusion he realized it was for removing the contents of a woman's uterus, probably after sex. She collected men's semen? Shortly after, he found a single stasis bottle containing that substance. It had to be his own. He suddenly he had an inkling of an idea—a possible explanation for his situation of the last five years. He took the bottle and poured its contents down the sink before turning to leave the apartment, but the delay had been enough.

Hirald looked at the man in the condensation bottle, her expression revealing nothing. He was alive beyond his time; some sadist had dropped a bottle of water in with him to prolong his suffering. He stared at Hirald with drying eyes, the empty bottle by his head, his body shrunken and badly sunburned, his black tongue protruding. Hirald looked around carefully—there were harsh penalties for what she was about to do—then placed a small chrome cylinder against the glass near the man's head. There was a brief flash. The man convulsed and the bottle was misted with smoke and steam. Hirald replaced the device in her pocket, stood and walked on. Her masters would not have been pleased at her risking herself like this, but they did not have complete control over her actions.

The gray-bearded proctor was crouched behind the sofa, his short-barreled riot gun resting on the back and sighted on the bathroom door. Songrel stood by the moisture lock, his own weapon also trained on Snow.

Songrel glanced across at the Androche's corpse. "You will be staying for the trial," he said, nodding to the proctor.

The man stood and moved across the room, not letting Snow out of his sights for a moment. Even as the barrel of the riot gun was pushed up under Snow's chin he noted how the man was careful not to block Songrel's field of fire. Snow allowed his weapon to be taken. Maybe he could have dealt with the proctor, but not Songrel as well. Now the proctor backed off, flicking one puzzled glance at the weapon he had taken before pocketing it.

Songrel opened the moisture lock and gestured Snow over. There, maybe, Snow thought. He walked over, stepped through the lock and glanced behind him. The proctor, staying well back, shook his head and grinned. Swearing under his breath, Snow shut his plastron mask and ducked out into the arid day.

They gave him no openings, not on the stairs nor out on the dusty street. Always, one of them would be covering him from a distance of two or three paces. Snow was fast; faster than most people had reason to suspect, but not fast enough to outrun a bullet or energy charge.

"You know you're killing me," he said to Songrel.

"There'll be guards during the trial, and we'll give you an escort after . . . if you're released," Songrel replied.

Opening his dust robes so both of them could see clearly what he was doing, he reached to the back of his belt and removed the holocorder Songrel had given him.

"You've got all the evidence you need here, and I have to wonder how many of your guards might be tempted by the merchant's reward."

Songrel appeared pained at this; he stepped closer to take the recording device, his weapon directed at Snow's mask.

The woman seemed to come out of nowhere: one moment all movement in the street was warily distant, then she was there, holding the proctor's riot gun as he stumbled and went face down. Songrel's aim slid aside to track her.

That was enough of an opening for Snow. He snapped his

boot forward, catching the man in the gut, then chopped down on the back of his neck as he bowed forward. Songrel's gun thudded into the dust. Snow dropped, snatched and rolled, coming up to get the woman in his sights. She wasn't there.

"I think this is yours," she said, to one side of him.

Turning his head only, he observed her. With one hand she was covering him with the riot gun. In her other hand she was holding his own weapon. She lowered the riot gun.

"Perhaps now would be a good time to leave?"

By the condensation jar Snow paused for breath. The woman, he noted, seemed not to need the rest, hardly seemed to be breathing at all. He shook his head and studied the jar. The man was now dead, his body giving up the last of its water for the public good. Snow paused for a moment longer to observe the greasy film on the inside of the jar before moving on. Someone had finished the poor bastard off.

"Why did you help me?" he asked the woman.

"Because you needed help."

Snow contained his annoyance. With a glance back toward the station he set out again, the woman easily keeping pace with him. She'd had her opportunity to kill him, so it was not the reward she was after. Time enough to find out what her angle was when they had put some distance between themselves and potential pursuit.

Once out of sight of the station they left the road, setting out across a spill of desert to a distant rock field. There, Snow felt, they would be able to lose themselves, unless a sand shark got them first. He drew his pistol as he walked and kept his eyes open. One sand shark twitched its motion-detecting palps above the sand, but shortly subsided. It must have fed in the last year; it would be quiescent for another year to come.

Having reached the rocks and firmer ground without event Snow slowed his pace while studying his companion. She was incongruously attractive and clean-looking and he found himself staring in fascination, reluctant to tell her, after what she had done for him, that he normally traveled alone. That, he supposed was the problem—he traveled alone by necessity, not choice. He gave an open-handed gesture and she walked on a pace ahead of him. Whatever danger she represented to him, at least he had her in sight.

Now studying her from the side he said, "I won't be going much farther. I want to set up camp before the Thira."

The woman nodded, but made no comment.

Snow made a fire from old carapaces and removed his mask in the light of evening. He was curious to note that the woman had not replaced her mask, yet her skin was clear and unblemished. She sank down next to him by the fire, with a grace that could only reflect superb physical condition.

"You never answered my question," he said.

With her head bowed the woman said, "You owe me, perhaps for your life. For that will you allow me to tell you in my own time?"

"People have been trying to kill me. I'm not sure I can afford to be that generous."

She shrugged. "I could have killed you."

Snow bit down on frustration: he did owe her for his life. She could have killed him and, without her help, killers would have gathered at the water station while slow due process brought him to court. He took a deep breath and searched for some stillness.

"What do I call you?" he asked eventually.

"Hirald."

He struggled on, "Where did you come from . . . before?"

"Across the Thira."

Snow had his doubts about that reply. He had crossed the Thira a couple of times and knew it to be rough going. Hirald looked like someone fresh from a month's sojourn in a water station.

"I see," he said.

"You are Snow," she said, turning and fixing him with blue eyes that appeared violet in the fading red light.

He felt his stomach lurch at that look, and then he imme-

diately felt self-contempt. After all these years he was still
susceptible to physical attraction . . . to beauty . . . "Yes, I
am."

"I would like to travel with you for a while."

"You know who I am, and I suspect you know why I am
suspicious of your motives."

She smiled at him and he felt that lurch again. He turned
and spat in the fire.

"I'm crossing the Thira," he said.

"I have no problem with that."

Snow lay back and rested his head on one of the packs. He
pulled a thermal sheet across his body and stared up at the
sky. The red-tinted swathe of stars was being encroached on
by the asteroids of the night—all that remained of Vatch's
moon after some long-ago cataclysm. A single sword of
light from an ion drive cut the sunset.

"Why?" he asked.

"Because I'm lonely, and I feel like a change."

Snow grunted and closed his eyes. She was not out to kill
him, but her motives remained unrevealed. Whatever, she
could never keep to the pace he set and would soon abandon
him, and the unsettling things he was feeling would soon go
away. He slept.

Sunlight on his face, bringing the familiar tingling prior to
burning, had his hand up and closing his mask across before
he was fully awake. He looked at Hirald across the dead
ashes of the fire and got the unsettling notion that she had
not changed position all night. He sat up, then after a muttered good morning, went behind a rock and urinated into
his condenser pack. Following the ritual of every morning
for many years now, he then emptied the moisture-collectors
of his undersuit into it as well. The collector bottle he emptied into his drinking bottle before dipping his toothbrush
and cleaning his teeth. By the time he had finished his ablu-
tions and come out from behind the rock, Hirald had opened
a breakfast-soup ration pack and it was bubbling under its
lid. Snow reached for another pack, but she held up her
hand.

"This is for you. I have already eaten."

"Did you sleep at all?"

"A little. Tell me, how do you come to be in possession of proscribed weaponry?"

"Took it off someone who tried to kill me," he lied. He could hardly tell her he had brought it here before the runcible proscription and modified it himself over many years thereafter. He sat down to drink his breakfast.

When he had finished they set out across the Thira. Hirald noted him looking at her after an hour's walking and closed her mask. He thought no more of it—lots of people disliked the masks, and were prepared to pay the price of water-loss not to wear them so much.

By midmorning the temperature had reached forty-five degrees and was still rising. A sand shark broke from the surface of a dune and came scuttling after them for a few meters, then halted, panting like a dog, tired or too well fed to continue—that, or it had sampled human flesh before.

When the temperature reached fifty and the cooling units of Snow's undersuit were laboring under the load, he noted that Hirald still easily matched his pace. When a crab-bird dropped clacking out of the sky at them she brought it down with one shot before Snow could even think of reaching for his weapon, and before he saw what weapon she shot the creature with. She was a remarkable woman.

Shortly after midday Snow called a halt. "We'll rest until evening, then continue through the night and tomorrow morning. The following night should bring us out the other side."

Hirald nodded in agreement, seemingly unconcerned.

They slept under the reflective shelter of Snow's day tent, then moved on at sunset after Snow had checked their position. They walked all night and most of the following morning, and when they finally set up the tent again Snow was exhausted. With a hint of irritation he told Hirald he wanted privacy in the tent and suggested she set up her own. Once inside his tent he sealed up and stripped naked. He then cleaned himself and the inside of his undersuit with a cycle sponge—a device that made it possible to stay clean with a quarter liter of water and little spillage. After this he pulled on a pair of toweling shorts and lay back with his miniature air cooler humming away at full power. It was luxury of a kind. After half an hour's sleep he woke and opened the tent to look outside. Hirald was sitting in the sand with her mask open. She was watching the horizon intently, her stillness quite unnatural.

"Don't you have a day tent?" Snow asked.

She shook her head.

"Come and join me then," he said, reversing back into his tent. Hirald stood and walked over, apparently unaffected by the baking sun. She entered the tent and closed it behind her, then, after a glance at Snow, she began to remove her survival suit. Snow turned away for a moment, then thought, *what the hell*, and turned back to watch. She had not asked him to turn his head. Under her suit she wore a single, skin-hugging garment. The material was like white silk, and almost translucent. Snow swallowed dryly, then tried to distract himself by wondering about her sanitary arrangements. As she lifted her legs up to remove her trousers from her feet he saw then how the matter was arranged and wondered if a blush was evident on his white skin. The garment was slit from the lower part of her pale pubic hair round to the top crease of her buttocks.

As she finally removed her trousers Hirald looked at him and noted the direction of his attention. He raised his gaze and met her eye to eye. She smiled at him and, still smiling, stretched the sleeves of the garment down and off over her hands and rolled it down below her breasts. Snow cleared his throat and tried to think of something witty to say. She was a succubus, a lonely desert man's fantasy. Still smiling she came across the tent on her hands and knees, put her hand against his chest and pushed him back, sat astride him, and with her pale hair falling either side of his head she leaned down and kissed him on the mouth. Her mouth was sweet and warm. Snow was thoroughly aware of her hard little nipples sliding from side to side against his chest. He touched the skin of her shoulders and found it dry and warm.

She sat back then and looked down at him for a moment. There was something strange about that look—a kind of cold curiosity. She slid forward onto his stomach, then turned and reached back to pull his shorts down and off his legs. He was amazed at just how far she could twist and bend her body. Once his shorts were removed she slid back until his penis rested between her buttocks, then, after raising herself a little, she continued to push back, bending it over until it hurt, then with a swift movement of her pelvis, took it inside her. Snow groaned, then gritted his teeth as she started to move, still staring down at him with that strange expression.

In the evening, when it was time to go, Snow felt a bone-deep lethargy. He had not slept much during the afternoon. Each time he had tried to relax after a session of sex, Hirald would do something he could not resist. Her last climax had been so intense that she had cried out and shuddered uncontrollably, and after it she had looked down at herself in surprise and shock. Thereafter she had been eager to repeat the experience. Snow felt sore and drained.

As they walked across the darkened violet sands they had talked little, but one conversation had raised Snow's suspicions.

"Your hand, how did you lose it?"

"Andronache challenge. It was shredded by a flack shell."

"How is it now?"

Snow had paused before replying. Did she know?

"What do you mean: how is it? It was amputated. It is no longer there."

"Yes," she had said, and no more.

The sun was crossing the horizon and the night asteroids fading out of the sky when they reached the rock-field at the edge of the Thira. With little energy for conversation, Snow set up his day tent and collapsed inside, instantly asleep. When he woke in the latter part of the day it was to discover himself undressed under a blanket, with Hirald lying beside him. She was up on her elbow, her head propped on her hand, studying his face. As soon as she saw that he was awake she handed him a carton of mixed juice. He sat up, the blanket sliding down. She was naked. He drank the juice.

"I'm glad you came along," he said, and the rest of the day was spent in pleasant activity.

That night they moved deep into the rock field. The following day passed much as the one before.

"I think it fair to tell you I have an implant," Snow said as he rested after some particularly vigorous activity. "You won't get pregnant by me, and my semen is little more than water and a few free proteins."

"Why do you feel it necessary to tell me this?" Hirald asked him.

"As you know, there is a reward out for my testicles, stasis preserved. This is not because Merchant Baris particularly wants me dead. I think it is because he is after my genetic tissue. At the water station the Androche . . . seduced me." Snow was uncomfortable with that. "She did it so she could collect my sperm, probably to sell."

"I know," Hirald said. Snow looked at her and she went on, "He is after your testicles or other body tissue to provide him with an endless supply of your genetic material."

Snow considered that. Of course there had to be more to Hirald than he had supposed, but the sex had clouded his thought-processes somewhat.

"It is the next best thing to having your entire living body. I suspect Baris thought it unlikely he could get away with that. He'd never get your entire body off-planet. This way he also corners the market."

"You know an awful lot about what Baris wants."

Hirald gazed at him very directly. "How is your hand?"

Snow looked down at the stump. He unclipped the covering and pulled it off. What he exposed was recognizably a hand, though deformed and almost useless. The covering had been cleverly made to conceal it, to make it appear as if the hand was missing.

"It will be no different from its predecessor in about six months. I intended to walk out of one water station without a hand, then into another station with a hand and a new identity."

"What about your albinism?"

"Skin dye and eye lenses."

"Of course. You cannot take transplants."

"No . . . I think you should explain yourself."

"The people I work for want the same as Baris: your genome."

"You've had opportunity . . ."

"No, they want the best option, which is you, willingly. I want you to gate back to Earth with me."

"Why?"

"You are regenerative. It is the source of your immortality. We know this now. You have known it for more than a thousand years."

"Still, why?"

"We have managed to keep your secret for the last three hundred years, ever since it was discovered. Ten years ago the knowledge was leaked. Now several organizations know about you, and what you represent: whoever can decode your genome has access to immortality, and through that access to unprecedented wealth and power. That's why Baris was the first to track you down. There will be others."

"You work for Earth Central."

"Yes."

"Wouldn't it be better just to kill me and destroy my body?"

"Earth Central does not suppress knowledge." Hirald smiled at him. "You should be old enough to understand the futility of that. It wants the knowledge disseminated so that it doesn't put power into the hands of the wrong people. It could do immense good. The projections are that in ten years a treatment would become available to make anyone regenerative, within limits."

"Yet prior to this it kept a lid on things," Snow said.

"It guarded your privacy. It did not suppress knowledge. Not to seek out knowledge is not the same as suppressing it."

"Is Earth Central so moral now?" Snow wondered, then could have kicked himself for his stupidity. Of course Earth Central was. Only human beings and other low-grade sentients could become corrupt, and Earth Central was the most

powerful AI in the human Polity. Hirald, noting his discom-
fiture, did not answer his question.

"Will you come?" she asked him.

Snow was gazing at the wall of the tent as if he could see
through it across the rock field. "This requires thought, not
instant decisions. Two days should bring us to my home. I'll
consider it."

Draped in chameleon cloth the hover transport vanished into
the surrounding dunes. Inside the transport Jharit shuffled a
pack of cards and played a game men like himself had
played in similar situations for many centuries. His wife,
Jharilla, slept. Trock was cleaning an antique revolver he
had picked up at an auction in the last water station. The bullets he had acquired with it were arrayed in neat, soldierly
rows on the table before him.

Canard Meck was plugged in, trying to pick up information from the net and the high-speed communications the
runcible AI exchanged with its subminds. The call came as a
relief to all of them but her—she resented dropping out of
that world of perfect logic and pure clarity of thought, back
into the sweat-stink of the transport.

"I am Baris," said the smiling face from the screen.

Coming straight to the point Jharit said, "You have the information?"

"I have," Baris confirmed, his smile only slightly less,
"and I will be coming to join you for the final chase."

Jharit and Trock exchanged a look.

"As you wish. You are paying."

"Yes, I am." The merchant's smile was gone now. "Turn
on your beacon and I will join you within the hour."

"How are you getting out here?" Canard Meck asked.

"By AGC of course," Baris said, turning to look toward
her.

"All AGCs are registered. The AI will know where you
are."

Baris flicked his fingers at this, assuming an expression of
contempt. "No matter. We will continue from your position
to . . . our destination, in the transport."

"Very well," Canard Meck agreed.

Baris waited for something more to be said. When nothing was he blanked the screen with a disappointed moue.

The merchant arrived in a fancy repro Macrojet AGC. He climbed out wearing sand fatigues and followed by two women dressed much the same. One carried a hunting rifle and ammunition belts; the other carried various unidentifiable packages. Baris struck a pose before them. He was a handsome man, but none of the four reacted to this foolish display. They knew that anyone who had reached the merchant's position was no fool. Jharit and Jharilla looked at him glassy-eyed. Trock inspected the rifle. Canard Meck glanced at one of the women, took in the imbecilic smile, then returned her attention to the merchant.

"Shall we be on our way then?" she said.

Baris nodded and, still smiling, clicked his fingers and walked to the transport. The two women followed him, obedient as dogs. The four came after: hounds of a different breed.

Out of the rock field reared the first of the stone buttes, carved by wind-blown sand into something resembling a man-like statue sunk up to its chest in the ground. In the cracks and divisions of its head, mica and quartz glittered like insectile eyes. Snow led the way to the base of the butte where slabs of the same stone lay tilted in the ground.

"Here," he said, holding his hand out to a sandwich of slabs. With a grinding noise, the top slab pivoted to one side to expose a stair dropping a short distance to the floor of a tunnel. "Welcome to my home."

"You live in a hole in the ground?" Hirald asked, with a touch of irony.

"Of course not. Follow me."

As they climbed down, the slab swung back across above them and wall lights clicked on. Hirald noted that the tunnel led under the butte and had already worked things out by the time they reached the chimney and the elevator car. They climbed inside the car and sprawled in plush seats as it hauled them up a chimney cut through the center of the butte.

"This must have taken you some time," Hirald observed.

"The chimney was already here. I first found it about two hundred years ago. Others had lived here before me, but in rather primitive conditions. I've been improving the place ever since."

The car arrived at its destination and they walked from it into a complex of moisture-locked rooms at the head of the butte.

With a drink in her hand Hirald stood at a polarized panoramic window and gazed out across the rock field for a moment, then returned her attention to the room and its contents. In a glass-fronted case along one wall was a display of weapons dating from the 22nd century, and at the center a sword from some prespace age. Hirald had to wonder where and when Snow had acquired it. She turned from the case as Snow returned to the room, dressed now in loose black trousers and a black, open-necked shirt. The contrast with his white skin and hair and pink eyes gave him the appearance of someone who might have a taste for blood.

"There's some clothing there for you to use if you like, and the shower. There's plenty of water here," he told her.

Hirald nodded, placed her drink on a glass-topped table, and headed back into the rooms Snow had come from. Snow watched her go. She would shower and change and be little fresher than she already was. He had noted with some puzzlement how she never seemed to smell bad, never seemed dirty.

"Whose clothing is this?" Hirald asked from the room beyond.

"My last wife's," said Snow.

Hirald came to the door with clothing folded over one arm. She looked at Snow questioningly.

"She killed herself about a century ago," he said in a flat voice. "Walked out into the desert and burned a hole through her head. I found her before the crab-birds and sand sharks."

"Why?"

"She grew old and I did not. She hated it."

Hirald didn't comment. She went to take her shower, and shortly returned wearing a skin-tight body-suit of translucent blue material, which she did not expect to be wearing for long once Snow saw her in it. He was occupied though—sitting in a swivel chair studying a screen. He was back in his dust robes, terrapin mask hanging open. She walked up behind him to see what he was looking at. She saw the hover transport on the sand and the two women pulling a sheet over it. She recognized Merchant Baris and the four hired killers.

"It would seem Baris has found me," Snow said, his tone cold and flat.

"You know him?"

"Met him once when he was younger. He hasn't changed much." He nodded at the screen. "The four with him look an interesting bunch."

"I met them: the Marsman and the Corporate woman are the leaders—mercenary group," said Hirald. "What defenses does this place have?"

"None, I never felt the need for them."

"Are you sure they are coming here?"

"It seems strange that he has chosen this particular rock field on the whole planet. I'll have to go and settle this."

"I'll change," said Hirald, and hurried back to get her suit. When she returned Snow was gone; when she tried to follow she found the elevator car locked at the bottom of the shaft.

"Damn you," she said flatly, smashing her fist against a doorjamb, leaving a fist-shaped dent in the steel. Then she walked back a few paces, turned, ran and leaped into the shaft. The rails pinned to the edge were six meters away. She reached them easily, her hands locking on the polished metal with a thump. Laboriously she began to climb down.

Jharit smiled at his wife and nodded to Trock, who stood beyond her, strapping on body armor. This was the one. They would be rich after this. He examined the narrow-beam laser he held. He would have preferred something with a little more power, but it was essential that the body not be too badly damaged. He turned to Baris as the merchant sent his two women back to the transport.

"We'll go in spread out. He probably has scanning equipment in the rock field and if there's an ambush we don't want him to get too many of us at once."

Baris smiled and thumbed bullets into his rifle, adjusted the scope. Jharit wondered about him, wondered how good he was. He gave the signal for them to spread out and enter the rock field.

They were coming to kill him. There were no rules, no challenges offered. Snow braced the butt of his pistol against the rock and sighted along it.

"Anything?" Jharit asked over the com.

"Pin cameras," Jharilla told him. "I burned a couple out, but there have to be more. He knows we're here."

"Remember, narrow-beam, we burn too much and there's no money. A clean kill. A head shot would be nice," Jharit added.

There was a whooshing sound, a brief scream, static over the com. Jharit hit the ground and moved behind a rock.

"What the hell was that?"

"He's got a fucking proton weapon. Fucking body armor's useless!"

Jharit felt a sinking sensation in his gut. They had expected projectile weapons, perhaps a laser.

"Who..?"

There was a pause.

"Trock?"

"Jharilla's dead."

Jharit swallowed dryly and edged on into the rock field.

"Position?"

"Don't know?"

"Meck?"

"Nothing here."

"Baris?"

There was no reply from the Merchant.

Snow dropped down off the top of the boulder and pulled some of the small but deadly grenades from his belt. Lacking a hand, he used his teeth to twist their tops right around.

The dark-skinned one was over to his left, the Marsman over to his right. The others were farther over to the right somewhere. He threw the two spheroids right and left and moved back, then flicked through multiple views on his wrist screen. A lot of the cameras were out, but he pulled up a view of the Marsman. Two detonations. As the Marsman hit the ground he realized he had thrown too far. He flicked through the views again and caught the other stumbling through dust and wreckage, rock splinters imbedded in his face. Ah, so.

Snow moved to his left, checking his screen every few seconds. He halted behind a tilted slab and after checking his screen once more, squatted down and waited. With little regard for his surroundings Trock stumbled out of the falling dust. Snow smiled grimly under his mask and sighted on him, but before he could fire, red agony cut his shoulder. The smell of burning flesh. Snow rolled to one side, came up onto his feet, ran. Rock to one side of him smoked, pinged as it heated. He dived for cover, crawled among broken rock. The firing ceased. Now I'm dead, he thought. His pistol lay in the dust back there somewhere.

"He dropped his weapon, Trock. He's over to your left. Take him down, I can't get a sighting on him at the moment."

Trock spat a broken tooth from his mouth and walked in the direction indicated, his antique revolver in his left hand and his laser in his right. This was it. The bastard was dead, or perhaps not. *I'll cut his arms and legs off, the beam should cauterize sufficiently*. But Trock did not get time to fire. The figure in dust robes came out of nowhere to drop-kick him in the chest. The body armor absorbed most of the blow, but Trock went over. Before he could rise the figure was above him, a split-fingered blow spearing down. After that Trock saw nothing. Sprawled back he lifted fingers to the bleeding mess behind his broken visor. Then the pain hit and he started screaming.

Snow coughed as quietly as he could, opened his mask and gasped in pain. The burn had started at his shoulder and ended in the middle of his chest, but luckily his dust robes had absorbed most of the heat. A second more and he would have been dead. The pain was crippling. He knew he would not have the energy to withstand another attack like that, nor would he be likely to take any of the others by surprise. His adversary had been stunned by the explosion, angered by injury. Snow edged back through the rock field, his mobility rapidly decreasing. When a shadow fell across him he looked up into the inevitable.

"Why didn't you take his weapon?" Jharit asked, nodding back toward Trock, who was no longer screaming. He was curled fetal by a rock, a field dressing across his eyes and his body pumped full of self-administered pain-killers.

"No time, no strength . . . could only get him through his visor," Snow managed.

Jharit nodded and spoke into his com.

"I have him. Home in on my signal."

Snow waited for death, but Jharit squatted in the dust, seemingly disinclined to kill him.

"Jharilla was a hell of a woman," said Jharit, removing a stasis bottle from his belt and pushing it into the sand next to him. "We were married in Viking City twenty years ago." Jharit pulled a wicked ceramal knife from his boot and held it up before his face. "This is for her you understand. After I've taken your testicles and dressed that wound I'll see to your other injury. I don't want you to die yet. I have so much to tell you about her, and there is so much I want you to experience. You know she—"

Jharit turned at a sound, rose to his feet and drew his laser again. He stepped away from Snow and gazed around. Snow looked beyond him but could see nothing.

"If you leave here now, Marsman, I will not kill you."

The voice was Hirald's.

Jharit fired into the rocks and backed toward Snow.

"I have a singun and I am in chameleonwear. I can kill you any time I wish. Drop your weapon."

Jharit paused for a moment of indecision, then whirled, pointing his laser at Snow. The expression on his face told all. Before he could press the trigger he collapsed into himself: a central point the size of a pinhead, a plume of sand standing where he stood, then all blasted away in a thunderclap and encore of miniature lightnings across the ground. Snow slowly shoved himself to his feet as he stared in awe at the spot Jharit had occupied. He had heard of such weapons but had not believed they existed. He looked across as Hirald flickered back into existence only a few meters away. She smiled at him, just before the first shot ripped the side of her face away.

Snow knew he yelled, he might have screamed. He watched in impotent horror as the second shot smacked into her back and knocked her to the ground. Then: Baris and the Corporate woman, walking out of the rock field. Baris sighted again as he walked, hit Hirald with another shot that ripped half her side away as he and his companion moved past her.

Snow felt his legs give way. He went down on his knees. Baris came before him, a self-satisfied smirk on his face. Snow gazed up at him, trying to pull the energy together, to throw it all into one last attempt. He knew it was what Baris was waiting for, but it was all he could do. He glanced aside at the woman, saw she had halted some way back. She was staring back past Baris at Hirald, horror on her face. Snow did not want to look there—he did not want to know.

"O my God! It's her!"

Snow pulled himself to his feet, dizziness making him lurch. Baris glanced at the Corporate woman in confusion, then pointed the rifle at Snow's face. The merchant relished his moment for the half a second it lasted. The hand punched through his body from the back, knocked the rifle aside, lifted him and hurled him against a rock with such force he stuck for a moment, then fell, leaving a man-shaped corona of blood. Hirald stood there, revealed. Where the syntheflesh had been blown away, glittering ceramal was exposed, her white enamel teeth, one blue eye complete in its socket, the ribbed column of her spine. She observed Snow for a moment, then turned toward the woman. Snow fainted before the scream.

* * *

He was in his bed and memories slowly dragged themselves into his mind. He lay there, his throat dry, and after a moment felt across to his numbed chest and the dressing. It was a moment before he dared open his eyes. Hirald sat at the side of the bed and when she saw he was awake she helped him up into a sitting position against his pillows. Snow observed her face. She had repaired the damage somehow, but the scars of that repair-work were still there. She looked just like a human woman who had been disfigured in an accident. She wore a loose shirt and trousers to hide the other repairs. As he studied her she reached up and self-consciously touched her face, before reaching for a glass of water to hand to him. That touch of vanity confused him for a moment. Gratefully, he drained the glass.

"You're a Golem android," he said in the end, unsure.

Hirald smiled, and it did not look so bad.

She said, "Canard Meck thought that." When she saw his confusion she explained, "The Corporate woman. She called me product, which is an understandable mistake. I am nearly indistinguishable from the Golem Twenty-Two."

"What are you then?" Snow asked as she poured him another glass of water.

"A cyborg discovering she's more human than she thought. No one owns me."

Snow sipped his drink as he considered that. He was not sure what he was feeling.

"Will you come to Earth with me?" she asked.

Snow turned and watched her for a long time. He remembered how it had been in the tent as she, he realized, discovered that she was still human.

"You know, I will never grow old and die," she said.

"I see."

She tilted her head questioningly and awaited his answer.

A slow smile spread across his face. "I'll come with you," he told her. He put his drink down and reached out to take hold of her hand. There was still blood under her fingernails and the tear duct in her left eye was not working properly. It didn't matter.

Singleton

GREG EGAN

*Greg Egan (www.netspace.net.au/~gregegan), who lives in Perth, West Australia, hit his stride in the early 1990s, and became one of the most interesting new hard SF writers of the decade. He is internationally famous for his stories and novels. His early fiction was supernatural horror, and his first novel (*An Unusual Angle—*not SF) was published in 1983, but his writing burst into international prominence in 1990, with several fine SF stories that focused attention on his writing. His SF novels to date are* Quarantine *(1992),* Permutation City *(1994),* Distress *(1995),* Diaspora *(1997),* Teranesia *(1999), and* Schild's Ladder *(2002); his short story collections are* Our Lady of Chernobyl *(1995),* Axiomatic *(1995), and* Luminous *(1999). He quit his job as a computer programmer to write full time in 1992. As of 2000, he had become the flagship hard SF writer of the younger generation.*

"Singleton," from Interzone, *is a hard SF quantum computer story. Egan assumes an Everett-Wheeler–type quantum mechanics—usually referred to as the Many Worlds Interpretation—but meticulously sets up a mechanism by which an individual AI could subvert the branching. But it is also a philosophical story on a human scale about making choices and accepting consequences. A married couple, a physicist and a mathematician, want to have a child, and they have one never before imagined in SF. There is enough material for a novel compressed into this provocative novella.*

2003

I was walking north along George Street toward Town Hall railway station, pondering the ways I might solve the tricky third question of my linear algebra assignment, when I encountered a small crowd blocking the footpath. I didn't give much thought to the reason they were standing there; I'd just passed a busy restaurant, and I often saw groups of people gathered outside. But once I'd started to make my way around them, moving into an alley rather than stepping out into the traffic, it became apparent that they were not just diners from a farewell lunch for a retiring colleague, putting off their return to the office for as long as possible. I could see for myself exactly what was holding their attention.

Twenty meters down the alley, a man was lying on his back on the ground, shielding his bloodied face with his hands, while two men stood over him, relentlessly swinging narrow sticks of some kind. At first I thought the sticks were pool cues, but then I noticed the metal hooks on the ends. I'd only ever seen these obscure weapons before in one other place: my primary school, where an appointed window monitor would use them at the start and end of each day. They were meant for opening and closing an old-fashioned kind of hinged pane when it was too high to reach with your hands.

I turned to the other spectators. "Has anyone called the police?" A woman nodded without looking at me, and said, "Someone used their mobile, a couple of minutes ago."

The assailants must have realized that the police were on their way, but it seemed they were too committed to their task to abandon it until that was absolutely necessary. They were facing away from the crowd, so perhaps they weren't entirely reckless not to fear identification. The man on the ground was dressed like a kitchen hand. He was still moving, trying to protect himself, but he was making less noise than his attackers; the need, or the ability, to cry out in pain had been beaten right out of him.

As for calling for help, he could have saved his breath.

A chill passed through my body, a sick cold churning sensation that came a moment before the conscious realization: *I'm going to watch someone murdered, and I'm going to do nothing.* But this wasn't a drunken brawl, where a few bystanders could step in and separate the combatants; the two assailants had to be serious criminals, settling a score. Keeping your distance from something like that was just common sense. I'd go to court, I'd be a witness, but no one could expect anything more of me. Not when 30 other people had behaved in exactly the same way.

The men in the alley did not have guns. If they'd had guns, they would have used them by now. They weren't going to mow down anyone who got in their way. It was one thing not to make a martyr of yourself, but how many people could these two grunting slobs fend off with sticks?

I unstrapped my backpack and put it on the ground. Absurdly, that made me feel more vulnerable; I was always worried about losing my textbooks. *Think about this. You don't know what you're doing.* I hadn't been in so much as a fist fight since I was 13. I glanced at the strangers around me, wondering if anyone would join in if I implored them to rush forward together. But that wasn't going to happen. I was a willowy, unimposing 18-year-old, wearing a T-shirt adorned with Maxwell's Equations. I had no presence, no authority. No one would follow me into the fray.

Alone, I'd be as helpless as the guy on the ground. These men would crack my skull open in an instant. There were half a dozen solid-looking office workers in their 20s in the crowd; if these weekend rugby players hadn't felt competent to intervene, what chance did I have?

I reached down for my backpack. If I wasn't going to help, there was no point being here at all. I'd find out what had happened on the evening news.

I started to retrace my steps, sick with self-loathing. This wasn't *kristallnacht*. There'd be no embarrassing questions from my grandchildren. No one would ever reproach me.

As if that were the measure of everything.

"Fuck it." I dropped my backpack and ran down the alley.

I was close enough to smell the three sweating bodies over the stench of rotting garbage before I was even noticed. The nearest of the attackers glanced over his shoulder, af-fronted, then amused. He didn't bother redeploying his weapon in mid-stroke; as I hooked an arm around his neck in the hope of overbalancing him, he thrust his elbow into my chest, winding me. I clung on desperately, maintaining the hold even though I couldn't tighten it. As he tried to prize himself loose, I managed to kick his feet out from un-der him. We both went down onto the asphalt; I ended up beneath him.

The man untangled himself and clambered to his feet. As I struggled to right myself, picturing a metal hook swinging into my face, someone whistled. I looked up to see the sec-ond man gesturing to his companion, and I followed his gaze. A dozen men and women were coming down the alley, advancing together at a brisk walk. It was not a particularly menacing sight—I'd seen angrier crowds with peace signs painted on their faces—but the sheer numbers were enough to guarantee some inconvenience. The first man hung back long enough to kick me in the ribs. Then the two of them fled.

I brought my knees up, then raised my head and got into a crouch. I was still winded, but for some reason it seemed vi-tal not to remain flat on my back. One of the office workers grinned down at me. "You fuckwit. You could have got killed."

The kitchen hand shuddered, and snorted bloody mucus. His eyes were swollen shut, and when he laid his hands down beside him, I could see the bones of his knuckles through the torn skin. My own skin turned icy, at this vision of the fate I'd courted for myself. But if it was a shock to realize how I might have ended up, it was just as sobering to think that I'd almost walked away and let them finish him off, when the intervention had actually cost me nothing.

I rose to my feet. People milled around the kitchen hand, asking each other about first aid. I remembered the basics from a course I'd done in high school, but the man was still breathing, and he wasn't losing vast amounts of blood, so I couldn't think of anything helpful that an amateur could do in the circumstances. I squeezed my way out of the gathering and walked back to the street. My backpack was exactly where I'd left it; no one had stolen my books. I heard sirens approaching; the police and the ambulance would be there soon.

My ribs were tender, but I wasn't in agony. I'd cracked a rib falling off a trail bike on the farm when I was twelve, and I was fairly sure that this was just bruising. For a while I walked bent over, but by the time I reached the station I found I could adopt a normal gait. I had some grazed skin on my arms, but I couldn't have appeared too battered, because no one on the train looked at me twice.

That night, I watched the news. The kitchen hand was described as being in a stable condition. I pictured him stepping out into the alley to empty a bucket of fishheads into the garbage, to find the two of them waiting for him. I'd probably never learn what the attack had been about unless the case went to trial, and as yet the police hadn't even named any suspects. If the man had been in a fit state to talk in the alley, I might have asked him then, but any sense that I was entitled to an explanation was rapidly fading.

The reporter mentioned a student "leading the charge of angry citizens" who'd rescued the kitchen hand, and then she spoke to an eye witness, who described this young man as "a New Ager, wearing some kind of astrological symbols on his shirt." I snorted, then looked around nervously in case one of my housemates had made the improbable connection, but no one else was even in earshot.

Then the story was over.

I felt flat for a moment, cheated of the minor rush that 15 seconds' fame might have delivered; it was like reaching into a biscuit tin when you thought there was one more chocolate chip left, to find that there actually wasn't. I considered phoning my parents in Orange, just to talk to them from within the strange afterglow, but I'd established a routine and it was not the right day. If I called unexpectedly, they'd think something was wrong.

So, that was it. In a week's time, when the bruises had faded, I'd look back and doubt that the incident had ever happened.

I went upstairs to finish my assignment.

Francine said, "There's a nicer way to think about this. If you do a change of variables, from x and y to z and z-conjugate, the Cauchy-Riemann equations correspond to the condition that the partial derivative of the function with respect to z-conjugate is equal to zero."

We were sitting in the coffee shop, discussing the complex analysis lecture we'd had half an hour before. Half a dozen of us from the same course had got into the habit of meeting at this time every week, but today the others had failed to turn up. Maybe there was a movie being screened, or a speaker appearing on campus that I hadn't heard about.

I worked through the transformation she'd described. "You're right," I said. "That's really elegant!"

Francine nodded slightly in assent, while retaining her characteristic jaded look. She had an undisguisable passion for mathematics, but she was probably bored out of her skull in class, waiting for the lecturers to catch up and teach her something she didn't already know.

I was nowhere near her level. In fact, I'd started the year poorly, distracted by my new surroundings: nothing so glamorous as the temptations of the night life, just the different sights and sounds and scale of the place, along with the bureaucratic demands of all the organizations that now impinged upon my life, from the university itself down to the shared house groceries subcommittee. In the last few weeks, though, I'd finally started hitting my stride. I'd got a part-time job, stacking shelves in a supermarket; the pay was lousy, but it was enough to take the edge off my financial anxieties, and the hours weren't so long that they left me with no time for anything but study.

I doodled harmonic contours on the notepaper in front of me. "So what do you do for fun?" I said. "Apart from complex analysis?"

Francine didn't reply immediately. This wasn't the first time we'd been alone together, but I'd never felt confident that I had the right words to make the most of the situation. At some point, though, I'd stopped fooling myself that there was ever going to be a perfect moment, with the perfect phrase falling from my lips: something subtle but intriguing slipped deftly into the conversation, without disrupting the flow. So now I'd made my interest plain, with no attempt at artfulness or eloquence. She could judge me as she knew me from the last three months, and if she felt no desire to know me better, I would not be crushed.

"I write a lot of Perl scripts," she said. "Nothing complicated; just odds and ends that I give away as freeware. It's very relaxing."

I nodded understandingly. I didn't think she was being deliberately discouraging; she just expected me to be slightly more direct.

"Do you like Deborah Conway?" I'd only heard a couple of her songs on the radio myself, but a few days before I'd seen a poster in the city announcing a tour.

"Yeah. She's great."

I started thickening the conjugation bars over the variables I'd scrawled. "She's playing at a club in Surrey Hills," I said. "On Friday. Would you like to go?"

Francine smiled, making no effort now to appear world-weary. "Sure. That would be nice."

I smiled back. I wasn't giddy, I wasn't moonstruck, but I felt as if I was standing on the shore of an ocean, contemplating its breadth. I felt the way I felt when I opened a sophisticated monograph in the library, and was reduced to savoring the scent of the print and the crisp symmetry of the notation,

understanding only a fraction of what I read. Knowing there
was something glorious ahead, but knowing too what a
daunting task it would be to come to terms with it.

I said, "I'll get the tickets on my way home."

To celebrate the end of exams for the year, the household
threw a party. It was a sultry November night, but the back
yard wasn't much bigger than the largest room in the house,
so we ended up opening all the doors and windows and distributing food and furniture throughout the ground floor and
the exterior, front and back. Once the faint humid breeze off
the river penetrated the depths of the house, it was equally
sweltering and mosquito-ridden everywhere, indoors and out.

Francine and I stayed close for an hour or so, obeying the
distinctive dynamics of a couple, until by some unspoken
mutual understanding it became clear that we could wander
apart for a while, and that neither of us was so insecure that
we'd resent it.

I ended up in a corner of the crowded backyard, talking to
Will, a biochemistry student who'd lived in the house for the
last four years. On some level, he probably couldn't help
feeling that his opinions about the way things were run
should carry more weight than anyone else's, which had annoyed me greatly when I'd first moved in. We'd since become friends, though, and I was glad to have a chance to talk
to him before he left to take up a scholarship in Germany.

In the middle of a conversation about the work he'd be doing, I caught sight of Francine, and he followed my gaze.

Will said, "It took me a while to figure out what finally
cured you of your homesickness."

"I was never homesick."

"Yeah, right." He took a swig of his drink. "She's changed
you, though. You have to admit that."

"I do. Happily. Everything's clicked, since we got together." Relationships were meant to screw up your studies,
but my marks were soaring. Francine didn't tutor me; she just
drew me into a state of mind where everything was clearer.

"The amazing thing is that you got together at all." I
scowled, and Will raised a hand placatingly. "I just meant,

when you first moved in, you were pretty reserved. And down on yourself. When we interviewed you for the room, you practically begged us to give it to someone more deserving."

"Now you're taking the piss."

He shook his head. "Ask any of the others."

I fell silent. The truth was, if I took a step back and contemplated my situation, I was as astonished as he was. By the time I'd left my home town, it had become clear to me that good fortune had nothing much to do with luck. Some people were born with wealth, or talent, or charisma. They started with an edge, and the benefits snowballed. I'd always believed that I had, at best, just enough intelligence and persistence to stay afloat in my chosen field; I'd topped every class in high school, but in a town the size of Orange that meant nothing, and I'd had no illusions about my fate in Sydney.

I owed it to Francine that my visions of mediocrity had not been fulfilled; being with her had transformed my life. But where had I found the nerve to imagine that I had anything to offer her in return?

"Something happened," I admitted. "Before I asked her out."

"Yeah?"

I almost clammed up; I hadn't told anyone about the events in the alley, not even Francine. The incident had come to seem too personal, as if to recount it at all would be to lay my conscience bare. But Will was off to Munich in less than a week, and it was easier to confide in someone I didn't expect to see again.

When I finished, Will bore a satisfied grin, as if I'd explained everything. "Pure karma," he announced. "I should have guessed."

"Oh, very scientific."

"I'm serious. Forget the Buddhist mystobabble; I'm talking about the real thing. If you stick to your principles, of course things go better for you—assuming you don't get killed in the process. That's elementary psychology. People have a highly developed sense of reciprocity, of the appropriateness of the treatment they receive from each other. If things work out too well for them, they can't help asking, 'What did I do to deserve this?' If you don't have a good answer, you'll sabotage yourself. Not all the time, but often enough. So if you do something that improves your self-esteem—"

"Self-esteem is for the weak," I quipped. Will rolled his eyes. "I don't think like that," I protested.

"No? Why did you even bring it up, then?"

I shrugged. "Maybe it just made me less pessimistic. I could have had the crap beaten out of me, but I didn't. That makes asking someone to a concert seem a lot less dangerous." I was beginning to cringe at all this unwanted analysis, and I had nothing to counter Will's pop psychology except an equally folksy version of my own.

He could see I was embarrassed, so he let the matter drop. As I watched Francine moving through the crowd, though, I couldn't shake off an unsettling sense of the tenuousness of the circumstances that had brought us together. There was no denying that if I'd walked away from the alley, and the kitchen hand had died, I would have felt like shit for a long time afterward. I would not have felt entitled to much out of my own life.

I hadn't walked away, though. And even if the decision had come down to the wire, why shouldn't I be proud that I'd made the right choice? That didn't mean everything that followed was tainted, like a reward from some sleazy, palm-greasing deity. I hadn't won Francine's affection in a medieval test of bravery; we'd chosen each other, and persisted with that choice, for a thousand complicated reasons.

We were together now; that was what mattered. I wasn't going to dwell on the path that had brought me to her, just to dredge up all the doubts and insecurities that had almost kept us apart.

2012

As we drove the last kilometer along the road south from Ar Rafidiyah, I could see the Wall of Foam glistening ahead of us in the morning sunlight. Insubstantial as a pile of soap bubbles, but still intact, after six weeks.

"I can't believe it's lasted this long," I told Sadiq.

"You didn't trust the models?"

"Fuck, no. Every week, I thought we'd come over the hill and there'd be nothing but a shriveled-up cobweb."

Sadiq smiled. "So you had no faith in my calculations?"

"Don't take it personally. There were a lot of things we could have both got wrong."

Sadiq pulled off the road. His students, Hassan and Rashid, had climbed off the back of the truck and started toward the Wall before I'd even got my face mask on. Sadiq called them back, and made them put on plastic boots and paper suits over their clothes, while the two of us did the same. We didn't usually bother with this much protection, but today was different.

Close up, the Wall almost vanished: all you noticed were isolated, rainbow-fringed reflections, drifting at a leisurely pace across the otherwise invisible film as water redistributed itself, following waves induced in the membrane by the interplay of air pressure, thermal gradients, and surface tension. These images might easily have been separate objects, scraps of translucent plastic blowing around above the desert, held aloft by a breeze too faint to detect at ground level.

The further away you looked, though, the more crowded the hints of light became, and the less plausible any alternative hypothesis that denied the Wall its integrity. It stretched for a kilometer along the edge of the desert, and rose an uneven 15 to 20 meters into the air. But it was merely the first, and smallest, of its kind, and the time had come to put it on the back of the truck and drive it all the way back to Basra.

Sadiq took a spray can of reagent from the cabin, and shook it as he walked down the embankment. I followed him, my heart in my mouth. The Wall had not dried out; it had not been torn apart or blown away, but there was still plenty of room for failure.

Sadiq reached up and sprayed what appeared from my vantage to be thin air, but I could see the fine mist of droplets strike the membrane. A breathy susurration rose up, like the sound from a steam iron, and I felt a faint warm dampness before the first silken threads appeared, crisscrossing the region where the polymer from which the Wall was built had begun to shift conformations. In one state, the polymer was soluble, exposing hydrophilic groups of atoms that bound water into narrow sheets of feather-light gel. Now, triggered by the reagent and powered by sunlight, it was tucking these groups into slick, oily cages, and expelling every molecule of water, transforming the gel into a desiccated web.

I just hoped it wasn't expelling anything else.

As the lacy net began to fall in folds at his feet, Hassan said something in Arabic, disgusted and amused. My grasp of the language remained patchy; Sadiq translated for me, his voice muffled by his face mask: "He says probably most of the weight of the thing will be dead insects." He shooed the youths back toward the truck before following himself, as the wind blew a glistening curtain over our heads. It descended far too slowly to trap us, but I hastened up the slope.

We watched from the truck as the Wall came down, the wave of dehydration propagating along its length. If the gel had been an elusive sight close up, the residue was entirely invisible in the distance; there was less substance to it than a very long pantyhose—albeit, pantyhose clogged with gnats.

The smart polymer was the invention of Sonja Helvig, a Norwegian chemist; I'd tweaked her original design for this application. Sadiq and his students were civil engineers, responsible for scaling everything up to the point where it could have a practical benefit. On those terms, this experiment was still nothing but a minor field trial.

I turned to Sadiq. "You did some mine clearance once, didn't you?"

"Years ago." Before I could say anything more, he'd caught my drift. "You're thinking that might have been more satisfying? Bang, and it's gone, the proof is there in front of you?"

"One less mine, one less bomblet," I said. "However

many thousands there were to deal with, at least you could tick each one off as a definite achievement."

"That's true. It was a good feeling." He shrugged. "But what should we do? Give up on this, because it's harder?"

He took the truck down the slope, then supervised the students as they attached the wisps of polymer to the specialized winch they'd built. Hassan and Rashid were in their 20s, but they could easily have passed for adolescents. After the war, the dictator and his former backers in the west had found it mutually expedient to have a generation of Iraqi children grow up malnourished and without medical care, if they grew up at all. More than a million people had died under the sanctions. My own sick joke of a nation had sent part of its navy to join the blockade, while the rest stayed home to fend off boatloads of refugees from this, and other, atrocities. General Mustache was long dead, but his comrades-in-genocide with more salubrious addresses were all still at large: doing lecture tours, running think tanks, lobbying for the Nobel peace prize.

As the strands of polymer wound around a core inside the winch's protective barrel, the alpha count rose steadily. It was a good sign: the fine particles of uranium oxide trapped by the Wall had remained bound to the polymer during dehydration, and the reeling in of the net. The radiation from the few grams of U-238 we'd collected was far too low to be a hazard in itself; the thing to avoid was ingesting the dust, and even then the unpleasant effects were as much chemical as radiological. Hopefully, the polymer had also bound its other targets: the organic carcinogens that had been strewn across Kuwait and southern Iraq by the apocalyptic oil well fires. There was no way to determine that until we did a full chemical analysis.

We were all in high spirits on the ride back. What we'd plucked from the wind in the last six weeks wouldn't spare a single person from leukemia, but it now seemed possible that over the years, over the decades, the technology would make a real difference.

* * *

I missed the connection in Singapore for a direct flight home to Sydney, so I had to go via Perth. There was a four-hour wait in Perth; I paced the transit lounge, restless and impatient. I hadn't set eyes on Francine since she'd left Basra three months earlier; she didn't approve of clogging up the limited bandwidth into Iraq with decadent video. When I'd called her from Singapore she'd been busy, and now I couldn't decide whether or not to try again.

Just when I'd resolved to call her, an email came through on my notepad, saying that she'd received my message and would meet me at the airport.

In Sydney, I stood by the baggage carousel, searching the crowd. When I finally saw Francine approaching, she was looking straight at me, smiling. I left the carousel and walked toward her; she stopped and let me close the gap, keeping her eyes fixed on mine. There was a mischievousness to her expression, as if she'd arranged some kind of prank, but I couldn't guess what it might be.

When I was almost in front of her, she turned slightly, and spread her arms. "Ta-da!"

I froze, speechless. *Why hadn't she told me?*

I walked up to her and embraced her, but she'd read my expression. "Don't be angry, Ben. I was afraid you'd come home early if you knew."

"You're right, I would have." My thoughts were piling up on top of each other; I had three months' worth of reactions to get through in 15 seconds. *We hadn't planned this. We couldn't afford it. I wasn't ready.*

Suddenly I started weeping, too shocked to be self-conscious in the crowd. The knot of panic and confusion inside me dissolved. I held her more tightly, and felt the swelling in her body against my hip.

"Are you happy?" Francine asked.

I laughed and nodded, choking out the words: "This is wonderful!"

I meant it. I was still afraid, but it was an exuberant fear. Another ocean had opened up before us. We would find our bearings. We would cross it together.

*   *   *

It took me several days to come down to Earth. We didn't have a real chance to talk until the weekend; Francine had a teaching position at UNSW, and though she could have set her own research aside for a couple of days, marking could wait for no one. There were a thousand things to plan; the six-month UNESCO fellowship that had paid for me to take part in the project in Basra had expired, and I'd need to start earning money again soon, but the fact that I'd made no commitments yet gave me some welcome flexibility.

On Monday, alone in the flat again, I started catching up on all the journals I'd neglected. In Iraq I'd been obsessively single-minded, instructing my knowledge miner to keep me informed of work relevant to the Wall, to the exclusion of everything else.

Skimming through a summary of six months' worth of papers, a report in *Science* caught my eye: "An Experimental Model for Decoherence in the Many-Worlds Cosmology." A group at Delft University in the Netherlands had arranged for a simple quantum computer to carry out a sequence of arithmetic operations on a register which had been prepared to contain an equal superposition of binary representations of two different numbers. This in itself was nothing new; superpositions representing up to 128 numbers were now manipulated daily, albeit only under laboratory conditions, at close to absolute zero.

Unusually, though, at each stage of the calculation the qubits containing the numbers in question had been deliberately entangled with other, spare qubits in the computer. The effect of this was that the section performing the calculation had ceased to be in a pure quantum state: it behaved, not as if it contained two numbers simultaneously, but as if there were merely an equal chance of it containing either one. This had undermined the quantum nature of the calculation, just as surely as if the whole machine had been imperfectly shielded and become entangled with objects in the environment.

There was one crucial difference, though: in this case, the experimenters had still had access to the spare qubits that had made the calculation behave classically. When they performed an appropriate measurement on the state of the computer *as a whole,* it was shown to have remained in a superposition all along. A single observation couldn't prove this, but the experiment had been repeated thousands of times, and within the margins of error, their prediction was confirmed: although the superposition had become undetectable when they ignored the spare qubits, it had never really gone away. *Both* classical calculations had always taken place simultaneously, even though they'd lost the ability to interact in a quantum-mechanical fashion.

I sat at my desk, pondering the result. On one level, it was just a scaling-up of the quantum eraser experiments of the '90s, but the image of a tiny computer program running through its paces, appearing "to itself" to be unique and alone, while in fact a second, equally oblivious version had been executing beside it all along, carried a lot more resonance than an interference experiment with photons. I'd become used to the idea of quantum computers performing several calculations at once, but that conjuring trick had always seemed abstract and ethereal, precisely because the parts continued to act as a complicated whole right to the end. What struck home *here* was the stark demonstration of the way each calculation could come to appear as a distinct classical history, as solid and mundane as the shuffling of beads on an abacus.

When Francine arrived home I was cooking dinner, but I grabbed my notepad and showed her the paper.

"Yeah, I've seen it," she said.

"What do you think?"

She raised her hands and recoiled in mock alarm.

"I'm serious."

"What do you want me to say? Does this prove the Many Worlds interpretation? No. Does it make it easier to understand, to have a toy model like this? Yes."

"But does it sway you at all?" I persisted. "Do you believe the results would still hold, if they could be scaled up indefinitely?" From a toy universe, a handful of qubits, to the real one.

She shrugged. "I don't really need to be swayed. I always

thought the MWI was the most plausible interpretation anyway."

I left it at that, and went back to the kitchen while she pulled out a stack of assignments.

That night, as we lay in bed together, I couldn't get the Delft experiment out of my mind.

"Do you believe there are other versions of us?" I asked Francine.

"I suppose there must be." She conceded the point as if it was something abstract and metaphysical, and I was being pedantic even to raise it. People who professed belief in the MWI never seemed to want to take it seriously, let alone personally.

"And that doesn't bother you?"

"No," she said blithely. "Since I'm powerless to change the situation, what's the use in being upset about it?"

"That's very pragmatic," I said. Francine reached over and thumped me on the shoulder. "That was a compliment!" I protested. "I envy you for having come to terms with it so easily."

"I haven't, really," she admitted. "I've just resolved not to let it worry me, which isn't quite the same thing."

I turned to face her, though in the near-darkness we could barely see each other. I said, "What gives you the most satisfaction in life?"

"I take it you're not in the mood to be fobbed off with a soppy romantic answer?" She sighed. "I don't know. Solving problems. Getting things right."

"What if for every problem you solve, there's someone just like you who fails, instead?"

"I cope with my failures," she said. "Let them cope with theirs."

"You know it doesn't work like that. Some of them simply *don't* cope. Whatever you find the strength to do, there'll be someone else who won't."

Francine had no reply.

I said, "A couple of weeks ago, I asked Sadiq about the time he was doing mine clearance. He said it was more satisfying than mopping up DU; one little explosion, right before your eyes, and you know you've done something worthwhile. We all get moments in our lives like that, with that pure, unambiguous sense of achievement: whatever else we might screw up, at least there's one thing that we've done right." I laughed uneasily. "I think I'd go mad, if I couldn't rely on that."

Francine said, "You can. Nothing you've done will ever disappear from under your feet. No one's going to march up and take it away from you."

"I know." My skin crawled, at the image of some less favored alter ego turning up on our doorstep, demanding his dues. "That seems so fucking selfish, though. I don't want everything that makes me happy to be at the expense of someone else. I don't want every choice to be like . . . fighting other versions of myself for the prize in some zero-sum game."

"No." Francine hesitated. "But if the reality is like that, what can you do about it?"

Her words hung in the darkness. What could I do about it? Nothing. So did I really want to dwell on it, corroding the foundations of my own happiness, when there was absolutely nothing to be gained, for anyone?

"You're right. This is crazy." I leaned over and kissed her. "I'd better let you get to sleep."

"It's not crazy," she said. "But I don't have any answers."

The next morning, after Francine had left for work, I picked up my notepad and saw that she'd mailed me an e-book: an anthology of cheesy "alternate (sic) history" stories from the '90s, entitled *My God, It's Full of Tsars!* "What if Gandhi had been a ruthless soldier of fortune? What if Theodore Roosevelt had faced a Martian invasion? What if the Nazis had had Janet Jackson's choreographer?"

I skimmed through the introduction, alternately cackling and groaning, then filed the book away and got down to work. I had a dozen minor administrative tasks to complete for UNESCO, before I could start searching in earnest for my next position.

By mid-afternoon, I was almost done, but the growing

sense of achievement I felt at having buckled down and cleared away these tedious obligations brought with it the corollary: someone infinitesimally different from me— someone who had shared my entire history up until that morning—had procrastinated instead. The triviality of this observation only made it more unsettling; the Delft experiment was seeping into my daily life on the most mundane level.

I dug out the book Francine had sent and tried reading a few of the stories, but the authors' relentlessly camp take on the premise hardly amounted to a *reductio ad absurdum*, or even a comical existential balm. I didn't really care how hilarious it would have been if Marilyn Monroe had been involved in a bedroom farce with Richard Feynman and Richard Nixon. I just wanted to lose the suffocating conviction that everything I had become was a mirage; that my life had been nothing but a blinkered view of a kind of torture chamber, where every glorious reprieve I'd ever celebrated had in fact been an unwitting betrayal.

If fiction had no comfort to offer, what about fact? Even if the Many Worlds cosmology was correct, no one knew for certain what the consequences were. It was a fallacy that literally everything that was physically possible had to occur; most cosmologists I'd read believed that the universe as a whole possessed a single, definite quantum state, and while that state would appear from within as a multitude of distinct classical histories, there was no reason to assume that these histories amounted to some kind of exhaustive catalog. The same thing held true on a smaller scale: every time two people sat down to a game of chess, there was no reason to believe that they played every possible game.

And if I'd stood in an alley, nine years before, struggling with my conscience? My subjective sense of indecision proved nothing, but even if I'd suffered no qualms and acted without hesitation, to find a human being in a quantum state of pure, unshakable resolve would have been freakishly unlikely at best, and in fact was probably physically impossible.

"Fuck this." I didn't know when I'd set myself up for this

bout of paranoia, but I wasn't going to indulge it for another second. I banged my head against the desk a few times, then picked up my notepad and went straight to an employment site.

The thoughts didn't vanish entirely; it was too much like trying not to think of a pink elephant. Each time they recurred, though, I found I could shout them down with threats of taking myself straight to a psychiatrist. The prospect of having to explain such a bizarre mental problem was enough to give me access to hitherto untapped reserves of self-discipline.

By the time I started cooking dinner, I was feeling merely foolish. If Francine mentioned the subject again, I'd make a joke of it. I didn't need a psychiatrist. I was a little insecure about my good fortune, and still somewhat rattled by the news of impending fatherhood, but it would hardly have been healthier to take everything for granted.

My notepad chimed. Francine had blocked the video again, as if bandwidth, even here, was as precious as water.

"Hello?"

"Ben? I've had some bleeding. I'm in a taxi. Can you meet me at St. Vincent's?"

Her voice was steady, but my own mouth went dry. "Sure. I'll be there in 15 minutes." I couldn't add anything: *I love you, it will be all right, hold on*. She didn't need that, it would have jinxed everything.

Half an hour later, I was still caught in traffic, white-knuckled with rage and helplessness. I stared down at the dashboard, at the real-time map with every other gridlocked vehicle marked, and finally stopped deluding myself that at any moment I would turn into a magically deserted side-street and weave my way across the city in just a few more minutes.

In the ward, behind the curtains drawn around her bed, Francine lay curled and rigid, her back turned, refusing to look at me. All I could do was stand beside her. The gynecologist was yet to explain everything properly, but the miscarriage had been accompanied by complications, and she'd had to perform surgery.

Before I'd applied for the UNESCO fellowship, we'd discussed the risks. For two prudent, well-informed, short-term visitors, the danger had seemed microscopic. Francine had never traveled out into the desert with me, and even for the locals in Basra the rates of birth defects and miscarriages had fallen a long way from their peaks. We were both taking contraceptives; condoms had seemed like overkill. *Had I brought it back to her, from the desert? A speck of dust, trapped beneath my foreskin? Had I poisoned her while we were making love?*

Francine turned toward me. The skin around her eyes was gray and swollen, and I could see how much effort it took for her to meet my gaze. She drew her hands out from under the bedclothes, and let me hold them; they were freezing.

After a while, she started sobbing, but she wouldn't release my hands. I stroked the back of her thumb with my own thumb, a tiny, gentle movement.

2020

"How do you feel now?" Olivia Maslin didn't quite make eye contact as she addressed me; the image of my brain activity painted on her retinas was clearly holding her attention.

"Fine," I said. "Exactly the same as I did before you started the infusion."

I was reclining on something like a dentist's couch, halfway between sitting and lying, wearing a tight-fitting cap studded with magnetic sensors and inducers. It was impossible to ignore the slight coolness of the liquid flowing into the vein in my forearm, but that sensation was no different than it had been on the previous occasion, a fortnight before.

"Could you count to ten for me, please."

I obliged.

"Now close your eyes and picture the same familiar face as the last time."

She'd told me I could choose anyone; I'd picked Francine. I brought back the image, then suddenly recalled that, the first time, after contemplating the detailed picture in my head for a few seconds—as if I was preparing to give a description to the police—I'd started thinking about Francine herself. On cue, the same transition occurred again: the frozen, forensic likeness became flesh and blood.

I was led through the whole sequence of activities once more: reading the same short story ("Two Old-Timers" by F. Scott Fitzgerald), listening to the same piece of music (from Rossini's *The Thieving Magpie*), recounting the same childhood memory (my first day at school). At some point, I lost any trace of anxiety about repeating my earlier mental states with sufficient fidelity; after all, the experiment had been designed to cope with the inevitable variation between the two sessions. I was just one volunteer out of dozens, and half the subjects would be receiving nothing but saline on both occasions. For all I knew, I was one of them: a control, merely setting the baseline against which any real effect would be judged.

If I was receiving the coherence disruptors, though, then as far as I could tell they'd had no effect on me. My inner life hadn't evaporated as the molecules bound to the microtubules in my neurons, guaranteeing that any kind of quantum coherence those structures might otherwise have maintained would be lost to the environment in a fraction of a picosecond.

Personally, I'd never subscribed to Penrose's theory that quantum effects might play a role in consciousness; calculations dating back to a seminal paper by Max Tegmark, 20 years before, had already made sustained coherence in any neural structure extremely unlikely. Nevertheless, it had taken considerable ingenuity on the part of Olivia and her team to rule out the idea definitively, in a series of clear-cut experiments. Over the past two years, they'd chased the ghost away from each of the various structures that different factions of Penrose's disciples had anointed as the essential quantum components of the brain. The earliest proposal—the microtubules, huge polymeric molecules that formed a kind of skeleton inside every cell—had turned out to be the hardest to target for disruption. But now it was entirely possible that the cytoskeletons of my very own neurons were dotted with molecules that coupled them strongly to a noisy microwave field in which my skull was, definitely, bathed. In which case, my microtubules had about as much chance of exploiting quantum effects as I had of playing a game of squash with a version of myself from a parallel universe.

When the experiment was over, Olivia thanked me, then became even more distant as she reviewed the data. Raj, one of her graduate students, slid out the needle and stuck a plaster over the tiny puncture wound, then helped me out of the cap.

"I know you don't know yet if I was a control or not," I said, "but have you noticed significant differences, with anyone?" I was almost the last subject in the microtubule trials; any effect should have shown up by now.

Olivia smiled enigmatically. "You'll just have to wait for publication." Raj leaned down and whispered, "No, never."

I climbed off the couch. "The zombie walks!" Raj declaimed. I lunged hungrily for his brain; he ducked away, laughing, while Olivia watched us with an expression of pained indulgence. Die-hard members of the Penrose camp claimed that Olivia's experiments proved nothing, because even if people *behaved* identically while all quantum effects were ruled out, they could be doing this as mere automata, totally devoid of consciousness. When Olivia had offered to let her chief detractor experience coherence disruption for himself, he'd replied that this would be no more persuasive, because memories laid down while you were a zombie would be indistinguishable from ordinary memories, so that looking back on the experience, you'd notice nothing unusual.

This was sheer desperation; you might as well assert that everyone in the world but yourself was a zombie, and you were one, too, every second Tuesday. As the experiments were repeated by other groups around the world, those people who'd backed the Penrose theory as scientific hypothesis, rather than adopting it as a kind of mystical dogma, would gradually accept that it had been refuted.

I left the neuroscience building and walked across the campus, back toward my office in the physics department. It was a mild, clear spring morning, with students out lying on the grass, dozing off with books balanced over their faces like tents. There were still some advantages to reading from old-fashioned sheaves of e-paper. I'd only had my own eyes chipped the year before, and though I'd adapted to the technology easily enough, I still found it disconcerting to wake on a Sunday morning to find Francine reading the *Herald* beside me with her eyes shut.

Olivia's results didn't surprise me, but it was satisfying to have the matter resolved once and for all: consciousness was a purely classical phenomenon. Among other things, this meant that there was no compelling reason to believe that software running on a classical computer could not be conscious. Of course, everything in the universe obeyed quantum mechanics at some level, but Paul Benioff, one of the pioneers of quantum computing, had shown back in the '80s that you could build a classical Turing machine from quantum mechanical parts, and over the last few years, in my spare time, I'd studied the branch of quantum computing theory that concerned itself with *avoiding* quantum effects.

Back in my office, I summoned up a schematic of the device I called the Qusp: the quantum singleton processor. The Qusp would employ all the techniques designed to shield the latest generation of quantum computers from entanglement with their environment, but it would use them to a very different end. A quantum computer was shielded so it could perform a multitude of parallel calculations, without each one spawning a separate history of its own, in which only one answer was accessible. The Qusp would perform just a single calculation at a time, but on its way to the unique result it would be able to pass safely through superpositions that included any number of alternatives, without those alternatives being made real. Cut off from the outside world during each computational step, it would keep its temporary quantum ambivalence as private and inconsequential as a daydream, never being forced to act out every possibility it dared to entertain.

The Qusp would still need to interact with its environment whenever it gathered data about the world, and that interaction would inevitably split it into different versions. If you attached a camera to the Qusp and pointed it at an ordinary object—a rock, a plant, a bird—that object could hardly be expected to possess a single classical history, and so neither would the combined system of Qusp plus rock, Qusp plus plant, Qusp plus bird.

The Qusp itself, though, would never initiate the split. In a given set of circumstances, it would only ever produce a single response. An AI running on the Qusp could make its decisions as whimsically, or with as much weighty deliberation as it liked, but for each distinct scenario it confronted, in the end it would only make one choice, only follow one course of action.

I closed the file, and the image vanished from my retinas. For all the work I'd put into the design, I'd made no effort to build the thing. I'd been using it as little more than a talisman: whenever I found myself picturing my life as a tranquil dwelling built over a slaughter house, I'd summon up the Qusp as a symbol of hope. It was proof of a possibility, and a possibility was all it took. Nothing in the laws of physics could prevent a small portion of humanity's descendants from escaping their ancestors' dissipation.

Yet I'd shied away from any attempt to see that promise fulfilled, firsthand. In part, I'd been afraid of delving too deeply and uncovering a flaw in the Qusp's design, robbing myself of the one crutch that kept me standing when the horror swept over me. It had also been a matter of guilt: I'd been the one granted happiness, so many times, that it had seemed unconscionable to aspire to that state yet again. I'd knocked so many of my hapless cousins out of the ring, it was time I threw a fight and let the prize go to my opponent instead.

That last excuse was idiotic. The stronger my determination to build the Qusp, the more branches there would be in which it was real. Weakening my resolve was *not* an act of charity, surrendering the benefits to someone else; it merely impoverished every future version of me, and everyone they touched.

I did have a third excuse. It was time I dealt with that one, too.

I called Francine.

"Are you free for lunch?" I asked. She hesitated; there was always work she could be doing. "To discuss the Cauchy-Riemann equations?" I suggested.

She smiled. It was our code, when the request was a special one. "All right. One o'clock?"

I nodded. "I'll see you then."

Francine was 20 minutes late, but that was less of a wait than I was used to. She'd been appointed deputy head of the mathematics department 18 months before, and she still had some teaching duties as well as all the new administrative work. Over the last eight years, I'd had a dozen short-term contracts with various bodies—government departments, corporations, NGOs—before finally ending up as a very lowly member of the physics department at our *alma mater*. I did envy her the prestige and security of her job, but I'd been happy with most of the work I'd done, even if it had been too scattered between disciplines to contribute to anything like a traditional career path.

I'd bought Francine a plate of cheese-and-salad sandwiches, and she attacked them hungrily as soon as she sat down. I said, "I've got ten minutes at the most, haven't I?"

She covered her mouth with her hand and replied defensively, "It could have waited until tonight, couldn't it?"

"Sometimes I can't put things off. I have to act while I still have the courage."

At this ominous prelude she chewed more slowly. "You did the second stage of Olivia's experiment this morning, didn't you?"

"Yeah." I'd discussed the whole procedure with her before I volunteered.

"So I take it you didn't lose consciousness, when your neurons became marginally more classical than usual?" She sipped chocolate milk through a straw.

"No. Apparently no one ever loses anything. That's not official yet, but—"

Francine nodded, unsurprised. We shared the same position on the Penrose theory; there was no need to discuss it again now.

I said, "I want to know if you're going to have the operation."

She continued drinking for a few more seconds, then released the straw and wiped her upper lip with her thumb, unnecessarily. "You want me to make up my mind about that, here and now?"

"No." The damage to her uterus from the miscarriage could be repaired; we'd been discussing the possibility for almost five years. We'd both had comprehensive chelation therapy to remove any trace of U-238. We could have children in the usual way with a reasonable degree of safety, if that was what we wanted. "But if you've already decided, I want you to tell me now."

Francine looked wounded. "That's unfair."

"What is? Implying that you might not have told me, the instant you decided?"

"No. Implying that it's all in my hands."

I said, "I'm not washing my hands of the decision. You know how I feel. But you know I'd back you all the way, if you said you wanted to carry a child." I believed I would have. Maybe it was a form of doublethink, but I couldn't treat the birth of one more ordinary child as some kind of atrocity, and refuse to be a part of it.

"Fine. But what will you do if I don't?" She examined my face calmly. I think she already knew, but she wanted me to spell it out.

"We could always adopt," I observed casually.

"Yes, we could do that." She smiled slightly; she knew that made me lose my ability to bluff, even faster than when she stared me down.

I stopped pretending that there was any mystery left; she'd seen right through me from the start. I said, "I just don't want to do this, then discover that it makes you feel that you've been cheated out of what you really wanted."

"It wouldn't," she insisted. "It wouldn't rule out anything. We could still have a natural child as well."

"Not as easily." This would not be like merely having workaholic parents, or an ordinary brother or sister to compete with for attention.

"You only want to do this if I can promise you that it's the only child we'd ever have?" Francine shook her head. "I'm not going to promise that. I don't intend having the operation any time soon, but I'm not going to swear that I won't change my mind. Nor am I going to swear that if we do this it will make no difference to what happens later. It will be a factor. How could it not be? But it won't be enough to rule anything in or out."

I looked away, across the rows of tables, at all the students wrapped up in their own concerns. She was right; I was being unreasonable. I'd wanted this to be a choice with no possible downside, a way of making the best of our situation, but no one could guarantee that. It would be a gamble, like everything else.

I turned back to Francine.

"All right; I'll stop trying to pin you down. What I want to do right now is go ahead and build the Qusp. And when it's finished, if we're certain we can trust it . . . I want us to raise a child with it. I want us to raise an AI."

2029

I met Francine at the airport, and we drove across Sao Paulo through curtains of wild, lashing rain. I was amazed that her plane hadn't been diverted; a tropical storm had just hit the coast, halfway between us and Rio.

"So much for giving you a tour of the city," I lamented. Through the windscreen, our actual surroundings were all but invisible; the bright overlay we both perceived, surreally colored and detailed, made the experience rather like perusing a 3D map while trapped in a car wash.

Francine was pensive, or tired from the flight. I found it

hard to think of San Francisco as remote when the time difference was so small, and even when I'd made the journey north to visit her, it had been nothing compared to all the ocean-spanning marathons I'd sat through in the past.

We both had an early night. The next morning, Francine accompanied me to my cluttered workroom in the basement of the university's engineering department. I'd been chasing grants and collaborators around the world, like a child on a treasure hunt, slowly piecing together a device that few of my colleagues believed was worth creating for its own sake. Fortunately, I'd managed to find pretexts—or even genuine spin-offs—for almost every stage of the work. Quantum computing, *per se*, had become bogged down in recent years, stymied by both a shortage of practical algorithms and a limit to the complexity of superpositions that could be sustained. The Qusp had nudged the technological envelope in some promising directions, without making any truly exorbitant demands; the states it juggled were relatively simple, and they only needed to be kept isolated for milliseconds at a time.

I introduced Carlos, Maria and Jun, but then they made themselves scarce as I showed Francine around. We still had a demonstration of the "balanced decoupling" principle set up on a bench, for the tour by one of our corporate donors the week before. What caused an imperfectly shielded quantum computer to decohere was the fact that each possible state of the device affected its environment slightly differently. The shielding itself could always be improved, but Carlos's group had perfected a way to buy a little more protection by sheer deviousness. In the demonstration rig, the flow of energy through the device remained absolutely constant whatever state it was in, because any drop in power consumption by the main set of quantum gates was compensated for by a rise in a set of balancing gates, and *vice versa*. This gave the environment one less clue by which to discern internal differences in the processor, and to tear any superposition apart into mutually disconnected branches.

Francine knew all the theory backward, but she'd never

seen this hardware in action. When I invited her to twiddle the controls, she took to the rig like a child with a game console.

"You really should have joined the team," I said.

"Maybe I did," she countered. "In another branch."

She'd moved from UNSW to Berkeley two years before, not long after I'd moved from Delft to Sao Paulo; it was the closest suitable position she could find. At the time, I'd resented the fact that she'd refused to compromise and work remotely; with only five hours' difference, teaching at Berkeley from Sao Paulo would not have been impossible. In the end, though, I'd accepted the fact that she'd wanted to keep on testing me, testing both of us. If we weren't strong enough to stay together through the trials of a prolonged physical separation—or if I was not sufficiently committed to the project to endure whatever sacrifices it entailed—she did not want us proceeding to the next stage.

I led her to the corner bench, where a nondescript gray box half a meter across sat, apparently inert. I gestured to it, and our retinal overlays transformed its appearance, "revealing" a maze with a transparent lid embedded in the top of the device. In one chamber of the maze, a slightly cartoonish mouse sat motionless. Not quite dead, not quite sleeping.

"This is the famous Zelda?" Francine asked.

"Yes." Zelda was a neural network, a stripped-down, stylized mouse brain. There were newer, fancier versions available, much closer to the real thing, but the ten-year-old, public domain Zelda had been good enough for our purposes.

Three other chambers held cheese. "Right now, she has no experience of the maze," I explained. "So let's start her up and watch her explore." I gestured, and Zelda began scampering around, trying out different passages, deftly reversing each time she hit a cul-de-sac. "Her brain is running on a Qusp, but the maze is implemented on an ordinary classical computer, so in terms of coherence issues, it's really no different from a physical maze."

"Which means that each time she takes in information, she gets entangled with the outside world," Francine suggested.

"Absolutely. But she always holds off doing that until the Qusp has completed its current computational step, and every qubit contains a definite zero or a definite one. She's never in two minds when she lets the world in, so the entanglement process doesn't split her into separate branches."

Francine continued to watch, in silence. Zelda finally found one of the chambers containing a reward; when she'd eaten it, a hand scooped her up and returned her to her starting point, then replaced the cheese.

"Here are 10,000 previous trials, superimposed." I replayed the data. It looked as if a single mouse was running through the maze, moving just as we'd seen her move when I'd begun the latest experiment. Restored each time to exactly the same starting condition, and confronted with exactly the same environment, Zelda—like any computer program with no truly random influences—had simply repeated herself. All 10,000 trials had yielded identical results.

To a casual observer, unaware of the context, this would have been a singularly unimpressive performance. Faced with exactly one situation, Zelda the virtual mouse did exactly one thing. So what? If you'd been able to wind back a flesh-and-blood mouse's memory with the same degree of precision, wouldn't it have repeated itself too?

Francine said, "Can you cut off the shielding? And the balanced decoupling?"

"Yep." I obliged her, and initiated a new trial.

Zelda took a different path this time, exploring the maze by a different route. Though the initial condition of the neural net was identical, the switching processes taking place within the Qusp were now opened up to the environment constantly, and superpositions of several different eigenstates—states in which the Qusp's qubits possessed definite binary values, which in turn led to Zelda making definite choices—were becoming entangled with the outside world. According to the Copenhagen interpretation of quantum mechanics, this interaction was randomly "collapsing" the superpositions into single eigenstates; Zelda was still doing just one thing at a time, but her behavior had ceased to be deterministic. According to the MWI, the interaction was transforming the environment—Francine and me included—into a superposition with components that were coupled to each eigenstate; Zelda was actually running the maze in many different ways simultaneously, and other versions of us were seeing her take all those other routes.

Which scenario was correct?

I said, "I'll reconfigure everything now, to wrap the whole setup in a Delft cage." A "Delft cage" was jargon for the situation I'd first read about 17 years before: instead of opening up the Qusp to the environment, I'd connect it to a second quantum computer, and let *that* play the role of the outside world.

We could no longer watch Zelda moving about in real time, but after the trial was completed, it was possible to test the combined system of both computers against the hypothesis that it was in a pure quantum state in which Zelda had run the maze along hundreds of different routes, all at once. I displayed a representation of the conjectured state, built up by superimposing all the paths she'd taken in 10,000 unshielded trials.

The test result flashed up: CONSISTENT.

"One measurement proves nothing," Francine pointed out.

"No." I repeated the trial. Again, the hypothesis was not refuted. If Zelda had actually run the maze along just one path, the probability of the computers' joint state passing this imperfect test was about one percent. For passing it twice, the odds were about one in 10,000.

I repeated it a third time, then a fourth.

Francine said, "That's enough." She actually looked queasy. The image of the hundreds of blurred mouse trails on the display was not a literal photograph of anything, but if the old Delft experiment had been enough to give me a visceral sense of the reality of the multiverse, perhaps this demonstration had finally done the same for her.

"Can I show you one more thing?" I asked.

"Keep the Delft cage, but restore the Qusp's shielding?"

"Right."

I did it. The Qusp was now fully protected once more

whenever it was not in an eigenstate, but this time, it was the second quantum computer, not the outside world, to which it was intermittently exposed. If Zelda split into multiple branches again, then she'd only take that fake environment with her, and we'd still have our hands on all the evidence.

Tested against the hypothesis that no split had occurred, the verdict was: CONSISTENT. CONSISTENT. CONSISTENT.

We went out to dinner with the whole of the team, but Francine pleaded a headache and left early. She insisted that I stay and finish the meal, and I didn't argue; she was not the kind of person who expected you to assume that she was being politely selfless, while secretly hoping to be contradicted.

After Francine had left, Maria turned to me. "So you two are really going ahead with the Frankenchild?" She'd been teasing me about this for as long as I'd known her, but apparently she hadn't been game to raise the subject in Francine's presence.

"We still have to talk about it." I felt uncomfortable myself, now, discussing the topic the moment Francine was absent. Confessing my ambition when I applied to join the team was one thing; it would have been dishonest to keep my collaborators in the dark about my ultimate intentions. Now that the enabling technology was more or less completed, though, the issue seemed far more personal.

Carlos said breezily, "Why not? There are so many others now. Sophie. Linus. Theo. Probably a hundred we don't even know about. It's not as if Ben's child won't have playmates." Adai—Autonomously Developing Artificial Intelligences—had been appearing in a blaze of controversy every few months for the last four years. A Swiss researcher, Isabelle Schib, had taken the old models of morphogenesis that had led to software like Zelda, refined the technique by several orders of magnitude, and applied it to human genetic data. Wedded to sophisticated prosthetic bodies, Isabelle's creations inhabited the physical world and learned from their experience, just like any other child.

Jun shook his head reprovingly. "I wouldn't raise a child

with no legal rights. What happens when you die? For all you know, it could end up as someone's property."

I'd been over this with Francine. "I can't believe that in ten or 20 years' time there won't be citizenship laws, somewhere in the world."

Jun snorted. "Twenty years! How long did it take the U.S. to emancipate their slaves?"

Carlos interjected, "Who's going to create an adai just to use it as a slave? If you want something biddable, write ordinary software. If you need consciousness, humans are cheaper."

Maria said, "It won't come down to economics. It's the nature of the things that will determine how they're treated."

"You mean the xenophobia they'll face?" I suggested.

Maria shrugged. "You make it sound like racism, but we aren't talking about human beings. Once you have software with goals of its own, free to do whatever it likes, where will it end? The first generation makes the next one better, faster, smarter; the second generation even more so. Before we know it, we're like ants to them."

Carlos groaned. "Not that hoary old fallacy! If you really believe that stating the analogy 'ants are to humans, as humans are to x' is proof that it's possible to solve for x, then I'll meet you where the south pole is like the equator."

I said, "The Qusp runs no faster than an organic brain; we need to keep the switching rate low, because that makes the shielding requirements less stringent. It might be possible to nudge those parameters, eventually, but there's no reason in the world why an adai would be better equipped to do that than you or I would. As for making their own offspring smarter . . . even if Schib's group has been perfectly successful, they will have merely translated human neural development from one substrate to another. They won't have 'improved' on the process at all—whatever that might mean. So if the adai have any advantage over us, it will be no more than the advantage shared by flesh-and-blood children: cultural transmission of one more generation's worth of experience."

Maria frowned, but she had no immediate comeback.

Jun said dryly, "Plus immortality."

"Well, yes, there is that." I conceded.

Francine was awake when I arrived home.

"Have you still got a headache?" I whispered.

"No."

I undressed and climbed into bed beside her.

She said, "You know what I miss the most? When we're fucking on-line?"

"This had better not be complicated; I'm out of practice."

"Kissing."

I kissed her, slowly and tenderly, and she melted beneath me. "Three more months," I promised, "and I'll move up to Berkeley."

"To be my kept man."

"I prefer the term 'unpaid but highly valued caregiver.'" Francine stiffened. I said, "We can talk about that later." I started kissing her again, but she turned her face away.

"I'm afraid," she said.

"So am I," I assured her. "That's a good sign. Everything worth doing is terrifying."

"But not everything terrifying is good."

I rolled over and lay beside her. She said, "On one level, it's easy. What greater gift could you give a child than the power to make real decisions? What worse fate could you spare her from than being forced to act against her better judgment, over and over? When you put it like that, it's simple.

"But every fiber in my body still rebels against it. How will she feel, knowing what she is? How will she make friends? How will she belong? How will she not despise us for making her a freak? And what if we're robbing her of something she'd value: living a billion lives, never being forced to choose between them? What if she sees the gift as a kind of impoverishment?"

"She can always drop the shielding on the Qusp," I said. "Once she understands the issues, she can choose for herself."

"That's true." Francine did not sound mollified at all; she would have thought of that long before I'd mentioned it, but she wasn't looking for concrete answers. Every ordinary human instinct screamed at us that we were embarking on something *dangerous, unnatural, hubristic*—but those instincts were more about safeguarding our own reputations than protecting our child-to-be. No parent, save the most willfully negligent, would be pilloried if their flesh-and-blood child turned out to be ungrateful for life; if I'd railed against my own mother and father because I'd found fault in the existential conditions with which I'd been lumbered, it wasn't hard to guess which side would attract the most sympathy from the world at large. Anything that went wrong with *our* child would be grounds for lynching—however much love, sweat, and soul-searching had gone into her creation—because we'd had the temerity to be dissatisfied with the kind of fate that everyone else happily inflicted on their own.

I said, "You saw Zelda today, spread across the branches. You know, deep down now, that the same thing happens to all of us."

"Yes." Something tore inside me as Francine uttered that admission. I'd never really wanted her to feel it, the way I did.

I persisted. "Would you willingly sentence your own child to that condition? And your grandchildren? And your great-grandchildren?"

"No," Francine replied. A part of her hated me now; I could hear it in her voice. It was *my* curse, *my* obsession; before she met me, she'd managed to believe and not believe, taking her acceptance of the multiverse lightly.

I said, "I can't do this without you."

"You can, actually. More easily than any of the alternatives. You wouldn't even need a stranger to donate an egg."

"I can't do it unless you're behind me. If you say the word, I'll stop here. We've built the Qusp. We've shown that it can work. Even if we don't do this last part ourselves, someone else will, in a decade or two."

"If *we* don't do this," Francine observed acerbically, "we'll simply do it in another branch."

I said, "That's true, but it's no use thinking that way. In the end, I can't function unless I pretend that my choices are real. I doubt that anyone can."

Francine was silent for a long time. I stared up into the darkness of the room, trying hard not to contemplate the near certainty that her decision would go both ways.

Finally, she spoke.

"Then let's make a child who doesn't need to pretend."

2031

Isabelle Schib welcomed us into her office. In person, she was slightly less intimidating than she was on-line; it wasn't anything different in her appearance or manner, just the ordinariness of her surroundings. I'd envisaged her ensconced in some vast, pristine, high-tech building, not a couple of pokey rooms on a back-street in Basel.

Once the pleasantries were out of the way, Isabelle got straight to the point. "You've been accepted," she announced. "I'll send you the contract later today."

My throat constricted with panic; I should have been elated, but I just felt unprepared. Isabelle's group licensed only three new adai a year. The short-list had come down to about a hundred couples, winnowed from tens of thousands of applicants. We'd traveled to Switzerland for the final selection process, carried out by an agency that ordinarily handled adoptions. Through all the interviews and questionnaires, all the personality tests and scenario challenges, I'd managed to half-convince myself that our dedication would win through in the end, but that had been nothing but a prop to keep my spirits up.

Francine said calmly, "Thank you."

I coughed. "You're happy with everything we've proposed?" If there was going to be a proviso thrown in that rendered this miracle worthless, better to hear it now, before the shock had worn off and I'd started taking things for granted.

Isabelle nodded. "I don't pretend to be an expert in the relevant fields, but I've had the Qusp's design assessed by several colleagues, and I see no reason why it wouldn't be an appropriate form of hardware for an adai. I'm entirely agnostic about the MWI, so I don't share your view that the Qusp is a necessity, but if you were worried that I might write you off as cranks because of it," she smiled slightly, "you should meet some of the other people I've had to deal with.

"I believe you have the adai's welfare at heart, and you're not suffering from any of the superstitions—technophobic *or* technophilic—that would distort the relationship. And as you'll recall, I'll be entitled to visits and inspections throughout your period of guardianship. If you're found to be violating any of the terms of the contract, your license will be revoked, and I'll take charge of the adai."

Francine said, "What do you think the prospects are for a happier end to our guardianship?"

"I'm lobbying the European parliament constantly," Isabelle replied. "Of course, in a few years' time several adai will reach the stage where their personal testimony begins contributing to the debate, but none of us should wait until then. The ground has to be prepared."

We spoke for almost an hour, on this and other issues. Isabelle had become quite an expert at fending off the attentions of the media; she promised to send us a handbook on this, along with the contract.

"Did you want to meet Sophie?" Isabelle asked, almost as an afterthought.

Francine said, "That would be wonderful." Francine and I had seen a video of Sophie at age four, undergoing a battery of psychological tests, but we'd never had a chance to converse with her, let alone meet her face to face.

The three of us left the office together, and Isabelle drove us to her home on the outskirts of the town.

In the car, the reality began sinking in anew. I felt the same mixture of exhilaration and claustrophobia that I'd experienced 21 years before, when Francine had met me at the airport with news of her pregnancy. No digital conception had yet taken place, but if sex had ever felt half as loaded with risks and responsibilities as this, I would have remained celibate for life.

"No badgering, no interrogation," Isabelle warned us as she pulled into the driveway.

I said, "Of course not."

Isabelle called out, "Marco! Sophie!" as we followed her through the door. At the end of the hall, I heard childish giggling, and an adult male voice whispering in French. Then Isabelle's husband stepped out from behind the corner, a smiling, dark-haired young man, with Sophie riding on his shoulders. At first I couldn't look at her; I just smiled politely back at Marco, while noting glumly that he was at least 15 years younger than I was. *How could I even think of doing this, at 46?* Then I glanced up, and caught Sophie's eye. She gazed straight back at me for a moment, appearing curious and composed, but then a fit of shyness struck her, and she buried her face in Marco's hair.

Isabelle introduced us, in English; Sophie was being raised to speak four languages, though in Switzerland that was hardly phenomenal. Sophie said, "Hello" but kept her eyes lowered. Isabelle said, "Come into the living room. Would you like something to drink?"

The five of us sipped lemonade, and the adults made polite, superficial conversation. Sophie sat on Marco's knees, squirming restlessly, sneaking glances at us. She looked exactly like an ordinary, slightly gawky, six-year-old girl. She had Isabelle's straw-colored hair, and Marco's brown eyes; whether by fiat or rigorous genetic simulation, she could have passed for their biological daughter. I'd read technical specifications describing her body, and seen an earlier version in action on the video, but the fact that it looked so plausible was the least of its designers' achievements. Watching her drinking, wriggling and fidgeting, I had no doubt that she felt herself inhabiting this skin, as much as I did my own. She was not a puppeteer posing as a child, pulling electronic strings from some dark cavern in her skull.

"Do you like lemonade?" I asked her.

She stared at me for a moment, as if wondering whether she should be affronted by the presumptuousness of this question, then replied, "It tickles."

In the taxi to the hotel, Francine held my hand tightly.

"Are you OK?" I asked.

"Yes, of course."

In the elevator, she started crying. I wrapped my arms around her.

"She would have been 20 this year."

"I know."

"Do you think she's alive, somewhere?"

"I don't know. I don't know if that's a good way to think about it."

Francine wiped her eyes. "No. This will be her. That's the way to see it. This will be my girl. Just a few years late."

Before flying home, we visited a small pathology lab, and left samples of our blood.

Our daughter's first five bodies reached us a month before her birth. I unpacked all five, and laid them out in a row on the living room floor. With their muscles slack and their eyes rolled up, they looked more like tragic mummies than sleeping infants. I dismissed that grisly image; better to think of them as suits of clothes. The only difference was that we hadn't bought pajamas quite so far ahead.

From wrinkled pink newborn to chubby 18-month-old, the progression made an eerie sight—even if an organic child's development, short of serious disease or malnourishment, would have been scarcely less predictable. A colleague of Francine's had lectured me a few weeks before about the terrible "mechanical determinism" we'd be imposing on our child, and though his arguments had been philosophically naïve, this sequence of immutable snapshots from the future still gave me goose bumps.

The truth was, reality as a whole was deterministic, whether you had a Qusp for a brain or not; the quantum state of the multiverse at any moment determined the entire future. Personal experience—confined to one branch at a time—certainly *appeared* probabilistic, because there was no way to predict which local future you'd experience when a branch split, but the reason it was impossible to know that in advance was because the real answer was "all of them."

For a singleton, the only difference was that branches never split on the basis of your personal decisions. The world at large would continue to look probabilistic, but every choice you made was entirely determined by *who you were* and *the situation you faced*.

What more could anyone hope for? It was not as if *who you were* could be boiled down to some crude genetic or sociological profile; every shadow you'd seen on the ceiling at night, every cloud you'd watched drift across the sky, would have left some small imprint on the shape of your mind. Those events were fully determined too, when viewed across the multiverse—with different versions of you witnessing every possibility—but in practical terms, the bottom line was that no private investigator armed with your genome and a potted biography could plot your every move in advance.

Our daughter's choices—like everything else—had been written in stone at the birth of the universe, but that information could only be decoded by *becoming her* along the way. Her actions would flow from her temperament, her principles, her desires, and the fact that all of these qualities would themselves have prior causes did nothing to diminish their value. *Free will* was a slippery notion, but to me it simply meant that your choices were more or less consistent with your nature—which in turn was a provisional, constantly-evolving consensus between a thousand different influences. Our daughter would not be robbed of the chance to act capriciously, or even perversely, but at least it would not be impossible for her ever to act wholly in accordance with her ideals.

I packed the bodies away before Francine got home. I wasn't sure if the sight would unsettle her, but I didn't want her measuring them up for more clothes.

* * *

The delivery began in the early hours of the morning of Sunday, December 14, and was expected to last about four hours, depending on traffic. I sat in the nursery while Francine paced the hallway outside, both of us watching the data coming through over the fiber from Basel.

Isabelle had used our genetic information as the starting point for a simulation of the development *in utero* of a complete embryo, employing an "adaptive hierarchy" model, with the highest resolution reserved for the central nervous system. The Qusp would take over this task, not only for the newborn child's brain, but also for the thousands of biochemical processes occurring outside the skull that the artificial bodies were not designed to perform. Apart from their sophisticated sensory and motor functions, the bodies could take in food and excrete wastes—for psychological and social reasons, as well as for the chemical energy this provided—and they breathed air, both in order to oxidize this fuel, and for vocalization, but they had no blood, no endocrine system, no immune response.

The Qusp I'd built in Berkeley was smaller than the Sao Paulo version, but it was still six times as wide as an infant's skull. Until it was further miniaturized, our daughter's mind would sit in a box in a corner of the nursery, joined to the rest of her by a wireless data link. Bandwidth and time lag would not be an issue within the Bay Area, and if we needed to take her further afield before everything was combined, the Qusp wasn't too large or delicate to move.

As the progress bar I was overlaying on the side of the Qusp nudged 98 percent, Francine came into the nursery, looking agitated.

"We have to put it off, Ben. Just for a day. I need more time to prepare myself."

I shook my head. "You made me promise to say no, if you asked me to do that." She'd even refused to let me tell her how to halt the Qusp herself.

"Just a few hours," she pleaded.

Francine seemed genuinely distressed, but I hardened my heart by telling myself that she was acting: testing me, seeing if I'd keep my word. "No. No slowing down or speeding up, no pauses, no tinkering at all. This child has to hit us like a freight train, just like any other child would."

"You want me to go into labor now?" she said sarcastically. When I'd raised the possibility, half-jokingly, of putting her on a course of hormones that would have mimicked some of the effects of pregnancy in order to make bonding with the child easier—for myself as well, indirectly—she'd almost bit my head off. I hadn't been serious, because I knew it wasn't necessary. Adoption was the ultimate proof of that, but what we were doing was closer to claiming a child of our own from a surrogate.

"No. Just pick her up."

Francine peered down at the inert form in the cot.

"I can't do it!" she wailed. "When I hold her, she should feel as if she's the most precious thing in the world to me. How can I make her believe that, when I know I could bounce her off the walls without harming her?"

We had two minutes left. I felt my breathing grow ragged. I could send the Qusp a halt code, but what if that set the pattern? If one of us had had too little sleep, if Francine was late for work, if we talked ourselves into believing that our special child was so unique that we deserved a short holiday from her needs, what would stop us from doing the same thing again?

I opened my mouth to threaten her: *Either you pick her up now, or I do it.* I stopped myself, and said, "You know how much it would harm her psychologically, if you dropped her. The very fact that you're afraid that you won't convey as much protectiveness as you need to will be just as strong a signal to her as anything else. *You care about her.* She'll sense that."

Francine stared back at me dubiously.

I said, "She'll know. I'm sure she will."

Francine reached into the cot and lifted the slack body into her arms. Seeing her cradle the lifeless form, I felt an anxious twisting in my gut; I'd experienced nothing like this when I'd laid the five plastic shells out for inspection.

I banished the progress bar and let myself free-fall through the final seconds: watching my daughter, willing her to move.

Her thumb twitched, then her legs scissored weakly. I couldn't see her face, so I watched Francine's expression. For an instant, I thought I could detect a horrified tightening at the corners of her mouth, as if she was about to recoil from this golem. Then the child began to bawl and kick, and Francine started weeping with undisguised joy.

As she raised the child to her face and planted a kiss on its wrinkled forehead, I suffered my own moment of disquiet. How easily that tender response had been summoned, when the body could as well have been brought to life by the kind of software used to animate the characters in games and films.

It hadn't, though. There'd been nothing false or easy about the road that had brought us to this moment—let alone the one that Isabelle had followed—and we hadn't even tried to fashion life from clay, from nothing. We'd merely diverted one small trickle from a river already four billion years old.

Francine held our daughter against her shoulder, and rocked back and forth. "Have you got the bottle? Ben?" I walked to the kitchen in a daze; the microwave had anticipated the happy event, and the formula was ready.

I returned to the nursery and offered Francine the bottle. "Can I hold her, before you start feeding?"

"Of course." She leaned forward to kiss me, then held out the child, and I took her the way I'd learned to accept the babies of relatives and friends, cradling the back of her head with my hand. The distribution of weight, the heavy head, the play of the neck, felt the same as it did for any other infant. Her eyes were still screwed shut, as she screamed and swung her arms.

"What's your name, my beautiful girl?" We'd narrowed the list down to about a dozen possibilities, but Francine had refused to settle on one until she'd seen her daughter take her first breath. "Have you decided?"

"I want to call her Helen."

Gazing down at her, that sounded too old to me. Old-fashioned, at least. Great-Aunt Helen. Helena Bonham-Carter. I laughed inanely, and she opened her eyes.

Hairs rose on my arms. The dark eyes couldn't quite search my face, but she was not oblivious to me. Love and fear coursed through my veins. *How could I hope to give her what she needed?* Even if my judgment had been faultless, my power to act upon it was crude beyond measure.

We were all she had, though. We would make mistakes, we would lose our way, but I had to believe that something would hold fast. Some portion of the overwhelming love and resolve that I felt right now would have to remain with every version of me who could trace his ancestry to this moment.

I said, "I name you Helen."

2041

"Sophie! *Sophie!*" Helen ran ahead of us toward the arrivals gate, where Isabelle and Sophie were emerging. Sophie, almost 16 now, was much less demonstrative, but she smiled and waved.

Francine said, "Do you ever think of moving?"

"Maybe if the laws change first in Europe," I replied.

"I saw a job in Zürich I could apply for."

"I don't think we should bend over backward to bring them together. They probably get on better with just occasional visits, and the net. It's not as if they don't have other friends."

Isabelle approached, and greeted us both with kisses on the cheek. I'd dreaded her arrival the first few times, but by now she seemed more like a slightly overbearing cousin than a child protection officer whose very presence implied misdeeds.

Sophie and Helen caught up with us. Helen tugged at Francine's sleeve. "Sophie's got a boyfriend! Daniel. She showed me his picture." She swooned mockingly, one hand on her forehead.

I glanced at Isabelle, who said, "He goes to her school. He's really very sweet."

Sophie grimaced with embarrassment. "Three-year-old *boys* are *sweet*." She turned to me and said, "Daniel is charming, and sophisticated, and *very* mature."

I felt as if an anvil had been dropped on my chest. As we crossed the car park, Francine whispered, "Don't have a heart attack yet. You've got a while to get used to the idea."

The waters of the bay sparkled in the sunlight as we drove across the bridge to Oakland. Isabelle described the latest session of the European parliamentary committee into adai rights. A draft proposal granting personhood to any system containing and acting upon a significant amount of the information content of human DNA had been gaining support; it was a tricky concept to define rigorously, but most of the objections were Pythonesque rather than practical. "Is the Human Proteomic Database a person? Is the Harvard Reference Physiological Simulation a person?" The HRPS modeled the brain solely in terms of what it removed from, and released into, the bloodstream; there was nobody home inside the simulation, quietly going mad.

Late in the evening, when the girls were upstairs, Isabelle began gently grilling us. I tried not to grit my teeth too much. I certainly didn't blame her for taking her responsibilities seriously; if, in spite of the selection process, we had turned out to be monsters, criminal law would have offered no remedies. Our obligations under the licensing contract were Helen's sole guarantee of humane treatment.

"She's getting good marks this year," Isabelle noted. "She must be settling in."

"She is," Francine replied. Helen was not entitled to a government-funded education, and most private schools had either been openly hostile, or had come up with such excuses as insurance policies that would have classified her as hazardous machinery. (Isabelle had reached a compromise with the airlines: Sophie had to be powered down, appearing to sleep during flights, but was not required to be shackled or stowed in the cargo hold.) The first community school we'd tried had not worked out, but we'd eventually found one close to the Berkeley campus where every parent involved was happy with the idea of Helen's presence. This had saved her from the prospect of joining a net-based school; they weren't so bad, but they were intended for children isolated by geography or illness, circumstances that could not be overcome by other means.

Isabelle bid us good night with no complaints or advice; Francine and I sat by the fire for a while, just smiling at each other. It was nice to have a blemish-free report for once.

The next morning, my alarm went off an hour early. I lay motionless for a while, waiting for my head to clear, before asking my knowledge miner why it had woken me.

It seemed Isabelle's visit had been beaten up into a major story in some east coast news bulletins. A number of vocal members of Congress had been following the debate in Europe, and they didn't like the way it was heading. Isabelle, they declared, had sneaked into the country as an agitator. In fact, she'd offered to testify to Congress any time they wanted to hear about her work, but they'd never taken her up on it.

It wasn't clear whether it was reporters or anti-adai activists who'd obtained her itinerary and done some digging, but all the details had now been splashed around the country, and protesters were already gathering outside Helen's school. We'd faced media packs, cranks, and activists before, but the images the knowledge miner showed me were disturbing; it was five a.m. and the crowd had already encircled the school. I had a flashback to some news footage I'd seen in my teens, of young schoolgirls in Northern Ireland running the gauntlet of a protest by the opposing political faction; I could no longer remember who had been Catholic and who had been Protestant.

I woke Francine and explained the situation.

"We could just keep her home," I suggested.

Francine looked torn, but she finally agreed. "It will probably all blow over when Isabelle flies out on Sunday. One day off school isn't exactly capitulating to the mob."

At breakfast, I broke the news to Helen.

"I'm not staying home," she said.

"Why not? Don't you want to hang out with Sophie?"

Helen was amused. "'Hang out'? Is that what the hippies used to say?" In her personal chronology of San Francisco, anything from before her birth belonged to the world portrayed in the tourist museums of Haight-Ashbury.

"Gossip. Listen to music. Interact socially in whatever manner you find agreeable."

She contemplated this last, open-ended definition. "Shop?"

"I don't see why not." There was no crowd outside the house, and though we were probably being watched, the protest was too large to be a moveable feast. Perhaps all the other parents would keep their children home, leaving the various placard wavers to fight among themselves.

Helen reconsidered. "No. We're doing that on Saturday. I want to go to school."

I glanced at Francine. Helen added, "It's not as if they can hurt me. I'm backed up."

Francine said, "It's not pleasant being shouted at. Insulted. Pushed around."

"I don't think it's going to be *pleasant*," Helen replied scornfully. "But I'm not going to let them tell me what to do."

To date, a handful of strangers had got close enough to yell abuse at her, and some of the children at her first school had been about as violent as (ordinary, drug-free, non-psychotic) nine-year-old bullies could be, but she'd never faced anything like this. I showed her the live news feed. She was not swayed. Francine and I retreated to the living room to confer.

I said, "I don't think it's a good idea." On top of everything else, I was beginning to suffer from a paranoid fear that Isabelle would blame us for the whole situation. Less fancifully, she could easily disapprove of us exposing Helen to the protesters. Even if that was not enough for her to terminate the license immediately, eroding her confidence in us could lead to that fate, eventually.

Francine thought for a while. "If we both go with her, both walk beside her, what are they going to do? If they lay a finger on us, it's assault. If they try to drag her away from us, it's theft."

"Yes, but whatever they do, she gets to hear all the poison they spew out."

"She watches the news, Ben. She's heard it all before."

"Oh, shit." Isabelle and Sophie had come down to breakfast; I could hear Helen calmly filling them in about her plans.

Francine said, "Forget about pleasing Isabelle. If Helen wants to do this, knowing what it entails, and we can keep her safe, then we should respect her decision."

I felt a sting of anger at the unspoken implication: having gone to such lengths to enable her to make meaningful choices, I'd be a hypocrite to stand in her way. *Knowing what it entails?* She was nine-and-a-half years old.

I admired her courage, though, and I did believe that we could protect her.

I said, "All right. You call the other parents. I'll inform the police."

The moment we left the car, we were spotted. Shouts rang out, and a tide of angry people flowed toward us.

I glanced down at Helen and tightened my grip on her. "Don't let go of our hands."

She smiled at me indulgently, as if I was warning her about something trivial, like broken glass on the beach. "I'll be all right, Dad." She flinched as the crowd closed in, and then there were bodies pushing against us from every side, people jabbering in our faces, spittle flying. Francine and I turned to face each other, making something of a protective cage and a wedge through the adult legs. Frightening as it was to be submerged, I was glad my daughter wasn't at eye level with these people.

"Satan moves her! Satan is inside her! Out, Jezebel spirit!" A young woman in a high-collared lilac dress pressed her body against me and started praying in tongues.

"Gödel's theorem proves that the non-computible, nonlinear world behind the quantum collapse is a manifest expression of Buddha-nature," a neatly dressed youth intoned earnestly, establishing with admirable economy that he had no idea what any of these terms meant. "Ergo, there can be no soul in the machine."

"Cyber nano quantum. Cyber nano quantum. Cyber nano quantum." That chant came from one of our would-be "supporters," a middle-aged man in Lycra cycling shorts who was forcefully groping down between us, trying to lay his hand on Helen's head and leave a few flakes of dead skin behind; according to cult doctrine, this would enable her to resurrect him when she got around to establishing the Omega Point. I blocked his way as firmly as I could without actually assaulting him, and he wailed like a pilgrim denied admission to Lourdes.

"Think you're going to live forever, Tinkerbell?" A leering old man with a matted beard poked his head out in front of us, and spat straight into Helen's face.

"Asshole!" Francine shouted. She pulled out a handkerchief and started mopping the phlegm away. I crouched down and stretched my free arm around them. Helen was grimacing with disgust as Francine dabbed at her, but she wasn't crying.

I said, "Do you want to go back to the car?"

"*No.*"

"Are you sure?"

Helen screwed up her face in an expression of irritation. "Why do you always ask me that? *Am I sure? Am I sure?* You're the one who sounds like a computer."

"I'm sorry." I squeezed her hand.

We plowed on through the crowd. The core of the protesters turned out to be both saner and more civilized than the lunatics who'd got to us first; as we neared the school gates, people struggled to make room to let us through uninjured, at the same time as they shouted slogans for the cameras. "Healthcare for all, not just the rich!" I couldn't argue with that sentiment, though adai were just one of a thousand ways the wealthy could spare their children from disease, and in fact they were among the cheapest: the total cost in prosthetic bodies up to adult size came to less than the median lifetime expenditure on healthcare in the U.S. Banning adai wouldn't end the disparity between rich and poor, but I could understand why some people considered it the ultimate act of selfishness to create a child who could live forever. They probably never wondered about the fertility rates

and resource use of their own descendants over the next few
thousand years.

We passed through the gates, into a world of space and silence; any protester who trespassed here could be arrested
immediately, and apparently none of them were sufficiently
dedicated to Gandhian principles to seek out that fate.

Inside the entrance hall, I squatted down and put my arms
around Helen. "Are you OK?"

"Yes."

"I'm really proud of you."

"You're shaking." She was right; my whole body was
trembling slightly. It was more than the crush and the con-
frontation, and the sense of relief that we'd come through
unscathed. Relief was never absolute for me; I could never
quite erase the images of other possibilities at the back of
my mind.

One of the teachers, Carmela Peña, approached us, looking stoical; when they'd agreed to take Helen, all the staff
and parents had known that a day like this would come.

Helen said, "I'll be OK now." She kissed me on the cheek,
then did the same to Francine. "I'm all right," she insisted.
"You can go."

Carmela said, "We've got 60 percent of the kids coming.
Not bad, considering."

Helen walked down the corridor, turning once to wave at
us impatiently.

I said, "No, not bad."

A group of journalists cornered the five of us during the
girls' shopping trip the next day, but media organizations
had grown wary of lawsuits, and after Isabelle reminded
them that she was presently enjoying "the ordinary liberties
of every private citizen"—a quote from a recent eight-figure
judgment against *Celebrity Stalker*—they left us in peace.

The night after Isabelle and Sophie flew out, I went in to
Helen's room to kiss her good night. As I turned to leave,
she said, "What's a Qusp?"

"It's a kind of computer. Where did you hear about that?"

"On the net. It said I had a Qusp, but Sophie didn't."

Francine and I had made no firm decision as to what we'd tell her, and when. I said, "That's right, but it's nothing to worry about. It just means you're a little bit different from her."

Helen scowled. "I don't want to be different from Sophie."

"Everyone's different from everyone else," I said glibly. "Having a Qusp is just like . . . a car having a different kind of engine. It can still go to all the same places." *Just not all of them at once.* "You can both still do whatever you like. You can be as much like Sophie as you want." That wasn't entirely dishonest; the crucial difference could always be erased, simply by disabling the Qusp's shielding.

"I want to be the same," Helen insisted. "Next time I grow, why can't you give me what Sophie's got, instead?"

"What you have is newer. It's better."

"No one else has got it. Not just Sophie; none of the others." Helen knew she'd nailed me: if it was newer and better, why didn't the younger adai have it too?

I said, "It's complicated. You'd better go to sleep now; we'll talk about it later." I fussed with the blankets, and she stared at me resentfully.

I went downstairs and recounted the conversation to Francine. "What do you think?" I asked her. "Is it time?"

"Maybe it is," she said.

"I wanted to wait until she was old enough to understand the MWI."

Francine considered this. "Understand it how well, though? She's not going to be juggling density matrices any time soon. And if we make it a big secret, she's just going to get half-baked versions from other sources."

I flopped onto the couch. "This is going to be hard." I'd rehearsed the moment a thousand times, but in my imagination Helen had always been older, and there'd been hundreds of other adai with Qusps. In reality, no one had followed the trail we'd blazed. The evidence for the MWI had grown steadily stronger, but for most people it was still easy to ignore. Ever more sophisticated versions of rats running mazes just looked like elaborate computer games. You couldn't travel from branch to branch yourself, you couldn't spy on your parallel alter egos—and such feats would probably never be possible. "How do you tell a nine-year-old girl that she's the only sentient being on the planet who can make a decision, and stick to it?"

Francine smiled. "Not in those words, for a start."

"No." I put my arm around her. We were about to enter a minefield—and we couldn't help diffusing out across the perilous ground—but at least we had each other's judgment to keep us in check, to rein us in a little.

I said, "We'll work it out. We'll find the right way."

2050

Around four in the morning, I gave in to the cravings and lit my first cigarette in a month.

As I drew the warm smoke into my lungs, my teeth started chattering, as if the contrast had forced me to notice how cold the rest of my body had become. The red glow of the tip was the brightest thing in sight, but if there was a camera trained on me it would be infrared, so I'd been blazing away like a bonfire, anyway. As the smoke came back up I spluttered like a cat choking on a fur ball; the first one was always like that. I'd taken up the habit at the surreal age of 60, and even after five years on and off, my respiratory tract couldn't quite believe its bad luck.

For five hours, I'd been crouched in the mud at the edge of Lake Pontchartrain, a couple of kilometers west of the soggy ruins of New Orleans. Watching the barge, waiting for someone to come home. I'd been tempted to swim out and take a look around, but my aide sketched a bright red moat of domestic radar on the surface of the water, and offered no guarantee that I'd remain undetected even if I stayed outside the perimeter.

I'd called Francine the night before. It had been a short, tense conversation.

"I'm in Louisiana. I think I've got a lead."

"Yeah?"

"I'll let you know how it turns out."

"You do that."

I hadn't seen her in the flesh for almost two years. After facing too many dead ends together, we'd split up to cover more ground: Francine had searched from New York to Seattle; I'd taken the south. As the months had slipped away, her determination to put every emotional reaction aside for the sake of the task had gradually eroded. One night, I was sure, grief had overtaken her, alone in some soulless motel room—and it made no difference that the same thing had happened to me, a month later or a week before. Because we had not experienced it together, it was not a shared pain, a burden made lighter. After 47 years, though we now had a single purpose as never before, we were starting to come adrift.

I'd learned about Jake Holder in Baton Rouge, triangulating on rumors and fifth-hand reports of barroom boasts. The boasts were usually empty; a prosthetic body equipped with software dumber than a microwave could make an infinitely pliable slave, but if the only way to salvage any trace of dignity when your buddies discovered that you owned the high-tech equivalent of a blowup doll was to imply that there was somebody home inside, apparently a lot of men leaped at the chance.

Holder looked like something worse. I'd bought his lifetime purchasing records, and there'd been a steady stream of cyber-fetish porn over a period of two decades. Hardcore and pretentious; half the titles contained the word "manifesto." But the flow had stopped, about three months ago. The rumors were, he'd found something better.

I finished the cigarette, and slapped my arms to get the circulation going. *She would not be on the barge.* For all I knew, she'd heard the news from Brussels and was already halfway to Europe. That would be a difficult journey to make on her own, but there was no reason to believe that she didn't have loyal, trustworthy friends to assist her. I had too many out-of-date memories burned into my skull: all the blazing, pointless rows, all the petty crimes, all the self-mutilation. Whatever had happened, whatever she'd been through, she was no longer the angry 15-year-old who'd left for school one Friday and never come back.

By the time she'd hit 13, we were arguing about everything. Her body had no need for the hormonal flood of puberty, but the software had ground on relentlessly, simulating all the neuroendocrine effects. Sometimes it had seemed like an act of torture to put her through that—instead of hunting for some magic shortcut to maturity—but the cardinal rule had been never to tinker, never to intervene, just to aim for the most faithful simulation possible of ordinary human development.

Whatever we'd fought about, she'd always known how to shut me up. "I'm just a thing to you! An instrument! Daddy's little silver bullet!" I didn't care who she was, or what she wanted; I'd fashioned her solely to slay my own fears. (I'd lie awake afterward, rehearsing lame counter-arguments. Other children were born for infinitely baser motives: to work the fields, to sit in boardrooms, to banish ennui, to save failing marriages.) In her eyes, the Qusp itself wasn't good or bad—and she turned down all my offers to disable the shielding; that would have let me off the hook too easily. But I'd made her a freak for my own selfish reasons; I'd set her apart even from the other adai, purely to grant myself a certain kind of comfort. "You wanted to give birth to a singleton? Why didn't you just shoot yourself in the head every time you made a bad decision?"

When she went missing, we were afraid she'd been snatched from the street. But in her room, we'd found an envelope with the locator beacon she'd dug out of her body, and a note that read: *Don't look for me. I'm never coming back.*

I heard the tires of a heavy vehicle squelching along the muddy track to my left. I hunkered lower, making sure I was hidden in the undergrowth. As the truck came to a halt with a faint metallic shudder, the barge disgorged an unmanned motorboat. My aide had captured the data streams exchanged, one specific challenge and response, but it had no clue how to crack the general case and mimic the barge's owner.

Two men climbed out of the truck. One was Jake Holder; I couldn't make out his face in the starlight, but I'd sat within a few meters of him in diners and bars in Baton Rouge, and my aide knew his somatic signature: the electromagnetic radiation from his nervous system and implants; his body's capacitative and inductive responses to small shifts in the ambient fields; the faint gamma-ray spectrum of his unavoidable, idiosyncratic load of radioisotopes, natural and Chernobylesque.

I did not know who his companion was, but I soon got the general idea.

"One thousand now," Holder said. "One thousand when you get back." His silhouette gestured at the waiting motor-boat.

The other man was suspicious. "How do I know it will be what you say it is?"

"Don't call her 'it'," Holder complained. "She's not an object. She's my Lilith, my Lo-li-ta, my luscious clockwork succubus." For one hopeful moment, I pictured the customer snickering at this overheated sales pitch and coming to his senses; brothels in Baton Rouge openly advertised machine sex, with skilled human puppeteers, for a fraction of the price. Whatever he imagined the special thrill of a genuine adai to be, he had no way of knowing that Holder didn't have an accomplice controlling the body on the barge in exactly the same fashion. He might even be paying 2,000 dollars for a puppet job from Holder himself.

"OK. But if she's not genuine . . ."

My aide overheard money changing hands, and it had modeled the situation well enough to know how I'd wish, always, to respond. "Move now," it whispered in my ear. I complied without hesitation; 18 months before, I'd pavloved myself into swift obedience, with all the pain and nausea modern chemistry could induce. The aide couldn't puppet my limbs—I couldn't afford the elaborate surgery—but it overlaid movement cues on my vision, a system I'd adapted from off-the-shelf choreography software, and I strode out of the bushes, right up to the motorboat.

The customer was outraged. "What is this?"

I turned to Holder. "You want to fuck him first, Jake? I'll hold him down." There were things I didn't trust the aide to control; it set the boundaries, but it was better to let me improvise a little, and then treat my actions as one more part of the environment.

After a moment of stunned silence, Holder said icily, "I've never seen this prick before in my life." He'd been speechless for a little too long, though, to inspire any loyalty from a stranger; as he reached for his weapon, the customer backed away, then turned and fled.

Holder walked toward me slowly, gun outstretched. "What's your game? Are you after her? Is that it?" His implants were mapping my body—actively, since there was no need for stealth—but I'd tailed him for hours in Baton Rouge, and my aide knew him like an architectural plan. Over the starlit gray of his form, it overlaid a schematic, flaying him down to brain, nerves, and implants. A swarm of blue fireflies flickered into life in his motor cortex, prefiguring a peculiar shrug of the shoulders with no obvious connection to his trigger finger; before they'd reached the intensity that would signal his implants to radio the gun, my aide said "Duck."

The shot was silent, but as I straightened up again I could smell the propellant. I gave up thinking and followed the dance steps. As Holder strode forward and swung the gun toward me, I turned sideways, grabbed his right hand, then punched him hard, repeatedly, in the implant on the side of his neck. He was a fetishist, so he'd chosen bulky packages, intentionally visible through the skin. They were not hard-edged, and they were not inflexible—he wasn't that masochistic—but once you sufficiently compressed even the softest biocompatible foam, it might as well have been a lump of wood. While I hammered the wood into the muscles of his neck, I twisted his forearm upward. He dropped the gun; I put my foot on it and slid it back toward the bushes.

In ultrasound, I saw blood pooling around his implant. I paused while the pressure built up, then I hit him again and the swelling burst like a giant blister. He sagged to his knees, bellowing with pain. I took the knife from my back pocket and held it to his throat.

I made Holder take off his belt, and I used it to bind his hands behind his back. I led him to the motorboat, and when the two of us were on board, I suggested that he give it the necessary instructions. He was sullen but cooperative. I didn't feel anything; part of me still insisted that the transaction I'd caught him in was a hoax, and that there'd be nothing on the barge that couldn't be found in Baton Rouge.

The barge was old, wooden, smelling of preservatives and unvanquished rot. There were dirty plastic panes in the cabin windows, but all I could see in them was a reflected sheen. As we crossed the deck, I kept Holder intimately close, hoping that if there was an armed security system it wouldn't risk putting the bullet through both of us.

At the cabin door, he said resignedly, "Don't treat her badly." My blood went cold, and I pressed my forearm to my mouth to stifle an involuntary sob.

I kicked open the door, and saw nothing but shadows. I called out "Lights!" and two responded, in the ceiling and by the bed. Helen was naked, chained by the wrists and ankles. She looked up and saw me, then began to emit a horrified keening noise.

I pressed the blade against Holder's throat. "Open those things!"

"The shackles?"

"Yes!"

"I can't. They're not smart; they're just welded shut."

"Where are your tools?"

He hesitated. "I've got some wrenches in the truck. All the rest is back in town."

I looked around the cabin, then I led him into a corner and told him to stand there, facing the wall. I knelt by the bed.

"Ssh. We'll get you out of here." Helen fell silent. I touched her cheek with the back of my hand; she didn't flinch, but she stared back at me, disbelieving. "We'll get you out." The timber bedposts were thicker than my arms, the links of the chains wide as my thumb. I wasn't going to snap any part of this with my bare hands.

Helen's expression changed: I was real, she was not hallucinating. She said dully, "I thought you'd given up on me. Woke one of the backups. Started again."

I said, "I'd never give up on you."

"Are you sure?" She searched my face. "Is this the edge of what's possible? Is this the worst it can get?"

I didn't have an answer to that.

I said, "You remember how to go numb, for a shedding?"

She gave me a faint, triumphant smile. "Absolutely." She'd had to endure imprisonment and humiliation, but she'd always had the power to cut herself off from her body's senses.

"Do you want to do it now? Leave all this behind."

"Yes."

"You'll be safe soon. I promise you."

"I believe you." Her eyes rolled up.

I cut open her chest and took out the Qusp.

Francine and I had both carried spare bodies, and clothes, in the trunks of our cars. Adai were banned from domestic flights, so Helen and I drove along the interstate, up toward Washington, D.C., where Francine would meet us. We could claim asylum at the Swiss embassy; Isabelle had already set the machinery in motion.

Helen was quiet at first, almost shy with me as if with a stranger, but on the second day, as we crossed from Alabama into Georgia, she began to open up. She told me a little of how she'd hitchhiked from state to state, finding casual jobs that paid e-cash and needed no social security number, let alone biometric ID. "Fruit picking was the best."

She'd made friends along the way, and confided her nature to those she thought she could trust. She still wasn't sure whether or not she'd been betrayed. Holder had found her in a transient's camp under a bridge, and someone must have told him exactly where to look, but it was always possible that she'd been recognized by a casual acquaintance who'd seen her face in the media years before. Francine and

I had never publicized her disappearance, never put up flyers or web pages, out of fear that it would only make the danger worse.

On the third day, as we crossed the Carolinas, we drove in near silence again. The landscape was stunning, the fields strewn with flowers, and Helen seemed calm. Maybe this was what she needed the most: just safety, and peace.

As dusk approached, though, I felt I had to speak.

"There's something I've never told you," I said. "Something that happened to me when I was young."

Helen smiled. "Don't tell me you ran away from the farm? Got tired of milking, and joined the circus?"

I shook my head. "I was never adventurous. It was just a little thing." I told her about the kitchen hand.

She pondered the story for a while. "And that's why you built the Qusp? That's why you made me? In the end, it all comes down to that man in the alley?" She sounded more bewildered than angry.

I bowed my head. "I'm sorry."

"For what?" she demanded. "Are you sorry that I was ever born?"

"No, but—"

"You didn't put me on that boat. Holder did that."

I said, "I brought you into a world with people like him. What I made you, made you a target."

"And if I'd been flesh and blood?" she said. "Do you think there aren't people like him, for flesh and blood? Or do you honestly believe that if you'd had an organic child, there would have been *no chance at all* that she'd have run away?"

I started weeping. "I don't know. I'm just sorry I hurt you."

Helen said, "I don't blame you for what you did. And I understand it better now. You saw a spark of good in yourself, and you wanted to cup your hands around it, protect it, make it stronger. I understand that. I'm not that spark, but that doesn't matter. I know who I am, I know what my choices are, and I'm glad of that. I'm glad you gave me that." She reached over and squeezed my hand. "Do you think I'd feel *better*, here and now, just because some other version of me handled the same situations better?" She smiled. "Knowing that other people are having a good time isn't much of a consolation to anyone."

I composed myself. The car beeped to bring my attention to a booking it had made in a motel a few kilometers ahead.

Helen said, "I've had time to think about a lot of things. Whatever the laws say, whatever the bigots say, all adai are part of the human race. And what *I* have is something almost every person who's ever lived thought they possessed. Human psychology, human culture, human morality, all evolved with the illusion that we lived in a single history. But we don't—so in the long run, something has to give. Call me old-fashioned, but I'd rather we tinker with our physical nature than abandon our whole identities."

I was silent for a while. "So what are your plans, now?"

"I need an education."

"What do you want to study?"

"I'm not sure yet. A million different things. But in the long run, I know what I want to do."

"Yeah?" The car turned off the highway, heading for the motel.

"You made a start," she said, "but it's not enough. There are people in billions of other branches where the Qusp hasn't been invented yet—and the way things stand, there'll always be branches without it. What's the point in us having this thing, if we don't share it? All those people deserve to have the power to make their own choices."

"Travel between the branches isn't a simple problem," I explained gently. "That would be orders of magnitude harder than the Qusp."

Helen smiled, conceding this, but the corners of her mouth took on the stubborn set I recognized as the precursor to a thousand smaller victories.

She said, "Give me time, Dad. Give me time."

Geropods

ROBERT ONOPA

*Robert Onopa (departmental website http://maven.english.
hawaii.edu/cw/page12.html) is associate professor of creative writing and literary theory at the University of Hawaii.
He has been a Fulbright lecturer in West Africa and a National Endowment for the Arts Fellow in Fiction Writing. In
1980, he co-edited (with David G. Hartwell) TriQuarterly
49, the special science fiction issue of that distinguished literary quarterly, which included stories by Gene Wolfe,
Thomas M. Disch, Samuel R. Delany, Ursula K. Le Guin,
and a first story by Michael Swanwick. The issue also set a
record at the time for generating subscription cancellations.
His SF novel,* The Pleasure Tube, *was published in 1979,
and he has since published a number of well-written stories
in F&SF over the last twenty years.*

*"Geropods," from F&SF, is an amusing variant on the
gestalt personality trope common in SF since the days of
Theodore Sturgeon's* More Than Human. *It is also an interesting contrast to Eleanor Arnason's story appearing earlier in this book. In the near future, a geropod is a legal
entity that constitutes a full human being: "any group of infirm old people whose combined physical and mental capacities constitutes the powers of a single, competent individual
is collectively entitled to act as an individual." So old Kaplan, in need of a posse to right a wrong done to his daughter,
forms a geropod.*

Grow old along with me, the best is yet to be. . . .
                                    —Robert Browning

Like me, my two elderly companions had outlived their wives, but I was new to Arcadia. You know the sort of place I'm talking about, somewhere between a nursing home and a morgue: pastel walls with prints of rolling hills in "quality" antiqued frames, sturdy plastic furniture, a tiled, low-maintenance floor. That afternoon, the digital holo in the corner of the sunroom was tuned to *The Young and the Old*, a trendy soap starring the ancient Macaulay Culkin, his already pale colors so washed out by the late afternoon glare he looked transparent. The air was laced with the odors of antiseptic and urine. Distant rattling and the indistinct conversations of the old echoed through the chip-array hearing aid I wore like a baseball cap.

I'd come out of a long stay in the hospital—my total deafness aside, a Parkinson's-like movement disorder was getting the best of me. Pinkie and I hadn't had any kids. After my long career as a shrink, it looked like I'd moved into my final home.

"*Bored*?" Kaplan said from his wheelchair. "Are you kidding? I used to be a Hollywood agent. Bored? It's so boring here it must be a new medical condition, right?"

"That evidence is accepted by this court," Judge Ortiz said from the couch, waving his red-and-white striped cane. The dot from its laser guidance flew around the room like a bug.

"I had depressives who literally put me to sleep," I recalled from my practice. "But, okay, maybe we do break new ground here. The question is, what's the alternative? We're disabled and technically incompetent. The law says we can't leave."

"Not quite right," Kaplan said. "Judge, tell him about Geropods."

"Geropods?"

The judge shushed me in a conspiratorial way as an orderly cruised in behind a trolley rattling with glass and plastic. I already knew him as Dennis, his hair the color of straw, his neck wider than his ears. He passed me my dopamine agonists in a little plastic cup and ticked his stylus on his palm chart. "DIDN'T SEE YOU AT THE LUAU LAST NIGHT, DOC," Dennis shouted, as if my hat was out of order.

"That's because I *lived* in Hawaii during the Aussie war," I muttered, watching my hand shake and water splash out of the cup. "Luau Night here is pathetic. Hawaii without the beach."

"*Exactly*," Judge Ortiz agreed.

Kaplan swung his wheelchair around, just missing Dennis's shin. "Casino Night without the money," he chimed in. "Casting without the couch."

Dennis, who'd gone a bit pink, tucked the palm chart into the trolley. "Valentine's Day coming up," he said ingenuously. "Let's see. That would be sex without the. . . ."

Kaplan pumped his arms and nailed him with a quick reverse sweep of his chair.

"Re . . . strictions . . . ," Dennis hissed when he could speak. "Going to talk to . . . Nurse Tucker . . . Re . . . strict . . . you all from . . . recreation . . . room. . . ."

When we were alone again, Kaplan wheeled over to the judge. "All right, *tell* him about Geropods. The Doc's been in the hospital."

"Okay," said Judge Ortiz. "Supreme Court decision last month. Civil rights case brought by the AARP. You're correct; the law says we can't leave as individuals—danger to ourselves, incompetent, all that crap. But the Court ruled that any *group* of infirm old people whose *combined* physical and mental capacities constitute the powers of a single, competent individual, is collectively entitled to act *as* an individual, as a single, legally defined human being."

· "A Geropod," Kaplan chimed in. "Free as a blue jay." ·

"Justice Kirkpatrick's term," Ortiz said. "I'm blind, but Kaplan here can see. Kaplan's in a wheelchair, but you're ambulatory. As a matter of fact, you're the one who's going to move us around."

"Me?"

"We've been looking for a guy like you. Of course, you're stone deaf without your hat, and you goddamned vibrate all the time. . . ."

"Parkinson's. . . ."

"So you need help yourself. But among us we've got all the parts."

"And where would we go?"

"Mr. Kaplan has a *burning mission*," the judge told me, his face swinging from side to side.

"My daughter Monica," Kaplan explained, "is in her late forties. Five years ago she marries a client of mine, 'Boots' Bacci. From that talk show on the Moon? Remember him? Always wore silver boots? I get admitted into Cedars with a stroke, the snake talks me into signing over the house in Brentwood. I get released from Cedars, and instead of taking me home, he gets behind my wheelchair, crams me into his sports car, then pushes me in here."

"Time for a little payback," Judge Ortiz said, pushing on his cane and rising from the couch. "Are you with us?"

A sharp animal sound, a yapping, came from the direction of the lobby. I adjusted my cap, feeling a bit frail. My companions didn't strike me as completely stable, but. . . . "Is that a dog?"

"No, it's a Yorkshire terrier. Animal therapy day."

I like animals, but I recalled how the previous week a pot-bellied pig had fouled the library floor. "I'm with you, gents. Let's roll."

And so I stood there the next morning, shaking on my walker, leaning on the gurney, fresh air just ten feet away.

Dennis was scanning our forms into the web station with a frown, Nurse Tucker looking over his shoulder. Partly because we were dressed in street clothes, my two partners in old suits, myself in cords and a cardigan, we'd attracted a bit of a crowd. There was Agnes Dorchester with her humped back and blue nightgown, Ted Makelena with his robe pockets filled with sweets, Marjorie Walters in her ridiculous tracksuit.

Nurse Tucker grimaced over the terminal. "What about him?" she asked, pointing to the gurney that Kaplan had instructed me to push.

"He's with us. Tiger Montelban," Judge Ortiz said. Even I remembered him as a screen playboy. He'd been Kaplan's most productive client.

"Medical data's in order, but what's he do for your 'pod? He's been comatose for a year."

"He can pee, which I can't," Kaplan said. "Wanna see my catheter?"

Tucker rolled her eyes. Actually, so did I.

"Look here," the judge snapped. "It doesn't matter if he can do anything. The law says that the sum of our powers merely has to replicate those of a normal adult."

Tucker sighed, puzzled over the terminal, then it beeped. "Admin says you guys can go," she said with quiet surprise. "What name?" As a new single legal entity, we had to provide a separate name.

"Story Musgrave," the judge answered. Musgrave had been my idea. The bald ex-marine, one of the first astronauts, had been active into his nineties, had six graduate degrees including one in medicine, and at ninety-seven was with the crew that went to Mars.

The sliding doors opened and we took our first step through.

It was surprisingly easy going at first. We weren't fast, exactly, but the gurney I was pushing stabilized my tremor and provided a platform for Judge Ortiz to walk along as he tapped his way. Kaplan was out in front, leading us to the parking lot. He'd been savvy enough to hire a van, a big one, into whose capacious back the driver helped us slide Tiger Montelban's gurney.

I took a deep breath and smelled the hot pavement, the wet grass under the sprinklers. I heard noise from traffic on Wilshire, and, yes, birds!, so loud I had to turn down my hat. The sunlight was amazing, the sky huge. I knew Pinkie would have been proud of me. I swung closed the rear door. "Why *are* we taking this guy along?" I wondered.

"Kaplan said he owed him one last ride," Ortiz shrugged. "Now help me in."

At the judge's suggestion, Miguel, our driver, first drove us toward the Pacific at Venice, then through the park in Santa Monica and up along the beach in Malibu. Ortiz had his head out the window like a Lab, his thin hair streaming in the wind. What a pleasure it was to be along the blue ocean, the wide stretches of sand, to see the girls on their maglev boards weaving down pedestrian tracks. Trees! Dogs! People whose hair wasn't white! At a crosswalk, an infant in a stroller made me realize how much I'd missed seeing children. When we turned back toward the city, I rolled down my own window and caught a scent on the breeze and remembered something else: Mexican food!

But before we could eat, Kaplan insisted, we had an assignment at his house in Brentwood.

"What's the plan?" I asked, not for the first time. The night before, Kaplan had prattled about "degrading assets," but he hadn't been entirely clear. I had him diagnosed as manic, the judge as suffering from cerebral arteriosclerosis, a side effect of which is senile dementia. I suppose I had a touch of that myself.

"First step, we shake him up. Ground zero, the garage," Kaplan said. "That sports car of his? He's got one of the first fuel cell Lamborghinis. The model that looks like a shuttle?"

I sucked in air between my teeth. "We'd stoop to petty vandalism?"

"No no no no. He loves that car more than he loves Monica. It's his financial security, see? His first two wives got all his money, and it's the only asset he has. Aside from my daughter." From a pocket of his wheelchair, Kaplan extracted a small black case. "I've still got a remote for the garage," he whispered.

"And?"

From another pocket, he pulled a spray can with an ugly, mustard-colored top. "Think you can handle this, Doc?" he said with glee. "The idea is, I open the door, then we . . . well, you . . . decorate the Lamborghini."

I raised a shaking hand. So vandalism it was. My first impulse was to refuse, but then I took a deep breath . . . and imagined Pinkie laughing. So what if we got caught? And maybe we could get it over with quick, like a prostate exam. We could have a wonderful day. "And then?" I asked.

Kaplan hesitated, his eyes glazed with confusion.

"And then the rest of the plan develops," Ortiz said gamely. He was still half out his open window, the breeze on his face, a self-absorbed smile on his lips. "We take it one step at a time."

From a block away, Kaplan's house looked to be an impressive small mansion in the Tudor style. It had a gabled portico, two stories with a large east wing, a sizable pool and a cabana in the side yard, and a four-car garage.

"Somebody's there!" Kaplan choked. Miguel pulled along the curb, and I watched a heavyset man heave himself out of the pool. I saw him slip on silver sandals and with a shock recognized that it was Boots Bacci himself. He had put on a lot of weight since he'd returned to Earth's gravity, and the way he scratched his ample belly, he was not expected at the studio anytime soon. He pushed his wet black hair back, and it seemed to lift from his scalp. "Say, how old's that guy?"

"Sixty-two," Kaplan muttered. "You'd think he'd have more consideration, right?"

Boots bent toward his towel and sunglasses, picked up a script, threw the towel around his shoulders, looked toward the street. He cast a quick, hostile glance at our van, and walked into the house.

We could follow his progress through a side window, see

him step half naked into a small room, ease his dripping body into a leather chair, hoist his feet up. . . .

"My teak desk," Kaplan said in a small, unhappy voice.

Then Boots pointed a remote toward the window and closed the blinds.

Kaplan had Miguel move up the block, putting a stand of bright pink oleander between us and his house.

Kaplan and Ortiz started bickering. Under the pretext of a battery problem, I took off my hat and fiddled with it as they talked. That's the one thing, the only thing, about my deafness for which I am grateful: I don't have to hear anything I don't want to hear. You can imagine what that did to my psychiatric practice toward the end. Now, though I'd lost confidence in Kaplan, I was still glad to be away from Arcadia. My jiggling foot tapped a rhythm on the van's floorboards.

After a while I realized that Kaplan was shouting at me.

"I can hear you now," I said, adjusting my hat.

Kaplan ordered Ortiz and me out, got out himself, and dispatched Miguel back to the house. His mission was to ring the doorbell and ascertain if Monica was at home. Kaplan's idea was that if she was home, we could discreetly enter through a side door and occupy the screening room, where we could lock ourselves in. The plan sounded lame.

Turned out *she* was at work, at her desk at the William Morris Agency in Studio City. And Boots Bacci made it clear to Miguel that if "that van" didn't "evaporate" from the neighborhood, he was calling the cops.

"Do you think he made us?" the judge asked as Miguel put the van in gear.

"I tol' him we was gardeners. You know, mow and blow?"

"Where now?" the judge asked.

"Weapons," Kaplan said. "Tasers. Pipe bomb."

"Dios," Miguel muttered under his breath.

"You're obsessing, Marv," I told Kaplan in my best professional voice. "You're going to give yourself another stroke. I prescribe lunch."

"All right, Miguel," Kaplan said with dismay. "Head for Casa Escobar. On Alvarado Street."

* * *

The new "old" Mexican part of town, for all its advertised ethnic uniqueness, looked a lot like the Beverly Hills Mall. Half the buildings were sand-colored stucco, with heavy black timbers, Mission-style arches, and red-tiled roofs. Many of the arches opened onto recessed mini-malls disguised as blocks of market stalls. Miguel maneuvered us into a disabled parking space, and we formed our pod again, Ortiz and Montelban and I in a wedge behind Kaplan's wheelchair.

We moved through the crowd fronting Pescado Mojado like a tanker in heavy seas, past Selena World, past Hologames 'R' Us, past Alberto's Secret. I had forgotten the theme park domesticity of the new old part of town, the fountains, the fishponds, the forests of cacti and rented ficus, the tidy upscale families with their matching body studs. Interiors were uniformly dense with epiphytes and those sheet-water walls that have become so big. Really, I hate it when I accidentally lean against one.

"Whoa," I heard Kaplan shout. "Señoritas at eleven o'clock!"

I looked ahead. Three elderly women were pushing along a narrow white table high with what I took to be catered food.

"What's he talking about?" Ortiz asked.

"Señoritas," Kaplan said. "Babes."

"Good grief," I said. "They're pushing a gurney."

"Tell me what they look like," Ortiz said.

"They look as old as we are. Except the one in front— Kaplan's right—she's some . . . babe. Big blue hair, leopard skin outfit, wide black belt, gold high heels. Great legs. Behind her, alongside the gurney, there's a woman who looks like . . . I guess you'd say a giant robin. Big bosom, big behind. Grandmotherly. She's got a red-and-white striped cane. Laser guidance."

"Come to Papito," I heard Ortiz say, to my surprise.

"The thin one on the other side reminds me of Pinkie. My late wife. She's using one of those electric canes. That woman up front, though. She's got to be somebody's daughter."

"Faster, Doc," Kaplan urged, leaning forward into his

wheelchair and pushing hard. "Let's cut them off at Orange Julio's."

"An all-woman Geropod?" Judge Ortiz marveled. "I'm absolutely charmed."

"Such a gentleman," the blind woman replied, feeling around the table discreetly for her venison burrito with one hand, fingering the straw in her fluorescent green margarita with the other.

We were clustered at the rear of Casa Escobar. There'd been some trouble about the gurneys, but we arranged to park them just outside, in a quiet alcove with a little birdbath. To my great relief, the woman who reminded me of Pinkie turned out to be a retired intensive care nurse. Between us we checked vital signs on Tiger and started a new IV line on her temporary patient, a one-hundred-and-twelve-year-old woman whose hair was so white, whose still smile was so beatific, she looked like a porcelain angel.

Kaplan had settled deep into the red booth alongside the woman with the blue hair. Her name was Bette. Her makeup was very thick, but expertly applied. She was as old as the rest of us, it turned out, and a marvel. Her artificial lungs gave her a breathy voice and she'd somehow managed to keep her figure, or at least had tucked and squeezed it into the leopard skin suit in a way that belied her age. Unless you looked closely, you might have easily mistaken her for a woman in her early fifties.

"Were you in the industry?" Kaplan asked. "Films? Holos?"

"I was on a poster once," she said coyly.

"If you'd had the right representation . . . " Kaplan speculated, flattering her in the easy way of an experienced professional.

Bette's false eyelashes fluttered so vigorously I thought I felt a breeze.

And so we ate and talked. By the time it came to coffee and flan, the restaurant was almost empty. Ostensibly to try one another's laser canes, Ortiz and the blind woman groped their way into a separate booth for dessert.

The ex-nurse and I went out to the alcove to check on our charges again. Her name was Barbara.

"So how do you like being old?" I asked, adjusting my hat.

"Today is fun," she said. "But it's hard to do things."

I nodded. "I suppose I had some training. In med school they had us put on scratched-up goggles—like we had cataracts. Plugged our ears with wax, gave us heavy rubber gloves. . . ."

"Like arthritis. . . ."

"Put marshmallows in our mouths. . . ."

"Mmmm. Post-stroke paralysis."

". . . corn kernels in our shoes, braces around our necks. The worst thing was the padded diapers."

She laughed and blushed. "Let me guess. They had you try to read prescription labels with the goggles on, count out pills with fat fingers, eat around the marshmallows."

"Exactly."

"In nursing school, we had to spend a morning in a hospital bed, got applesauce shoved into our mouths every half hour. Isn't it great to be out here?"

"Want to walk down Alvarado?" I asked.

It took us forever, but not since Pinkie died have I spent such a pleasant hour with a woman. We lingered in Casa DIY, admiring the lawn furniture and the barbecue grills. Outside Burrito Loco her electric cane got confused by a passing maglev scooter. She started to stumble, and I reached out to hold her arm to steady her.

When she regained her balance, she slipped her warm fingers into mine, and we made our way back down the sidewalk holding hands.

"I'd give you my heart," she said as we approached the restaurant, "but it's plastic and I think it needs a new battery."

I laughed. "Like my kidney," I said. "But how about if I ask you for a date sometime?"

Back at the big red booth in Casa Escobar, Kaplan announced that he had a plan.

"I hope you don't have too much for me to do," I admitted. "I'm bushed."

"Not necessary," Kaplan said. "Bette here's going in."

Kaplan explained that he'd sent Miguel over to the office supply store next door and was faxing over some forged NASA stationery from an FX vault he used to work with. The idea was to mock up a letter from Story Musgrave Junior to Boots Bacci—as Kaplan recalled, Junior had been a guest on Boots's talk show some years earlier during a tribute to his dad. The letter would personally introduce Bette as a talented performer whose career just wanted the kind of help Bacci could provide through his extensive contacts. "Let's see," Kaplan muttered as he scribbled notes. "We'll put in something about using Boots to host an old astronaut special. 'Please give this warm lady your special attention, the Boots Bacci boost we all know about, that big, stiff rocket. . . . '"

Bette was going to take a cab and present herself at the front door of the Brentwood house with the letter in hand.

Kaplan set down his notes. "Then we let Nature take its course."

"What was—uh, is—your career?" I asked Bette.

"She was an exotic dancer." Barbara giggled.

"Use what you've got, honey," Bette said. "Just get me to Casa Charo on the way so's I can get a blond wig and some sunglasses. And I'd like another Margarita."

Kaplan was radiant. "She's gonna be a star."

We all wanted to be there in Brentwood, if only down the block, to see if she'd get into the house. But we were stumped about the gurneys.

"We could get arrested for harassment," the judge said. "I'd hate to see them in a cell."

Barbara pointed out that our charges had been in comas for months. Kaplan said he didn't see anything wrong with leaving the gurneys side by side in the alcove, and giving the busboy a hundred dollars to page us if there was any noticeable change in their condition.

The busboy was not only willing, but even trained in CPR. Though it was a little irresponsible, Barbara and I went along. Kaplan hacked away at the letter, and when it was finished, Miguel moved the van around and helped us in.

I really was tired. There in the back of the van, I settled in for a bit of a nap. I woke up with the mid-afternoon sun in my eyes and realized that we'd stopped. My companions were hushed. When I looked down the street, I saw a blonde in a leopard skin outfit at the front door of the Brentwood house—the blonde was Bette—falling into a big hug from Boots Bacci and being ushered in.

"I still don't get it," I admitted.

From the front of the van, Kaplan placed a call to Studio City, telling Monica that Boots had had a seizure and was unable to get out of bed and that she needed to rush right home.

What really frosted Monica, she told us later, was the way Boots hadn't even folded back the family quilt (an heirloom in colorful interlocking circles, the classic "wedding ring" pattern). When she burst in, distraught, limping on a shoe whose high heel she'd broken during her breathless climb up the stairs, he was sitting right on it, back against the teak headboard, stark naked except for the silk bathrobe Monica had only recently given him for Christmas (strike two). From behind a hand-held holocorder, he was apparently directing Bette in some sort of "audition" (strike three). The holodisc, of course, left as little doubt about his guilt as the famous bin Laden tape from before the Aussie War. In a somewhat empty tribute to virtue, leggy Bette had never in fact had to get out of her leopard skin outfit, which was probably just as well, even though she'd closed the drapes and dimmed the lights. Monica confessed that the affair confirmed growing suspicions she'd had about her husband, who had been taking uncommon interest in a series of female trainers though he never seemed to exercise, and had started locking himself in the screening room.

From the street, the sequence was elegant in its economy—Monica running in the front door, Boots ejected from the rear, hopping past the pool and cabana, struggling to pull

on his clothes. He nearly lost it all together when Kaplan
punched the garage door's remote.

There were repercussions, of course. Bacci maintained that
he had been harassed, entrapped, and defrauded. Before
the day was out, we actually had to answer some questions
posed to us by an investigator at the L.A. prosecutor's office.

Bacci himself was there, his eyes puffy, his silver boots
scuffed, his anger palpable. He'd inflicted a long scrape on
the side of the silver Lamborghini as he'd peeled out of the
garage.

"Okay," the investigator, an anorexic attorney, began,
"Who's Story Musgrave?"

"I am," the judge said.

"I am," Kaplan added, then he pointed to me.

I waved. "Did you say Story Musgrave?" I asked, adjusting my cap. "That's me."

She sighed. "Mr. Bacci maintains that earlier today, Feb-
ruary 7th, you gentlemen, particularly Mr. Kaplan and
Judge Ortiz, colluded to defraud him. Now, Mr. Kaplan, I
want you to tell me your precise whereabouts from the
hours of. . . ."

"Excuse me," he interrupted. "Let's cut to the chase. The
medical record will show that I have suffered a massive, debilitating stroke, and the legal record will show that special-
ists under Mr. Bacci's own supervision had me declared
incompetent as an individual not six months ago. Any testimony I might give can't have standing in the State of California."

"Mmm," she mused, consulting her softscreen for a long
moment. Then she turned to me. "Doctor, did you hear any
conversation between Mr. Kaplan and Judge Ortiz that
would suggest such a conspiracy?"

I fiddled with my cap. "Would you please put your question in writing?" I asked.

When she did so, I read the sentence, fiddled with my hat
again, and replied. "I'm so sorry for the trouble, counselor. I

was trained to be a good listener, but, you see, I've become stone deaf, and my hat's not entirely reliable. So I could hardly. . . ."

"Judge Ortiz," she said, looking down at her softscreen again, sucking her upper lip. "Did you see anything today to call into question the legal standing of the woman known as Bette Waters as a legitimate entertainer seeking professional advice from Mr. Bacci?"

Ortiz twirled his red and white cane, and a bright red dot flew around the room. The dot finally got her attention. "Justice is blind," he said, setting his cane on the floor and rising. "Now can we go?"

That hour at the prosecutor's office, however, wasn't the strangest thing that happened toward the end of that day. Miguel, who said he'd never had a better time in his life, and who still is with us as our driver, ran us back to Casa Escobar to retrieve the gurneys.

They were there in the alcove, all right. But Tiger Montelban wasn't, and neither was the one-hundred-and-twelve-year-old lady.

The busboy was distraught. He'd checked every quarter hour, he told us. He'd been a bit late just after five because he'd had to help set up for dinner. When he'd finally looked in the alcove, they were gone—the tops of the gurneys empty landscapes of rumpled sheets and dented pillows punctuated by a trailing IV line. The restaurant staff had searched the neighborhood. People on the street spoke of an elderly couple in white who looked to be romantically involved, but it was just impossible. There was no report back at the nursing home, nothing from the nearby hospitals, nothing from the police or the morgue. To this day, we don't have a clue as to what happened to them, except for a series of charges that appeared on Montelban's credit chip at a resort in Cabo San Lucas. The chip had been embedded in his wrist.

These days we count on Arcadia for our medical care three days out of every seven, but otherwise we spend extended weekends at the house in Brentwood, sitting in leather furniture, watching sports in the den, taking in old movies with Barbara and Bette and Ramona in the screening room—that's really a treat, as Marv has remastered digital holos of all the great ones from the past hundred and fifty years, from *Birth of a Nation* to the ten Lucas *Star Wars* sequels. Monica's a regular angel, kind and considerate and a world-class caterer, though we do our best to look after ourselves as much as we can.

Barbara and I have taken to light exercise in the pool and lounging beside the cabana. Every once in a while, lying on my back, relaxed and at peace—a third try with stem cells has reduced my tremor—I look up and think of them, Tiger Montelban and his angel. Occasionally I see them in the shapes of clouds rolling in the sky, soft and free as floating gauze or down, white as bright moonlight on a snow-covered mountain, drifting in the heavens together, arm in arm.

Afterlife

JACK WILLIAMSON

Jack Williamson lives in Portales, New Mexico, near the Jack Williamson Library and SF collection at the University of New Mexico, which sponsors an annual Jack Williamson lecture on SF. The first age of SF genre heroes is not over as long as Jack Williamson is alive and writing. Williamson's first SF story was published in the 1920s, and he has been a leading figure in the field in every decade since, all eight of them. He is a legendary pioneer of SF now in his nineties, who has never ceased learning his craft and producing fiction of high quality.

Published in F&SF, *which had a particularly strong year in 2002, "Afterlife" is a good old-fashioned SF moral tale about believing in reason and science, and being rewarded by a better, longer life. Not an easy life, nor one with immediate rewards, but a deeper, richer one. This is one of the core messages of science fiction as a genre. There is also a level of satire in the subtext about con men who promise immediate salvation through science, a message just as relevant today as it has always been.*

"**W**e live on faith," my father used to say. "The afterlife is all we have."

I wasn't sure of any afterlife. My questions troubled my father, who was pastor of our little church. He made me kneel with him to pray and listen to long chapters from the Bible on the altar. That sacred book, he said, had come from the holy Mother Earth. It looked old enough, the brittle yellow pages breaking loose from the cracked leather binding, but if its miracles had ever really happened, that had been a hundred light-years away and long millennia ago.

"If there is a God," I told him, "and if he heard our prayers, we'd all be dead before we ever got his answer."

With an air of tragic sorrow, he warned me that such reckless words could put my immortal soul in danger.

"We ourselves are miracles," he told me, "happening every day. Our whole planet was the Lord's miraculous answer to the prayers of the first Earthmen to land here. They found it rich in everything, and spoiled it with their own greed and folly."

I heard the history of that from our one-legged schoolmaster. Our first dozen centuries had been a golden age. We settled both great continents, harvested the great forests, loaded fleets of space freighters with precious hardwoods and rare metals. All that wealth was gone two thousand years ago.

Sadly, he showed us a few precious relics he kept in the dusty cupboard he called a museum. There was a little glass tube that he said had shone with the light of a hundred candles when there was power to make it burn, and a dusty telephone that once had talked around the world.

We were born poor, in a poor little village. On the Sabbaths, my father preached in the adobe-walled church. On weekdays, he got into his dusty work clothes and ground corn on a little grist mill turned by a high waterwheel. His pay was a share of the meal.

Wheat grew on the flat land down in the valley below us, but the soil in our hill country had eroded too badly for wheat. Through most of the week we ate cornmeal mush for breakfast and corn pones for bread. Sometimes my mother made white bread or even honey cakes, when church members from the valley gave us wheat flour.

On the Sabbaths she played a wheezy old organ to accompany the hymns. I used to love the music and the promise of a paradise where the just and good would live happily forever, but now I saw no reason to believe it. With no life here at home, I longed to get away into the wider universe, but I saw no chance of that.

It's seven light-years to the nearest settled star system. The trade ships quit coming long ago, because we had nothing left to trade. There's only the mail ship, once every Earth year. It arrives nearly empty and leaves with every sling filled with those lucky people who find money for the fare.

It lands at the old capitol, far across the continent. I'd never been there, nor seen any kind of starship till the year I turned twelve. That quiet Sabbath morning, the rest of the family was gone in the wagon with my father to a revival meeting in another village down the river. Expecting no miracle there or anywhere, I'd been happy to stay home and do the chores.

Awakened by a rooster crowing, I was walking out to the barn to milk our three cows. I heard something thundering across the sky. In a moment I found it, a flash of silver when it caught the sun. I dropped the milk bucket, staring while it wheeled low over the crumbled ruins of something that had stood on the hill west of us.

It turned and dived straight at me.

With no time to run, I stood frozen while it sank over the west pasture and the apple orchard. It struck the cornfield and plowed on through a cloud of dust and flying rocks till it stopped at the edge of my mother's kitchen. Its thunder ceased. It lay still, a smoking mass of broken metal.

I stood there watching, waiting for something more to happen. Nothing did. I caught my breath at last, and walked uneasily toward it. Nothing about it made any kind of sense until I looked into the long furrow it had dug and found a torn and bleeding human arm. A leg farther on, most of the skin torn off. Another naked leg, still attached to the mangled body. Finally a hairless skull grinning from the bottom of the ditch.

Dazed by the sudden strangeness of it, I thought I ought to call my father or the constable or the schoolmaster, but they were all away at the revival. I was still there, wondering what to do, when I saw a carrion bird hovering over the body. I shouted and threw stones to keep it away till some of the neighbors came from up the river. We gathered up what we could, the smallest red scraps in my milk bucket, and carried them into the church.

The sheriff came on horseback, the doctor with him. They frowned over the body parts, laid out on a long table made of planks laid across the benches. The doctor fitted them closer together to see if anything was missing. The sheriff picked up pieces of broken metal, scowled at them uneasily, threw them back in the ditch.

They all left at last, for their dinners or whatever they had to do. I think they were afraid of too much they didn't understand. So was I, but I didn't like the flies buzzing around the body. I went home for a sheet to cover it. After a cold corn pone and a bowl of clabbered milk for lunch, I came back to look at the wreck again, and watch the empty sky. Nothing else came down.

Evening came. I milked the cows again, fed the pig, found a dozen eggs in the nests. I heard dogs barking and went back to the church to be certain the door was closed. Night fell as I was walking home. Our planet has no moon. In the sudden darkness, the stars were a blaze of diamonds.

I stopped to look up at them, wondering about the stranger. Where was his home? Why had he come here? What could have gone so terribly wrong when he tried to land? The answers were beyond me, but I stood there a long time, wishing I'd been born somewhere else, with a chance to see worlds more exciting than our own.

In the empty house, I lit a candle, ate another corn pone and a piece of fried chicken my mother had left for me, went to bed. Trying to forget the vulture circling over that skinned skull in the ditch, I lay listening to the tick of the old clock in the hall till I heard the rattle of my father's wagon.

My mother and my sister came in the house while he drove on to stable the team. News of the dead stranger stopped their chatter about the meeting. My father lit a candle lantern when he heard about it, and we all walked across the road to the church. My mother lifted the sheet to look at the body.

She screamed and my father dropped the lantern.

"Alive! It's alive!"

The candle had gone out. I shivered when I heard some small creature scurry away in the dark. My father's hands must have been shaking; it took him a long time to find a match to light the candle again. The long naked body was a man's, black with dried blood and horribly scarred, but somehow whole again.

The bald skull had hair again, a short pale fuzz. The eyes were open, staring blindly up into the dark. The body seemed stiff and hard, but I saw the blood-caked chest rise and slowly fall. My mother reached to touch it, and said she felt a heartbeat.

My father made me saddle my pony and go for the doctor. I had to hammer at the door a long time before he came out in his underwear to call me crazy for waking him in the middle of the night with such a cock-and-bull story. If we had a live man there at the church, it had to be some drunk who had crept inside to sober up.

Still angry, he finally dressed and saddled a horse to come back with me. My mother had lit candles at the altar. My father was on his knees before it, praying. The doctor threw the sheet off the man, felt his wrist, and said he'd be damned.

"The hand of God!" my father whispered, backing away and dropping back to his knees. "A holy miracle! We prayed at the meeting for a sign to help us persuade the unbelievers. And the good Lord has answered!"

"Maybe." The doctor squinted at me. "Or is it some trick of Satan?"

My mother brought a basin of warm water and helped him wash off the clots of blood and mud. His eyes closed, the man seemed to be sleeping. He woke when day came, and sat up to stare blankly at the empty benches around him. His blond hair and beard had grown longer. The scars had disappeared.

My mother asked how he felt.

He blinked at her and shivered, wrapping the sheet around himself.

"Are you the Son of God?" My father knelt before him. "Have you come to save the world?"

He shook his head in a puzzled way.

My mother asked if he was hungry. He nodded, and rose unsteadily when she asked if he could. She took his hand and led him out of the church and down the street to our house. He limped slowly beside her, peering around him as if everything was strange.

"Sir?" The doctor came up beside him. "Can you tell us who you are?"

He made a strange animal grunt and shook his head again.

At our house, my mother brought him a glass and a pitcher of apple juice. He gulped it thirstily and sat watching her fix breakfast. My father brought clothing for him, and a pair of shoes. He sat frowning at them and finally stood up to dress himself, slow and clumsy about it, and let me tie the shoes.

"Sir?" The doctor stood watching. "Where are you from?"

"Earth." He spoke at last, his voice deep and slow. "I am here from Mother Earth."

My mother set a plate for him. He studied the knife and

fork as if they were new to him, but plied them ravenously when she brought a platter of ham and scrambled eggs. She had set plates for the doctor and my father, but they forgot to eat.

"You were dead." My father was hoarse with awe. "How can you live again?"

"I was never dead." He reached to stab another slice of ham. "I am eternal."

"Eternal?" The doctor blinked and squinted at him. "Do you mean immortal?"

"I—" He paused as if he had to search for words. "I do not die."

"I saw you dead." The doctor swallowed hard and watched him slice the ham. "What brought you back?"

"The power." Smiling as though glad to find what to say, he wiped his lips with a slice of white bread. "The immortal power that moves the mortal body."

"I see," the doctor muttered, as if he really did. "Why are you here?"

"If immortality interests you, that is what I bring."

The doctor blinked, startled into silence. My father muttered something under his breath and moved to a chair across the room. My mother had made a pot of tea. The man drained a tall glass of it, sweetened with honey. Seeming to grow stronger and brighter, he began asking questions. He wanted to know about our history, cities, industries, governments, ways of travel. Did ships from Earth ever land here? I thought he looked pleased that the mail skipper was not due soon. Our neighbors had crowded the kitchen by then, and we all moved into the front room. Somebody asked his name.

"Who cares?" He shrugged, standing tall in the middle of the room. "Your world is new to me. I come to you as a new man, an agent of eternity. I bring you the gift of eternal life."

"Eternal?" The doctor had recovered his voice. "Just what do you mean?"

"My secrets are my own." He was suddenly smiling, his voice resonant and strong. "But if you wish to live forever, follow me."

Too many people had pushed into our house by then, and the blacksmith wanted to take him to speak at the church. Stubbornly, my father shook his head.

"I don't know what he is, but he claims no power from God. He could be a son of Satan, scheming to trap our souls for hell. I don't want him in my church. Get him out of my house!"

"He's slick as a barrel of eels," the doctor agreed. "I wouldn't believe him if he swore the sun came up this morning. But I don't—" He shrugged uneasily toward the wreckage in the cornfield. "I want to know more about him."

The sheriff escorted him to a vacant lot. My father stayed away, but I followed with my sister. The sheriff helped him to the top of an old stone slab that must have supported some public monument when our world was great. We all crowded around. He stood silent while the blacksmith spoke to tell how he had risen from the dead. The murmur of voices died into breathless expectation as we waited for him to speak. I heard a dog barking somewhere, and a rooster crowing. I thought he looked handsome, even in the misfit garments.

"He can't be the demon Dad says he is." I saw a glow of awed admiration on my sister's face. "I believe he's an angel sent from Heaven to save us."

He spread his arms to beckon us closer.

"I see that your world has suffered misfortune."

His voice rang loud and clear, but he paused to gesture at the muddy ruts we called a street and our straggle of mud-walled, straw-roofed homes. He turned to nod at the rubble mounds of what had been a city on the hill behind him.

"I knew poverty like yours back on the mother world. It is ruled by the rich. They live in great mansions, with swarms of servants and every luxury. Skipping time on space flights to their estates on other planets, they stretch their lives almost forever. The very richest can pay for microbots."

"Microbots?" the doctor shouted. "What are they?"

"Tiny robots." He slowed his voice to help us understand. "They circulate like cells in the blood, repairing all the damage of illness and age. Their owners are immortal, gathering wealth and knowledge and power as they live through century after century. They have everything.

"We mortals were poor as you are."

He shrugged at the shabby streets with a grimace of remembered pain.

"Poorer, because they have kept us down, generation after generation born to toil and die in ignorance of all that might have helped us. To keep us humble, they have allowed us to learn no more than our tasks required. Most have no escape except to breed another generation to suffer and die as we have always done.

"I was lucky. My mother's husband worked as a janitor in a university that taught the children of the rich. He stole books and holo cubes to let me learn at home. She was a housemaid for an immortal scientist. They had an affair they never confessed, but my mother told me I am his son. He made me his lab assistant when I was old enough, finally made me his subject for the experiment that made me eternal."

I heard a buzz of excitement in the crowd, and then a volley of breathless questions.

"If you don't believe, ask those who saw me arrive." He paused to let his eyes search out the doctor, the sheriff, me. "They saw my body heal from what they thought was death."

"I saw a dead man," the doctor muttered uneasily. "But I don't know how—"

His voice trailed off.

"I'll tell you how." The stranger smiled, and his voice pealed louder. "I bring you my father's secret gift to me, something simpler than the microbots and a better way to immortality. It has alarmed the old immortals, who have made laws and broken laws to keep the microbots for themselves forever.

"They raided and wrecked my father's lab, left me for dead. I recovered. My mother brought me the keys to his private skipship. I am not a pilot, but I had watched him drive the ship. The robotic controls got me here, though I botched the landing and injured myself."

Wryly, he gestured toward the twisted metal in the cornfield.

"You have seen how I recovered."

He spread his arms again and posed to display his body. Splendid now, it showed no scars. I saw a flash of gold from his hair, now grown almost to his shoulders, and heard a soft cry from my sister. Awe had hushed the crowd. Far off, I heard the rooster crow again.

"A child of God!" my sister whispered. "Here to save us!"

People stood frozen for a moment, then pushed anxiously closer. I heard a babble of questions.

"Can you make me whole again?" That was the blacksmith's crippled son, caked with smoke and sweat from the forge. "How can we repay you?"

"Just follow me," he said. "Do as I say."

He had brought his gift for all mankind, he said. He wanted to carry it on to the capitol. The blacksmith passed a hat for money to buy him a horse. The tailor gave him a jacket. The sheriff deputized the schoolmaster to be his bodyguard and show him the way. He slept that night at the doctor's house. When he left next morning, the doctor, the blacksmith, and the schoolmaster rode away with him. My sister came out with me to watch them go by. She broke into tears as they passed.

"An angel!" she whispered. "I'd die to be with him."

She stood in the dusty street looking after them till he was gone from sight, and waited with the rest of us, hoping for him to return. He never did. She grew up to be a beautiful woman and the mistress of our one-room school. The blacksmith's son courted her devotedly, but she never forgot the stranger.

An artist of some talent, she painted a portrait of him, standing on a planet out in starry space, a golden halo shining above his head. It hung in her room, above a candle and a scrap of twisted metal from his ship. Once I caught her kneeling to it.

With nowhere else to go, most of us stayed at home in the village. The doctor's young bride learned to make her living as a midwife. The blacksmith's son got his younger brother to help at the forge and became a smith himself. News moves slowly on our planet, but we began to hear tales of the miraculous Agent who had risen from death, won new believers by the thousand, built a magnificent Temple of Eternity at the capitol. My sister longed to follow him there, and cried when my father called him the Agent of Satan.

The doctor and the schoolmaster returned at last, in a coach drawn by four fine black horses, a uniformed driver seated in front and a footman standing behind. Another four-horse team pulled a long, black-painted wagon. They stopped on the village square. Half a dozen men in long black robes climbed out of the wagon to set up a platform on one side of the coach and a black tent on the other. They unpacked drums and trumpets and instruments I had never seen, and brought the street to life with music I had never heard.

When a curious crowd had gathered, the schoolmaster hopped out of the black wagon, still nimble on his wooden leg. No longer the shabby little mouse I remembered, he was robed in gold and black velvet.

"My father?" The blacksmith's son limped anxiously to meet him. "Is he coming home?"

The trumpets drowned anything the schoolmaster said.

"Is he—is he dead?"

"Alive." The schoolmaster waved his hand. The music stopped, and he lifted his voice for the rest of us. "Alive forever, safe in Eternity."

He strutted to the coach and climbed to stand on the driver's seat. His voice pealed louder. Our village was a sacred place, he said, because here the Agent had died and risen again from death. He and the doctor had been blessed to witness that first miracle. As chosen Voices of Eternity, they had now returned to share the blessing of eternal life with all of their old friends who wished it.

My father had pushed to the front of the crowd.

"By what power, and by what name," he demanded, "do you preach the resurrection of the dead?"

"The Agent has power enough of his own." Glaring down at him, schoolmaster waved as if to knock him aside. "He needs no other name, and some of you here witnessed his own resurrection."

"I call him by his true names," my father shouted. "Satan! Lucifer! Beelzebub! The Prince of Darkness!" He dropped his voice. "I am sorry to hear you repeating his lies, because all of you were once true children of our true Lord. I beg you to repent and confess, that your mortal sins may be blotted out—"

The schoolmaster gestured, and a bray of trumpets drowned the words.

"You call yourselves Voices," my father tried again. "I beg you to listen for the voice of God. Listen to Him in your hearts, speaking through the Holy Ghost."

"I never met a holy ghost."

My father flushed red at the mockery.

"Listen to the words of Eternity!" The schoolmaster raised his head to look beyond my father. "We bring you something better than myth and ignorant superstition. I pray you to heed the verities of scientific truth and save your own precious lives. Learn the new science of veronics. For you with open minds, let me lay out the actual facts."

"Facts?" my father shouted. "Or Satanic lies?"

The blacksmith's son caught his arm.

"The words of the Agent." The schoolmaster frowned as if we were backward students. "He has taught the simple truth. The veron is an energy particle. Carrying neither mass nor dimension, it is mind without matter. The so-called human soul in fact the veronic being. The Agent has taught us how to liberate it into Eternity. Freed from slavery to the mortal flesh, with all its faults and ills, your immortal minds can live forever."

He paused for a paean of rousing music, and asked for questions when it ceased.

What proof could he offer?

"Look inside yourselves." He paused, with nods and smiles of recognition for my mother and my sister. "Haven't every one of you hated the limits and pains of your bodies? Haven't you all enjoyed moments of liberty from space and time, as you recalled the past, looked into the future, thought of far-off friends? Those were precious glimpses of your future freedoms in eternity!

"If you want to live forever, step forward now!"

The doctor came down from the coach to a table set up in front of the black tent. Robed like the schoolmaster in gold and black velvet, he had grown grayer and fatter than I recalled him. Silently, he spread his arms to urge us forward. The music rose again. The blacksmith's deserted wife hobbled toward him. Arthritic and blind, she leaned on her limping son.

"Eat. Drink." Intoning the words, the doctor gestured at a platter and a pitcher on the table. "One little wafer and one small sip of this veronic fluid will break the chains of flesh to set you free. But you must be warned."

He dropped his voice and raised his hands.

"This final feast is only for those who trust the Agent and accept the miracle of his resurrection. Once you have felt the joy of eternity, there is no turning back. I must remind you also that you take nothing with you."

Tears washing white channels down his dark-grimed face, the blacksmith's son shouted the warning into his mother's ear. She mumbled and opened her mouth. He dropped jingling coins into a basket on the table. The doctor laid a tiny white wafer on her tongue, put a little glass of a blood-red liquid to her drooling lips. She gulped it down. Two men in black took her arms to help her into the tent.

Next came the baker's old and helpless father, moaning on a stretcher carried by the baker and his helper. A dozen others shuffled forward. Finally my sister. Tears on her face, she hugged our mother and our father, darted to startle the blacksmith's son with a kiss and a quick embrace, and fell into the line. I caught her arm to pull her back.

"Let her go." My father was hoarse with pain. "She has damned herself."

The solemn music rose again. The line crept forward, my sister the last. My father knelt on the ground, murmuring a prayer. My mother stood silently sobbing. My sister dropped something into the basket, the gold necklace and gold earrings the blacksmith's son had given her. I heard a stifled moan from him. Smiling, she swallowed the wafer and the liquid. My mother cried out, shrill with pain. My sister looked back and tried to speak, but her voice was already gone. Her features stiffened. She staggered. The black robes hustled her into the tent.

With a final flourish, the music ceased. The doctor intoned a solemn assurance that these beloved beings were happy now, forever free from grief and care. He and the schoolmaster climbed back into the coach. The musicians dismantled their instruments and knocked down the platform where they had stood. They rolled up the black tent, loaded everything on the wagon, and followed the coach back to the road down the river.

The bodies were left lying in a row on the ground. My mother knelt to close my sister's eyes. My father stood above them to beg the Lord that all their sins and blunders might be forgiven and their souls received into God's own paradise. Neighbor men toiled all night, nailing coffins together. Next day a pastor came from the village below to preach a farewell service before the boxes were lowered into the row of new graves.

One morning next spring, while my mother was making breakfast, we saw a bright silver skipship lying in the cornfield where the stranger's craft had fallen. Another tall stranger was poking into the tangle of tall weeds and rusted metal where it had stopped. He came across the garden to our door.

When I answered his knock, he displayed a holo card that showed the bright round Earth spinning in starry black space. Silver print across it identified him as a field inspector for the Pan-Terran Police. Pointing back at the wreck, he asked for anything we knew about it. My mother asked him to share our grits and bacon while we told him what we could about the ship and the Agent and the Church of Eternity.

"We believed—" She broke into tears when she spoke of my sister's death. "We had seen him risen from the dead. She trusted him."

"Satan!" my father rasped. "He dragged my daughter down to Hell!"

"He was a criminal." The inspector nodded in sober sympathy. "The tale he told you was largely a hoax. It's true that he was a native Earthman, but no verons exist, no veronic bodies either. Though he did have microbots in his blood, he had no skills or know-how to share them with anybody else."

Sobbing, my mother rose to leave the room.

"Listen to him!" My father was hoarse with his own emotion. "The Lord will help us bear the truth."

"A vicious criminal." Regretfully, the inspector shook his head. "But also the victim of tragedy. He was the offspring of a mortal woman's illicit affair with an immortal. He inherited his father's microbots. They should have been destroyed, but that would have crippled or probably killed him. It must have been a desperate choice, but his mother kept him as he was and kept his secret till he was grown. She was arrested when the truth came out, but he escaped in his father's skipship. I regret the harm he did here, but at least his evil career is over."

"Over?" My father stared at him. "If he is immortal—"

"His church officials will no doubt claim that he's still alive in some veronic paradise." The inspector grinned. "But microbots aren't magic. They are only electronic devices. When we located him here, we were able to shut them down with a radio signal. His natural body functions had become dependent on the microbots. His heart stopped when they did.

"He will trouble you no longer."

"Thank you, sir." My father reached over the table to shake his hand. "You have served as a faithful agent of the Lord."

"Or the Pan-Terran Police."

After breakfast, the inspector asked me to clear the weeds around the wreckage to let him take holos of it. He walked with my father over our little farm and wanted to see the farm tools and the mules in the barn. He looked at my mother's garden and asked about the plants she grew. He had me show him the windmill and the water wheel and the grist mill, and tell him how they worked.

He watched me slop the hogs and milk the cows that night, and went with my parents to the hymn service at the church while I stayed home to finish the chores. My mother let him sleep in the room that had been my sister's. Next morning he watched my father kindle the fire in the old cast iron stove and watched my mother fix the breakfast. When we had eaten, he looked sharply at me and asked what I planned for the future.

"I never had a future," I told him. "I always longed to get away, but never had a chance."

"If he had a chance—" He turned to my parents. "Could you let him go?"

They stared at him and whispered together.

"If he could really get away—" My mother tried to smile at my father. "We have each other."

My father nodded solemnly. "The Lord's will be done."

The inspector let his shrewd eyes measure me again.

"It would be forever," he told me gravely. "As final as death."

"Let him go," my father said. "He has earned his own salvation."

The inspector took me out to see his skipship. It was strange and wonderful, but I was too dazed and anxious to understand what he said about it. He had me sit, looked me in the eye, and asked for more about my life.

"I stay alive," I told him. "I'm the janitor for my father's church, though I've never caught his faith. I help him at the mill and help my mother in her garden."

My heart thumping, I waited again until he asked, "Would you like to be immortal?"

Hardly breathing, I found no words to say.

"Perhaps you can be," he said. "If you want the risk. The immortals have to guard their own future. They want no rivals here, but they have agreed to let us send an expedition to colonize the Andromeda galaxy. There's a two-million-year skip each way, which leaves them safe from any harm from us."

He frowned and shook his head.

"We ourselves can't feel so confident. No skip so far has

ever been attempted. It's a jump into the dark, with no data to let us compute any sure destination. We may be lost forever from our own universe of space, with no way back. Even if we're lucky, we'll have new frontiers to face, with our industrial infrastructure still to build. We're likely to need the skills and the knowledge you have learned here. I can sign you on, if you want the chance."

I said I did.

My mother dried her tears and kissed me. My father made us kneel and pray together. I hugged them both, and the inspector took me with him to board the departing mother ship.

All that was two million years ago and two million lightyears behind us. That long jump dropped us into the gravity well of a giant black hole, but we were able to coast around it in free fall, with no harm at all. The third skip brought us into low orbit around our new planet, a kind world that had no native life and needed no terraforming. My low-tech skills did help us stay alive. The microbots have learned them, and we are well established now.

I have recalled this story for our children and their microbots to remember. I was at first uneasy about letting the microbots into my body. For a long time I hardly felt them, but they're beginning now to give me a new zest for life, a new happiness with all my new friends, an endless delight in the wonders of our new world.

Our new sky blazes with more stars than I ever imagined, all in strange constellations, but on a clear night we can make out our home galaxy, a faint fleck of brightness low in the south. Remembering my parents, who lived so far away and long ago, I wish they could have known the true afterlife we've discovered here.

Shields of Mars

GENE WOLFE

Gene Wolfe (tribute site: http://www.op.net/~pduggan/ wolfe.html and www.ultan.co.uk/) lives in Barrington, Illinois, and is widely considered the most accomplished writer in the fantasy and science fiction genres. His four-volume The Book of the New Sun is an acknowledged masterpiece. Some people consider him among the greatest living American writers. His most recent book is Return to the Whorl, the third volume of The Book of the Short Sun (really a single huge novel), which many of his most attentive readers feel is his best book yet. He has published many fantasy, science fiction, and horror stories over the last thirty-six years, and has been given the World Fantasy Award for Life Achievement. Collections of his short fiction include The Island of Dr Death and Other Stories and Other Stories, Storeys from the Old Hotel, Endangered Species, and Strange Travelers.

"Shields of Mars" is from Mars Probes, along with the DAW 30th Anniversary SF Anthology, and somewhat by default the most significant SF anthology of the year. The story is an homage to the planetary romance tradition, to space opera, to the value system of honor and loyalty in a racially mixed culture. But in contrast to the Moorcock story later in this book, it is not space opera but ironic science fiction. It transcends the disappointments of Mars as it turned out to be without denying scientific reality, and reinvigorates the SF tropes Mars.

435

Once they had dueled beneath the russet Martian sky for the hand of a princess—had dueled with swords that, not long before, had been the plastic handles of a rake and a spade.

Jeff Shonto had driven the final nail into the first Realwood plank when he realized that Zaa was standing six-legged, ankle-deep in red dust, watching him. He turned a little in case Zaa wanted to say something; Zaa did not, but he four-legged, rearing his thorax so that his arms hung like arms (perhaps in order to look more human) before he became a glaucous statue once again, a statue with formidable muscles in unexpected locations.

Zaa's face was skull-like, as were the faces of all the people from his star, with double canines jutting from its massive jaw and eyes at its temples. It was a good face, Jeff thought, a kind and an honest face.

He picked up the second Realwood plank, laid it against the window so it rested on the first, and plucked a nail from his mouth.

Zaa's gray Department shirt ("Zaa Leem, Director of Maintenance") had been dirty. No doubt Zaa had put it on clean that morning, but there was a black smear under the left pocket now. What if they wanted to talk to Zaa, too?

Jeff's power-hammer said *bang*, and the nail sank to the head. Faint echoes from inside the store that had been his father's might almost have been the sound of funeral drums. Shrugging, he took another nail from his mouth.

436

A good and a kind face, and he and Zaa had been friends since Mom and Dad were young, and what did a little grease matter? Didn't they want Zaa to work? When you worked, you got dirty.

Another nail, in the diagonal corner. *Bang*. Mind pictures, daydream pictures showed him the masked dancers who ought to have been there when they buried Dad in the desert. And were not.

Again he turned to look at Zaa, expecting Zaa to say something, to make some comment. Zaa did not. Beyond Zaa were thirty bungalows, twenty-nine white and one a flaking blue that had once been bright. Twenty-eight bungalows that were boarded up, two that were still in use.

Beyond the last, the one that had been Diane's family's, empty miles of barren desert, then the aching void of the immense chasm that had been renamed the Grand Canal. Beyond it, a range of rust-red cliff that was in reality the far side of the Grand Canal, a glowing escarpment lit at its summit by declining Sol.

Jeff shrugged and turned back to his plank. A third nail. *Bang*. The dancers were sharp-edged this time, the drums louder. "You're closing your store."

He fished more nails from his pocket. "Not to you. If you want something I'll sell it to you."

"Thanks." Zaa picked up a plank and stood ready to pass it to Jeff.

Bang. Echoes of thousands of years just beginning.

"I've got one in the shop that feeds the nails. Want me to get it?"

Jeff shook his head. "For a little job like this, what I've got is fine."

Bang.

"Back at the plant in a couple hours?"

"At twenty-four ten they're supposed to call me." Jeff had said this before, and he knew Zaa knew it as well as he did. "You don't have to be there . . ."

"But maybe they'll close it."

And I won't have to be the one who tells you.

Jeff turned away, staring at the plank. He wanted to drive

more nails into it, but there was one at each corner already. He could not remember driving that many.

"Here." Zaa was putting up another plank. "I would have done this whole job for you. You know?"

"It was my store." Jeff squared the new plank on the second and reached to his mouth for a nail, but there were no nails there. He positioned his little ladder, leaning it on the newly nailed one, got up on the lowest step, and fished a fresh nail from his pocket.

Bang.

"Those paintings of mine? Give them back and I'll give you what you paid."

"No." Jeff did not look around.

"You'll never sell them now."

"They're mine," Jeff said. "I paid you for them, and I'm keeping them."

"There won't ever be any more tourists, Jeff."

"Things will get better."

"Where would they stay?"

"Camp in the desert. Rough it." *Bang.*

There was a silence, during which Jeff drove more nails.

"If they close the plant, I guess they'll send a crawler to take us to some other town."

Jeff shrugged. "Or an orthopter, like Channel Two has. You saw *Scenic Mars*. They might even do that."

Impelled by an instinct he could not have described but could not counter, he stepped down—short, dark, and stocky—to face Zaa. "Listen here. In the first place, they can't close the plant. What'd they breathe?"

Even four-legging, Zaa was taller by more than a full head; he shrugged, massive shoulders lifting and falling. "The others could take up the slack, maybe."

"Maybe they could. What if something went wrong at one of them?"

"There'd be plenty of time to fix it. Air doesn't go that fast."

"You come here."

He took Zaa by the arm, and Zaa paced beside him, intermediate armlike legs helping support his thorax and abdomen.

"I want to show you the plant."

"I've seen it."

"Come on. I want to see it myself." Together, the last two inhabitants of the settlement called Grand Canal went around the wind-worn store and climbed a low hill. The chain-link fence enclosing the plant was tall and still strong, but the main gate stood open, and there was no one in the guard shack. A half mile more of dusty road, then the towers and the glassy prisms, and the great pale domes, overshadowed by the awe-inspiring cooling stack of the nuclear reactor. On the left, the spherical hydrogen tanks and thousands upon thousands of canisters of hydrogen awaiting the crawler. Beyond those, nearly lost in the twilight, Number One Crusher. It would have been a very big plant anywhere on Earth; here, beneath the vastness of the russet sky, standing alone in the endless red-and-black desert, it was tiny and vulnerable, something any wandering meteor might crush like a toy.

"Take a good look," Jeff said, wishing Zaa could see it through his eyes.

"I just did. We might as well go now. They'll be wanting to call you pretty soon."

"In a minute. What do you suppose all that stuff's worth? All the equipment?"

Zaa picked his teeth with a sharp claw. "I don't know. I guess I never thought about it. A couple hundred million?"

"More than a billion. Listen up." Jeff felt his own conviction growing as he spoke. "I can lock the door on my store and board up the windows and walk away. I can do that because I'm still here. Suppose you and I just locked the gate and got on that crawler and went off. How long before somebody was out here with ten more crawlers, loading up stainless pipe, and motors, and all that stuff? You could make a better stab at this than I could, but I say give me three big crawlers and three men who knew what they were doing and I'd have ten million on those crawlers in a week."

Zaa shook his head. "Twelve hours. Eight, if they never took a break and really knew their business."

"Fine. So is the Department going to lock the door and walk away? Either they gut it themselves—not ten million, over a billion—or they'll keep somebody here to keep an eye on things. They'll have to."

"I guess."

"Suppose they've decided to stop production altogether. How long to shut down the pile and mothball everything? With two men?"

"To do it right?" Zaa fingered the point of one canine. "A year."

Jeff nodded. "A year. And they'd have to do it right, because someday they might have to start up again. We're pretty well terraformed these days. This out here isn't much worse than the Gobi Desert on Earth. A hundred years ago you couldn't breathe right where we're standing."

He studied Zaa's face, trying to see if his words were sinking in, if they were making an impression. Zaa said, "Sure."

"And everybody knows that. Okay, suppose one of the other plants went down. Totally. Suppose they lost the pile or something. Meltdown."

"I got it."

"Like you say, the air goes slow now. We've added to the planetary mass—covered the whole thing with an ocean of air and water vapor three miles thick, so there's more gravity." Jeff paused for emphasis. "But it goes, and as it goes, we lose gravity. The more air we lose, the faster we lose more."

"I know that."

"Sure. I know you do. I'm just reminding you. All right, they lose one whole plant, like I said."

"You never lose the pile if you do it right."

"Sure. But not everybody's as smart as you are, okay? They get some clown in there and he screws up. Let's take the Schiaparelli plant, just to talk about. How much fossil water have they got?"

Zaa shrugged.

"I don't know either, and neither do they. They could give you some number, but it's just a guess. Suppose they run out of water."

Zaa nodded and turned away, four-legging toward the main gate.

Jeff hurried after him. "How long before people panic? A week? A month?"

"You never finished boarding up."

"I'll get it later. I have to be there when they call."

"Sure," Zaa said.

Together, as they had been together since Jeff was born, they strode through the plant gate upon two legs and four, leaving it open behind them. "They're going to have to give us power wagons," Jeff said. "Suppose we're at home and we have to get here fast."

"Bikes." Zaa looked at him, then looked away. "In here you're the boss. All right, you had your say. I listened to everything."

It was Jeff's turn to nod. He said, "Uh-huh."

"So do I get to talk now?"

Jeff nodded again. "Shoot."

"You said it was going to get better, people were going to come out here from Elysium again. But you were boarding up your store. So you know, only you're scared I'll leave."

Jeff did not speak.

"We're not like you." To illustrate what he meant, Zaa began six-legging. "I been raised with you—with you Sol people is what I mean. I feel like I'm one of you, and maybe once a week I'll see myself in a mirror or someplace and I think, my gosh, I'm an alien."

"You're a Martian," Jeff told him firmly. "I am, too. You call us Sols or Earthmen or something, and most of my folks were Navajo. But I'm Martian, just like you."

"Thanks. Only we get attached to places, you know? We're like cats. I hatched in this town. I grew up here. As long as I can stay, I'm not going."

"There's food in the store. Canned and dried stuff, a lot of it. I'll leave you the key. You can look after it for me."

Zaa took a deep breath, filling a chest thicker even than Jeff's with thin Martian air that they had made. "You said we'd added to the mass with our air. Made more gravity. Only we didn't. The nitrogen's from the rock we dig and crush. You know that. The oxygen's from splitting water. Fossil water from underground. Sure, we bring stuff from Earth, but it doesn't amount to shit. We've still got the same gravity we always did."

"I guess I wasn't thinking," Jeff conceded.

"You were thinking. You were scraping up any kind of an argument you could to make yourself think they weren't going to shut us down. To make me think that, too."

Jeff looked at his watch.

"It's a long time yet."

"Sure."

He pressed the combination on the keypad—nine, nine, two, five, seven, seven. You could not leave the door of the Administration Building open; an alarm would sound.

"What's that?" Zaa caught his arm.

It was a voice from deep inside the building. Zaa leaped away with Jeff after him, long bounds carrying them the length of the corridor and up the stair.

"Mister Shonto? Administrator Shonto?"

"Here I am!" Panting, Jeff spoke as loudly as he could. "I'm coming!"

Undersecretary R. Lowell Bensen, almost in person, was seated in the holoconference theater; in that dim light, he looked fully as real as Zaa.

"Ah, there you are." He smiled; and Jeff, who was superstitious about smiles, winced inwardly.

"Leem, too. Good. Good! I realized you two might be busy elsewhere, but good God, twenty-four fifteen. A time convenient for us, a convenient time to get you two out of bed. Believe me, the Department treats me like that, too. Fourteen hours on a good day, twice around the clock on the bad ones. How are things in Grand Canal?"

"Quiet," Jeff said. "The plant's running at fifteen percent, per instructions. We've got a weak hydraulic pump on Number One Crusher, so we're running Number Two." All this would have been on the printout Bensen had undoubtedly read before making his call, but it would be impolite to mention it. "Zaa Leem here is making oversized rings and a new piston for that pump while we wait for a new one." Not in the least intending to do it, Jeff gulped. "We're afraid we may not get a new pump, sir, and we want to be capable of one hundred percent whenever you need us."

Bensen nodded, and Jeff turned to Zaa. "How are those new parts coming, Leem?"

"Just have to be installed, sir."

"You two are the entire staff of the Grand Canal Plant now? You don't even have a secretary? That came up during our meeting."

Jeff said, "That's right, sir."

"But there's a town there, isn't there? Grand Canal City or some such? A place where you can hire more staff when you need them?"

Here it came. Jeff's mouth felt so dry that he could scarcely speak. "There is a town, Mr. Bensen. You're right about that, sir. But I couldn't hire more personnel there. Nobody's left besides—besides ourselves, sir. Leem and me."

Bensen looked troubled. "A ghost town, is it?"

Zaa spoke up, surprising Jeff. "It was a tourist town, Mr. Bensen. That's why my family moved here. People wanted to see aliens back then, and talk to some, and they'd buy our art to do it. Now—well, sir, when my folks came to the Sol system, it took them two sidereal years just to get here. You know how it is these days, sir. Where'd you take your last vacation?"

"Isis, a lovely world. I see what you mean."

"The Department pays me pretty well, sir, and I save my money, most of it. My boss here wants me to go off to our home planet, where there are a lot more people like me. He says I ought to buy a ticket, whenever I've got the money, just to have a look at it."

Bensen frowned. "We'd hate to lose you, Leem."

"You're not going to, Mr. Bensen. I've got the money

now, and more besides. But I don't speak the language or
know the customs, and if I did, I wouldn't like them. Do you
like aliens, sir?"

"I don't dislike them."

"That's exactly how I feel, sir. Nobody comes to Grand
Canal anymore, sir. Why should they? It's just more Mars,
and they live here already. Me and Mr. Shonto, we work
here, and we think our work's important. So we stay. Only
there's nobody else."

For a moment no one spoke.

"This came up in our meeting, too." Bensen cleared his
throat, and suddenly Jeff understood that Bensen felt almost
as embarrassed and self-conscious as he had. "Betty Collins
told us Grand Canal had become a ghost town, but I wanted
to make sure."

"It is," Jeff muttered. "If you're going to shut down our
plant, sir, I can draw up a plan—"

Bensen was shaking his head. "How many security bots
have you got, Shonto?"

"None, sir."

"None?"

"No, sir. We had human guards, sir. The Plant Police.
They were only police in Grand Canal, actually. They were
laid off one by one. I reported it—or my predecessor and I
did, sir, I ought to say."

Bensen sighed. "I didn't see your reports. I wish I had.
You're in some danger, I'm afraid, you and Leem."

"Really, sir?"

"Yes. Terrorists have been threatening to wreck the plants.
Give in to their demands, or everyone suffocates. You know
the kind of thing. Did you see it on vid?"

Jeff shook his head. "I don't watch much, sir. Maybe not
as much as I should."

Bensen sighed again. "One of the news shows got hold of
it and ran it. Just one show. After that, we persuaded them to
keep a lid on it. That kind of publicity just plays into the terrorists' hands."

For a moment he was silent again, seeming to collect his
thoughts; Zaa squirmed uncomfortably.

"Out there where you are, you're safer than any of the others. Still, you ought to have security. You get supplies each thirty-day?"

Jeff shook his head again. "Every other thirty-day, sir."

"I see. I'm going to change that. A supply crawler will come around every thirty-day from now on. I'll see to it that the next one carries that new pump."

"Thank you, sir."

"But you'll be getting a special resupply as quickly as I can arrange it. Security bots. Twenty, if I can scrape that many together. Whatever I can send."

Jeff began to thank him again, but Bensen cut him off. "It may take a while. Weeks. Until you get them, you'll have to be on guard every moment. You're running at fifteen percent, you said. Could you up that to twenty-five?"

"Yes, sir. To one hundred within a few days."

"Good. Good! Make it twenty-five now, and let us know if you run into any problems."

Abruptly, Bensen was gone. Jeff looked at Zaa, and Zaa looked at Jeff. Both grinned.

At last Jeff managed to say, "They're not shutting us down. Not yet anyhow."

Zaa rose, two-legging and seeming as tall as the main cooling stack. "These terrorist have them pissing in their pants, Jeff. Pissing in their pants! We're their ace in the hole. There's nobody out here but us."

"It'll blow over," Jeff found he was still grinning. "It's bound to, in a year or two. Meanwhile we better get Number One back on line."

They did, and when they had finished, Zaa snatched up a push broom, holding it with his right hand and his right intermediate foot as if it were a two-handed sword. "Defend yourself, Earther!"

Jeff backed away hurriedly until Zaa tossed him a mop, shouting, "They can mark your lonely grave with this!"

"Die, alien scum!" Jeff made a long thrust that Zaa parried just in time. "I rid the spaceways of their filth today!" Insulting the opponent had always been one of the best parts of their battles.

This one was furious. Jeff was smaller and not quite so strong. Zaa was slower; and though his visual field was larger, he lacked the binocular vision that let Jeff judge distances.

Even so, he prevailed in the end, driving Jeff through an open door and into the outdoor storage park, where after more furious fighting he slipped on the coarse red gravel and fell laughing and panting with the handle of Zaa's push broom at his throat.

"Man, that was fun!" He dropped his mop and held up his hands to indicate surrender. "How long since we did this?"

Zaa considered as he helped him up. "Ten years, maybe."

"Way too long!"

"Sure." Sharp claws scratched Zaa's scaly chin. "Hey, I've got an idea. We always wanted real swords, remember?"

As a boy, Jeff would have traded everything he owned for a real sword; the spot had been touched, and he found that there was still—still—a little, wailing ghost of his old desire.

"We could make swords," Zaa said. "Real swords. I could and you could help." Abruptly, he seemed to overflow with enthusiasm. "This rock's got a lot of iron in it. We could smelt it, make a crucible somehow. Make steel. I'd hammer it out—"

He dissolved in laughter beneath Jeff's stare. "Just kidding. But, hey, I got some high-carbon steel strip that would do for blades. I could grind one in an hour or so, and I could make hilts out of brass bar stock, spruce them up with file work, and fasten them on with epoxy."

Though mightily tempted, Jeff muttered, "It's Department property, Zaa."

Zaa laid a large, clawed hand upon his shoulder. "Boss boy, you fail to understand. We're arming ourselves. What if the terrorists get here before the security bots do?"

The idea swept over Jeff like the west wind in the Mare Erythraeum, carrying him along like so much dust. "How come I'm the administrator and you're the maintenance guy?"

"Simple. You're not smart enough for maintenance. Tomorrow?"

"Sure. And we'll have to practice with them a little before we get them sharp, right? It won't be enough to have them, we have to know how to use them, and that would be too dangerous if they had sharp edges and points."

"It's going to be dangerous anyhow," Zaa told him thoughtfully, "but we can wear safety helmets with face shields, and I'll make us some real shields, too."

The shields required more work than the swords, because Zaa covered their welded aluminum frames with densely woven plastic-coated wire, and wove a flattering portrait of Diane Seyn (whom he had won in battle long ago) into his, and an imagined picture of such a woman as he thought Jeff might like into Jeff's.

Although the shields had taken a full day each, both swords and shields were ready in under a week, and the fight that followed—the most epic of all their epic battles— ranged from the boarded up bungalows of Grand Canal to the lip of the Grand Canal itself, a setting so dramatic that each was nearly persuaded to kill the other, driving him over the edge to fall—a living meteor—to his death tens of thousands of feet below. The pure poetry of the thing seemed almost worth a life, as long as it was not one's own.

Neither did, of course. But an orthopter taped them as it shot footage for a special called *Haunted Mars*. And among the tens of billions on Earth who watched a few seconds of their duel were women who took note of their shields and understood.

Patent Infringement

NANCY KRESS

Nancy Kress [www.sff.net/people/nankress] lives in Silver Spring, Maryland. She is one of today's leading SF writers. She is known for her complex medical SF stories, and for her biological and evolutionary extrapolations in such classics as Beggars in Spain *(1993),* Beggars and Choosers *(1994), and* Beggars Ride *(1996). In recent years, she has written* Maximum Light *(1998),* Probability Moon *(2000), and* Probability Sun *(2001), and last year published* Probability Space, *the final book in a trilogy of hard SF novels set against the background of a war between humanity and an alien race. Her stories are rich in texture and in psychological insight, and have been collected in* Trinity and Other Stories *(1985),* The Aliens of Earth *(1993) and* Beaker's Dozen *(1998). She has won two Nebulas and a Hugo for them, and been nominated for a dozen more of these awards.*

"Patent Infringement," from Asimov's, *is a short, amusing story told in memos and letters, about a guy whose genes are used to create a medicine. He asks for a share of the royalties. Pohl and Kornbluth, still the models in SF, were never more sharply satirical than this.*

PRESS RELEASE

Kegelman-Ballston Corporation is proud to announce the first public release of its new drug, Halitex, which cures Ulbarton's Flu completely after one ten-pill course of treatment. Ulbarton's Flu, as the public knows all too well, now afflicts upward of thirty million Americans, with the number growing daily as the highly contagious flu spreads. Halitex "fluproofs" the body by inserting genes tailored to confer immunity to this persistent and debilitating scourge, whose symptoms include coughing, muscle aches, and fatigue. Because the virus remains in the body even after symptoms disappear, Ulbarton's Flu can recur in a given patient at any time. Halitex renders each recurrence ineffectual by "fluproofing" the body.

The General Accounting Office estimates that Ulbarton's Flu, the virus of which was first identified by Dr. Timothy Ulbarton, has cost four billion dollars already this calendar year in medical costs and lost work time. Halitex, two years in development by Kegelman-Ballston, is expected to be in high demand throughout the nation.

New York Post
KC ZAPS ULBARTON'S FLU
NEW DRUG DOES U'S FLU 4 U

Jonathan Meese
538 Pleasant Lane
Aspen Hill, MD 20906

Dear Mr. Kegelman and Mr. Ballston,

I read in the newspaper that your company, Kegelman-Ballston, has recently released a drug, Halitex, that provides immunity against Ulbarton's Flu by gene therapy. I believe that the genes used in developing this drug are mine. Two years ago, on May 5, I visited my GP to explain that I had been exposed to Ulbarton's Flu a lot (the entire accounting department of The Pet Supply Catalog Store, where I work, developed the flu. Also my wife, three children, and mother-in-law. Plus, I believe my dog had it, although the vet disputes this). However, despite all this exposure, I did not develop Ulbarton's.

My GP directed me to your research facility along I-270, saying he "thought he heard they were trying to develop a med." I went there, and samples of my blood and bodily tissues were taken. The researcher said I would hear from you if the samples were ever used for anything, but I never did. Will you please check your records to verify my participation in this new medicine, and tell me what share of the profits are due me.

Thank you for your consideration.

Sincerely,

Jon Meese

Jonathan J. Meese

From the Desk of Robert Ballston
Kegelman-Ballston Corporation

To: Martin Blake, Legal
Re: attached letter

Marty—

Is he a nut? Is this a problem?

Bob

Internal Memo

To: Robert Ballston
From: Martin Blake
Re: gene-line claimant Jonathan J. Meese

Bob—

I checked with Records in Research and yes, unfortunately this guy donated the tissue samples from which the gene line was developed that led to Halitex. Even more unfortunately, Meese's visit occurred just before we instituted the comprehensive waiver for all donors. However, I don't think Meese has any legal ground here. Court precedents have upheld corporate right to patent genes used in drug development. Also, the guy doesn't sound very sophisticated (his *dog*?). He doesn't even know Kegelman's been dead for ten years. Apparently Meese has not yet employed a lawyer. I can make a small nuisance settlement if you like, but I'd rather avoid setting a corporate precedent for these people. I'd rather send him a stiff letter that will scare the bejesus out of the greedy little twerp.
   Please advise.

Marty

From the Desk of Robert Ballston
Kegelman-Ballston Corporation

To: Martin Blake, Legal
Re: J. Meese

Do it.

Bob

Martin Blake, Attorney at Law
Chief Legal Counsel, Kegelman-Ballston Corporation

Dear Mr. Meese:

Your letter regarding the patented Kegelman-Ballston drug
Halitex has been referred to me. Please be advised that you
have no legal rights in Halitex; see attached list of case precedents. If you persist in any such claims, Kegelman-
Ballston will consider it harassment and take appropriate
steps, including possible prosecution.

Sincerely,

Martin Blake

Martin Blake

Jonathan Meese
538 Pleasant Lane
Aspen Hill, MD 20906

Dear Mr. Blake,

But they're my genes!!! This can't be right. I'm consulting a
lawyer, and you can expect to hear from her shortly.

Jon Meese

Jonathan Meese

Catherine Owen, Attorney at Law

Dear Mr. Blake,

I now represent Jonathan J. Meese in his concern that Kegelman-Ballston has developed a pharmaceutical, Halitex, based on gene-therapy that uses Mr. Meese's genes as its basis. We feel it only reasonable that this drug, which will potentially earn Kegelman-Ballston millions if not billions of dollars, acknowledge financially Mr. Meese's considerable contribution. We are therefore willing to consider a settlement and are available to discuss this with you at your earliest convenience.

Sincerely,

Catherine Owen

Catherine Owen, Attorney

From the Desk of Robert Ballston
Kegelman-Ballston Corporation

To: Martin Blake, Legal
Re: J. Meese

Marty—

Damn it, if there's one thing that really chews my balls it's this sort of undercover sabotage by the second-rate. I played golf with Sam Fortescue on Saturday, and he opened my eyes (you remember Sam; he's at the agency we're using to benchmark our competition). Sam speculates that this Meese bastard is really being used by Irwin-Lacey to set us up. You know that bastard Carl Irwin has had his own Ulbarton's drug in development, and he's sore as hell because we beat him to market. Ten to one he's paying off this Meese patsy.
    We can't allow it. Don't settle. Let him sue.

Bob

Internal Memo

To: Robert Ballston
From: Martin Blake
Re: gene-line claimant Jonathan J. Meese

Bob—

I've got a better idea. *We* sue *him*, on the grounds he's walking around with our patented genetic immunity to Ulbarton's. No one except consumers of Halitex have this
immunity, so Meese must have acquired it illegally, possibly
on the black market. We gain several advantages with this
suit: We eliminate Meese's complaint, we send a clear message to other rivals who may be attempting patent infringement, and we gain a publicity circus to both publicize
Halitex (not that it needs it) and, more important, make the
public aware of the dangers of black market substitutes for
Halitex, such as Meese obtained.

Incidentally, I checked again with Records over at Research. They have no documentation on any visit from a
Jonathan J. Meese on any date whatsoever.

Marty

From the Desk of Robert Ballston
Kegelman-Ballston Corporation

To: Martin Blake, Legal
Re: J. Meese

Marty—

Brilliant! Do it. Can we get a sympathetic judge? One who
understands business? Maybe O'Connor can help.

Bob

The New York Times
HALITEX BLACK MARKET
CASE TO BEGIN TODAY

This morning the circuit court of Manhattan County is scheduled to begin hearing the case of *Kegelman-Ballston v. Meese*. This case, heavily publicized during recent months, is expected to set important precedents in the controversial areas of gene patents and patent infringement of biological properties. Protesters from the group FOR US: CANCEL KIDNAPPED-GENE PATENTS, which is often referred to by its initials, have been in place on the court steps since last night. The case is being heard by Judge Latham P. Farmingham III, a Republican who is widely perceived as sympathetic to the concerns of big business.

This case began when Jonathan J. Meese, an accountant with The Pet Supply Catalog Store. . . .

Catherine Owen, Attorney at Law

Dear Mr. Blake,

Just a reminder that Jon Meese and I are still open to a settlement.

Sincerely,

Catherine Owen

Martin Blake, Attorney at Law, Chief Legal Counsel, Kegelman-Ballston Corporation

Martin Blake, Attorney at Law
Chief Legal Counsel, Kegelman-Ballston Corporation

Cathy—

Don't they teach you at that law school you went to (I never can remember the name) that you don't settle when you're sure to win?

You're a nice girl; better luck next time.

Martin Blake

The New York Times
MEESE CONVICTED
PLAINTIFF GUILTY OF "HARBORING" DISEASE-FIGHTING GENES WITHOUT COMPENSATING DEVELOPER KEGELMAN-BALLSTON

From the Desk of Robert Ballston
Kegelman-Ballston Corporation

To: Martin Blake, Legal
Re: Kegelman-Ballston v Meese

Marty—

I always said you were a genius! My God, the free publicity we got out of this thing, not to mention the future edge. . . . How about a victory celebration this weekend? Are you and Elaine free to fly to Aruba on the Lear, Friday night?

Bob

The New York Times
BLUE GENES FOR DRUG THIEF
JONATHAN J. MEESE SENTENCED TO SIX MONTHS
FOR PATENT INFRINGEMENT

From the Desk of Robert Ballston
Kegelman-Ballston Corporation

To: Martin Blake, Legal
Re: Halitex

Marty! I just had a brilliant idea I want to run by you. We got
Meese, but now that he's at Ossining the publicity has died
down. Well, my daughter read this squib the other day in
some science magazine, how the Ulbarton's virus has in it
some of the genes that Research combined with Meese's to
create Halitex. I didn't understand all the egghead science,
but apparently Halitex used some of the flu genes to build its
immune properties. And we own the patent on Halitex. As I
see it, that means that Dr. Ulbarton was working with OUR
genes when he identified Ulbarton's flu and published his
work. Now, if we could go after *Ulbarton* in court, the publicity would be tremendous, as well as strengthening our
proprietorship position. . . .

Lost Sorceress of the Silent Citadel

MICHAEL MOORCOCK

Michael Moorcock (www.multiverse.org/ and www.eclipse. co.uk/sweetdespise/moorcock/) lives in Bastrop, Texas. Once the firebrand editor of New Worlds, *and the polemicist behind the British New Wave of the 1960s, and still one of the great living SF and fantasy writers, Moorcock is known more for his avant-garde work, and his support of other writers pushing the boundaries of genre, than for his genre work. He is now a recognized literary figure in the UK, a significant contemporary writer. Nevertheless, he has deep roots in genre fiction, and his love for certain genre works and writers (for instance Leigh Brackett, Charles Harness, and Alfred Bester) is long-term and enduring.*

"Lost Sorceress of the Silent Citadel" is another story from Mars Probes. *It is an exercise in nostalgia, a swashbuckling planetary romance that brings back Mars as an exciting setting for SF adventure for an audience that knows better but is still willing to indulge in it. It is primarily an homage to Leigh Brackett, but also to her honorable tradition, which now (we say with some regret) prospers more in the media than in the SF literature—though not entirely: see the Neal Asher story earlier in this book. Moorcock succeeds both because of his sincere feelings for Brackett's achievements and because of his sheer talent and experience at writing fantasy and science fiction adventure.*

*T*hey came upon the Earthling naked, somewhere in the Shifting Desert when Mars' harsh sunlight beat through thinning atmosphere and the sand was raw glass cutting into bare feet. His skin hung like filthy rags from his bloody flesh. He was starved, unshaven, making noises like an animal. He was raving—empty of identity and will. What had the ghosts of those ancient Martians done to him? Had they traveled through time and space to take a foul and unlikely vengeance? A novella of alien mysteries—of a goddess who craved life—who lusted for the only man who had ever dared disobey her. A tale of Captain John MacShard, the Half-Martian, of old blood and older memories, of a restless quest for the prize of forgotten centuries. . . .

CHAPTER ONE

Whispers of an Ancient Memory

"That's Captain John MacShard, the tomb-thief." Schomberg leaned his capacious belly on the bar, wiping around it with a filthy rag. "They say his mother was a Martian princess turned whore, and his father—"

Low City's best-known antiquities fence, proprietor of the seedy Twenty Capstans, Schomberg murmured wetly through lips like fresh liver. "Well, Mercury was the only

459

world would take them. Them and their filthy egg." He flicked a look toward the door and became suddenly grave.

Outlined against the glare of the Martian noon a man appeared to hesitate and go on down the street. Then he turned and pushed through the entrance's weak energy gate. Then he paused again.

He was a big, hard-muscled man, dressed in spare ocher and brown, with a queer, ancient weapon, all baroque unstable plastics and metals, prominent on his hip.

The Banning gun was immediately recognized and its owner identified by the hardened spacers and *krik* traders who used the place.

They said only four men in the solar system could ever handle that weapon. One was the legendary Northwest Smith; the second was Eric John Stark, now far off-system. The third was Dumarest of Terra, and the fourth was Captain John MacShard. Anyone else trying to fire a Banning died unpleasantly. Sometimes they just disappeared, as if every part of them had been sucked into the gun's impossible energy cells. They said Smith had given his soul for a Banning. But MacShard's soul was still apparent, behind that steady gray gaze, hungering for something like oblivion.

From long habit Captain John MacShard remained in the doorway until his sight had fully adjusted to the sputtering naphtha. His eyes glowed with a permanent feral fire. He was a lean-faced, slim-hipped wolf's head whom no man could ever tame. Through all the alien and mysterious spheres of interplanetary space, many had tried to take the wild beast out of Captain John MacShard. He remained as fierce and free as in the days when, as a boy, he had scrabbled for survival over the unforgiving waste of rocky crags and slag slopes that was Mercury and from the disparate blood of two planets had built a body which could withstand the cruel climate of a third.

Captain John MacShard was in Schomberg's for a reason. He never did anything without a reason. He couldn't go to sleep until he had first considered the action. It was what he had learned on Mercury, orphaned, surviving in those terrible caverns, fighting fiercely for subsistence where nothing would grow and where you and the half-human tribe which had adopted you were the tastiest prey on the planet.

More than any Earthman, he had learned the old ways, the sweet, dangerous, old ways of the ancient Martians. Their descendants still haunted the worn and whispering hills which were the remains of Mars' great mountain ranges in the ages of her might, when the Sea Kings ruled a planet as blue as turquoise, as glittering red as rubies, and as green as that Emerald Isle which had produced Captain John Mac-Shard's own Earth ancestors, as tough, as mystical and as filled with wanderlust as this stepson of the shrieking Mercurian wastelands, with the blood of Brian Borhu, Henry Tudor, and Charles Edward Stuart in his veins. Too, the blood of Martian Sea Kings called to him across the centuries and informed him with the deep wisdom of his Martian forebears. That long-dead kin had fought against the Danes and the Anglo-Saxons, been cavaliers in the Stuart cause and marshals in Napoleon's army. They had fought for and against the standard of Rhiannon, in both male and female guise, survived blasting sorcery and led the starving armies of Barrakesh into the final battle of the Martian pole. Their stories, their courage and their mad fearlessness in the face of inevitable death were legendary.

Captain John MacShard had known nothing of this ancestry of course and there were still many unsolved mysteries in his past, but he had little interest in them. He had the instincts of any intelligent wild animal, and left the past in the past. A catlike curiosity was what drove him and it made him the best archaeological hunter on five planets—some, like Schomberg, called him a grave-looter, though never to his face. There was scarcely a museum in the inhabited universe which didn't proudly display a find of Captain John MacShard's. They said some of the races which had made those artifacts had not been entirely extinct until the captain found them. There wasn't a living enemy who didn't fear him. And there wasn't a woman in the system who had known him that didn't remember him.

To call Captain John MacShard a loner was something of a tautology. Captain John MacShard was loneliness personified. He was like a spur of rock in the deep desert, resisting everything man and nature could send against it. He was endurance. He was integrity, and he was grit through and through. Only one who had tested himself against the entire fury of alien Mercury and survived could know what it meant to be MacShard, trusting only MacShard.

Captain John MacShard was very sparing in his affections but gave less to himself than he gave to an alley-*brint*, a wounded ray-rat, or the scrawny street kid begging in the hard sour Martian sun to whom he finally tossed a piece of old silver before striding into the bar and taking his usual, which Schomberg had ready for him.

The Dutchman began to babble something, but Captain John MacShard placed his lips to the shot glass of Vortex Water, turned his back on him, and surveyed his company.

His company was pretending they hadn't seen him come in.

From a top pocket MacShard fished a twisted pencil of Venusian talk-talk wood and stuck it between his teeth, chewing on it thoughtfully. Eventually his steady gaze fell on a fat merchant in a fancy fake *skow*-skin jerkin and vivid blue tights who pretended an interest in his fancifully carved flagon.

"Your name Morricone?" Captain John MacShard's voice was a whisper, cutting through the rhythmic sound of men who couldn't help taking in sudden air and running tongues around drying mouths.

His thin lips opened wide enough for the others to see a glint of bright, pointed teeth before they shut tight again.

Morricone nodded. He made a halfhearted attempt to smile. He put his hands on either side of his cards and made funny shrugging movements.

From somewhere, softly, a *shtrang* string sounded.

"You wanted to see me," said Captain John MacShard. And he jerked his head toward a corner where a filthy table was suddenly unoccupied.

The man called Morricone scuttled obediently toward the

table and sat down, watching Captain John MacShard as he picked up his bottle and glass and walked slowly, his antique *ghat*-scale leggings chinking faintly.

Again the *shtrang* string began to sound, its deep note making peculiar harmonies in the thin Martian air. There was a cry like a human voice which echoed into nowhere, and when it was gone the silence was even more profound.

"You wanted to see me?" Captain John MacShard moved the unlit stogie from one side of his mouth to the other. His gray, jade-flecked eyes bore into Morricone's shifting black pupils. The fat merchant was obviously hyped on some kind of Low City "head chowder."

There wasn't a drug you couldn't buy at Schomberg's where everything was for sale, including Schomberg.

The hophead began to giggle in a way that at once identified him as a *cruffer*, addicted to the fine, white powdered bark of the Venusian high tree cultures, who used the stuff to train their giant birds but had the sense not to use it themselves.

Captain John MacShard turned away. He wasn't going to waste his time on a druggy, no matter how expensive his tastes.

Morricone lost his terror of Captain John MacShard then. He needed help more than he needed dope. Captain John MacShard was faintly impressed. He knew the kind of hold *cruff* had on its victims.

But he kept on walking.

Until Morricone scuttled in front of him and almost fell to his knees, his hands reaching out toward Captain John Mac-Shard, too afraid to touch him.

His voice was small, desperate, and it held some kind of pain Captain John MacShard recognized. "Please . . ."

Captain John MacShard made to move past, back into the glaring street.

"Please, Captain MacShard. Please help me . . ." His shoulders slumped, and he said dully: "They've taken my daughter. The Thennet have taken my daughter."

Captain John MacShard hesitated, still looking into the street. From the corner of his mouth he gave the name of one of the cheapest hotels in the quarter. Nobody in their right mind would stay there if they valued life or limb. Only the crazy or desperate would even enter the street it was in.

"I'm there in an hour." Captain John MacShard went out of the bar. The boy he'd given the silver coin to was still standing in the swirling Martian dust, the ever-moving red tide which ran like a bizarre river down the time-destroyed street. The boy grinned up at him. Old eyes, young skin. A slender snizzer lizard crawled on his shoulder and curled its strange, prehensile tail around his left ear. The boy touched the creature tenderly, automatically.

"You good man, Mister Captain John MacShard."

For the first time in months, Captain John MacShard allowed himself a thin, self-mocking grin.

CHAPTER TWO

Taken by the Thennet!

Captain John MacShard left the main drag almost at once. He needed some advice and knew where he was most likely to find it. There was an old man he had to visit. Though not of their race, Fra Energen had authority over the last of the Memiget Priests whose Order had discovered how rich the planet was in man-made treasure. They had also been experts on the Thennet as well as the ancient Martian pantheon.

His business over with, Captain John MacShard walked back to his hotel. His route took him through the filthiest, most wretched slums ever seen across all the ports of the spaceways. He displayed neither weakness nor desire. His pace was the steady, relentless lope of the wolf. His eyes seemed unmoving, yet took in everything.

All around him the high tottering tenement towers of the Low City swayed gently in the glittering light, their rusted metal and red terra cotta merging into the landscape as if they were natural. As if they had always been there.

Not quite as old as Time, some of the buildings were older

than the human race. They had been added to and stripped and added to again, but once those towers had sheltered and proclaimed the power of Mars' mightiest sea lords.

Now they were slums, a rat warren for the scum of the spaceways, for half-Martians like Captain John MacShard, for stranger genetic mixes than even Brueghel imagined.

In that thin atmosphere you could smell the Low City for miles and beyond that, in the series of small craters known as Diana's Field, was Old Mars Station, the first spaceport the Earthlings had ever built, long before they had begun to discover the strange, retiring races which had remained near their cities, haunting them like barely living ghosts, more creatures of their own mental powers than of any natural creation—ancient memories made physical by act of will alone.

Millennia before, the sea lords and their ladies and children died in those towers, sensing the end of their race as the last of the waters evaporated and red winds scoured the streets of all ornament and grace. Some chose to kill themselves as their fine ships became so many useless monuments. Some had marshaled their families and set off across the new-formed deserts in search of a mythical ocean which welled up from the planet's core.

It had taken less than a generation, Captain John Mac-Shard knew, for a small but navigable ocean to evaporate rapidly until it was no more than a haze in the morning sunlight. Where it had been were slowly collapsing hulls, the remains of wharfs and jetties, endless dunes and rippling deserts, abandoned cities of poignant dignity and unbelievable beauty. The great dust tides rose and fell across the dead sea bottoms of a planet which had run out of resources. Even its water had come from Venus, until the Venusians had raised the price so only Earth could afford it.

Earth was scarcely any better now, with water wars turning the Blue Planet into a background of endless skirmishes between nations and tribes for the precious streams, rivers, and lakes they had used so dissolutely and let dissipate into space, turning God's paradise into Satan's wasteland.

And now Earth couldn't afford Venusian water either. So Venus fought a bloody civil war for control of what was left of her trade. For a while MacShard had run bootleg water out of New Malvern. The kind of money the rich were prepared to pay for a tiny bottle was phenomenal. But he'd become sickened with it when he'd walked through London's notorious Westminster district and seen degenerates spending an artisan's wages on jars of gray reconstitute while mothers held the corpses of dehydrated babies in their arms and begged for the money to bury them.

"Mr. Captain John MacShard."

Captain John MacShard knew the boy had followed him all the way to the hotel. Without turning, he said: "You'd better introduce yourself, sonny."

The boy seemed ashamed, as if he had never been detected before. He hung his head. "My dad called me Milton," he said.

Captain John MacShard smiled then. Once. He stopped when he saw the boy's face. The child had been laughed at too often and to him it meant danger, distrust, pain. "So your dad was Mr. Eliot, right?"

The boy forgot any imagined insult. "You knew him?"

"How long did your mother know him?"

"Well, he was on one of those long-haul ion sailors. He was a great guitarist. Singer. Wrote all his own material. He was going to see a producer when he came back from Earth with enough money to marry. Well, you know that story." The boy lowered his eyes. "Never came back."

"I'm not your pa," said Captain John MacShard and went inside. He closed his door. He marveled at the tricks the street kids used these days. But that stuff couldn't work on him. He'd seen six-year-old masters pulling the last Uranian *bakh* from a tight-fisted New Nantucket blubber-chaser who had just finished a speech about a need for more workhouses.

A few moments later, Morricone arrived. Captain John MacShard knew it was him by the quick, almost hesitant rap.

"It's open," he said. There was never any point in locking doors in this place. It advertised you had something worth stealing. Maybe just your body.

Morricone was terrified. He was terrified of the neighborhood and he was terrified of Captain John MacShard. But he was even more terrified of something else. Of whatever the Thennet might have done to his daughter.

Captain John MacShard had no love for the Thennet, and he didn't need a big excuse to put a few more of their number in hell.

The gaudily dressed old man shuffled into the room, and his terror didn't go away. Captain John MacShard closed the door behind him. "Don't tell me about the Thennet," he said. "I know about them and what they do. Tell me when they took your daughter and whatever else you know about where they took her."

"Out past the old tombs. A good fifty or sixty versts from here. Beyond the Yellow Canal. I paid a breed to follow them. That's as far as he got. He said the trail went on, but he wasn't going any farther. I got the same from all of them. They won't follow the Thennet into the Aghroniagh Hills. Then I heard you had just come down from Earth." He made some effort at ordinary social conversation. His eyes remained crazed. "What's it like back there now?"

"This is better," said Captain John MacShard. "So they went into the Aghroniagh Hills? When?"

"Some two days ago . . ."

Captain John MacShard turned away with a shrug.

"I know," said the merchant. "But this was different. They weren't going to eat her or—or—play with her . . ." His skin crawled visibly. "They were careful not to mark her. It was as if she was for someone else. Maybe a big slaver? They wouldn't let any of their saliva drip on her. They got me, though." He extended the twisted branch of burned flesh that had been his forearm.

Captain John MacShard drew a deep breath and began to take off his boots. "How much?"

"Everything. Anything."

"You'll owe me a million hard *deens* if I bring her back alive. I won't guarantee her sanity."

"You'll have the money. I promise. Her name's Mercedes. She's sweet and decent—the only good thing I ever helped create. She was staying with me . . . the vacation . . . her mother and I . . ."

Captain John MacShard moved toward his board bed. "Half in the morning. Give me a little time to put the money in a safe place. Then I'll leave. But not before."

After Morricone had shuffled away, his footsteps growing softer and softer until they faded into the general music of the rowdy street outside, Captain John MacShard began to laugh.

It wasn't a laugh you ever wanted to hear again.

CHAPTER THREE

The Unpromised Land

The Aghroniagh Hills had been formed by a huge asteroid crashing into the area a few million years earlier, but the wide sweep of meadowland and streams surrounding them had never been successfully settled by Captain John Mac-Shard's people. They were far from what they seemed.

Many settlers had come in the early days, attracted by the water and the grass. Few lasted a month, let alone a season. That water and grass existed on Mars because of Blake, the terraplaner. He had made it his life's work, crossing and re-crossing one set of disparate genes with another until he had something which was like grass and like water and which could survive, maybe even thrive and proliferate, in Mars' barren climate. A sort of liquid algae and a kind of lichen, at root, but with so many genetic modifications that its mathematical pedigree filled a book.

Blake's great atmosphere pumping stations had transformed the Martian air and made it rich enough for Earthlings to breathe. He had meant to turn the whole of Mars into the same lush farmland he had seen turn to dust on Earth. Some believed he had grown too ambitious, that instead of doing God's work, he was beginning to believe he, himself, was God. He had planned a city called New Jerusalem and had designed its buildings, its parks, streams, and ornamental lakes. He had planted his experimental fields and brought his first pioneer volunteers and given them seed he had made and fertilizer he had designed, and something had happened under the unshielded Martian sunlight which had not happened in his laboratories.

Blake's Eden became worse than Purgatory.

His green shoots and laughing fountains developed a kind of intelligence, a taste for specific nutrients, a means of finding them and processing them to make them edible. Those nutrients were most commonly found in Earthlings. The food could be enticed the way an anemone entices an insect. The prey saw sweet water, green grass and it was only too glad to fling itself deep into the greedy shoots, the thirsty liquid, which was only too glad to digest it.

And so fathers had watched their children die before their eyes, killed and absorbed in moments. Women had seen hard-working husbands die before becoming food themselves.

Blake's seven pioneer families lasted a year and there had been others since who brought certain means of defeating the so-called Paradise virus, who challenged the hungry grass and liquid, who planned to tame it. One by one, they went to feed what had been intended to feed them.

There were ways of surviving the Paradise. Captain John MacShard had tried them and tested them. For a while he had specialized in finding artifacts which the settlers had left behind, letters, deeds, cherished jewelry.

He had learned how to live, for short periods at least, in the Paradise. He had kept raising his price until it got too high for anybody.

Then he quit. It was the way he put an end to his own boredom. What he did with all his money nobody knew, but he didn't spend it on himself.

The only money Captain John MacShard was known to exchange in large quantities was for modifications and repairs to that ship of his, as alien as his sidearm, which he'd picked up in the Rings and claimed by right of salvage. Even the scrap merchants hadn't wanted the ship. The metal it was made of could become poisonous to the touch. Like the weapon, the ship didn't allow everyone to handle her.

* * *

Captain John MacShard paid a halfling phunt-renter to drive him to the edge of the Paradise, and he promised the sweating driver the price of his phunt if he'd wait for news of his reappearance and come take him back to the city. "And any other passenger I might have with me," he had added.

The *phunter* was almost beside himself with anxiety. He knew exactly what that green sentient weed could do, and he had heard tales of how the streams had chased a man halfway back to the Low City and consumed him on the spot. *Drank him, they said.* No sane creature, Earthling or Martian, would risk the dangers of the Paradise.

Not only was the very landscape dangerous, there were also the Thennet.

The Thennet, whose life-stuff was unpalatable to the Paradise, came and went comfortably all year round, emerging only occasionally to make raids on the human settlements, certain that no posse would ever dare follow them back to their city of tunnels, Kong Gresh, deep at the center of the Aghroniagh Crater, which lay at the center of the Aghroniagh Hills, where the weed did not grow and the streams did not flow.

They raided for pleasure, the Thennet. Mostly, when they craved a delicacy. Human flesh was almost an addiction to them, they desired it so much. They were a cruel people and took pleasure in their captives, keeping them alive for many weeks sometimes, especially if they were young women. But they savored this killing. Schomberg had put it graphically enough once: *The longer the torment, the sweeter the meat.* His customers wondered how he understood such minds.

Captain John MacShard knew Mercedes Morricone had a chance at life. He hoped, when he found her, that she would still want that chance.

What had Morricone said about the Thennet not wishing to mark her? That they were capturing her for someone else?

Who?

Captain John MacShard wanted to find out for himself. No one had needed to pay the Thennet for young girls in years. The wars among the planets had given the streets plenty of good-looking women to choose from. Nobody ever noticed a few missing from time to time.

If the Thennet were planning to sell her for the food they would need for the coming Long Winter, they would be careful to keep their goods in top quality, and Mercedes could well be a specific target. The odds were she was still alive and safe. That was why Captain John MacShard did not think he was wasting his time.

And it was the only reason he would go this far into the Aghroniaghs, where the Thennet weren't the greatest danger.

CHAPTER FOUR

Hell Under The Hill

It was hard to believe the Thennet had ever been human, but there was no doubt they spoke a crude form of English. They were said to be degenerated descendants of a crashed Earth ship which had left Houston a couple of centuries before, carrying a political investigative committee looking into reports that Earth mining interests were using local labor as slaves. The reports had been right. The mining interests had made sure the distinguished senators never got to see the evidence.

Captain John MacShard was wearing his own power armor. It buzzed on his body from soles to crown. The silky energy, soft as a child's hand, rippled around him like an atmosphere. He flickered and buzzed with complex circuitry outlining his veins and arteries, following the course of his blood. This medley of soft sounds was given a crazy rhythm by the ticking of his antigrav's notoriously dangerous regulators as he flew an inch above the hungry, whispering grass, the lush and luring streams of Paradise.

Only once did he come down, in the ruins of what was to have been the city of New Jerusalem and where the grass did not grow.

Here he ran at a loping pace which moved him faster over the landscape and at the same time recharged the antigrav's short-lived power units.

He was totally enclosed in the battlesuit of his own design, his visible skin a strange arsenical green behind the overlapping energy shields, his artificial gills processing the atmosphere to purify maximum oxygen. Around him as he moved was an unstable aura buzzing with gold and misty greens, skipping and sizzling as elements in his armor mixed and reacted with particles of semi-artificial Martian air, fusing them into toxic fumes which would kill a man if taken straight. Which is why Captain John MacShard wore his helmet. It most closely resembled the head of an ornamental dolphin, all sweeping flukes and baroque symmetry, the complicated, delicate wiring visible through the thin plasdex skin, while the macro-engineered plant curving from between his shoulder blades looked almost like wings. He could have been one of the forgotten beasts of the Eldren which they had ridden against Bast-Na-Gir when the first mythologies of Mars were being made. The transparent steel visor plate added to this alien appearance, enlarging and giving exaggerated curve to his eyes. He had become an unlikely creature whose outline would momentarily baffle any casual observer. There were things out here which fed off Thennet and human alike. Captain John MacShard only needed a second's edge to survive. But that second was crucial.

He was in the air again, his batteries at maximum charge. He was now a shimmering copper angel speeding over the thirsty grass and the hungry rivers of Paradise until he was at last standing on the shale slopes of the Aghroniagh Mountains.

The range was essentially the rim of a huge steep-sided crater. At the crater's center were peculiar pockets of gases which were the by-product of certain rock dust interacting with sunlight. These gases formed a breeding and sleeping environment for the Thennet, who could only survive so long away from what the first Earth explorers had called their "clouds." Most of the gas, which had a narcotic effect on humans, was drawn down into their burrows by an ingenious system of vents and manually operated fans. It was the only machinery they used. Otherwise they were primitive enough, though inventive murderers who delighted in the slow, perverse death of anything that lived, including their own sick and wounded. Suicide was the commonest cause of death.

As Captain John MacShard raced through the crags and eventually came to the crater walls, he knew he might have a few hours left in which to save the girl. The Thennet had a way of letting the gases work on their human victims so that they became light-headed and cheerful. The Thennet knew how to amuse humans.

Sometimes they would let the human feel this way for days, until they began to get too sluggish.

Then they would do something which produced a sudden rush of adrenaline in their victim. And thereafter it was unimaginable nightmare. Unimaginable because no human mind could conceive of such tortures and hold the memory or its sanity. No mind, that is, except Captain John MacShard's. And it was questionable now that Captain John MacShard's mind was still in most senses human.

Here's where I was too late. There's her bone and necklace again. That's the burrow into middle chamber. Gas goes low there. All these thoughts passed through his head as he retraced steps over razor rocks and unstable shale. He had been paid four times to venture into Thennet territory. Twice he had successfully brought out living victims, both still relatively sane. Once he had brought out a corpse. Once he had left a corpse where he found it. Seven times before that, curiosity had taken him there. The time they captured him, his chances of escape had been minimal. He was determined not to be captured again.

Now, however, there was something different about the sinister, smoking landscape of craters and spikes. There was a kind of silence Captain John MacShard couldn't explain. A sense of waiting. A sense of watching.

Unable to do anything but ignore the instinct, he dropped down into the fissures and began to feel his way into the first flinty corridors. He had killed five Thennet guards almost without thought by the time he had begun to descend the great main passage into the Thennet underworld. He always killed Thennet at a distance, if he could. Their venom could sear into delicate circuitry and destroy his armor and his lifelines.

Three more Thennet fell without knowing they were dead. Captain John MacShard felt no hesitation about killing them wherever he came across one. He killed them on principle, the way they killed by habit. The less of the Thennet there were, the better for everyone. And each corpse offered something useful to him as he crept on downward into the subsidiary tunnels, following still familiar routes.

The walls of the caverns were thick with flaking blood and ordure, which the Thennet used for building materials. Mostly it had hardened, but every so often it became soft and slippery. Captain John MacShard had to adjust his step, glad of his gills as well as his armor, which meant he did not have to smell or touch any of the glistening stuff, though every so often his air system overloaded and he got just a hint of the disgusting stench.

But something was wrong. His armor began to pop and tremble. It was a warning. Captain John MacShard paused in the slippery passage and considered withdrawing. There would normally be more Thennet, males and females, shuffling through the passages, going about their business, tending their eggs, tormenting their food.

He had a depressing feeling that he couldn't easily get back, that he was already in a trap. Was it a trap which had been set for him specifically? Or could anyone be the prey? This wasn't the Thennet. Could it be the Thennet had new leadership and wider goals? Captain John MacShard could smell intelligence. This was intelligence. And it wasn't a kind he'd smelled before. Not in Thennet territory. Mostly what you smelled was terror and ghastly glee.

There was something else down here. Something which had a personality. Something which had ambitions. Something which was even now gathering power.

Captain John MacShard had learned to trust his instincts,

and his instincts told him he would have to fight to return to the surface. What was more, he had an unpleasant feeling about what he might have to fight. . . .

His best chance was to pretend he had noticed nothing, but keep his attention on that intelligence, even as he sought out the merchant's daughter. What was her name? Mercedes?

The narrow, fetid tunnels of the Thennet city were familiar, but now they were opening up, growing wider and taller, as if the Thennet had been working on them. But why?

And then, suddenly, a wave of thought struck against his own mind—a wave which boomed with the force of a tidal wave. It almost stopped him moving forward. It was a moment before the sense of the thoughts began to filter in to him.

No longer. No longer. I am the one. And I am more than one. I am Shienna Sha Shanakana of the Yellow Price, and I shall again become the goddess I once was when Mars was young. I have paid the Yellow Price. I claim this star system as my own. And then I shall claim the universe. . . .

The girl? Captain John MacShard could not stop the question.

All he received was a wave of mockery which again struck, with an almost physical weight.

CHAPTER FIVE

Ancient and Modern

A voice began to whisper through the serpentine tunnels. It was cold as space, hard and sharp as Mercurian steel.

The female Mercedes is gone. She is gone, Earther. There is nothing of her, save this flesh, and I am already changing the flesh so that it is more to my taste. She'll produce the egg. First the body, then the entire planet. Then the system. Then the stars. We shall thrive again. We shall feast at will among the Galaxies.

So that was it! Yet another of Mars' ancient ghosts trying

to regain its former power. These creatures had been killed, banished, imprisoned long ago, during the last of Mars' terrible wars.

They had reached an enormous level of intellectual power, ruling the planet and influencing the whole system as they became capable of flinging their mental energy through interplanetary space, to control distant intelligences and rule through them.

They considered themselves to be gods, though they were mortal enough in many respects. It had been their arrogance which had brought them low.

So abstract and strange had become their ambitions that they had forgotten the ordinary humans, those who had chosen not to follow their bizarre path, whose lives became wretched as the Eldren used all the planet's resources to increase their powers. They had grown obsessed with immortality, recording themselves onto extraordinary pieces of jewelry containing everything needed to reconstitute the entire individual. Everything but ordinary humans to place the jewels in their special settings and begin the process, which required considerable human resources, ultimately taking the lives of all involved. For most of the ordinary humans had died of starvation and dehydration as those powers plundered their planet of all resources, melting the poles so that first there was an abundance of water, the time of the beginnings of the Sea Kings' power, but then, as quickly, the evaporation had begun, dissipating into empty space, no longer contained by the protective layers of ozone and oxygen. The water could not come back. It was a momentary shimmer in the vastness of space as it was drawn inevitably toward the sun.

Captain John MacShard knew all this because his mother had known all this. He had not known his mother, had not known he had emerged, a brawling, bawling independent creature from the egg she had saved, even as she and her husband died, victims of the planet's unforgiving climate. He had not known how he had come to live among the aboriginal ape people. The fiercely tribal Mercurians had been fascinated by his tanned, pale hide, so unlike their own dark green skins. They had never thought him anything but one of themselves. They had come to value him. He had been elected a kind of leader. He had taken them to food and guarded them against the giant rock snakes. He had taught them to kill the snakes, to preserve their meat. They named him Tan-Arz or Brown-Skin.

Tan-Arz was his name until the Earthlings found him at last. His father's brother had paid for the search, paid to bring him back to Earth during that brief Golden Age before the planet again descended into civil war. Back to the Old Country. Back to Ireland. Back to Dublin and Trinity College. Then to South London University.

Dublin and London had not civilized Captain John MacShard, but they had taught him the manners and ways of a gentleman. They had not educated Captain John MacShard, but they had informed his experience. Now he understood his enemies as well as his friends. And he understood that the law of the giant corporations was identical to the law he had learned on Mercury.

Kill or be killed. Trust nothing and no one. Power is survival. He smelled them. He was contemptuous of most of them, though they commanded millions. They were his kind. They were his kind gone soft, obscenely greedy, decadent to the marrow.

His instinct was to wipe them out, but they had trained him to serve them. And he had served them. At first, when the wars had begun, he had volunteered. He had served well and honorably, but as the wars got dirtier and the issues less clear, he found himself withdrawing.

He realized that he had more sympathy, most of the time, with the desperate men he was fighting than with the great patricians of Republican Earth.

His refusal to take part in a particularly bloody operation had caused him to be branded a traitor.

It was as an outlaw he had arrived on Mars. They had hunted him into the red wastelands and known he could not have lived.

But Mars was a rest cure compared to Mercury. Captain John MacShard had survived. And Captain John MacShard had prospered.

Now he captained his own ship, the gloriously alien *Duchess of Malfi*, murmuring and baroque in her perpetually shifting darkness. Now he could pick and choose whom he killed and whom he didn't kill.

He had no financial need to continue this dangerous life, no particular security to be derived, even the security of familiarity. Nothing to escape from. Nothing within him he could not confront. He did it because he was who he was.

He was Captain John MacShard and Captain John MacShard was a creature of action, a creature which only came fully alive when its own life was in the balance. A wild creature that longed for the harsh, savage places of the universe, their beauties and their dangers.

But Captain John MacShard had no wish to die here in the slimey burrows of the unhuman Thennet. He had no desire to serve the insane ends of the old Martian godlings who saw their immortality slowly fading and longed for all their power again.

You, Captain John MacShard, will help me. And I will reward you. Before you die, I will make you the sire of the supernatural. Already the blood of my Martians mingles with your own. It is why you are so perfect for my plans.

John MacShard: You are no longer the Earthboy who grew up wild with the submen of Mercury. You are of our own blood, for your mother drew her descent directly from the greatest of the Sea Kings and the Sea Kings were our own children—so much of our blood has mingled with yours that you are now almost one of us.

Let your blood bring you home, John MacShard.

"My blood is my own! It belongs to nobody but me! Every atom has been fought for and won."

It is the blood of gods and goddesses, John MacShard. Of kings and queens.

"Then it's still mine. By right of inheritance!" John MacShard was all aggression now, though the voices speaking to him were patient, reasonable. He had heard similar voices before. As he lay writhing in his own filthy juices on one of the Old Ones' examining slabs.

It is your Earth blood, however, which will give us our glory back. That vital, sturdy, undiluted stuff will bring us back our power and make Mars know her old fear of the un-humans who ruled her before the Sea Kings ruled.

Welcome home, Captain John MacShard, last of the Sea Kings. Welcome home to the Palace of Queen Shienna Sha Shanakana, Seventh of the Seven Sisters who guard the Shrine of the Star Pool, Seventh of the Seven Snakes, Sorcer-ess of the Citadel of Silence where she has slept for too many centuries.

The little mortal did its job well, though unconsciously. I needed its daughter's womb and I needed you, John Mac-Shard. And now I have both. I will reemerge from the great egg fully restored to my power and position.

Behold, Captain John MacShard! The Secrets of the Silent Citadel!

CHAPTER SIX

Queen of the Crystal Citadel

All at once the half-Martian was surrounded by crystal. Crystal colored like rainbows, flashing and murmuring in a cold wind that blew from all directions toward the center where a golden woman sat, smiling at him, beckoning to him, and driving all thought momentarily from his mind as he began to stumble forward. He wanted nothing else in the world but to mate with her. He would die, if necessary, to perform that function.

It took Captain John MacShard a few long seconds to bring himself back under control. Faces formed within the crystal towers. Familiar faces. The faces of friends and ene-mies who welcomed Captain John MacShard and bid him join them, in their good company, for eternity. These were the siren voices which had tempted Ulysses and his men across the void of space. Powerful intelligences trapped within indestructible crystal. Intelligences which, legend had it, could be freed by the stroke of a sacred sword held in the hand of one man.

Captain John MacShard shuddered. He had no such sword. Only his jittering Banning cannon in its heavy webbing. He laid his hand on the gun and seemed to draw reassurance from it.

His white wolf's teeth were clenched in his lean jaw. "No. I'm not your dupe and I'm not Earth's dupe. I'm my own man. I'm Captain John MacShard. There is no living individual more free than me in the universe and no one more ready to fight to keep that freedom."

Yes, murmured the voice in his head. It was a seductive voice. *Think of the power and therefore the freedom you have when we are combined . . . Power to do whatever you desire, to possess whatever you desire, to achieve whatever you desire. You will be reborn as Master of the Universe. The whole of existence will be yours, to satisfy your rarest appetites. . . .*

The voice was full of everything feminine. He could almost smell it. He could see the figure outlined at the center of the crystal palace. The lithe young body with its waves of golden hair, clad in gold, with golden threads cascading down her perfect thighs, with golden cups supporting her perfect breasts and golden sandals on her perfect feet. He could see her quite clearly, yet she seemed the length of a football field away. She was beckoning to him.

"All I want is the power to be free," said Captain John MacShard. "And I already have that. I got it long ago. Nobody gave it to me. I took it. I took it on Mercury. I took it on Earth. I took it on Mars, and I took it on Venus. Not a year goes by when I do not take that freedom again, because that is the only way you preserve the kind of freedom I value. My very marrow is freedom. Everything in me fights to maintain that freedom. It is unconscious and as enduring as the universe itself. I am not the only one to possess it or to know how to fight to keep it. It is the power of all the human heroes who overcame impossible odds that I carry in my blood. You cannot defeat that. Whatever you do, Shienna Sha Shanakana, you cannot defeat that."

She was laughing somewhere in his mind. That laughter coursed along his spine, over his buttocks, down his legs. It was directed. She was displaying the powers of her own incredible mentality.

Captain John MacShard examined the body of the girl he had come to rescue. Of course the Martian sorceress possessed her, probably totally. But was there anything of the girl left? It was crucial that he know.

He forced himself to push forward and thought he saw something like astonishment in the girl's eyes. Then another intelligence took control of her face and the eyes blazed with eager fury, as if the goddess had found a worthy match. There was an ancient knowledge in those eyes which, when they met Captain John MacShard's, saw its equal in experience.

But all Captain John MacShard cared about was that he had glimpsed human eyes, a human face. Somewhere, Mercedes Morricone still existed. That body which pulsed with strange, stolen life and glaring intelligence, still contained the girl's soul. That was what he had needed to know.

"Give the human its body back," said Captain John Mac-Shard, switching to servos so that his arm whined up, automatically bringing the Banning cannon to bear on the golden goddess who now smiled at him with impossible promises. "Or I will destroy it and in so doing destroy you. I am Captain John MacShard, and you must know I have never made a threat I was not prepared to follow through."

You cannot destroy me with that, with a mere weapon. I draw my strength from all this—all these—from all my companions still imprisoned in the crystal. Ultimately, of course, I may release them. As they come to acknowledge that I am Mistress of the Silver Machine.

And now Captain John MacShard looked up. It was as if someone had tilted him by the chin. And above him stretched the vibrating wires and twisting ribbons of silver that told him the terrible truth. Inadvertently he had stepped into the core of one of the ancient Martian machines.

The sorceress had set a trap. And it had been a subtle trap, a trap which showed the mettle of his enemy.

The trap had used his own stupid pride against him.

He cursed himself for an idiot, but already he was inspecting the peculiar twists and loops of the machine, which seemed to come from nowhere and disappear into nothing. A funnel of silver energy was at the apex, high above.

Yet, perhaps most impressively, this silver citadel of science was absolutely silent.

Silent, save for the faintest whisper, like the hiss of a human voice, far away, the sweet, persuasive suggestions of this seductive sorceress slipping into his synapses, soothing his ever-wary soul, preparing him for the big sleep, the long good-bye. . . .

Everything that was savage. Everything that had made him fight to survive in the wastelands of Mercury. Everything that he had learned in the cold depths of space and the steamy seas of Venus. Everything he had been taught in the seminaries of Dublin and the academies of London. Everything came to Captain John MacShard's aid then. And there was a possibility that everything would not be enough.

The silent crystals around him began to vibrate, almost in triumph. And there, below the pulsing silver fire, the goddess danced.

He knew why Shienna Sha Shanakana danced and he tried desperately to take his eyes off her. He had never seen anything quite so beautiful. He had never desired a woman more. He felt something close to love.

With a strangled curse which peeled his lips back from his teeth, he took the Banning in both hands, his fingers playing across the weird lines and configurations of the casing as if he drew music from an instrument.

The goddess smiled but did not stop dancing. Neither did the crystals of her citadel stop dancing. Everything moved in delicate, subtle silence. Everything seduced him. If there had been music, he might have resisted more easily. But the music was somewhere in his head. There was a tune. It was taking charge of his arms and legs. Taking over his mind.

Was he also dancing? Dancing with her in those strange, sinuous movements so reminiscent of the snakes which had pursued them on Mercury until he had become the hunter and turned them into food for himself and his tribe?

Oh, you are strong and resourceful and mighty and everything a hero should be. A true demigod to mate with a demigoddess and create a mighty god, a god who in turn will create entire new universes, an infinity of power. Look how beautiful you are, Captain John MacShard, what a perfect specimen of your kind.

A silver mirror appeared before him and he saw not what she described but the wild beast which had survived the deadly wastes of Mercury, the demonic creature who had slain the Green Emperor of Venus and wrested a planet from the grip of Grodon Worbn, the pious and vicious Robot Chancellor of Ganymede.

But the sweetness of her perfume, the sound of those golden, silky threads brushing against her skin, the rise and fall of her breasts, the promise in her eyes . . .

All this Captain John MacShard shook off, and he thought he saw a look of some astonishment, almost of admiration, in those alien orbs. His fingers would scarcely obey him, but they moved without thought, from pure habit, flicking across the Banning, touching it here, adjusting something there. An instrument made for aliens.

No human hand had ever been meant to operate the Banning, which was named not for its maker but for the first man who had died trying to find out how it worked. General Banning had prided himself on his expertise with alien artifacts. He had not died immediately, but from the poisons which had eaten into his skin and slowly digested his flesh. Captain John MacShard had never bothered to find out how the Banning worked. He simply knew how to work it. The way so many Spanish boys simply know how to coax the most beautiful music from the guitar.

The same intelligences, who Captain John MacShard believed to have perished out beyond Pluto, had also made his ship. There was a philosophy inherent to his ship, which rejected most who tried to board her vast, echoing interior, whose very emptiness was essential to her function, to her existence, and the weapon, and somehow Captain John MacShard understood the philosophy and loved the purity of the minds which had created it.

His respect was what had almost certainly saved his life more than once as he learned the properties and sublime beauty of the Banning and the ship.

He was panting. What had he been doing? Dancing? Before a mirror? The mirror was gone now. The goddess had stopped dancing. Indeed, she was leaning forward, fixing Captain John MacShard with strange eyes in which flecks of rainbow colors flashed and flared. The red lips parted to show white, even teeth. The young flesh glowed with inner desires, impossible promises . . .

Come, John MacShard. Come to me and fulfill your noble destiny.

Then Captain John MacShard was sweeping the Banning around him in an arc. He aimed at the crystals while the gun's impossible circuits and surfaces plated and replated in a blur of changes, from gold to copper to jade to silver to gold as the great gun seemed to expand under Captain John MacShard's urgent caresses. Yet nothing dramatic happened to the crystals. They darkened, but they did not break. The light went from glaring day to misty night.

A terrifying silence fell.

He swept the gun again. Still the crystal held. And whatever was within the crystal held, too. It was harder to see movement, perhaps because the inhabitants were protecting themselves. But the gun had done nothing.

The silence continued.

Then the golden girl laughed. Her laughter was the sweetest music in the universe.

Did you think, Captain John MacShard, your famous gun could conquer Shienna Sha Shanakana, Priestess of the Silent Citadel, Sorceress of the Seven Dials? The stupid Knights of the Balance who came against us from far Cygnus met their match. They planned to conquer us, but we killed them all, even before they reached the inner planets. . . .

He looked up. She was so much closer now. Her wonderful beauty loomed over him. He gasped. He refused to take a step back.

Those human lips were filled with the stored energy of ancient Mars as they smiled down at him. *Oh, yes, Captain John MacShard. You are not here by accident. I did not send the Thennet to take the girl until I knew you were about to land at Old Mars Station. And it was I who let the father know you were the only creature alive that could find his daughter. And you did find her, didn't you? You found me. You found Shienna Sha Shanakana who has been dust, who has not known this desire for uncountable millennia, who has not felt such need, such joyous lust. . . .*

Now Captain John MacShard took that backward step, the great Banning cannon loose on its webbing, swinging as his hands sought something in his clothing. Now his fists were clenched at his sides.

The goddess licked her sublime lips.

Is that sweat I see on your manly brow, Captain John MacShard? A hand reached out and whisked lightly across his forehead. He felt as if a flaming knife had been drawn through his flesh. Yet he would have given his whole life to experience that touch again.

He tasted a tongue that was not a human tongue. It licked at his flesh. It reveled in his smell, the feel of his hard, muscular body, the racing blood, the pounding heart, the sight of his perfect manhood. He was everything humans or Martians could be; everything the female might desire in a male.

Her touch yielded to him, offered him a power he knew she would never really give up. He had enjoyed the most expert seductresses, but this creature brought the experience of centuries, the instincts of her stolen body, the cravings of a female which had not known any kind of feeling, only a burning ambition, for longer than most of Earth's greatest civilizations had come and gone. And those cravings were centered on Captain John MacShard.

You will sire the new Martian race, she promised, as she moved her golden breastplates against his naked chest. *You will die knowing that you have fulfilled your greatest possible destiny.*

And Captain John MacShard believed her. He believed her to the depths of his being. He wanted nothing else. Nothing but to serve her in any way she demanded. The gun hung forgotten at his side. He reached out his arms to receive from her whatever she desired to give, to give to her whatever she needed to take. It was true. He was hers. Hers to use and then to bind so that later his own son might feed upon his holy flesh and become him. That was his destiny. The eternal life which lay before him.

But first, she whispered, *you must entertain me.*

Then he suddenly knew the son must be sired, the remains of the humans driven from the bodies and the blood mingled in the painful and protracted mating rituals of those first Martians.

She moved to enfold him in that final, lethal embrace.

CHAPTER SEVEN

The Poisoned Chalice

They came upon the Earthling naked, somewhere in the Shifting Desert, almost a hundred *versts* from the Aghroniagh Hills. He had no armor, no weapons. His skin hung like filthy rags on his bloody, blistered flesh. Both his legs had long, deep red lines running from thigh to heel, as if a white-hot sword blade had been placed on the limbs. He could see, but his eyes were turned inward. He was mumbling to himself. There was foam on his mangled lips. He was raving, seemingly empty of identity and will, and the noises that came occasionally from deep in his chest were the sounds a wild beast might make. At other times, he seemed amused.

The patrol which found him had been looking for Venusian *chuff* runners and couldn't believe anything lived in his condition. They were superstitious fellows. They thought at first he was a ghost. Then they decided he had fallen among ghosts, within the influence of those mythical Martians frozen in jewels and dreaming deep within the planet. Some of the customs people had seen Earthling explorers who had returned from expeditions in a state not much better than this.

But then one of the patrol recognized Captain John Mac-Shard and they knew that whatever enemy he had met out here, it must have been a powerful one. They identified the long scars down his legs and on his hands as burns from Thennet venom. But how had they gotten there? The marks did not look typical of Thennet torture.

They began to take him back to Old Mars Station where there was a doctor, but he roused himself, gathered his senses and pointed urgently toward the Aghroniaghs. It seemed he had a companion.

They had gone seventy *versts* before their instruments detected a human figure lying in the shade of a rock, a small bottle nearby. Indications were that the figure was barely alive.

Captain John MacShard sank back into the craft as soon as he saw Mercedes Morricone. He let go. He allowed oblivion at last to overcome him.

He would never deliberately recall and would never tell anyone what Shienna Sha Shanakana, Sorceress of the Silent Citadel, had made him do, as she took hold of his mind. He would never admit what he had allowed her to do in order to ensure the success of a desperate, maybe suicidal, plan.

She knew she could not fully control him and it had whetted her curiosity, made her test her powers in ways she had never expected to test them. She fed off him. She tasted at his brain the way a wealthy woman might take a delicate bite of a chocolate to see if it suited her. Some of what she took from him she discarded as so much waste. Memories. Affections. Pride.

But then she had become puzzled. Her own power seemed to ebb and flow. He was naked, and he had torn his own flesh for her amusement, had capered and drooled for her amusement. John MacShard was no longer a thinking being. She had sucked him dry of everything she herself lacked. Dry of everything human.

Or so it had seemed . . .

For Captain John MacShard had learned all he had needed to learn from the veteran priest he had talked to in Old City before he left. He had kept some of his wits by tapping the venom from the Thennet he had killed, keeping it in crushable vials until the moment came when he needed that level of pain to keep his mind from the likes of Shienna Sha Shananaka's seductions. It had been her embrace that had seared them both. But he intended to reverse her spell. He had reversed the path of most of the energy she had been drawing from her compatriots in their crystal prisons. He had absorbed it in the gun.

For the gun didn't merely expel energy, it also attracted energy. It processed its own power from the planet's energy, wherever that energy was to be found. The blood and soul she had sucked from him was still under his control. He had let her draw him in, let her take his very soul, somehow keeping his own consciousness as he was absorbed into her, somehow linking with that other terrified fragment of soul-mind that was the girl to whom he was able to give strength, a chance at life.

Somewhere in that ruined, apparently lunatic skull, there was a battle still taking place, through the twists and turns of an alien space and time—a battle for control of a human creature that had perished so that a goddess might survive. It was not only Captain John MacShard's vigorous blood she had sucked, nor his diamond-hard mind, but his will. A will which, ironically, she could not control. A will strong enough to take possession of a demigoddess.

Captain John MacShard was still there. Actually inside her. Actually working to destroy her. There had never been an individual more ruggedly determined to maintain its identity against all odds. He had summoned everything he possessed as she embraced him and had broken the vials containing the venom he had gathered from the Thennet. The venom burned his body as well as hers. The girl's body became useless to her. She began to remove herself from it. And Captain John MacShard, the skin of his hands and legs bubbling as the venom ate into them, kept his will directed to his goal.

She had been astonished to discover a mind as power-ful as her own—as thoroughly trained as her own in the Martian forms of mental control and counter-control which Earthers had nicknamed "brain-brawling" and which more subtle observers knew as a combination of mental fencing and mental chess whose outcome could annihilate the de-feated.

But the searing venom kept his mind free enough from her dominance and ultimately allowed him to break from her embrace. She had advanced on him, a roaring, shouting thing of raw energy, the ruined human body abandoned.

Then Captain John MacShard forced himself toward his fallen Banning cannon. The gun lay in a heap of clothing and circuitry which he had stripped from his own body be-fore beginning to strip the flesh as she had demanded.

But all the while his iron will had kept the crucial parts of himself free. Now he had the gun in his hands and the golden whirlwind that was the true form of Shienna Sha Shanakana, Sorceress of the Silent Citadel, was advancing toward him, triumphant in the knowledge that the gun had already failed to break the crystal coffins in which her kin-folk were still imprisoned.

But Captain John MacShard knew more about the people who had made the Banning than she did. Her folk had merely killed them. Captain John MacShard had examined the culture they had left behind in their great, empty ship. Captain John MacShard had a human quality which the an-cient Martians, for all their powers, always lacked and which would always undo them. They had no curiosity about those they fed upon. Captain John MacShard had the curiosity of the Venusian saber-tooth whose reactions matched his own. He had learned so much from *The Duchess of Malfi*.

He had never meant to destroy the crystal tombs with his gun. That would have released even more of the greedy im-mortals from their already fragile captivity. Instead he had used the gun's powering devices, the cells which sucked in energy of cosmic proportions, which in turn powered the gun when it was needed. The instrument in his hands could contain the raw power of an entire universe—and expel that same power wherever it was directed.

The gun hadn't failed to break the crystals, but it had absorbed their enormous energy.

It had gathered the power of the silent crystals into the gun so that the Sorceress could no longer call upon it. Her energy, uncontained, began to dissipate. She began to return to the body of the girl. But she had reckoned without the power of the Banning cannon.

She was held in balance between her own desperate lust for flesh and the relentless draw of the Banning.

MacShard's last act had been to take the girl's apparently lifeless body and carry it through the winding, filthy tunnels of the Thennet, who had all long since fled, and somehow get her up to the surface as a goddess shrilled and boomed in the crystal chamber. The whole planet seemed to shake with her frustrated attempts to draw more strength from her imprisoned brothers and sisters.

She was outraged. Not because she knew she might actually die, but because a puny little halfling threatened to best her. She could not bear the humiliation.

He saw an intense ball of light pursue him for a few moments and then become a face. Not the face he had seen before but a face at once hideous and obscenely beautiful. She was being dragged down to him, down to where the alien gun sucked at her very soul. Then she stopped resisting it. She might have lived on, as she had lived for millennia, but she chose oblivion. She let go of her consciousness. Only her energy remained in the gun's energy cells. But Captain John MacShard would never be sure.

Nothing but natural hazards blocked his progress to the top. At last he was stretched, gasping on the thin, sour air, staring upward.

Suddenly a sad wind began to stretch a curtain of dark blue across the sky. It seemed for a moment that Mars lived again, lived when the seas washed her wealthy, mysterious beaches.

At the surface, Captain John MacShard realized he would have to leave the Banning behind if he was to get the girl to safety. He must risk it. It had enough charge to do extraordinary damage. If mishandled, it would not only destroy any living thing within a hundred yards, it would probably destroy a good-sized portion of the planet or worse. He suspected that it was as safe from the Thennet as it was from the Sorceress of the Silent Citadel. He hoped to cross the Paradise before he smelled human again.

It had not been until the following night that he had stopped. The girl was just conscious, a shoulder and leg raw from Thennet venom, though her face, by a miracle, had not been touched. He had left her what little water he had brought and had stumbled on. He had been walking toward the Old City when the customs patrol found him.

The port doctors shook their heads. They could see no hope of saving him. But then Morricone stepped in. He flew Captain John MacShard to Phobos and the famous Clinique Al Rhabia, where his daughter was already recovering. They had worked on him. A billion *deen* had been spent on him, and they had saved him.

And in saving Captain John MacShard they instilled the germ of a new kind of anger, a profound understanding of the injustice which could let crippled boys beg in the Martian dust but fly the privileged to Phobos and the finest new medicine science could create.

He wasn't ungrateful to Morricone. Morricone had kept his bargain, paid the price and better. He didn't blame Morricone for his failure to understand, for not having the imagination to see that for every hero's life he saved, there were millions of ordinary people who would never be given the chance to be heroes.

They found his gun for him. Nobody dared handle it, but they picked it out of a dune with their waldos and brought it to him in a sealed canister.

Captain John MacShard saw Mercedes Morricone a couple of times after he left the Clinique and was waiting for his ship to be recircuited according to his new instructions. Plastic surgery had rid her of most of the scars. She was more than grateful to him. She knew him in a way no woman had ever known him before. And she loved him. She couldn't help herself. She understood Captain John Mac-Shard had nothing to offer her now that he had given her back her life.

Yet maybe there was something. A clear feeling of affection, almost a father's love for a daughter. He realized, to his own surprise, that he cared about her. He even let her come along when he took the kid aboard *The Duchess of Malfi* and showed him the wild, semistable gases and gemstones which were her controls. He wanted the boy to remember that the ship could be understood and handled. And Mercedes had fallen in love all over again, for the ship had a beauty that was unique.

Pretending to joke, she said they could be a hardy little pioneer family, the three of them, setting off for the worlds beyond the stars. How marvelous it would be to stand at his side as he took the alien ship into the echoing corridors of the multiverse, following fault lines created in the impossibly remote past through the infinitely layered realities of intraspatial matter. How marvelous it would be to see the sights that he would see.

He was loading the heavy canister down into a cradle he'd made for it and which fitted beside his compression bed. He had commissioned himself a new power suit. It rippled against his body, outlining muscles and sinews as he moved gracefully to his familiar tasks, checking screens and globes, columns of glittering force.

The boy was content to look, wide-eyed. And maybe he understood. Maybe he just pretended.

And maybe Captain John MacShard pretended not to understand her when she spoke of that impossible future. He didn't tell her what you had to become to steer *The Duchess* through time and space. What you must cease to be. What you must learn never to desire, never to think about.

He was gentle when he escorted her home from the spaceport, took her and the boy to her father's big front door, kissed her cheek, and bade her good-bye for the last time.

She held the boy's hand tight. He was her link to her dream. He might even become her best dream. She was going to get him educated, she said, as best you could these days.

The girl and the boy watched Captain John MacShard leave.

His perfect body was suddenly outlined against the huge, scarlet sun as it settled on the Martian horizon. Ribbons of red dust danced around his feet as he strode back up the drive of her father's mansion, between the artificial cedars and the holograph fountains. He walked to the gates, seemed about to turn, changed his mind, and was gone.

The girl and the boy were standing there again in the morning at Old Mars Station as *The Duchess* blasted off en route for the new worlds beyond Pluto where Captain John MacShard thought he might find what he was looking for.

He had gained something more than the cosmic power which resided in his gun. He now knew what love—ordinary, decent, celebratory human love—was. He had felt it. He still felt it.

The ship was cruising smoothly, her own intelligence taking over. He turned away from his instruments and poured himself a much-needed shot of Vortex Water.

Staring up at the great tapestry of stars, thinking about all the worlds and races which must inhabit them, Captain John MacShard turned away from his instruments.

Like the wild creature that he was, he shook off the dust and the horror and the memory of love.

By the time his alien ship was passing Jupiter, Captain John MacShard was his old self again. He patted the gun in its special case; his Banning was now powered by the life-stuff of the gods.

Soon he could start hunting the really big game.

The interstellar game.

Story Copyrights